P9-CEJ-006

# A BETTER MAN

## ALSO BY LOUISE PENNY

# Louise Penny

# A BETTER MAN

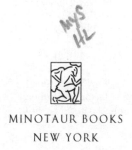

MINOTAUR BOOKS
NEW YORK

First published in the United States by Minotaur Books, an imprint of St. Martin's Publishing Group

A BETTER MAN. Copyright © 2019 by Three Pines Creations, Inc. All rights reserved. Printed in the United States of America. For information, address St. Martin's Publishing Group, 120 Broadway, New York, NY 10271.

www.minotaurbooks.com

Endpaper art by MaryAnna Coleman / www.maryannacolemandesign.com

Library of Congress Cataloging-in-Publication Data

Names: Penny, Louise, author.
Title: A better man : a Chief Inspector Gamache novel / Louise Penny.
Description: First Edition. | New York : Minotaur Books, 2019.
Identifiers: LCCN 2019012651 | ISBN 9781250066213 (hardcover) |
ISBN 9781250265074 (signed) | ISBN 9781250257833 (international, sold outside
the U.S., subject to rights availability) | ISBN 9781466873711 (ebook)
Classification: LCC PR9199.4.P464 B48 2019 | DDC 813/.6—dc23
LC record available at https://lccn.loc.gov/2019012651

Our books may be purchased in bulk for promotional, educational, or business use. Please contact your local bookseller or the Macmillan Corporate and Premium Sales Department at 1-800-221-7945, extension 5442, or by email at MacmillanSpecialMarkets@macmillan.com.

First U.S. Edition: August 2019
First International Edition: August 2019

10  9  8  7  6  5  4  3  2  1

*This book is dedicated to Bishop, our golden.*
*No better dog, no more loving companion.*

# A BETTER MAN

# CHAPTER ONE

⌒

*M*erde."

"*Merde?*" Myrna Landers looked over her bowl of café au lait at her friend.

"I'm sorry," said Clara Morrow. "I meant to say fuck. Fuckity fuck fuck."

"That's my girl. But why?"

"Can't you guess?"

"Is Ruth coming?" Myrna looked around the bistro in mock panic. Or maybe not-so-mock.

"Worse."

"That's not possible."

Clara gave Myrna her phone, though the bookstore owner already knew what she'd find.

Before meeting Clara for breakfast, she'd checked her Twitter feed. On the screen, for the world to see, was the quickly cooling body of Clara's artistic career.

As Myrna read, Clara wrapped her large, paint-stained hands around her mug of hot chocolate, a *specialité de la maison*, and shifted her eyes from her friend to the mullioned window and the tiny Québec village beyond.

If the phone was an assault, the window was the balm. While perhaps not totally healing, it was at least comforting in its familiarity.

The sky was gray and threatened rain. Or sleet. Ice pellets or snow. The dirt road was covered in slush and mud. There were patches of snow on the sodden grass. Villagers out walking their dogs were clumping around in rubber boots and wrapped in layers of clothing, hoping to keep April away from their skin and out of their bones.

It was not possible. Somehow, having survived another bitterly cold Canadian winter, early spring always got them. It was the damp. And the temperature swings. And the illusion and delusion that it must be milder out, surely, by now.

The forest beyond stood like an army of winter wraiths, skeleton arms dangling, limbs clacking together in the breeze.

Woodsmoke drifted from the old fieldstone, brick, clapboard homes. A signal to some higher power. Send help. Send heat. Send a real spring and not this crapfest of slush and freezing, teasing days. Days of snow and warmth.

April in Québec was a month of cruel contrasts. Of sublime afternoons spent sitting outside in the bright sunshine with a glass of wine, then waking to another foot of snow. A month of muttered curses and mud-caked boots and splattered cars and dogs rolling, then shaking. So that every front entrance was polka-dotted with muck. On the walls. On the ceilings. On the floors. And people.

April in Québec was a climatological shitstorm. A mindfuck of epic proportions.

But what was happening outside the large windows was comforting compared to what was happening on the small screen of Clara's phone.

Clara's and Myrna's armchairs were pulled close to the hearth, where logs popped and sent embers fluttering up the fieldstone chimney. The village bistro smelled of woodsmoke and maple syrup and strong fresh coffee.

*Clara Morrow is going through her brown period,* Myrna read. *To say her latest offerings are shit is to be unfair to effluent. Let's hope it is just a period, and not the end.*

"Oh," said Myrna. Putting down the phone, she reached for her friend's hand. *"Merde."*

*"Tabernac.* Someone from Serious Crimes just sent a link. Listen to this."

The other agents in the conference room looked over as he read off his cell phone, *"This is Armand Gamache's first day back at the Sûreté du Québec after a suspension of nine months following a series of ill-advised and disastrous decisions."*

"Disastrous? That's bullshit," said one of the officers.

"Well, it's bullshit retweeted by hundreds."

Other agents and inspectors scrambled for their phones, tapping away while glancing out the open door. To make sure . . .

It was eleven minutes to eight, and members of the homicide department were gathering for the regular Monday morning meeting to discuss ongoing investigations.

Though there was very little "regular" about this meeting. About this morning. The room was electric with anticipation. Now heightened even further by what was blowing up on their phones.

*"Merde,"* muttered an agent. *"Having achieved the pinnacle of power as Chief Superintendent of the Sûreté,"* she read, *"Gamache promptly abused it. Deliberately allowing catastrophic amounts of opioids onto the streets. After an investigation, he was demoted."*

"They have no idea what they're talking about. Still, that's not too bad."

"It goes on. *He should have been fired, at the very least. Probably put on trial and thrown in prison."*

"Oh."

"That's insane," said one of the senior officers, grabbing the phone and reading it for herself. "Who's writing this crap? They don't even mention he got the stuff back."

"Of course they don't."

"I hope he doesn't see it."

"Are you kidding? He'll see it."

The room fell silent, except for the soft clicking from each device. Like the sound of near-dead tree limbs in the breeze.

Words were muttered under their breaths as they read. Words their grandparents had considered sacred but were now profane. *Tabernac. Câlice. Hostie.*

One senior officer put his head in his hands and massaged his temples. Then, dropping them, he reached for his phone. "I'm going to write a rebuttal."

"Don't. Better if it comes from the leadership. Chief Superintendent Toussaint will set them straight."

"She hasn't yet."

"She will. She trained under Gamache. She'll defend him."

Off in the far corner, one agent was staring at her phone, a deep line forming between her brows.

While the others were pale, she was flushed as she read not a text or tweet but an email.

Though in her mid-forties, Lysette Cloutier was one of the newer recruits to homicide, having been transferred from the Sûreté's accounting department. She'd spent years quietly keeping track of the budget, now surpassing a billion dollars, until Chief Superintendent Gamache had noticed her work and thought she'd be helpful tracking down killers.

While she couldn't follow a DNA trail or a suspect to save her life, she could follow the money. And that often led to the same place.

Everyone else in that conference room had worked hard to get into the most prestigious department in the Sûreté du Québec.

Agent Lysette Cloutier was doing her best to get out. And get back to nice, safe, predictable, understandable numbers. And away from the daily horrors, the physical violence, the emotional chaos of murder.

Cloutier always chose the same seat at these meetings. Making sure her back was to the long whiteboard, on which were tacked photographs.

She considered the email she'd just received, then typed a response and hit send before she had time to reconsider.

"What do you wanna bet some of these tweets are from Beauvoir?" said one of the younger agents.

"You mean Chief Inspector Beauvoir?"

All heads turned to the doorway. And then there was a scramble and a scraping of chairs as everyone got to their feet.

Isabelle Lacoste stood, cane in hand, staring at the young agent. Then her expression softened to a smile as she looked around at the familiar faces.

The last time she'd been in the Monday-morning meeting, she'd chaired it, as head of homicide. Now she entered limping.

Her injuries, though almost healed, were not completely gone. And never would be.

Officers and agents crowded around, welcoming her back, while she tried to explain she wasn't really back. Promoted to Superintendent, she was in the building for meetings to discuss the timing and conditions of her return to active duty.

But it was no coincidence, everyone in that room knew, that she was there this Monday. Not just any old day. Not just any old meeting.

She took a chair by the head of the table and nodded to the others to retake their seats. Then she looked at the young agent who'd made the comment about Chief Inspector Beauvoir.

"What did you mean by that?"

Her voice was calm, but she sat unnaturally still. Veteran homicide agents who'd served under Chief Inspector Lacoste recognized the look. And almost pitied the foolish young agent who found himself in her crosshairs.

"I mean that we all know Chief Inspector Beauvoir is leaving the Sûreté," he said. "Moving to Paris. But not for another couple of weeks. What happens before then? With Gamache coming back. I'd rather be in a firefight than be Chief Inspector Beauvoir walking into this meeting today. I bet he feels the same way."

"You'd lose," said Lacoste.

The room grew quiet.

*He's young and foolish,* Lacoste thought. Probably longing for some desperate glory.

She knew this agent had never been in a so-called firefight. Even using the ridiculous phrase gave him away. Anyone who'd actually raised a weapon, sighted another human, and shot. Again, and again. And been shot at. Would never consider that glory, nor call it a firefight.

And would never, ever wish to be there again.

Those in the room who'd been on that last raid were looking at the agent. Some with outrage. But some almost wistfully. Remembering when they'd been that young. That naïve. That immortal.

Nine months ago.

They thought back to the summer afternoon. In the pretty forest by the Vermont border. How the sun broke through the trees and they could feel the warmth on their faces.

That moment that seemed to hang in midair before all hell broke loose.

As weapons were raised and fired. And fired. Cutting down the saplings. Cutting down the people.

The screams. The chocking, acrid stench of smoke from the weapons. Of wood and flesh burned by bullets.

Chief Inspector Lacoste was one of the first to fall. Her actions giving Chief Superintendent Gamache that one moment he needed to act. And act he had.

Isabelle Lacoste hadn't seen what Chief Superintendent Gamache had done. By then she was unconscious. But she'd heard about it. She'd read the transcripts of the investigation, after he'd been suspended.

Gamache had survived the events that day.

Only to be cut down by his own people.

And the attacks were continuing, even as he returned to work.

Isabelle Lacoste, and every veteran officer in that room, knew that the decisions Chief Superintendent Gamache had made were audacious. Daring. Unconventional. And, unlike what the tweets claimed, hugely effective.

But it could very well have gone the other way.

It had been a coup de grâce. The last desperate act of the most senior officer in Québec, who felt there was no other option.

Had Gamache failed, and for a while it appeared he would, the Sûreté would have been crippled, leaving Québec defenseless against an onslaught of gang violence, trafficking, organized crime.

Gamache had prevailed. But just barely, and at a cost.

Any reasonable person making those decisions would expect a

consequence, no matter the outcome. The Chief Superintendent was reasonable. He must've expected to be suspended. Investigated.

But had he expected to be humiliated?

In their own coup de grâce, the political leadership had decided to save their own skins by putting Gamache's career out of its misery. Though vindicated in the investigation, he would be offered a job he could not possibly accept. Chief Inspector of homicide. A position he'd held for many years. One he'd handed over to Lacoste when he'd been promoted to head of the Sûreté. After she'd been wounded, it was a job now filled by Jean-Guy Beauvoir.

It was a demotion, the leadership knew, that Armand Gamache could not agree to. The humiliation would be too great. The cut too deep. He would resign. Retire. Disappear.

But Armand Gamache refused to go. To their astonishment, he'd accepted their offer.

His fall from grace would be completed here. In this room. Today.

And it appeared he'd land, with a thump, right on top of Jean-Guy Beauvoir.

It was seven minutes to eight. The two men would soon walk through the door. Both holding the rank of head of homicide.

And then what would happen?

Even Isabelle Lacoste found herself glancing at the door. Wondering. She didn't expect trouble but couldn't help thinking about what George Will called the "Ohio Event."

In 1895 there were only two automobiles in the whole state. And they'd collided.

No one knew better than Lacoste that the unexpected happened. And now she found herself bracing for the collision.


"It's your own fault," said Ruth Zardo. "You should never have agreed to it, if you ask me."

No one had.

"Listen to this one," the elderly poet continued, reading off the phone. *"Clara Morrow's contribution is trite, derivative, and banal.* They left out clichéd and pedestrian. Or maybe someone says that further down the thread."

"I think that's enough, Ruth," said Reine-Marie Gamache.

She glanced at her watch. Nearly eight. She wondered how her husband was getting on. It did not take a savant to know how Clara was doing.

Her friend had dark circles under her eyes and looked drawn. And slightly painted. There were dabs of cadmium red and burnt umber on her face and in her hair.

Clara was wearing her usual jeans and a sweater. Success as an artist had not changed her fashion sense. Such as it was. Perhaps because recognition had come later in Clara's life. In her late forties now, she'd been working in her studio for decades, creating works that went unnoticed. Her greatest success had been her Warrior Uterus series. She'd sold one. To herself. And given it to her mother-in-law. Thereby weaponizing her art. And her uterus.

Then, after an evening in the bistro with women friends from the village, Clara had gone back to her studio and started something different. Portraits. Oil paintings. Of those women.

She'd painted them as they really were, their lines and lumps and wrinkles. But what she'd really captured, in her bold strokes, were their feelings.

The portraits burst onto the art scene, lauded as revolutionary. Bringing back a traditional form but revitalizing it. Her portraits were luminous. Joyous. Vibrant. Unsettling at times, as the loneliness and brute sorrow in some faces became apparent.

Her portraits of the women were challenging and bold and audacious.

And now, this April morning, many of those same women had joined Clara in the bistro. They'd celebrated her successes here. Today they came to comfort.

"They don't know what they're talking about," said Myrna. "It's just mean, malicious."

"But if I believed them when they loved the works, shouldn't I believe them now?" asked Clara. "Why were they right then but wrong now?"

"But these aren't art critics," said Reine-Marie. "I bet most of them haven't even seen the exhibition."

"The art critic for the *New York Times* just posted," reported Ruth. "He says in light of this disaster, he's going to go back to your earlier works, the portraits, to see if he'd been wrong about them. Shit. He can't mean the portrait you did of me, can he?"

"Fuck, fuck, fuck," muttered Rosa. The duck was sitting on Ruth's lap and looked irritated. But then, ducks often did.

"It'll be fine," said Myrna.

"That I believe," said Clara, running her hands through her thick hair so that it stood out from her head. Making her look like a mad madwoman.

Perversely, Ruth, who almost certainly really was mad, looked perfectly composed.

"The good thing is, nobody will see your crap," said Ruth. "Who goes to an exhibition of miniatures? Why in the world would you agree to contribute to a group show of tiny oil paintings? It's what bored society women in the 1700s painted."

"And many were far better than their male counterparts," said Myrna.

"Right," said Ruth. "Like that can be true."

Rosa rolled her duck eyes.

"You paint portraits on large canvases," Ruth persisted. "Why do tiny landscapes?"

"I wanted to stretch myself," said Clara.

"By doing miniatures?" asked Ruth. "Bit ironic."

"Did you see Clara's works?" Reine-Marie asked.

"Don't have to. I can smell them. They smell like—"

"You might want to take a look before you comment."

"Why? Apparently they're trite and banal."

"Do you write the same poem over and over?" asked Myrna.

"No, of course not," said Ruth. "But neither do I try to write a novel. It's all words, but I know what I'm good at. Great at."

Myrna Landers heaved a sigh and shifted her considerable weight in her armchair. As much as she longed to contradict Ruth, she couldn't. The fact was, their drunk and disorderly old neighbor in Three Pines was a brilliant poet. Though not much of a human being.

Ruth made a noise that could have been a laugh. Or indigestion.

"I'll tell you what is funny. You crash and burn trying to do something different while Armand destroys his career by agreeing to go back and do the same old thing."

"No one's crashing and burning," said Reine-Marie, glancing at her watch again.

The atmosphere in the conference room was crackling.

"So how's this going to work?" asked one of the agents. "Are we going to have two Chief Inspectors?"

They looked at the visiting Superintendent. "*Non*. Chief Inspector Beauvoir will be in charge until he leaves for Paris."

"And Gamache will be . . . ?" asked another agent.

"Chief Inspector Gamache. This's a transition for a few weeks, that's all," said Lacoste, trying to sound more confident than she actually was. "This is a good thing. There'll be two experienced leaders."

But the men and women in the room weren't idiots. One strong leader was great. Two led to power struggles. Conflicting orders. Chaos.

"They've worked together for years," said Lacoste. "They'll have no trouble working together now."

"Would you be okay taking orders from someone who'd been your subordinate?"

"Of course I would."

But despite her annoyance, Lacoste knew it was a legitimate question.

Could Beauvoir bring himself to give orders to his former boss and mentor?

And, more to the point, could the former Chief Superintendent take them? Gamache, as respectful as he might be, was used to being in charge. And in charge of Beauvoir.

"But it's not just that, is it?" said a senior officer.

"There's more?" asked an agent.

"You don't know?" The officer looked around, intentionally, it seemed, avoiding the warning in Lacoste's eyes. "Gamache wasn't just Beauvoir's boss. He's his father-in-law."

"You're kidding," said the agent, knowing that the officer was not.

"*Non*. He's married to Gamache's daughter, Annie. They have a kid."

While the personal connection between Gamache and Beauvoir

wasn't exactly a secret, neither did the two men go out of their way to advertise it.

There was a snort from down the table, and an agent looked up from his cell phone. "They're really going after the man. Listen to this—"

"*Non*," said Lacoste. "I don't want to hear it."

There was movement by the door.

They looked over, then jumped to their feet.

The senior officers saluted. The younger ones looked momentarily taken aback.

Some in the room had never seen Armand Gamache in person. Others had not seen him in months. Not since that steamy hot July afternoon in the forest. The air filled with the stench of gun smoke and the cries of the wounded. When it had cleared, they'd seen the head of the Sûreté, weapon in hand. Hauling a body through the pretty woods.

Had Gamache known when he'd dressed that summer morning, putting on the clean white shirt and the suit and tic, that that was how the day would end? With blood on his clothing. And on his hands.

He'd risen that sultry day the Chief Superintendent of the Sûreté du Québec. A confident leader. Unhappy about, but committed to, a dangerous course of action.

He left the woods, late that afternoon, shattered.

And now he was back.

A better man? A bitter man?

They were about to find out.

# CHAPTER TWO

⁓

The man they saw at the door was in his late fifties. Tall, not heavy but sturdy. Clean-shaven. And while not classically handsome, he was more attractive, certainly more distinguished, than the pictures on social media that morning had led the younger agents to believe.

Armand Gamache's hair, once dark, was mostly gray and slightly wavy. His complexion was that of someone who'd spent hours in open fields, in damp forests, in knee-deep snow, staring at bodies. And tracking down those who'd made them.

He had the appearance of someone who'd spent years shouldering heavy responsibility. Weighing dreadful choices.

The lines down his face spoke of determination. Of concentration. Of worry spread over years. And sorrow. Spread over decades.

But as the agents watched, Gamache smiled, and they saw that the deepest of those lines ran from the corners of his eyes.

Laugh lines. Far more pronounced than those caused by worry and pain. Though they did meet, mix, intersect.

And then there was the unmistakable, unmissable scar at his temple. Like a calling card. A mark that distinguished him. It cut across the worry lines and laugh lines. And told a story all its own.

That's what the newer agents saw.

For the veterans it was different. They didn't so much see as feel.

There was silence, stillness, as Armand Gamache stood on the threshold, looking at them, meeting eyes that were suddenly moist.

The agents in the room never thought he'd return. Not to the Sûreté

and certainly not to homicide. This senior officer they'd worked alongside for years. Who'd mentored most. Who'd taught them how to catch
killers. And not lose themselves in the process. How to be great officers and even better men and women.

He'd taken each for a leisurely walk, early in their placement in homicide, and told them the four statements that led to wisdom.

Never repeating them.

I was wrong. I'm sorry. I don't know. I need help.

They'd watched, impotent, as Gamache had been brought down.
Then thrown aside.

But today he'd come back. To them.

He always wore a suit and tie, a crisp white shirt, as he did today.
Even in the field. As a sign of respect for victim and family. And as a
symbol of order in the face of the chaos that threatened.

He looked unchanged. But that, they knew, was superficial. Who
knew what was going on underneath?

Gamache stepped into the conference room. *"Bonjour."*

*"Bonjour, patron,"* came the response.

He nodded, subtly acknowledging the salutes, while also indicating
they weren't necessary.

"Superintendent, I didn't expect to see you here." He put out his
hand, and Isabelle Lacoste took it. A far more formal greeting than the
one they'd exchanged when she and her family visited the Gamaches in
Three Pines.

"I was in the neighborhood," she said.

"I see." He glanced at the wall clock. "Your first appointment is in
half an hour, I believe."

Isabelle Lacoste smiled. He knew. Of course he'd know. That she was
there that morning for a round of interviews, speaking to various de-
partments. To see which one she'd head up once her leave was over in a
few weeks.

Though it wasn't a complete coincidence she'd scheduled the appointment on Chief Inspector Gamache's first morning back.

"It is. I'm starting at the top."

"The janitorial service?"

"Of course. A girl can dream."

"All your years cleaning up my messes—"

"Finally paying off, *oui*."

He laughed.

Gamache knew that Isabelle was actually starting with the Serious Crimes division. Which would make her, in effect, his boss.

"You have your pick of positions, Superintendent. Any one of them would be lucky to have you."

"*Merci*." She was genuinely moved by what he said.

He turned then and offered his hand to the young agent closest to him. "We haven't met. I'm Armand Gamache."

The agent froze, staring at the hand, then into the smiling face. Into his eyes.

Not the eyes of the moron some were claiming in the tweets. Not the eyes of the cold-blooded killer others were depicting.

As the agent introduced himself, he caught a very slight scent of sandalwood and rose.

"Ah, *oui*," said Gamache. "You were with the security detail at the National Assembly in Québec City."

"*Oui, patron.*"

"Settling into Montréal all right?"

"Yes, sir."

Leaving the agent slightly stunned, and more than a little ashamed of what he'd said earlier, Gamache circled the table. Introducing himself to those he hadn't met. Chatting briefly with the officers who'd worked under him in the past.

Then he looked around.

The chair at the head of the table was empty, and Gamache walked toward it, all eyes on him. Then, pulling out the seat to the right of it, he sat and nodded to the others to also take their places.

He'd arrived a few minutes early for the meeting, knowing it might be necessary to clear the air. And answer some questions. Get it out of the way before Jean-Guy Beauvoir arrived.

Truth be told, he had not expected that the air would be so foul.

"You were talking about a blog post, I believe," he said.

He'd brought out a handkerchief and was wiping his eyes.

"A tweet, actually," said the agent, and got a filthy look from the others. "Not important, sir."

He put the phone down on the table.

"We're not going to start out by hiding the truth from each other, are we? It was important enough to mention before I arrived. I'd rather colleagues didn't talk behind my back." He met their eyes, then smiled. "I know this's awkward. I've read some of the posts. I know what they're saying. That I should've been fired. That I should've been put in jail. That I'm incompetent, perhaps even criminally so. Is that right?"

He was no longer smiling, but neither was he angry. Armand Gamache was simply stating facts. Clearing the air by exposing the crap.

He leaned forward. "You can't possibly think I have a thin skin, do you?"

Heads shook.

"Good. I doubt you're going to read anything I haven't heard before. Let's get it out in the open. I'll answer your questions, once, and then we can put it behind us. *D'accord?*"

The unhappy young man was again clutching his phone and willing the building to collapse.

No one reached the top rank of a police force as large and powerful as the Sûreté without being ambitious. And ruthless. And the agent knew what Gamache had had to do to get to the top. He also knew what they were saying about Gamache on social media. That he was no better than a sociopath.

And now that man was staring at him. Inviting him to walk into what was almost certainly a trap.

"I'd rather not, *patron.*"

"I see." Gamache lowered his voice, though all could still hear the words. "When I was Chief Superintendent, I had a framed poster in my office. On it were the last words of a favorite poet, Seamus Heaney. *Noli timere.* It's Latin. Do you know what it means?"

He looked around the room.

"Neither did I," he admitted when no one spoke. "I had to look it up. It means 'Be Not Afraid.'" His eyes returned to the unhappy young agent. "In this job you'll have to do things that scare you. You might be afraid, but you must be brave. When I ask you to do something, you must trust there's a good reason. And I need to trust that you will do it. *D'accord?*"

The agent looked down at his phone, clicked it on, and began reading.

"*Gamache is a madman. A coward,*" he read. His voice was strong and steady, but his face was a bright red. "*He should be locked up, not sent back to duty. Québec isn't safe as long as he's there.*"

The agent looked up, his eyes pleading to be allowed to stop. "They're just comments, sir. Responding to some article. These aren't real people."

Gamache raised his brows. "Unless you're suggesting they're bots—"

The agent shook his head.

"—then they are real people. I'm just hoping they're not Québécois."

"That one's from Trois-Rivières."

Gamache grimaced. "Go on. Anyone else have one?"

They went around the table, reading wildly insulting posts.

"*Gamache doesn't even want to be back,*" one agent read. "*I heard he turned the job down. He doesn't care about the people of Québec. He only cares about himself.*" The agent looked up and saw a slight wince.

"Others are saying the same thing. That you didn't want to come back to homicide. To work with us. Is that true?"

"Partly, yes."

No one in the room expected that answer. All phones were lowered to the table as they stared.

"I did turn down the offer to return to homicide as Chief Inspector," said Gamache. "But not because I didn't want it."

"Then why?"

"Because you have an exceptional leader in Chief Inspector Beauvoir. I would never displace him. I wouldn't do that to him, or to you."

There was silence as the officers took that in.

"You're wondering if I really want to be here or if I took the job to spite those who only offered it to humiliate me?"

Now they stared at him, clearly surprised by his candor. At least the younger ones were. Isabelle Lacoste and other veterans looked on with amusement at their amazement.

"Did you?" asked an agent.

"No. I turned the offer down when I thought Chief Inspector Beauvoir

was staying. But when he told me he was taking up a job in private industry, in Paris, he and I talked. I spoke to my wife and decided to accept the
position." He looked around the room. "I understand your concern, but
I wouldn't be here unless I wanted to be. Working in the Sûreté, in any
capacity, is a privilege. It's been the greatest honor of my life. I can think
of no better way to be useful, or better people to serve with."

He said it with such conviction, such unabashed sincerity, that the
motto on their warrant cards, their vehicles, their badges, suddenly had
real meaning.

*Service, Intégrité, Justice.*

Gamache turned his attention to the long whiteboard covering a wall.
He'd come in over the weekend, when it was quiet, and sat in this
conference room studying the files. The photographs. Going over the
cases, the faces on the wall.

He knew where the investigations stood and what each lead investigator had done—or not done.

Just then all eyes shifted to behind Gamache.


When Jean-Guy Beauvoir had arrived twenty minutes earlier, he'd
gone directly to his office and closed the door. It wasn't something he
normally did. Normally his door was wide open. Normally he went
straight to the conference room. Normally he was the only Chief Inspector of homicide there.

But this was not a normal day. How the next half hour or so went
would set the tone going forward.

He needed to gather himself.

How would his agents and inspectors react to having not just their
former Chief Inspector back but one so storied? A private man who'd
become a public figure.

But, even more complex for Beauvoir, he wasn't really sure how he
himself would react. He and Armand had discussed it, of course, at
length, but theory and reality were often very different.

In theory, this would go smoothly. He would not be intimidated,
prickly, which he knew he tended to be when feeling insecure. He would
not be defensive or resort to sarcasm.

Chief Inspector Beauvoir would be confident. Calm. In control of the meeting and, even more vitally, of himself.

That was the plan. The theory.

But the reality was that the vast majority of his career had been spent working alongside, and slightly behind, Gamache. It was natural for him, at this point almost instinctive, to give Gamache the final word. The authority.

Jean-Guy took a deep breath in. Deep breath out. And wondered if he should call his sponsor but decided to just repeat the Serenity Prayer a few times.

He opened his eyes when a familiar ding sounded on his phone. An email from Annie.

*Are you with Dad? You need to see this.*

Clicking on the link, he read. Following the thread. Tweet after tweet. Comment, reply. Like some demented call and response. A liturgy gone wrong.

"Christ," he muttered, and closed the link.

He was glad his wife had sent it. She was a lawyer and understood the importance of preparation and information. Even things, especially things, we didn't really want to know.

The clock in front of him said one minute to eight. He rubbed his sweaty hands on his slacks and looked at the photo on his desk. Of Annie and Honoré. Taken at the Gamache home in Three Pines. In the background, unnoticed except by someone who knew it was there, was a framed picture on the bookcase. A smiling family shot of Annie, Honoré, Jean-Guy, Reine-Marie, and Armand.

Armand. Always there. Both a comfort and an undeniable presence.

Taking a deep breath, Jean-Guy placed both hands on the desk and thrust himself out of the chair. Then he opened his door and walked, strode, across the huge open space, past near-empty desks piled with reports and photographs and laptops.

He walked into the conference room. *"Salut tout le monde."*

Everyone got to their feet, including Gamache.

Without hesitation, Jean-Guy put out his hand, and Armand took it. "Welcome back."

*"Merci."* Gamache nodded. *"Patron."*

# CHAPTER THREE

⌇

They looked to Chief Inspector Gamache first, of course. Speaking to him. Reporting to him. Looking for his comments, his approval, as they went through their cases.

Gamache, for his part, listened closely but did not speak. Instead he looked to his left. To Chief Inspector Beauvoir.

For direction.

And Chief Inspector Beauvoir gave it. Calmly, thoughtfully. He asked clear questions when needed. Guiding, at times prodding. But otherwise he just listened.

He did not become defensive, or prickly.

Though, to be fair, he did feel no small annoyance, but not at Gamache. Not even at his investigators. Just at the situation. And the higher-ups he suspected had done this on purpose. Pitting two senior officers against each other. For the sake of the force? *Non.* For fun. To see if they could drive a wedge between them. Create enemies from friends in a kind of malevolent alchemy.

And perhaps, a slight warning voice suggested, for more than fun.

To his left, Superintendent Lacoste watched all this. Aware of the forces at work. Hoping for the best but half bracing for the collision.

Yet as the meeting went on, Jean-Guy Beauvoir was showing a side to himself she hadn't seen before.

She'd seen him display incredible bravery. Fierce loyalty. Dogged, often brilliant commitment to finding killers.

What she'd never seen before, in this kinetic man, was restraint.

Until today.

Somewhere along the line, probably in that sunny Québec forest, Beauvoir had learned which battles needed to be fought. And which did not. What mattered and what did not. Who were true allies and who were not.

He'd entered the woods a second-in-command. He'd left it a leader.

It was a shame, Lacoste thought, that it should happen just as he was about to leave the Sûreté.

They went through the cases, one by one, each lead investigator speaking succinctly about the homicide they were heading up. Giving updates on forensics, interrogations. Motives. Suspects.

As always, cell phones had been turned off and put away, banned for the life of the meeting.

As the gathering went on, the investigators slowly stopped looking to Gamache. Stopped glancing toward Superintendent Lacoste. And turned their full attention to Chief Inspector Beauvoir. Who gave them his.

Where arrests had been made and they were going to court, Beauvoir wanted to know what the Crown Prosecutor thought of the case. Though the fact was, he already knew. No homicide went to trial without Chief Inspector Beauvoir's being completely aware of the strengths and weaknesses of the case.

His questions were for the benefit of the team.

Beauvoir sat now with his elbows on the shiny table, hands clasped, leaning forward. Intent, focused. He hoped he gave off an aura of calm and steady leadership. The truth was, he gave off a sense of energy. Vitality. Extreme alertness.

As he glanced at his investigators, Jean-Guy Beauvoir's eyes were bright and encouraging. His glasses gave the impression he was older than he actually was. In his late thirties, he was younger than many of the senior investigators in the room.

Twenty years younger than the man to his right.

Slender and well-groomed, Beauvoir had dark hair that was just beginning to show some gray. And his once-lithe frame was filling out slightly.

As he'd approached the conference room, he'd heard some of the comments. And knew who they came from. It was no surprise. These were the agents most likely to question.

When Gamache was the Chief Superintendent, Lacoste and Beauvoir had gone to him asking that these same troublesome agents be removed.

"Remember what happened before," said Beauvoir.

There was, within the Sûreté du Québec, a before and after. A line drawn in their collective and institutional memory.

"Before" was a time of fear. Of distrust. Of enemies disguised as allies. It was a time of vast and rampant brutality. Of senior officers sanctioning beatings and even murders.

Gamache had led the resistance, at huge personal risk, and had eventually agreed to become Chief Superintendent himself.

No one left standing in the Sûreté who'd been through that could ever forget what had gone "before."

"We have to get rid of these agents," Lacoste had said. "They were transferred into homicide when things were out of control, just to cause trouble."

Gamache nodded. He knew that was true.

But he also knew that few were more loyal than those who'd been given a chance.

"Keep them on," Gamache had said. "And train them properly."

They had. And now, under Chief Inspector Beauvoir, those agents had become leaders themselves. Battle-hardened and trusted.

Which wasn't to say they didn't have their own opinions, opinions they were keen to voice.

Those had been the very homicide agents Beauvoir had heard questioning Gamache, just before he had arrived in the conference room.

With the Monday-morning meeting about to wrap up, something caught Beauvoir's attention, and he looked down the long conference table.

"Are we boring you?"

Agent Lysette Cloutier looked up, and her eyes grew round.

*"Désolée,"* she said, fumbling with her phone.

Chief Inspector Beauvoir continued to stare at her until she put it down.

The meeting continued, but only for another minute, before Beauvoir stopped it again.

"Agent Cloutier, what're you doing?"

Though it was clear what she was doing. She was typing on her phone. Again.

She looked up, flustered.

"I'm sorry. So sorry, but—"

"Is it a personal emergency?" Beauvoir asked.

"No, not really. I don't think—"

"Then put it away."

She lowered the phone to the table, then picked it up again. "I'm sorry, sir, but there is something."

"For us?"

"I don't know. Maybe."

The final report was wrapping up, and the others in the meeting wanted to finish and get out of there. Which meant they wanted her to put down the damned phone and shut up.

Feeling all eyes on her. Feeling her heart pounding in her chest. In her neck. In the vein at her temple. Agent Cloutier clutched the phone and spoke up.

"A friend has emailed me. His daughter is missing. Been gone since Saturday night."

"Where?" asked Beauvoir, pulling a pad of paper toward him.

"In the Eastern Townships."

"How old is she?"

"Twenty-five."

His pen stopped. He was expecting a child. He was relieved, but also slightly annoyed. Agent Cloutier could see this and tried to get him onside.

"She was on her way to visit him up north but never arrived."

"Is she married?"

"Yes."

"What does her husband say?"

24

"Nothing. Homer, her father, has called him over and over, but Carl just says there's nothing wrong and to stop calling."

"But she isn't at home?"

"Apparently not. Carl won't say where she is. He just hangs up on Homer. Now he isn't answering at all." She was talking rapidly, trying to get it all in. Searching the Chief Inspector's face for some sign of concern. Some sign she was getting through to him.

"Where does the father live?"

"North of Montréal. In the Laurentians. Ste.-Agathe."

"Has he gone down?"

"No. He wanted to give it until today."

Beauvoir considered the woman at the far end of the table. This was, as far as he could remember, the first time Agent Cloutier had spoken in a meeting.

"I can see why you'd be concerned, but this is a local issue. Let the local detachment handle it."

Beauvoir returned his attention to the inspector, who was just wrapping up her report.

"Homer called the local Sûreté. They sent a car but didn't find anything. That was yesterday. She's still missing. He's getting really worried."

"Then he needs to file a missing-persons report. You can help him with that."

He didn't mean to sound callous, but there were clear delineations of duties, and best not to step into someone else's lane.

"Please, *patron*," said Cloutier. "Can I go down? Take a look around?" She could see that Chief Inspector Beauvoir was undecided. Teetering. "She's pregnant."

Cloutier felt everyone turn to her. Flushing wildly, she kept her eyes on the Chief Inspector.

Beauvoir considered her again and weighed his options.

The fact this woman was pregnant shouldn't change anything. And yet, for Beauvoir, it did.

Missing. Pregnant. Unhelpful husband.

These were worrying signs. Warning signs.

Lysette Cloutier was not an experienced or, let's face it, effective criminal investigator. If he freed her up to look into it, just for the day, she'd come back with nothing. Probably because there was nothing to find.

The missing woman had probably just gone away for the weekend. Told her husband she was visiting her family but was really with girlfriends. Or a lover.

Far from the first person to do that.

"What do I tell her father?" Cloutier pressed. "He's really worried. It's not like her."

"He might not know her as well as he thinks he does."

"But he knows his son-in-law."

"What does that mean?"

"He's never said it outright, but I know he doesn't like him."

"That's not a reason to engage the resources of the homicide department, Agent Cloutier."

"He thinks something bad's happened." She could see she was losing him. She racked her brains for something else to say. "How would you feel, sir? If your child didn't come home?"

She could see that the words had hit home, but not in the way she'd hoped.

Chief Inspector Beauvoir now looked angry.

Beside him, Superintendent Lacoste watched and braced. There'd be a collision after all, but not with Gamache. Chief Inspector Beauvoir was about to run over Agent Cloutier.

"My son is an infant," Beauvoir said, his voice cold. "There's a difference."

"But if you love them, age doesn't matter, does it? Really?" she persisted, barely believing she was doing this. "They're still our children."

Beauvoir stared at her, the whole room holding its breath while the Chief Inspector weighed the options.

"What's the name?"

"Vivienne. Vivienne Godin."

Beauvoir wrote that down. "And husband?"

"Carl Tracey."

If this Vivienne Godin really was missing, then something bad had happened, and time counted.

Unfortunately, Cloutier was pretty much their Clouseau. She would not find the woman, even if standing next to her in line for a Double Double at Tim Hortons.

It wasn't that Cloutier was an idiot, just that this was not her strength. It wasn't why she was brought into homicide.

In a swift glance, Beauvoir took in the officers around the table. All had their hands full with active murder investigations. Where murders had indeed been committed and killers needed to be found. Urgently.

His eyes came to rest on the one officer as yet unassigned.

*Jeez*, thought Beauvoir, *am I really going to do this to him?*

"Would you work with Agent Cloutier and see if there's anything there? Just for the day?"

"With pleasure," said Chief Inspector Gamache.

# CHAPTER FOUR

⁓

I'm sorry," Beauvoir said under his breath as they left the meeting.
"Why?" asked Gamache.

"You know why." Beauvoir cocked his head toward Cloutier, who was at her desk. "She stapled her transfer papers to her thigh the first day here."

"She isn't armed, is she?" asked Gamache.

"Are you kidding?"

"Is she working out?" Gamache asked. After all, it had been his decision to transfer this desk agent into homicide.

"Actually, if kept off the streets and away from any citizens or anything sharp, yes."

"Good to know."

Gamache watched Agent Cloutier sitting at her desk, staring into space. He tried to believe she was thinking, but the look on her face said that she was paralyzed by indecision.

"*Noli timere*," said Beauvoir with a grin.

"Huh. Well, maybe just a little *timere*," admitted Gamache. As he considered Agent Cloutier, he thought about her question.

*How would you feel . . . ?*

How would he feel if his daughter, a grown woman, a married woman, had been missing for a day and a half?

He'd be frantic. He'd hope and pray that someone would pay attention. Someone would help.

Agent Cloutier's persistence had shown courage. Her question had shown empathy.

Both were extremely valuable, he told himself, even as he watched her knock her phone off the desk. Into the garbage.

She was nervous, that much was obvious. About the missing young woman? About working with him? About failing? Or was there something else?

"I've arranged for another desk to be put into the office," said Beauvoir. He'd almost said "my office" but had stopped himself.

"*Merci*. I appreciate the thought, but I'd like to sit out here."

"Really?" Beauvoir looked around.

Desks were placed together, facing each other, two by two. Some neat, some with documents piled high. Some personalized, with family photos and memorabilia. Others antiseptic.

Gamache followed Beauvoir's gaze. It had been years, decades, since he'd sat in an open bullpen. At a desk like any other.

An investigator like any other.

Far from the humiliation it was meant to be, this actually felt comfortable. Comforting, even. Someone else was in charge, and he could just concentrate on the job at hand.

"If it's all right with you, I'll take that desk." He pointed to the empty one across from Cloutier.

"It's all yours." Putting his hand on Gamache's back, Beauvoir said, "If you need anything, or just want to talk, my door's always open."

Gamache recognized it as something he said to raw recruits. "When's your last day again?"

Beauvoir laughed. "It's good to have you back. Sir."

Gamache took a deep breath. The place smelled of sweat. Of coffee burned to the bottom of the glass pot. Every day. For years.

For intelligent people, no one in homicide, it seemed, ever learned to turn the thing off. Or make a fresh pot.

It smelled of paper and files, and feet.

It smelled familiar.

When a nervous Agent Gamache had walked in, his first day at homicide, the place had been a riot of noise. Of agents yelling to each other. Phones ringing. Typewriters clacking.

Now there was a murmur of voices, the soft buzz of cell phones, and the tippity-tap of laptops.

*Plus ça change, plus c'est la même chose.*

The more things change, the more they stay the same.

While the technology had changed, the job had not.

Killers were still killing, and Sûreté agents were still hunting them down.

Only then did Gamache realize how much, deep in his core, he'd missed this.


They left the island of Montréal, driving over the Champlain Bridge to the south shore.

He was in the passenger seat while Cloutier drove. Below them, the St. Lawrence River was packed with broken ice, as the spring melt took hold. Rivers across Québec were freezing and thawing, then freezing again. Creating massive ice jams. The rivers, swollen with melting snow and April showers, had nowhere to go. Except to burst their banks.

It happened every spring, the flooding. But this, he could see, was different.

Gamache hated heights, preferring to look straight ahead whenever he drove across the impressive bridge. But now he forced himself to look down. Feeling light-headed and slightly dizzy, he gripped the door handle and stared over the edge, at the huge, jagged columns of ice thrusting toward him out of the river.

As far down the St. Lawrence as he could see, there was ice. Cracked and heaved. And heading their way.

Turning to the front, he began breathing again, and with each breath he prayed to God the warm weather would take hold and melt the jams. Melt the dams. Relieve the rivers before they burst free.

But it didn't look promising, he thought as the wipers of their vehicle swept wet snow off the windshield. And the sky ahead was choked with cloud.

"Tell me what you know," he said to Agent Cloutier.

"Vivienne Godin and Carl Tracey live on a farm in the countryside

31

not far from Cowansville. Before we left, I did a bit of digging. The local Sûreté detachment sent someone to her place yesterday, after Homer called them. They searched but found nothing. No evidence of violence."

"And no Madame Godin."

"*Non.* They'd been called to the home three times in the past, all for domestic violence. But each time they arrived, Madame Godin withdrew the complaint and refused to let them in."

So her father had been right, thought Gamache. Something bad was happening.

"Officers no longer need a formal complaint," he said. "They can make an arrest if they themselves see evidence of abuse."

"Yes, but I guess there wasn't enough evidence."

"So no arrests?"

"*Non.*"

They rode in silence, each looking out at the gray, damp day. Thinking.

Gamache about this young woman, Vivienne Godin.

Cloutier about Vivienne's father, Homer.

When she went to turn off the highway, Gamache instructed her to continue on.

"We need to get as much information as possible before visiting her home and speaking to her husband. We'll get one shot at that before he kicks us off the property. We have to make each question count. Take the next turnoff, please, and head for the local detachment. They're the ones who took the calls, right?"

"Yes, but I've already spoken to them."

"Speaking on the phone and doing it in person are two different things. There's also the issue of respect. This's their territory. We shouldn't just barge in and start questioning people. Besides, we'll probably need their help."

A few minutes later they turned in to the town.

"Down here, please," said Gamache, pointing to a side street and then at a low building with the Sûreté emblem out front.

# CHAPTER FIVE

—

*Bonjour.* I'm Chief Inspector Gamache, this is Agent Cloutier." He slipped his Sûreté ID under the glass partition, and the receptionist took it. "We'd like to see Commander Flaubert, *s'il vous plaît.*"

The man behind the glass, a civilian, glanced at the ID, then at them, and pointed to a hard bench where a drunk was slumped.

"Wait over there."

*"Merci,"* Gamache said, and took a seat under a photo of the Premier Ministre du Québec, the man responsible for his demotion.

Crossing his legs, he leaned back on the bench and waited. Apparently just staring into space.

Cloutier paced, checking her phone for messages, gazing at posters, photographs, warnings, commendations on the walls. Photos of the Sûreté hockey team. She checked her phone for messages. Again.

Finally an officer came out and hurried across the entrance hall. Her hand extended. "Chief Superintendent—"

"Inspector," Gamache corrected, and wondered how many times he'd have to do that. "Chief Inspector." He was on his feet.

"Brigitte Flaubert," she said, shaking his hand.

"Yes, I remember," said Gamache.

As Chief Superintendent, he'd made it a point to visit each detachment in the province. To sit down with the commander, and especially the agents. To get their take on what needed improving.

"Sorry to keep you waiting." Commander Flaubert looked at Gamache with an increasingly familiar searching gaze. He suspected he'd have to get used to it.

Different from the curious looks he normally got on the street, as passersby tried to place this familiar face. The looks today were not so much to place him as to judge him.

Flaubert shot a displeased glance at the receptionist, who did not seem to care, then she turned to Agent Cloutier, as Gamache introduced her.

"If you'll come with me," said Flaubert.

They followed her into the back of the station and to her office, walking past desks occupied by busy Sûreté officers, who glanced up as they passed, then back down.

Then up again. Realizing that the large man in the parka wasn't a stranger at all but the former head of the whole damn force.

For his part, Gamache scanned the room, meeting eyes that quickly dropped.

But one officer caught his attention. He was hefty though not fat. Solidly built, he sat at his desk, and when the others dropped their gaze, he did not.

Gamache's eyes moved on, but not before thinking he knew the man. Recognized him from somewhere.

He'd be about thirty. Short, dark hair. Built like a truck. Six feet tall, maybe six-one, Gamache guessed, though it was hard to tell with him sitting down.

Where had he met this officer? The academy? Had he taught him? Had he presented him with a medal? Service? Bravery? Distinction?

Gamache didn't think so. He'd remember. And yet he knew this man.

There was also the issue of his eyes. Where the other officers in the room seemed curious, this one seemed wary.

The commander waved them to chairs on the other side of her desk and closed the door.

"How can I help you?" Flaubert asked.

Gamache took off his coat and nodded to Agent Cloutier to start.

"Ummm. Well." She tried to gather herself. "We're interested in a local woman. Vivienne Godin. We understand she's missing."

She placed a photo of Vivienne on the commander's desk.

Flaubert saw a young woman. Straight brown hair pulled back in a ponytail. Her eyes were a clear, almost piercing blue. She didn't look particularly happy, but neither did she look angry or upset. Vivienne Godin looked almost blank.

While she might have been attractive in real life, this picture drained all the life from her, leaving her pretty features dulled.

Commander Flaubert looked up from it, then from one to the other, eyes resting back on Agent Cloutier.

"I'm sorry, I'm not familiar with her. She's local, you say?"

"Yes. Married to Carl Tracey."

"Ahh. Tracey I know." Flaubert went to the door and called another officer over. The one who'd caught Gamache's attention when they'd arrived.

"This's Agent Cameron."

Gamache rose and saw immediately that he'd been wrong. This man wasn't six feet tall or even six-one. He'd be at least six-three. And formidably built.

His face from a distance was unremarkable.

But that changed once up close. What was remarkable about it was the scarring. There was a permanent cut through his lip and another through his left brow. His left cheekbone was slightly flattened, as was his nose.

Gamache also noticed, though it was admittedly hard to miss, the ring on Cameron's finger.

That's where he knew him from.

"*Patron*," said Cameron.

Gamache pointed to the ring. "A great game. I was there. Alouettes came from behind. You had some very impressive blocks. One at the end of the third quarter, right? Allowed the quarterback to run for a touchdown."

"Right." Cameron smiled as his beefy hand released Gamache's grip. He remained standing, squeezed into the small room. "That was a long time ago."

"Not so long. It's Robert Cameron, *n'est-ce pas?*"

"Bob. Yes."

This man had been a tackle with the Montréal Alouettes. Helped them win the Canadian Football League's Grey Cup a few years back.

And now he was with the Sûreté.

His brown hair was cut short, and his eyes had a sharp focus. An athlete's eyes. Always aware of his surroundings. Prepared to act and react.

Also a useful quality in a Sûreté agent, thought Gamache. As long as react didn't become overreact. In a man this size, it could be brutal. Even fatal.

But when Cameron spoke, it was almost in a whisper. His voice was deep, audible, more gentle than soft. Many large men enjoyed lording over, looming over, lesser beings. Intimidating with their height and girth. But Bob Cameron seemed anxious to put people at ease. To try to fit into a world not made for him.

It was both endearing and perplexing. Because Gamache had seen this man play football.

Had seen what Cameron was capable of. What he was good at. What he clearly enjoyed. And that was not just blocking and tackling. It was doing damage, to flesh and bone.

Gamache was pleased to see that off the field, and in a Sûreté uniform, Bob Cameron was not a natural brute. In fact, he reminded Gamache of his own son, Daniel. Taller than his father. Heftier. But gentle and thoughtful. Though there was that other side to him.

Gamache knew it was folly to assume Agent Cameron had the same qualities as his son, but still, he found himself warming to the man. While keeping an image in his mind of the left tackle in action. Grabbing hold of opponents. Slamming them to the ground.

"Bob, are you aware of a missing woman?" the commander asked. "Vivienne—"

"Godin," said Cameron. "*Oui.* Her father called yesterday, and I spoke to an agent from Montréal this morning." He turned to Cloutier. "You?"

"*Oui.*"

"Has something else happened? She's not—"

He knew that Gamache had been returned to homicide. And like

36

everyone else in the station, in the Sûreté, probably in the province, he'd also seen the posts on social media that morning.

But he hadn't heard that a body had been found, never mind this body.

"No," said Gamache. "But we thought we'd look around, if it's all right with you."

"Fine with me, but like I told her father, we don't consider her missing."

"Why not?"

"After his call, agents went to the place. Spoke to Tracey. When told his wife never arrived at her father's home, he apparently laughed. Said he wasn't surprised. He said she was probably off with some lover."

"That's not—" Cloutier began before Gamache signaled her to be quiet.

"And they believed him?" he asked.

"Not completely, of course. They looked in the house and the outbuildings. There was no sign of her. Her car was gone, and they also didn't see any sign of violence. They had to leave it at that."

"You say 'they,'" said Gamache. "You weren't with them?"

"No. I had other assignments."

"I see," said Gamache. "We hear there were complaints of domestic abuse."

"Yes. I answered those calls, but Madame Godin would never press charges."

"You don't need her to," Gamache pointed out.

"I know, but she didn't want us to do anything. Asked us to leave."

"Madame Godin isn't at home and isn't with her father," said Gamache. "So where do you think she went?"

"Honestly?"

"Yes, please."

"She was obviously being abused. I tried to help. First time she called, I gave her the number for the local shelter."

"You think she might be there?" Cloutier asked.

"I called and asked. She isn't. I think she just took off. She's holed up in some motel, trying to get as far from Tracey as possible."

"Then why didn't she go to her father?" asked Cloutier.

"Maybe she just needed time to herself."

It seemed a strangely unsatisfactory answer.

Gamache thought for a moment. "Does she have a cell phone?"

"No. There's no reception up there in the mountains."

"You don't seem particularly worried, Agent Cameron," said Gamache. "An abused woman disappears and you just go about your day?"

"I'm worried," snapped Cameron, then pulled back. "*Désolé.*"

Not so slow to anger after all, thought Gamache.

"Yes, I'm worried," said Cameron. "I know what a piece of work Tracey is. But she'd been gone only a few hours at the time. I was going to give it until noon today, then alert missing persons."

They looked at the clock. It was ten thirty in the morning.

"Do you mind my asking why you're here?" he asked. "How did you even hear about this?"

"Her father emailed me this morning," said Cloutier. "We're old friends."

"So this's unofficial?" asked Cameron.

"Oh, no," said Gamache. "This's official. You might be right and she's safe in a motel. But let's be certain." He turned to the commander. "Can you send out an alert, please? And make sure the information gets to all the shelters in the province."

"*Oui, absolument.*"

"What did her friends tell you?"

"I didn't ask," said Cameron.

"Why not?"

"Because it wasn't an active investigation," said Cameron. "Look, if Vivienne needs time away, I for one can't blame her. I'm not going to track her down for her husband."

"But it's not for him," said Cloutier. "It's for her father. He was expecting her Saturday night. It's now Monday. You don't think she'd have called him by now, if she was safe?"

"Maybe she's afraid of him, too," said Cameron. "Maybe they didn't get along."

"Then why would she say she was going to him? She must've been in trouble. Where else would she turn? Where else would she feel safe?"

Gamache suspected that was true. But he also knew, from experience, people escaping abusive situations often made a fatal, though understandable, error.

They went to where they felt safe. Their families, their best friends.

Obvious places for support. But also obvious places to be found.

Where would the abuser look first, except family and friends?

If Vivienne Godin was leaving her abusive husband, Gamache hoped she'd changed her mind and instead of going to her father, she'd gone to some motel. Or shelter.

"Is that the woman you met?" He pointed to the photo on the desk.

"That's her," Cameron said in his gentle voice.

But Gamache wasn't fooled. He'd seen the man play. Had watched, cheered, as the Alouettes won the Grey Cup on that snowy day. Had seen how ferociously, certainly gleefully, this man had plowed into oncoming defensive tackles. Protecting his quarterback with all his might. And he was certainly mighty, even now.

Though something perplexed Gamache. That scarring. Football players wore helmets with grilles to protect their faces. While they could get concussions and twisted arms and legs, it would be almost impossible to get injuries like that to his face.

Those came, Gamache knew, from other types of blows.

"When was the first time she called for help?"

"Last summer sometime. I answered the call."

"You obviously remember it," said Gamache. He saw Cameron flush and tucked that away.

"And she called you more than once?" said Cloutier.

"Not me, 911. But yes, mostly when welfare checks came out."

"They're unemployed?" asked Gamache.

"Yeah, but Tracey does pottery."

"Pottery?" said Gamache, far from sure he'd heard right. "Like clay?"

"Yes. He makes things that people can't use. Useless. Like the man."

Carl Tracey was an artist, thought Gamache. But then, why not? Having known many artists in his life, especially through Clara, he'd grown to realize they were often not the most stable, or house-trained, individuals.

"When was the last time you were called to the home?" Gamache asked.

"Two weeks ago. Again she refused help."

"Why would she call, then refuse help?" asked Cloutier. "It doesn't make sense."

"She just wanted the beating to stop," said Cameron. "But she didn't want him arrested. I think she knew he'd be out in hours and then things would get really bad."

Gamache nodded. It was the terrible flaw in the system. It appeared to help the abused while actually just piling on more abuse. Worse abuse.

"There was nothing more we could do, really," said Cameron.

"Really?"

"Sir?" asked Cameron.

"You said there was nothing you could do . . . really." Gamache let that sit for a moment. "But was there something you did do?"

Cameron hesitated before finally answering. "I took Carl aside when I saw him in town last week. I warned him."

"What did you say?" asked Gamache.

"I told him I knew what he was doing to his wife and if there was one more complaint, I'd beat the shit out of him."

"You did what?" asked Gamache while beside him Cloutier muttered, "Good."

Gamache stood up and faced the mammoth man.

The small room grew even smaller. Suffocating.

"That was the wrong thing to do," said Commander Flaubert, recognizing that something needed to be said, though her tone was without real reproach.

"Why was it wrong?" asked Cameron, addressing Gamache. "He needed to know."

"Know what?" asked Gamache. "That cops with an ID card and a gun will be judge and jury and carry out the sentence? Did you want him to know that punishing one beating with another is the way we do things in the Sûreté? Did you want to cede all moral high ground?"

Gamache spoke clearly. And slowly. Choosing his words carefully and swallowing the ones that were screaming to get out. Though his outrage was evident. In his extreme stillness. And in each tightly. Controlled. Word.

"Threats of violence will not be tolerated. You're an officer in the Sûreté du Québec, not a thug. You set the tone, the atmosphere. You act as a role model, either consciously or unconsciously."

"My concern was for a vulnerable woman, a pregnant woman and her unborn child. Not for the entire population of Québec."

"The two are the same. No citizen is safe in a state where police feel free to beat those they don't like. Who take the law into their own hands."

"And you didn't?" asked Cameron.

"Agent Cameron!" snapped Commander Flaubert.

It was too late. The words were out, the line had been crossed.

Cloutier's mouth dropped open, but she said nothing. Just stared at the two men, staring at each other.

"I did," said Gamache. "And paid the price. Knew I would. Knew I should. You seem to think you're perfectly within your rights to threaten assault. To maybe even do it. Without censure."

Cameron couldn't deny that.

"At what stage did you think a threat of violence was appropriate?"

"At the stage, sir, when I realized the law could not protect Vivienne Godin."

"So you would? By piling violence on violence?"

"If you'd seen her—"

"I've seen worse."

The truth of that, the horror of that, pressed up against them in the tiny room.

"I'm not saying what was happening to Vivienne Godin was all right," Gamache went on. More gently. "Of course it wasn't. Of course it's tempting to do something, anything, to stop it. It's horrific when, as people sworn to protect, we cannot. When someone we know to be guilty is beyond our reach. When they can keep doing it and we can't stop it. But it's even worse if the cops become criminals, too. Do you understand?"

"Yessir."

"Do you really?" asked Gamache.

There was a pause as Agent Cameron considered, then finally nodded.

"There's one other thing," said Gamache, his voice now back to normal. "Did you consider what a threat like that would do to a man like Carl Tracey? Did you really think it would stop him from abusing his wife? Or would it, could it, enrage him even more? And who would he take it out on? You—or her?"

There was silence as Cameron considered a question he hadn't thought of before.

"Consequences," said Gamache. "We must always consider the consequences of our actions. Or inaction. It won't necessarily change what we do, but we need to be aware of the effect. That's the contract we have with the people of Québec. That those who have an ID card and a gun also have self-control."

"Yessir."

"*Bon.*"

He at least now understood why Cameron hadn't gone to the farmhouse himself yesterday.

Gamache sat down again. "Go on, Agent Cloutier."

The room, still tingling, settled back to near normal.

"Do you know if Vivienne has any friends we can contact?" Cloutier asked. "Anyone she might be with?"

Cameron shook his head. "Tracey didn't provide any names, and no one's come forward or shown concern."

They were getting a picture of Vivienne Godin's life, and what they saw was not good.

A woman isolated in a remote farmhouse. It was, they knew, one of the warning signs of extreme abuse. Control.

"Any gossip?" Cloutier asked.

"You mean an affair?" asked Cameron. "Again, if there was, I never heard it."

"And Tracey, does he have any friends?"

"Drinking buddies," said Cameron. "But even they seem to have disappeared. Last time I saw him in town, he was drinking alone at the joint on the edge of town."

"Name?" asked Cloutier. She was getting the hang of this.

"Le Lapin Grossier."

"The Dirty Rabbit?" she asked as he wrote.

"More like filthy," said Cameron.

"The Obscene Rabbit," said Flaubert. "It's a strip joint."

The interview was winding down.

"Thank you for your help," said Gamache as he stood and took his coat off the back of the chair.

"What're you going to do now, if you don't mind my asking?" said Cameron.

"We're going to visit Monsieur Tracey," said Gamache.

"Would you like me there?"

Gamache paused. He'd been about to decline, given Cameron's last encounter with Carl Tracey, but now wondered if it mightn't work in their favor. While Cameron's threat to beat Tracey was wrong, it was done. Gamache, the realist, knew that showing up with this agent might just shake some truth loose.

"If you don't mind," he asked the commander, who nodded, "that would be helpful. You can show us the way."

"I'll get my coat," said Cameron.

After he left, the commander said, "I'm sorry he threatened Tracey. I didn't know about that."

"Are you? Sorry?"

Commander Flaubert reddened. "I understand why he did it."

Gamache thought for a moment, looking at the closed door through which the large man had disappeared.

"The scars on his face?" he said. "Not from football."

"*Non.* Those are thanks to his father."

Gamache took a deep breath and shook his head. Had Bob Cameron turned that hurt, that pain, that betrayal, into something useful? Into sport? And now into protecting others?

Or had he learned something else from his father?

That day in the bitterly cold stands in Montréal again came to mind. Wrapped in blankets with Reine-Marie and their son, Daniel, watching the Grey Cup final. Hearing the crashes and grunts and shouts from the field.

The brutality. As the massive left tackle found his quarry. And decked him. Standing over the body and opening his arms in a primal display of domination.

To wild applause. To approval.

Was he still doing it, only now in a Sûreté uniform?

Once in the car, following Agent Cameron's vehicle, Gamache asked Agent Cloutier, "What do you think of him?"

"Cameron? I don't know."

"Think about it."

She thought. "He called her Madame Godin, but when he got angry, he called her Vivienne."

"*Oui.* When you spoke with him this morning, did you mention she was pregnant?"

Cloutier went back over the conversation. "No."

"I see."

And yet, thought Gamache, Agent Cameron knew that Vivienne was going to have a baby.

Now, how was that?

As they got closer to the farmhouse, the wipers pushing the wet flakes off the windshield, Agent Cloutier did what she always did in times of extreme stress.

Two times four is eight.

Three times five is fifteen.

Her times tables. Laid out neatly, in rows and columns.

Five times four is . . .

Her meditation. Her happy place. No chaos could survive in the tightly packed numbers. Everything in its place. In its home. Safe. Predictable. Known. Every question had an answer.

Twenty.

Terrible things did not happen to the pregnant daughter of an old friend, in the times table.

Six times six is . . .

Only, Cloutier knew, something had happened. And it was up to them to find the answer.

. . . thirty-six.

Thirty-six hours Vivienne was now missing.

# CHAPTER SIX

———

"What do you think?" Gabri asked Clara as they stood on the stone bridge and looked into the Rivière Bella Bella below.

He had to speak up, over the roar.

The water rushing beneath them, so clear and gentle in summer, was seething. Frothing with brown foam and great chunks of ice and tree limbs swept into it in the spring runoff.

All very natural. All very predictable.

But there was a problem.

There was too much of it. Too much water. Too much ice. Far too much forest swirling in the waters.

Gabri and Clara turned around and looked downriver.

"Damn," muttered Clara, and then, raising her voice, she turned to Gabri. "A dam is forming. I think it's time to start sandbagging."

"Did someone say sandbagging?" asked Ruth as she joined them on the bridge.

She'd put a moth-eaten woolen scarf over her short white hair and tied it at her chin, so that she looked like an elderly Victorian gentleman with a toothache. And a duck.

"Now, Ruth." Gabri spoke with exaggerated patience. "We've been through this before. When we call for volunteers to sandbag, we don't mean to hit each other over the head with sand-filled socks."

"Shit," said Ruth.

"No," said Gabri. "Not shit either, as we learned last spring."

Clara had returned to the other side of the bridge and looked at her garden, which backed onto the Rivière Bella Bella. The river had risen rapidly in the last hour and was now just inches from the top.

"I've never seen it so high so early," said Gabri, joining her.

"Are you talking about the river or Ruth?" asked Clara.

Gabri laughed, then regarded their neighbor more closely.

Ruth looked fairly sober, somber even. Though the duck looked bleary. But then, ducks often did.

"What do you think, Ruth?" Gabri asked, raising his voice so she could hear over the rushing waters and her natural inclination to not listen.

She was the oldest resident of Three Pines. But how old was a matter of some debate.

"We found her under a rock," Gabri's partner, Olivier, was fond of explaining. And she did appear more than a little fossilized.

She also happened to be the chief of the volunteer fire department. Not because she was a natural leader but because most villagers would rather run into a burning building or a river in full flood than face Ruth Zardo's sharp tongue.

She tipped her head back and looked into the sky. It had stopped snowing but was still threatening moisture of some sort. Exactly what they did not need.

"I think we should order more sand," she said, dropping her eyes to consider the river below. "I checked yesterday, and we have enough in the pile behind the old railway station for a normal flood, but this doesn't look normal to me."

If anyone had a knowledge of abnormal, it was Ruth.

"I've only seen it this high once before," she said. "Yes, I guess it's time."

"For what?" asked Clara.

"Another hundred-year flood."

"Oh, shit," said Gabri. "Fuckity fuck fuck. *Merde.*" Then he paused. "What's a hundred-year flood?"

"Surely the name is a giveaway," said Clara.

They followed Ruth as she turned toward the bistro.

"A hundred-year flood happens every hundred years, right?" Gabri whispered to Clara.

"I'd have to say yes."

"Then how could Ruth have seen one before?" He dropped his voice still further. "How old is she?"

"Not a clue. I'm still trying to figure out how old the duck is," said Clara.

Just then Rosa, in Ruth's arms a few paces ahead, turned her head 180 degrees. And glared at them.

"The Devil Duck," whispered Gabri. "If her head spins all the way around, I'm running for the hills."

But Rosa just turned back and nestled into the crook of Ruth's arm. And went to sleep.

Unaware of, or unconcerned about, the rising waters.

But then, thought Clara, as they entered the bistro, ducks could fly. And people could not.

Their tires spun in the thick mud, and the car slewed sideways on the hill.

The spring thaw had once again brought hope and muck. It was a beautiful filthy season.

"Stop, stop," said Gamache. *"Arrêt,"* he commanded when Cloutier gunned it one more time. And the car slipped a few more feet sideways, toward the gully.

Up ahead, Cameron's patrol car was sliding backward. Toward them.

"Back up," said Gamache. "Slowly."

He kept his voice calm and level, even as he watched Cameron's vehicle gather speed on the steep slope.

"What you want to do," he said, "is—"

"I know, I know."

As he watched, she put the car in reverse and touched the gas. Nursing it backward. Gamache braced, watching Cameron's car coming at them even as Cloutier applied gas and theirs sped up.

There was a small thud as the Sûreté vehicles met. Cloutier expertly nursed the brakes as both slowed down and came to a halt on the shoulder.

She'd executed the maneuver perfectly. Gamache doubted he could have done nearly as well.

"*Formidable,*" he said, and saw her smile.

"Please don't ask me to do that again."

He laughed. "Believe me, Agent Cloutier, if that ever needs to be done again, you're the one I'll call."

Cameron had gotten out and was sliding toward them, gripping the cars as he went. Finally stopping at Gamache's window.

"That was impressive. *Merci.*" Bending in, he looked at Gamache. "What now?"

"Now"—Gamache grabbed his hat and gloves—"we walk."

Cloutier looked up the hill. "It's at least half a kilometer to their place."

"Then we'd better get going," said Gamache, already out of the car and looking around.

The plump April snowflakes had stopped, and the air was cool and fresh. He took a deep breath and smelled sweet pine needles and musky leaves and mud.

And heard—

"What's that?" asked Cloutier, cocking her head.

"A river," said Cameron. "It must've broken up. The spring runoff's started."

Gamache turned toward the sound coming from deep in the woods.

While the river could not be seen, it could be heard. The waters rushing down the side of the mountain. It was a sound as familiar to those in the Québec countryside as sirens were in the city.

When he'd left Three Pines early that morning to get into Montréal, all had been silent. Except for the gentle tap-tap-tapping as the huge flakes landed on the trees and homes and vehicles.

But something had broken, something had woken, in the meantime. Something not at all gentle.

He took another deep breath, but with less pleasure.

All sorts of things woke up in the spring. With the warmer weather. Bears. Chipmunks. Skunks and racoons. And rivers.

They came to life.

There were few things more powerful, or destructive, or terrifying, than a hungry bear or a river in full flood.

Gamache knew exactly where the river was heading. While he'd never been along this road before, he knew the area. They weren't all that far from his own village.

Which meant the roar they heard was the Rivière Bella Bella, heading straight into Three Pines.

He took out his phone to call Reine-Marie, to warn her and find out how things were, but Cameron was right. There was no signal.

He clicked the phone off, put it back in his pocket, and turned to look up the muddy road.

"Come on," he said, and started the climb.


"The lottery ticket," said Isabelle Lacoste, looking over the file at Jean-Guy Beauvoir.

"What?"

Lacoste was between meetings. She'd dropped by to chat, and instead he'd put her to work, tossing her files and saying, "Take a look at these and tell me what you think."

The two sat in companionable silence, reading about sometimes gruesome, sometimes straightforward, always tragic murders. Every now and then, Superintendent Lacoste had asked a question. Or made a note. Or a comment.

"In the Anderson case," she said. "The victim was found with a lottery ticket in her pocket."

"*Oui*. A group of co-workers were in a pool."

"Which she organized."

"Yes." He leaned over so he could read the file she was holding. "But it was a losing ticket."

"Doesn't matter."

"Then what does?"

"Everyone in her section was in the lottery pool, right? Ten people?"

"Yes."

"But it says here there're eleven in that division. One was left out. Which one?"

Beauvoir sat back and thought. It seemed a tiny detail, but that was the thing about murders. And murderers. They hid in the details. The small things easily overlooked.

"You think whoever was left out killed her for the lottery ticket? But why not take it?"

"*Non.*" Isabelle was shaking her head. Then she suddenly looked at her watch. "I'm going to be late for the next meeting."

"But wait, why leave the ticket behind if that was the motive?" asked Beauvoir, calling after Lacoste as she made for the door.

"Because the ticket wasn't the motive. Being left out was. And it probably wasn't the first time. What happens when someone is shunned, over and over?"

He grabbed the dossier and scanned it, muttering, "*Merde.* She might be right."

Chief Inspector Beauvoir called the lead investigator and suggested he find out all he could about the co-worker who had not been included.

Then he sat back down and continued to go over the files.

He was damned if he was going to leave a mess for his replacement. Especially since he'd be spending holidays with that replacement for years to come.

In ten days' time, he and Annie would get on a flight to Paris with Honoré, to start their new lives. And he to start a new job in private industry.

It was almost impossible to believe.

April in Paris. The trees would be in leaf. The gardens, laid out so formally, would be in bloom. Parisians would be sitting at sidewalk cafés enjoying the warmth and their aperitifs.

The City of Light at its most luminous.

He looked out his large window at Montréal. He couldn't see the top of Mont Royal for the low-hanging clouds.

While the snow had stopped, the gloom had not.

Late spring in Québec was beautiful.

Early spring, on the other hand, was a pile of shit. Literally, in some cases. Some places.

He could almost smell it now. In the city it was not really noticeable. But in the countryside?

After years visiting the Gamaches at their home in the tiny village of Three Pines, Jean-Guy had gotten much closer to nature. To the rhythms. The surprises. The miracles.

Close enough to confirm that he hated the countryside. It was dirty and unpredictable. And it smelled.

Beauvoir still harbored the suspicion that those who could live in Montréal or Québec City but chose the countryside had at least one screw loose. This was confirmed when he'd first met the residents of Three Pines, and especially the old poet. Who seemed to have lost all her screws and, as a result, spent her time screwing with others. Or at least with Jean-Guy.

It didn't help that many of the villagers were Anglophones. And Jean-Guy was an Anglophobe.

They scared him. Partly because while his English was good, he rarely caught the nuances. Or the cultural references. Who was Captain Crunch? Captain Kangaroo? Why so many captains? Why not generals? And why did they eat frites with ketchup and not mayonnaise? And how do you begin to explain plum pudding? It looked, and smelled, like early spring.

And they ate it.

Over time, he'd grown to not just like the village but love the villagers. To accept their foibles. As they accepted his.

But still, plum pudding? It sounded so good and tasted so bad.

Anglos.

His cell phone rang, and he answered immediately.

"*Salut*," came the cheerful voice. "Am I calling at a bad time?"

"If it was, I wouldn't answer."

Though they both knew that wasn't true. Short of being in the middle of a shoot-out, when Annie called, he answered.

A successful lawyer, Annie had arranged a transfer to the Paris office and was now studying to get her license to become an *avocat* in France.

"Do you think you can go to Three Pines tonight?" she asked.

"I wasn't planning to. Why?"

"I just called Mom, and she told me the Bella Bella's going to flood."

"It does every spring."

"This seems different. She tried to sound casual, but I could hear that she's worried. She wanted to make sure Honoré and I weren't going down."

"That bad?"

It would have to be near catastrophic for his mother-in-law to give up precious time with them.

Jean-Guy dropped his feet off the desk and leaned forward.

"They'll need help sandbagging," said Annie. "Still, how bad can it be? It's the Bella Bella, not the St. Lawrence or the Mighty Mississippi. The worst that can happen is water in the basements, right? It's never completely flooded before."

Beauvoir walked to the window.

Lots of things never happened before, he knew. Then suddenly did. It only took once. Murder, for instance. A person was only killed once. And that was enough.

Yes, just because something had never happened, that didn't mean it couldn't. Or wouldn't.

And Annie was worried. Otherwise she'd never have called and asked him to go down.

After he hung up, he continued to look out the window. She'd mentioned the St. Lawrence. If the Bella Bella was flooding, what was the huge river that encircled the island of Montréal doing?

Through the skyscrapers, he could see the river was still frozen. He sighed with some relief. Now, that would be a problem. . . .

But then he looked more closely, and as his eyes adjusted, he could see fissures. And long shadows. That meant columns of ice had pushed their way up and out. Great chunks were piling up, and unless something happened soon, the St. Lawrence would also flood. And worse. The force of it could crush the pylons holding the bridges in place.

He picked up the phone. As he waited for Chief Superintendent Toussaint to answer, he thought again about Paris. Where the flowers were in bloom.

Where his little, growing family would live. In peace.

# CHAPTER SEVEN

~

Awful! Arrogant poseur #MorrowSucks

Overrated. No talent. #MorrowSucks

Just plain shit. #MorrowSucks

Lock him up #GamacheSux

The donkeys noticed first.

They turned in the field and started forward. Toward the fence. One or two were braying.

Carl Tracey came out and stood in the doorway of the barn and watched as three figures, covered in mud, trudged down the drive.

They looked like something out of a horror film. Golems, heading his way.

Tracey reached over and took hold of the pitchfork.

Gamache raised his hand in a fist, to signal them to stop.

Cameron, familiar with the silent combat gesture, did.

Cloutier did not.

"Agent Cloutier."

When she turned, Gamache nodded forward, and she saw it then.

Framed in the open barn door was a man straight out of some horror film.

He was disheveled. Filthy. With a pitchfork.

~

Tracey watched them closely. The two men were large. Disheveled. Filthy. The woman was small and filthy.

He tightened his grip on the pitchfork.


"Monsieur Tracey?"

"What do you want?" he shouted. In English.

Gamache lifted his hands, to show they held no weapon, and stepped forward. Cameron instinctively went to join him, to protect his quarterback, but once again Gamache gave him a signal.

To stand down. But remain alert.

The Chief Inspector took a few steps toward Tracey. There were at least fifteen paces to go before they'd be face-to-face, but already he could smell the booze.

"We're with the Sûreté du Québec—" Gamache began, in English.

"Get off my land."

"My name is Chief Inspector Armand Gamache. This is Agent Cloutier. And this—"

"I know who that is." Now that they were closer, Tracey recognized the man who'd threatened him with a beating not long ago. "Get him the fuck off my land."

He lifted the pitchfork and pointed it toward Cameron. Making a small jabbing movement. It was a futile, almost comic gesture.

But Gamache wasn't smiling. Instead he put his arms out at his sides and took a few steps closer.

Carl Tracey was in his mid-thirties. Slightly shorter, slightly lighter than Gamache. But where Gamache was solid, this man was not. As he jabbed, he jiggled.

Still, Gamache knew it was never wise to underestimate anyone. Especially someone with a pitchfork.

He stopped.

"We'd like to speak with your wife, please. Vivienne Godin. Is she here?"

"No. I already told the cops that she's gone away."

"And you haven't heard from her? She hasn't called?"

"No."

The only one who'd called him was her crazy father. Every hour, on the hour. Even through the night. Threatening him. But he wouldn't tell them that.

He noticed Cameron had opened his jacket. To reveal a gun on his belt.

Shit.

But the man standing just a few feet away, the guy in charge, displayed no weapon. In fact, he seemed to be trying to lull Tracey into some sort of trance. So deep and calm was his voice.

When Gamache took another step toward him, Tracey also stepped forward and thrust the pitchfork at the cop. "Stop right there."

The sharp tines stopped within a foot of Gamache's face. But he didn't flinch. Instead he looked right past the points. Straight into Tracey's eyes.

His gaze, Tracey saw with some alarm, wasn't angry. Wasn't threatening. Certainly wasn't frightened. It was thoughtful.

Anger, rage, violence Tracey could handle. But this was just confusing. And off-putting. And a little frightening.

Gamache, a pitchfork away from Tracey, could see the bloodshot eyes. And sense the havoc.

"I'm going to reach into my pocket and bring out my Sûreté ID." As he spoke, he did just that, watching the man closely. Tracey's nostrils flared with each breath. Longing to attack. And he probably would have, Gamache knew, if it weren't for Cameron. And his earlier threat to beat Tracey. This man obviously knew it was not an empty threat.

While Gamache did not have a loaded gun, he did have Cameron. A biological weapon.

Bringing out the card, he offered it to Tracey, who pushed his head forward and read.

"It says here you're Chief Superintendent."

"My new card hasn't arrived."

"So you were the big boss, but not anymore?"

Tracey was more with-it than Gamache had given him credit for. Replacing the card, Gamache shrugged and smiled.

"I messed up. It happens."

He looked at Tracey now with a slightly conspiratorial gaze. Wanting Tracey to try to guess what he could possibly have done to warrant such a demotion.

Gamache knew what a man like Tracey would naturally assume.

It would have to be something illegal. Almost certainly brutal. If Tracey thought Cameron was threatening, just wait for it . . .

So now Tracey was well and truly confused.

Gamache's manner was courteous, calm. But he intimated he was capable of something else.

"What do you want?" demanded Tracey.

"Do you know what I'd really like?"

"What?"

"Water. And to use your phone."

"What?"

"Do you mind?" asked Gamache.

It appeared such a reasonable, though random, request that Tracey was struck dumb for a moment.

"There's a hose over there." He gestured to the side of the barn. "I'll bring the phone out. Make your call, then leave."

"*Merci.* I'm most grateful."

Everyone in the farmyard was now staring at Gamache with open astonishment, including the donkeys. But human behavior often astonished them.

"Are you okay, *patron*?" asked Cameron when Tracey left.

He'd walked over to the Chief and scanned him for blood, concerned he might have hit his head on a rock in one of the many falls as they'd made their way, slipping and sliding, up the hill.

"How would you have had me handle this?" Gamache asked as they walked over to the hose. "Grab the pitchfork and beat him with it?"

Cameron flushed. It was, actually, exactly what he'd expected. And would have done.

Gamache gestured to the others to take the water first.

"You could've demanded to see Vivienne," said Cloutier, reaching for the hose.

"I did ask."

"Ask, yes, but couldn't you have pushed harder?"

"To what end? Do you know what he'd have done? Run us off his property, and he'd have had every right. We have no warrant." Gamache glanced behind him to make sure Tracey wasn't approaching. Then he lowered his voice.

"We have to assume we're dealing with a person capable of murdering his pregnant wife. And everything we've heard about him confirms he's abusive. Violent."

Gamache reached over and patted a donkey, taking in the barnyard as he did. He also assumed Tracey was watching them from the house.

There were a lot of places to bury a body here. Though he doubted that Carl Tracey would be stupid enough to put her on their own property.

But then, people did stupid things. Like kill each other. And Carl Tracey did not strike him as the brightest of people.

Besides, he held out some hope that Vivienne Godin was indeed alive and had fled this terrible place.

"Violence, threats, he understands," said Gamache quietly, as though speaking to the donkey, who was now nuzzling him. Leaving a slimy trail of drool and grass on his already filthy coat. "The best way to keep Carl Tracey off balance is to be courteous. Didn't you notice how confused he became?"

"So you want us to be nice to him?" asked Cameron.

"Exactly. We can always ratchet it up later. Steps. Degrees. And always keep something in reserve. And," said Gamache as he took the hose once Cameron had finished. "We have to keep something else in mind."

"That he's a killer," said Cloutier.

Gamache bent over and drank. He was parched, and as he gulped, it struck him as ironic, and so like nature, to provide Tracey, a rancid man, with such sweet water.

"That he might be innocent," said Gamache, lowering the hose, washing off his muddy hands, and turning off the tap.

"Of murder, let's hope," said Cloutier. "But not of beating his wife. His pregnant wife."

"True," said Gamache. "But we're here to investigate, not convict. Try to keep your emotions in check. A clear head, right, Agent Cloutier?"

"*Oui, patron.*"

"You want the phone or not," shouted Tracey, stepping off the porch and holding the handset out. "Make the call and get off my fucking land."

Gamache clicked it on and heard a dial tone. Finally, a phone that worked. In the background, almost unnoticed by now, was the sound of the Rivière Bella Bella, rushing toward Three Pines.

As Gamache dialed the number from memory, he watched Carl Tracey walk over to the donkeys, who nuzzled him, pushing him playfully. Tracey produced huge carrots and gave one to each.

The phone rang a few times before being answered.

"*Oui, allô,*" Gamache said, clearly relieved. "Yes, everything's fine. No cell-phone coverage here, so I've had to borrow a phone. How are things with you? . . . I see. . . . Yes. Sandbagging. Good idea. . . . I will." He looked at Tracey, who'd, at the mention of sandbagging, turned from the donkeys with a look of some alarm.

"But I do need a favor," said Gamache. "I'm at the farm where Vivienne Godin and her husband live. Carl Tracey refuses to answer questions or let us into the house or barn. I need a search warrant immediately. T-R-A-C-E-Y. . . . *Oui.*"

Tracey's face went slack. As though he'd been sandbagged.

"You can call back at this number," continued Gamache. "If you don't get an answer, send patrol cars up. They know the place. In fact, when the search warrant comes through, send them up to help search. But tell them the road is pretty much impassable. . . . No, everything's fine. I'll let you know when we have more news about Madame Godin. *Au revoir.*"

At Sûreté headquarters, Jean-Guy Beauvoir hung up and quickly made out a warrant request, then put in a call to a judge.

"Yes, Your Honor, we need it immediately. Chief Inspector Gamache is on-site and waiting. A woman is missing and perhaps murdered by her husband. I'm sending the request now."

He hit the send key. "Please let me know."

Then he hung up and looked out the window.

The rain had begun. It was pissing April showers.

# CHAPTER EIGHT

―

Gamache handed the phone back to Tracey, with a smile. *"Merci.* Most helpful."

"What the fuck was that?"

"You heard, Mr. Tracey. In a few minutes, that phone will ring again. It'll be about a warrant to search your property. Best to answer it. Let's go into your house, and while we wait for the call confirming the search warrant, you can answer some questions."

Tracey's face hardened. He looked like an obstinate child.

"Or not," said Gamache pleasantly. "But we're cold and wet and would appreciate your cooperation."

He could almost hear Cameron and Cloutier gagging at his courteous tone.

Tracey, it seemed, had gotten the point. He gestured for them to follow.

The mud had hardened onto their coats and pant legs and boots. They looked and felt like Québec's version of the Terra-Cotta Warriors. The Sûreté officers took off their coats and boots, leaving them on the porch. But they couldn't very well remove their wet and filthy slacks.

Tracey had no such hesitation about trailing muck through his house and had kept his rubber boots on.

It was hot in the home, almost stifling. An elderly mutt lay by the woodstove in the kitchen.

"Beer walk soon," said Tracey, gesturing toward the dog.

Gamache knew what that meant, though the others did not. He

looked past the gray muzzle into the tired old eyes and thought of the walk into the woods, with the rifle.

And wondered if the same fate had befallen the dog's mistress.

Dishes, pots, and pans were piled into and out of the sink. The place stank of grease and rotting food. Booze and old dog and cigarettes. The smell was almost overpowering.

Gamache took a deep breath through his nose. Wondering if, in the sweltering heat, he could pick up another scent.

Something familiar. Something unmistakable. Something far worse.

But he could not. It was, perhaps, masked by the other rotting odors. But he doubted it. There was really no masking that one putrid stench.

The three Sûreté officers had joined Tracey at the Formica kitchen table. Tracey lit a cigarette while Cloutier and Cameron waited for Gamache to do something.

But he was doing something. Armand Gamache was listening.

For a sound, however remote, telling him that there was someone else in the home. A tapping. A muffled call.

Anything.

But there was only silence.

Finally he said, "Monsieur Tracey, you say your wife isn't here. Do you know where she is?"

Cloutier had brought out her iPhone and was recording everything.

"I already told you cops. All I know is when I woke up yesterday morning, she was gone. No note, no nothin'."

"Any ideas?"

Tracey laughed. "She could be anywhere. On a bender. Shacked up with some guy. I'll tell you, when she comes back—"

He remembered, too late, who he was talking to.

"Yes?" said Gamache. "Go on."

"Nothin'."

Armand Gamache had looked across lots of tables, at lots of murderers. He didn't kid himself that he had, even after all these years, some sort of special talent. To spot a killer.

He didn't really know if he was looking at one now. But he found himself increasingly repulsed by Carl Tracey.

"We understand from Vivienne's father that she's pregnant."

"Yeah. Who knows who knocked her up? Doubt it's mine. And if she thinks I'm going to raise the bastard, she has another thing coming."

"And what would she have coming?" asked Gamache.

Tracey smirked. "How would you feel if your wife screwed another man and got pregnant?"

Gamache raised his chin and stared at Tracey.

And Carl Tracey stared back across the table into those calm, focused eyes and knew that while that shot had missed, this Sûreté officer was human. And therefore vulnerable. And he'd find that chink eventually.

"Aren't you worried at all about her?" asked Agent Cloutier.

Tracey took his eyes from Gamache and shifted to the woman cop. "Why should I be? Look, like I said, she's probably just taken off, and when that guy gets tired of her, she'll come back. I don't even know why it's any of your business."

Just then the phone rang.

"You might as well answer it," said Tracey. "It's for you."

Gamache clicked it on, but before he could say anything, he was met with a torrent of abuse. Culminating in the man shouting, "Where's my daughter? If you don't tell me, I'm coming down, and I'm going to beat it out of you. You understand?"

Everyone in the room heard the voice, and Gamache could see Tracey looking triumphant.

*See what I have to put up with?* his expression said.

"Monsieur Godin?" Gamache began.

"Who is this?"

"My name is Gamache, I'm with the Sûreté—"

"Oh, God, has something happened? Have you found her? Oh, God—"

"*Non, monsieur.* We have no news of your daughter. I'm here with Lysette Cloutier. She's a friend of yours, I understand. Agent Cloutier asked us to investigate."

There was heavy breathing on the other end as Godin composed himself.

"We're interviewing Monsieur Tracey right now."

"Monsieur Tracey? Monsieur? The man's a monster and you call him 'monsieur'? He might've . . . he could've . . . Do you know she's pregnant?"

"Yes. Please, calm yourself. We're doing all we can. I promise you, we'll find her."

"You will. Alive?"

It was said so pathetically. Not just a word but a world. Alive. Alive. And all that meant. For him. For her. For the child. A life spread out before them. With birthdays and holidays. Celebrations.

Alive.

"We'll find her," Gamache repeated, and wondered if Monsieur Godin noticed he hadn't said "alive." "Do you have someone with you?"

"*Non, non.* Vivienne's my only child. My wife died a few years ago. I was expecting her here, you know. She was going to leave him. I'd begged her for years to leave that son of a bitch."

There was a pause. Gamache heard heavy breathing, almost sobs, before Monsieur Godin was able to speak again.

"What has he done with her? Ask him. He knows. Make him tell you. If you don't, I will."

"Stay at home, Monsieur Godin. In case she calls."

Even as he said it, Gamache recognized it as cheap, potentially cruel manipulation. But he had to keep Godin away from Tracey. And there was still a chance his daughter was alive and would call her father.

"I'll be in touch with you when we're finished here. *D'accord?*"

There was a deep, deep breath on the other end of the line. And finally, "*D'accord.*"

"Can I speak to him?" whispered Cloutier, her hand out for the phone. "Homer, it's Lysette. . . . *Oui. Oui.* . . . I promise. . . . *Oui.*"

She'd dropped her eyes to the table and was listening intently. Homer Godin's voice was now quieter, so the others couldn't hear what he was saying.

"Chief Inspector Gamache will call you as soon as possible," said Cloutier once Vivienne's father had stopped talking. "*Oui.* I promise."

Her voice, gentle, calming, seemed to be having an effect. After saying goodbye, she placed the phone on the table.

"The man's a shithead," said Tracey, speaking to the phone as though it were his father-in-law. "You heard him threaten me. He's the dangerous one."

"Enough," said Cameron, hitting the table with such force that the ceramic roosters took flight and spilled salt and pepper over the table.

"Agent Cameron," said Gamache sharply.

"Sorry," he muttered, bringing himself under control.

Gamache shifted his attention back to where it belonged. "How long have you and Madame Godin been together?"

"I dunno. Four, five years."

"How did you meet?"

"It was in a bar. Where did you think? Church? The gym? Look, I have things to do around the farm. Those animals need to be fed, and this one needs to be taken into the woods."

He gestured toward the old dog, who looked up and gave a single, tired flop of his tail.

"Like you took Vivienne?" asked Cloutier.

"What? Kill her?" He made a dismissive noise. "Why would I? Believe me, she's alive."

Try as he might, Gamache couldn't get Monsieur Godin's voice out of his head. The deep breaths, the attempt to control the terror that seeped out anyway. The desperation of a father.

*How would he feel if . . .*

"You said she had lovers." He was careful to keep his tone neutral. "Can you give us names?"

"Of course not. She didn't exactly list them."

"And women friends?" Gamache asked.

"Women? No. Why would she?"

It was as Cameron had said. Tracey had isolated his wife here, and since there was no one to contradict him, he was free to say anything he wanted about her.

"We're going to need the make, model, and license-plate number of her car," said Cameron.

Tracey gave them the information.

"Where were you on Saturday?" Gamache asked.

"I was here, working on my pots. Where else?"

"Anybody see you?"

"Vivienne did. You can ask her when she gets back."

"Anyone besides your wife."

"No. Who'd come here?"

Who indeed? thought Gamache.

"So you never left the property on Saturday?"

"No. Wait a minute, I did go into town to buy supplies. Needed to get them before the road turned shitty. Can't drive on it now." He eyed them closely. "But that's probably not news to you."

"And yet," said Cloutier, "you say your wife managed to drive out later in the day."

There was silence, and they could see Tracey's brain skidding in the muck.

"She could, but you couldn't?" Cloutier pressed.

"She left at night, when the roads had frozen again."

He'd hit on an explanation bordering on reasonable. After Tracey had given them the names of the stores he'd visited, Gamache asked, "When was the last time you saw your wife?"

"Saturday night, like I said. We'd been drinking. Vivienne got pissed and started yelling abuse. Told me the kid wasn't mine. I went into my studio to do some work and get away from her. When I got up next morning, she was gone."

The phone rang.

"You take it," said Tracey.

Gamache picked it up and listened. *"Bon. Merci."* He hung up. "We have the warrant."

# CHAPTER NINE

Like the rest of the house, the bedroom was a shambles. Bed unmade, bedding dirty. A partly drunk bottle of beer was on the floor next to the bed. An ashtray was overflowing with butts.

In the bedside table, there was a small stash of pot. And rolling papers.

"Yours?" Gamache asked Tracey.

"Hers."

Gamache nodded, taking that in but not necessarily believing it.

The clock radio blinked 12:00.

Gamache stood in the middle of the room and turned full circle. Clothing was left on the floor where it fell. Socks, underwear, sweaters, jeans. Not just one day's worth but days. And days.

An agent was going through the closet and the dresser drawers, photographing and cataloging what was there.

It was very difficult to tell if anything had been taken.

Gamache asked Tracey about the clothes. Were they all his? Were some Vivienne's?

"All mine."

In Vivienne's closet clothing was hung up. Her drawers were a bit haphazard, with underwear and turtlenecks and jeans shoved in. But at least clean and off the floor.

Looking at the top of the dresser, he noticed jewelry. Inexpensive. Bright. Bulbous. No photographs, though.

She might've taken those with her.

Gamache hoped that was true.

"Is there a suitcase missing?" Gamache asked.

"Suitcase? We don't have any of those. Why would we?"

Gamache nodded. That alone was pretty telling. And slightly chilling.

In the bathroom, Gamache pointed to a toothbrush. "Is this hers?"

"No. That's mine. This's hers." Tracey pointed to the other one in the holder. The bristles were worn almost flat.

Maybe she'd left this one and bought a new one, Gamache thought. He hoped that was true.

The forensics officer bagged both brushes. For DNA testing.

Gamache opened the medicine cabinet. Nothing extraordinary there. No prescriptions, just cold meds and ointments. There were no gaps on the narrow shelves. Nothing obviously missing.

Then he left and walked from room to room, with Tracey following him. A shadow.

Other officers arrived and were searching the outbuildings.

"There's no sign of her, *patron*," reported Agent Cloutier. She found him in the living room, kneeling by the sofa. "But they have found something, just off the kitchen."

"I'll be right along, *merci*." He brought out a pen and moved a potato-chip wrapper aside. Then, standing up, he called to the forensics officer in the room. "Can you check this, please?"

He stepped away and turned to Tracey. "I think it's blood. Is it?"

"Could be. Might be hers. Might be mine. Who knows?"

"We will, soon. What happened here?"

"I told you. We got into a fight."

"You hit her?"

"And she hit me. Gave as good as she got. Look, I know you think I've done something, but I didn't. I left her here." He pointed to the sofa. "Alive."

"Check the rest of the room carefully," Gamache advised the officer.

Brushing past Tracey without a word, Gamache followed Agent Cloutier into the kitchen and through a door he'd assumed was a pantry. But instead it led into what had once maybe been an outhouse. Or a pigsty or chicken coop. It had been knocked through to connect to the main house.

He stood at the door and prepared himself. Clearly there was no body inside. He'd have been told right away. Nor was this an obvious crime scene. Again, he'd have been told.

But it did strike him as a place where unpleasant things might have happened. To animals. Or people.

He went in.

What struck him first was the extraordinary heat.

The agents working in there were perspiring and trying not to drip sweat and contaminate the room. On seeing him they stood up and started to salute. But with a gesture he stopped them and indicated they should continue working.

Then he looked around.

Not a slaughterhouse at all. Not an old outhouse. It was much larger than that. An old garage. Converted into a workshop.

No, not a workshop. A studio.

He saw a potter's wheel. He saw plastic bags filled with clay, their tags still on. The walls were lined with shelves holding unglazed pieces. He saw what Cameron had meant. No one could possibly use Tracey's works for anything practical. They wouldn't hold food or drink or flowers.

But they did hold the attention. Not unlike the man himself.

Carl Tracey seemed an unfinished, partially formed man. Soft. Useless. And yet there was also something about the man. Not attractive. In fact, Gamache felt repulsed by him. But he also felt his eyes returning to him. Carl Tracey was a presence. There was no denying that. A statement piece. Like his works.

But while his pottery looked, to Gamache's eye, good, Tracey did not.

Gamache turned and saw, in the corner, the source of the extraordinary heat.

A kiln.

It had obviously been fired up in the last day or so.

Kneeling down, he looked into the opening in the bottom of the kiln. It was filled with ash.

"Make sure you collect this," he said, straightening up. "Have you found anything?"

"Not yet," said the agent in charge. "If there's any blood here, it'd be impossible to hide or clean. The bricks and clay are porous. If it's here, we'll find it."

"*Bon. Merci.*"

He turned and saw Carl Tracey looking in.

"The kiln's been used recently," said Gamache.

"Yes. I was firing some works."

"When?"

"Saturday night."

"It's still hot."

"Takes a long time to cool down. Needs to be really hot to bake the clay." He examined Gamache, then laughed. "You don't think . . ." He looked astonished. "You actually think I stuck Vivienne in there? Piece by piece? Are you crazy? Do you know how much work that would be? And imagine the mess."

Gamache knew Tracey was trying to get under his skin. Denying the murder and cremation of a woman and her unborn child not because it was abhorrent but because it was too much work.

"Look," Tracey said as he followed Gamache into the kitchen, "it wasn't much of a marriage, but she did her thing, I did mine. Why would I kill her?"

"Why would you kill him?" Gamache pointed to the old dog, still lying by the warm stove.

"Because he's no use anymore. He can't hunt and isn't gonna guard the place. He just eats and shits. Gonna get a new dog. A better dog."

"Maybe that's why you'd kill your wife," said Gamache. "So that you could get a new one."

"Why kill her? I'd just chuck her out."

"Because she'd take you to court and get half the property," said Gamache.

"Yes," said Tracey, nodding. "That would be a good reason."

It was as close to a confession, without actually being one, that the head of homicide had heard.

Tracey looked down at the dog. "He's not mine. He's hers. Came with her, and he can leave with her. The sooner the better."

He made a shooting gesture with his hand. The dog struggled up, took a step closer to Tracey, and licked the trigger finger.

They found nothing. After conferring with the local agents, it was decided they'd done all they could. It was time to leave.

"What do we do now?" asked Agent Cameron as they put on their coats and boots.

They stepped onto the porch and looked around, at the acres and acres. Miles and miles. Of forest. At the donkeys in the field. Patiently watching them.

And they heard, again, the growl of the Bella Bella, from deep in the woods.

It seemed louder. Closer.

"First step is to declare Vivienne Godin missing," said Gamache. "And then to visit her father."

A large drop landed with a plop at the foot of the steps. Then another.

He looked up. It was early afternoon, but the clouds were so thick, and the sun so obscured, that it felt like dusk. Or an eclipse.

Gamache put his hand in his pocket but remembered that there was no cell-phone coverage.

"Can you give us a lift back to our cars?" Gamache asked one of the agents.

"Absolutely, sir. I saw them when we arrived. Just down the hill."

"Right. How'd you manage to get up the hill?"

"We didn't. We came around and down from the other side."

She glanced again at the Chief Inspector's clothing. He and the others looked like they'd crawled up the muddy slope on their hands and knees to this terrible place.

Which they practically had.

"Do you have a radio in your car?" asked Gamache.

"Yessir. We're all equipped with them, in case our phones don't work."

"Good." Gamache turned to Carl Tracey, who'd just stepped onto the porch. The old dog at his side. "We'll be in touch with more questions, I'm sure."

"He's done it, hasn't he?" said Agent Cloutier as they walked to the Sûreté vehicle. "Killed her."

Gamache said nothing but looked grim.

Once at the car, he leaned in and, taking the handset off its hook, identified himself and asked to be put through to Chief Inspector Beauvoir of homicide.

As he waited, more rain fell. Tracey disappeared off the porch and reappeared with a .22 rifle.

"How does he have that?" asked Gamache. "Does he have a permit?"

"Unfortunately, yes," said Cameron. "He's never been convicted of an offense, so there was no way to take it from him. We didn't find any others."

Gamache shook his head. As strict as the laws were governing firearms in Canada, they could be tighter. Here was a man known to abuse his wife, and he's allowed to have a gun?

"Did you test it? Has it been fired recently?"

"We tested, and no, it hasn't been fired in a while."

Gamache looked into the dog's eyes and knew that was about to change.

"There you are, finally," Beauvoir's voice came out the tinny speaker. "Did you get my messages?"

"No, we're out of cell-phone coverage. About what?"

"A state of emergency's been declared. Leaves have been canceled. There's flooding across the province. Looks bad."

"The dams?"

"Hydro's sending engineers up there now to assess the situation."

If they burst . . .

But Gamache didn't say it. They all knew what would happen if the massive hydroelectric dams in James Bay were breached.

But that wasn't the only potential disaster.

"Where's the worst flooding?"

Beauvoir detailed it. As he spoke, Gamache visualized the map of Québec and saw the danger points. Where rivers met larger rivers. Inevitably that was also where towns and cities had been built. At the junction of the great waterways.

"The St. Lawrence?" he asked. And held his breath. Though in his heart he knew the answer already. He'd seen the ice buildup just a few hours earlier and had called it in.

Beauvoir quickly and succinctly described the affected areas. Ending with the worst-hit.

"Montréal."

"Montréal," repeated Gamache.

"I've been trying to reach you. There's a meeting here they want you at. Starting in half an hour. How soon can you get back?"

Gamache looked at his watch. "I can be there in forty minutes."

"Hurry."

"Jean-Guy?"

"*Oui?*"

"The Bella Bella?"

"Still rising."

Gamache looked south. Toward his village. He could be there in minutes. Then he looked north. To Montréal.

"*Merci,*" said Gamache. "I'll be there as soon as possible."

He gave the handset back to the agent and started to walk around to the passenger side. But paused.

"Sir?" asked the agent. The car was running. Waiting.

"*Un moment,*" said Gamache.

As the others watched, the Chief Inspector walked back to the porch, took out his wallet, placed bills at Tracey's feet. Then walked back to the car. The old dog in his arms.

As he got in, he said, "His name's Fred."

# CHAPTER TEN

⌒

The patrol car slid down the road, but the agent managed to guide it to where they'd left their vehicles. She dropped them off and continued down the hill. Opening the windows to air out her once-pristine vehicle. That now smelled of old wet dog, and mud, and donkeys.

"What do we do now, *patron?*" asked Cameron as they stood in the rain outside their cars.

"You return to your station. You'll be needed for flood control or evacuations. We're heading back to Montréal."

Once in the car, Agent Cloutier asked, "What about Vivienne? What do I tell Homer?"

"I'll call him once we're out of the mountains and have communications."

Rain was hitting the windshield. The clouds were low, mingling with the mist clinging to the forest.

"Can I stay on it, though? Keep looking for her?"

"You'll do as you're ordered, Agent Cloutier," said Gamache. "As will I."

He turned toward the woods, where the Bella Bella, invisible, was rushing toward the valley. And the village.

Ruth stood at the top of the fieldstone bridge and watched the activity around her.

The whole village was out, filling sandbags. It was something they

77

did most springs, but until now it had been a precaution, that had morphed into a tradition, that had become a party. A celebration. To mark the end of a long winter.

The spring runoff often coincided with the running of the maple sap.

They'd fill sandbags and hold a sugaring-off party, with baked beans and crêpes and cauldrons boiling down the sap into syrup. A fiddler played as children, and Gabri, stood around the pots waiting to pour the sweet liquid onto snow, where it turned into a sort of soft caramel called *tire d'erable*.

While mothers and fathers, friends and neighbors filled sandbags to build walls along the Bella Bella, children, and Gabri, used twigs to roll the *tire*, then ate the maple candy and watched horses return from the forest bearing buckets brimming with more sap.

It was a festive end to winter. After all, the river had never broken her banks. There'd never been reason to worry.

But today was different. The fiddler was holding a shovel. The kids were safely in St. Thomas's Church, their evacuation center. There was no *tire*. Only tired and sodden villagers.

Ruth stood in the rain, almost sleet, and watched as they bowed, then straightened, then bowed again, filling the sandbags in what looked like a pagan ritual.

But if this was a ritual, it was to an angry, vindictive deity.

*I just sit where I'm put, composed / of stone and wishful thinking*, Ruth muttered one of her own poems as she watched her neighbors and friends bow and lift. Bend and shovel. *That the deity who kills for pleasure / will also heal.*

Villagers, under Ruth's direction, had formed two lines and were passing the bags along, then piling them one on top of the other. Building a wall on either side of the Bella Bella.

The old poet turned from surveying her dripping and dirty neighbors and looked upstream.

She tried not to let her face reflect her feelings. Gnawing her cheek to stop the fear from showing, she looked at the Bella Bella. Until recently it had been beige with froth, but now it was almost black. As the churning became more and more violent. Dredging up muck and sediment and God knew what else from the river bottom. Things left

78

undisturbed for decades, centuries perhaps, were now roiling to the surface. Rotten. Decayed.

Ruth watched as the bloated river swept great chunks of ice and tree limbs down the mountain. Crashing toward them. Jamming, then breaking apart.

But eventually, she knew, the jam would be too dense. The debris too solid. It would hold. And then . . . ?

Until this day, the villagers had considered the Bella Bella a friendly, gentle presence. It would never hurt them.

Now it was as though someone they thought they knew well, someone they loved and trusted, had turned on them. The only thing more shocking would be if the three huge pine trees in the center of the village broke free and began to attack them.

Gabri and Olivier were handing out hot drinks. Tea, coffee, hot chocolate, and soup. Monsieur Béliveau, the grocer, and Sarah the baker, were taking around trays of sandwiches. Brie and thick slices of maple-cured ham, and arugula on baguettes and croissants, and *pain ménage*.

Though the most popular proved to be the ones Reine-Marie had made before she took a place in the line, filling sandbags.

"God," said Clara, taking a huge bite. "These are delicious."

Her gloves were wet through, and her large hands trembled in the cold.

"What do you have?" asked Myrna as she swallowed a huge bite of baguette.

"Peanut butter and honey on Wonder Bread," said Clara, barely intelligible through the thick peanut butter.

"Oh, jeez," said Myrna, breaking from the line and turning to look for Sarah the baker. "I'm going to get one of those."

"Here," said Billy Williams. "Take mine."

Though he was famished, he offered her half his sandwich.

Myrna smiled and shook her head. "It's okay. I'll get my own. But thanks."

Billy looked after her, then down at his damp sandwich. And understood that he had nothing that Myrna wanted.

She was unattainable, and he worried he'd love her for the rest of his life.

Gabri walked over to the bridge and offered Ruth a coffee. "I put a shot of brandy in it."

"That's okay," shouted the old poet over the sound of the river. She reached for a steaming mug. "I'll take the soup."

Gabri paled. It was, he knew, a sign of the End of Days. Ruth refusing booze.

He looked down and saw that the river was not just angry, there was a madness about it. As though all the indignities visited on all the waterways in the New World, by generations of settlers, were coming to the surface.

The waters were rising up, not in protest but in revenge.

He could barely hear himself think for the howling.

It was, he thought as he walked off the bridge, the sound a soul might make as it approached hell.

Gamache's mind was racing. Had they thought to open the spillways for the dams across the province?

Hospitals needed to be put on alert. Other provinces contacted and asked for possible assistance. The water-filtration plants needed to be protected. Hydro crews needed to be ready to restore power. Military reserves and first responders called out. Emergency measures put in place.

A sudden catastrophic event, natural or otherwise, brought with it turmoil. Places so pastoral and pretty one minute became war zones the next.

A populace unused to these sudden emergencies needed to be rallied and directed. And kept calm.

It was vital to take control.

Gamache tried to stop his mind from going there. And his hand from reaching for his phone to call Emergency Management. Call his successor at the Sûreté. Call the Premier Ministre. And tell them what to do.

Instead he took a deep breath and forced himself to sit back in the passenger seat.

This was no longer his job. No longer his responsibility. They knew what they were doing. They did not need him.

Still, he felt like a swimmer treading water offshore. Watching some terrible event unfold on the mainland and being unable to stop it. Or even help.

Once out of the mountains, his phone had gone wild with emails. Texts. Phone messages.

He tried Reine-Marie first and finally got through to Olivier in the bistro, who called Reine-Marie in.

"We're all right, Armand. Sandbagging, of course. But there's no panic."

"Ruth didn't—"

"Put valium in the hot chocolate again?" asked Reine-Marie. "*Non.* But I am feeling very, very calm."

Actually, she sounded tired.

"How is it really?" he asked.

"We're getting the barriers built. The Bella Bella's higher than anyone's ever seen it. A few inches from the top. But even if it floods, it won't be too bad."

Reine-Marie had never been in a flood. He had. It wasn't just a few inches of water in basements. A wave of water, even a small one, that had traveled that distance contained almost unimaginable energy. The force of even a minor breach could knock down walls. Buildings. Wells would be contaminated. Power lines knocked over. People, animals swept away.

It didn't take as much water as people thought.

"I'll get there as soon as I can."

"Where are you?"

"There's a state of emergency. I'm on my way into Montréal."

There was the briefest of pauses. "Of course."

She'd tried to sound upbeat, but the disappointment in her voice took his breath away. He was heading away from her, not to her.

"I'm sorry."

"Don't you dare be sorry. We're fine. We really are. Be careful. You have your water wings?"

"The blow-up swan? Always."

"Good. Make sure you wear it."

He laughed. "Now, that would be a photo for social media."

Hearing her laughter as she imagined her husband in suit, tie, and pink swan around his waist, directing emergency operations, went some way to healing his heart. They talked another minute or so before hanging up.

Then he phoned Monsieur Godin. It was a difficult call. He had to tell Vivienne's father that the search for his daughter was temporarily on hold, during the emergency. But would be resumed as soon as possible.

"You can't stop," said Homer. "You have to find her. You promised."

"I'm sorry," said Gamache. "There's nothing we can do right now, but believe me—"

"I'm coming down."

"No, don't." Gamache's voice was sharp. "The roads will wash out soon. Bridges will be closed. You'll be trapped away from home. Stay where you are. In case she calls."

There it was again. Giving Vivienne's father what Gamache suspected was false hope. For a call he was more and more convinced would never come.

But he had to keep the man away. For any number of reasons, not just the flooding.

As soon as he hung up, Agent Cloutier put the siren on. They were on the autoroute now, racing toward the city. As they headed over the Champlain Bridge, he asked her to pull over and put the flashers on.

"But there's no emergency lane, sir. We'll block traffic."

"This won't take long."

Once the car stopped, he got out quickly, before he could change his mind.

Hardly believing he was doing this, he made for the side of the bridge.

It was only a few steps away, but he had to fight for every inch.

Terrified of heights and suffering from vertigo, he felt himself grow instantly light-headed. And wondered if he'd pass out.

But he had to look. Had to see.

He battled his way forward, just a few feet that felt like miles. Reaching out, he gripped the concrete wall that separated him from the void.

The wind and rain hit his face. Closing his eyes, he took a deep breath. Then, opening them, he leaned out.

And gasped. His eyes wide, his knuckles white.

The world seemed to spin, and he realized, with horror, that he was in danger not of falling but of throwing himself off the bridge. The vertigo was dragging him over the edge. And there was nothing to stop his fall. Nothing between the bridge and the water.

He could hear, as though from very, very far away, cars honking. He thought he heard his own name called and had the peculiar feeling it was coming from the void below.

But still he stared, willing his eyes to focus.

And when they did, he saw. It was worse than that morning. Much worse. Ice was heaving, pushing against the pylons of the bridge. Halfway up already, and climbing.

He looked out at the wide, wide expanse of river. Some open water was visible, dark jagged lines between the fissures. The ice floes, many feet thick, were crashing together. Mounting each other. Forcing huge shards of ice to jut out.

Then he heard the rumble and forced himself to look farther out, farther downriver. The sound grew louder and louder, moving quickly now. A frost quake was tearing toward the bridge.

Gamache took a couple of deep breaths. And tightened his grip on the low concrete wall.

Trying not to close his eyes. Trying not to flinch.

He stood up slightly straighter as the rumble turned into a roar.

And then the boom. Like cannon fire, as the ice ruptured under the pressure. About fifty meters away.

He exhaled.

If it was this bad here, it must be just as bad, if not worse, all around the island of Montréal. Never mind all the other rivers. All the other bridges, across Québec.

He needed to leave. To make it to that meeting at headquarters. But first he had to get back to the car. Across the vast three feet of asphalt. He found that his grip was so tight he couldn't let go.

He ripped his hands off the concrete and, turning, took a few shaky steps, then practically threw himself the last few feet.

*"Patron?"* asked Agent Cloutier on seeing his face.

"It's all right," Gamache said, his hands in tight fists so that the trembling wouldn't show. "But we need to hurry."

Sûreté headquarters was buzzing. Officers rushing along the hallways.

Bullpens on each floor were all but empty, only skeleton crews remaining to answer calls and continue the most urgent of investigations.

Everyone else had been reassigned to the flooding.

Gamache went directly to homicide and met briefly with Jean-Guy.

On entering the office, he saw Beauvoir on the phone, looking energized, in his element. Though the younger man would no doubt fiercely deny it, Jean-Guy Beauvoir liked nothing better than an emergency.

He hung up and raised his brows. "Been to a spa?"

"Spa?"

"Mud bath."

"Oh, that." Gamache looked down at his caked coat and slacks. He'd forgotten that he was covered in muck. "More like mud wrestling."

"Who won?"

"Not me." He took off his heavy coat and hung it on the hook at the back of the door. "I'll tell you about it later. Oh, there is one thing I'd like to leave here with you. Do you mind?"

"Not at all."

"His name's Fred. He might like some water."

He left the bedraggled dog and the befuddled man staring at each other and hurried upstairs.

The meeting in Chief Superintendent Toussaint's office was well under way by the time Gamache arrived.

He'd made a quick trip to the bathroom and tried to clean up, but the facilities and time didn't allow for much more than a good scrub of his hands and face.

He looked in the mirror and ran his hands through his hair.

Then shook his head and gave up. There were far more important things to focus on.

"Chief Inspector."

Chief Superintendent Madeleine Toussaint greeted her predecessor. If she noticed his unusually disheveled appearance, she didn't show it. "You know everyone here."

She was confident enough to invite her predecessor to the meeting and savvy enough about the realpolitik of power to highlight Gamache's diminished status by emphasizing his new rank.

There were senior representatives from the Corps of Military Engineers, from the RCMP, from Hydro-Québec. Environment Canada's chief meteorologist was there, as was the Deputy Premier of Québec.

All men and women Gamache knew well.

"I see some of the crap thrown at you today on Twitter has stuck," said the senior officer from the RCMP, gesturing at Gamache's clothing.

Gamache smiled. "Fortunately, it won't stain."

"But it does smell," said the Mountie, with a wry smile. "Helluva first day back on the job, Armand."

"It is that."

"We were going over the situation," said Toussaint, bristling slightly at the obvious familiarity and warmth between Gamache and the RCMP officer.

She waved him to the huge ordnance map of the province, where the others had gathered.

It didn't just show where the problems were now, but also the knock-on effects farther downriver. And Québec had a lot of rivers, a lot of water.

Gamache had bent over many such maps, from his time occupying this very office. Ones that showed criminal activity and natural disasters.

But he'd never seen anything quite like this.

There were so many markings the map was almost unrecognizable.

"I was just about to show this," said the chief meteorologist. She nodded to a colleague who was sitting at a laptop. After a few taps, another map of Québec appeared, projected on the wall. "These are our predictions of what we think could happen in the next twenty-four hours."

An animation began playing, but nothing Disney would recognize.

It showed a natural disaster of epic scope. As rivers flowed into each other. As ice jams piled up. As tributaries broke their banks.

Whole islands disappeared.

Populated islands, Gamache knew.

His eyes widened, and his stomach twisted. Cities and towns that had stood for centuries, along the St. Lawrence in particular, were engulfed.

And then it stopped. And the water receded. Leaving mud and rubble.

Below the animation was a timeline. All this took just a day.

There was silence in the room. And finally the chief meteorologist spoke.

"Would you like to see it again?"

"*Non,*" they said in unison.

*Non.* It wasn't necessary. Everyone in that room would go to their graves with those images playing.

"That's the worst-case scenario," said the meteorologist. "If the dams burst. Unlikely, but possible."

Gamache wanted to ask the Hydro rep the only question that mattered at the moment.

Will they hold?

But he refrained, knowing this was Toussaint's meeting. Not wanting to undermine her.

While the others looked to him, he turned to her. And slowly they all looked at the new Chief Superintendent.

"Will they hold?" the Mountie finally asked.

The Hydro-Québec rep gave a curt nod. Her face grim. "They're holding for now. The thaw hasn't reached that far north yet. And when it does, we can open the floodgates and relieve the pressure."

Gamache turned to Toussaint, who was clearly thinking.

*Ask,* he thought. *Ask.*

"Will it work?" she asked.

"If the gates don't jam, and if the ice pressure on the structure isn't too great, yes."

If, if, if . . .

There was silence in the room while they replayed the animation in their heads, if the ifs didn't happen.

"But even if they hold," the meteorologist continued, "what we're looking at is a catastrophic combination of record snowfall through the winter, record cold creating thick ice, a flash thaw and freeze-up, and now heavy rains. So that the melt is pouring into the rivers before the ground has thawed and the ice has left. Backing everything up."

"Right," said the Deputy Premier. "We can see that. The question is, what do we do about it?"

"There're emergency measures—"

"Yes, yes," he said. "I know that. That's how we're responding. I want to know how to stop this. Or at least lessen the impact. What can we do?"

His voice wasn't just urgent, it was tinged with panic and some petulance. A child who suspects he won't be getting what he wants.

Silence met his pleas.

Gamache had put on his reading glasses and now glanced over at the chief meteorologist. He'd had many meetings with her, in this very room. Leaning over ordnance maps.

But never had he heard the dry, precise, careful scientist use that word. Catastrophic.

"What do you think?" he asked.

"It's our worst fear realized," said the meteorologist, her voice weak with exhaustion. Her shoulders sagged. "What wakes any forecaster in the small hours. *All that most maddens and torments.*"

"What're you talking about?" demanded the politician. "Was that some quote? Have you lost your mind?"

Gamache recognized the quote, though he couldn't quite place where it was from.

"Maybe," said the meteorologist, rubbing her face. "I've been up for two days solid running simulations. I do feel as though my brain is caked."

"You wanted to say something, Chief Inspector?" Once again Toussaint emphasized his rank.

He'd removed his glasses and was looking at her intently.

But she'd also been watching him. From the moment he arrived, she'd been waiting for Gamache to take over.

But instead he'd held off. Deferring to her.

It appeared respectful, but now she wondered if he had another reason.

Did he see, even before she did, that whoever was in charge would be blamed?

Madeleine Toussaint was beginning to appreciate her mistake. And the near-impossible position she found herself in. If she took charge, she'd be blamed if her ideas failed. If she let Gamache take over, all her authority would disappear.

She'd invited him to the meeting partly for his expertise, but she'd also seen her chance to make a point in front of the other senior officials.

There was a new sheriff in town. The old one was weakened, diminished. Demoted.

She hadn't counted on the fact that the others in the room would naturally turn to him. Out of habit, perhaps. Or because he still commanded their respect.

Except for the Deputy Premier, of course. Who despised the man.

Nor had she counted on the fact Gamache would voluntarily hand the lead to her. In an act of apparent humility.

Toussaint hadn't seen her former boss in months, but now, seeing him again, she felt some shame at doing this to him. But mostly she felt annoyance. That he didn't seem to notice he'd been diminished.

Gamache tapped the map with his glasses, then looked at her. "We might have less time than you think."

He told them about the ice and the Champlain Bridge.

"How do you know about it?" Toussaint asked.

"Because I looked."

"How?"

"I got out of the car just now and looked."

"Over the edge?" she asked. "You stood on the bridge and looked over?"

While Gamache's fear of heights was not generally known, those who served with him longest knew, or at least suspected, he had that phobia.

"I did."

"That means the bridges will have to be closed soon," she said to him. "And roads, I expect."

Gamache gave the tiniest of nods. Of agreement. And Toussaint felt both gratified and annoyed at herself, for wanting, needing, his approval.

"Demolition teams are on their way to the major trouble spots," said the head of the Corps of Engineers for the Armed Forces. "Including the Hydro dams, of course. We'll blow the ice jams, if necessary."

"Good. Thank you, Colonel," said Toussaint, regaining control.

"Wait a minute," said the Deputy Premier. "You're suggesting setting off explosions all over the province? Can you imagine the panic?"

"I'd rather be panicked than drowned," said the military officer.

"But can't we do anything else?" asked the politician.

"Like stop the rain, sir?" asked the chief meteorologist. "I've tried. Doesn't work."

"I have a thought." Gamache turned to the Hydro rep. "You talked about the floodgates. Can we do the same thing farther south?"

"There are no dams farther south. No gates to open."

"I know, but we can dig runoffs, can't we? It comes to the same thing." He looked around for support.

"I can't see that working," said Toussaint.

"Why not?" Gamache asked, apparently genuinely interested. "What're you thinking?"

"I think it would take far too much equipment to do anything effective," she said. "We'd have to divert some from the dams, and that's just too dangerous. It would leave them vulnerable."

"That's a good point," said Gamache, returning to stare at the map.

"Still," said the RCMP officer. "If we could, it would relieve some of the smaller rivers. We could divert the water before it gets to the big rivers."

"Chief Superintendent Toussaint is right," said the head of the Corps of Engineers. "It would take a huge amount of equipment and personnel, and we just don't have the resources for that. The crisis is moving quickly and is widespread. Emergencies have just been declared in Ontario and the Maritime provinces. We're deploying across the east."

"Wait a minute," said the politician. "Are you saying that not only are you not giving us more people and equipment, you're actually taking some away?"

"I was going to tell you," said the colonel.

"When? When we're treading water?"

"The Van Doos will be assigned to help, but that's all," said the colonel, refusing to be provoked. "We need the other regiments for other areas."

Gamache straightened up. The Royal 22$^e$ Régiment of the Canadian Armed Forces was based just outside Québec City. A storied regiment, affectionately nicknamed the Van Doos, they'd be, Gamache knew, a formidable help in any emergency and had already been deployed.

But they would not be enough. Not nearly.

He, along with everyone else in the room, looked with some dismay at the senior armed forces engineer, who dropped her eyes before meeting their stares again.

"*Désolée.*"

As were they.

"But if you redirect most of the resources we do have, it could be done," pressed the RCMP officer.

"I don't like the sound of that," said the Deputy Premier.

"You don't like the idea of setting off explosions, you don't like redirecting resources," said the Mountie. "You demand action, then refuse to actually act."

Toussaint turned to Gamache, seeing her chance. "What do you suggest?"

Two people could play at humility, and this would put him not in the driver's seat but in the hot seat.

"It's a risk," agreed Gamache. "But one I think we need to take."

"Just to be clear," said the Hydro rep. "Are you suggesting removing the equipment and teams from the dams?"

"Yes," said Gamache, nodding slowly. He turned to the chief meteorologist. "You said it yourself. The thaw hasn't hit there yet. Might not. Why keep precious resources there when they're needed down south, where the crisis isn't just imminent, it's upon us."

"Because if the dams go, we're blown back into the Stone Age," said Toussaint. "If there's a flash thaw, like there has been down south, we're screwed. We won't be able to get the workers and equipment back up there fast enough. If even one of those dams breaks . . ."

She didn't need to say more. They all finished her thought.

Hundreds of millions of tons of water would be released, shooting straight down the province. Gathering ice and debris. Trees. Houses, cars, bridges. Animals. People.

Until much of Québec was smeared across Vermont.

"So we have a choice," said the colonel. "Keep the dams safe and guarantee terrible flooding down south. Or risk the dams."

"Like you say," said the RCMP officer. "One's a risk, the other's a certainty."

"To put it another way," said the colonel. "One's catastrophic, the other's Armageddon."

It sounded melodramatic, but anyone who'd witnessed a tidal wave, a tsunami, would know it was no exaggeration.

The Deputy Premier moaned.

"Bet you're glad you're not sitting in my seat now," Toussaint said to Gamache.

He smiled. "I'm glad you're in this office, yes. We all are."

She doubted that was true. "Any more advice, Armand?"

He thought, looking at the map. "I think you should open the sluice gates at the dams now. As a precaution—"

"But we'd lose power," said the Hydro rep, and the politician moaned again.

"*Non.* You'd lose money. But we both know you have plenty of power in reserve you could use." Gamache stared at the executive. "We won't be shivering in the cold and dark just yet."

That had been a threat, by Hydro, by politicians, for decades, justifying all sorts of draconian measures by the massive utility.

There was a long silence before the Hydro exec gave a curt nod. The politician just glared at Gamache. The old lie exposed.

"You keep one team at the most vulnerable dam," said Gamache. "In case opening the gates isn't enough. Then redirect all possible resources to digging those runoffs, the spillways along the tributaries."

"*Merci,*" Toussaint said, in an attempt to interrupt. To stop this torrent of advice.

"There're clearly key spots," the colonel from the Corps of Engineers said, taking up the suggestion and pointing to several rivers.

"We can choose a dozen of the most significant tributaries. Maybe here . . . and here."

"*Oui*," said Gamache, familiar with the terrain. "We don't have to divert all of them." He looked up from the map and held Toussaint's eyes. "And we could get local farmers to help. Use their equipment to dig—"

"We?" she asked, and once again the room grew still. Except for the smile that was spreading across the politician's face.

"You," said Armand, straightening up and removing his reading glasses. "This's your operation, Chief Superintendent. You asked for my help and advice. I'm simply giving it."

"Thank you."

"A battle might be won on a single front," he pressed on. "But a war is won on many. You're concentrating your forces on the most urgent need. Which makes sense. But you can also get out in front of the crisis. Though it is a risk."

"Not just a risk, Gamache," said the Deputy Premier. "It's reckless."

While the others watched, Gamache raised his head and turned to the politician.

"This would be a calculated risk, *monsieur.*" His voice formal, freezing. Those listening were surprised the words didn't come out in an icy vapor. "There's more risk in paralysis. In reckless indecision."

"You think so? Maybe we should ask those under your command who were wounded and killed because of your so-called calculated risks. You shouldn't even be here. You should be at home, or guarding some Walmart. Or in prison."

No one spoke, no one breathed. Eyes opened wide. Even Madeleine Toussaint was shocked by the vitriol.

"Chief Superintendent Gamache did—" she began, but a look from the politician silenced her.

"When your committee offered me the chance to return as head of homicide, sir," said Gamache, glaring at the Deputy Premier, "you must've known there was a risk that I'd take it."

At least two in the room snorted in amusement. Or it might have been amazement.

"We never thought you'd be that desperate. Or that stupid," said the politician.

"Well, you took your best shot," said Gamache, with a thin smile. "And yet here I am. Still standing. Right in front of you."

"You think that was our best shot, Armand?"

There was shocked silence then, until Chief Superintendent Toussaint jumped in.

"I think we hold the course. Keep the equipment at the Hydro dams to prevent a catastrophe and dynamite as it's necessary down south."

The Deputy Premier, ignoring her, leaned over the map. "I see in your scenario, Gamache, one of the villages spared would be your own. Don't you live in some tiny backwater in the townships? I can smell it on you. Smells like shit."

"Actually, it's donkey." He stared at the politician. "What's your point, Pierre?"

"Oh, Armand, I think you know my point. Once again you would misuse power for your own gain. And . . ." The Deputy Premier paused and inhaled. "I think what I smell isn't a donkey. It's an ass."

The room bristled.

"You're right," said Gamache. "One of the places in the path of the flooding is mine. A small village, insignificant by your standards, called Three Pines. No one's ever heard of it, and if it disappeared in the deluge, I suspect it wouldn't be missed. But it would still be a tragedy. As it would for all the other towns and villages you're ignoring."

"Thank you for coming, Chief Inspector." Toussaint put out her hand. "We'll take it from here. I'll let you get back to your own work now."

They stared at each other. The former occupant and the current occupant of the highest office in the Sûreté.

He was dismissed.

He found himself unceremoniously on the other side of the door as it closed.

Armand Gamache had been put in his place.

When he walked into Beauvoir's office to get his coat and boots and dog, Jean-Guy stood up at the desk. Isabelle Lacoste was also there.

"Interviews over?" Gamache asked.

"Interviews canceled," she said. "Because of the emergency."

"Meeting over?" asked Beauvoir.

"Not yet. I gave my opinion, and we'll see. There're smart people in there."

"So why're you out here?" asked Beauvoir.

"I guess I'm not so smart," said Gamache with a smile.

"I'm sorry," said Lacoste. "They shouldn't—"

"It's all right," Gamache assured her. Then noticed that Jean-Guy's suit, his papers, his chair, and the ceiling had little brown dots all over them.

"Your dog shook," explained Beauvoir.

"Oh, dear."

"Yes. That's pretty much what I said as I washed myself off and scraped down my desk. Gosh, I said. Bit of a mess." His eyes widened in a crazed look, and Lacoste laughed.

"By the way, do you mind my asking why you have a dog?"

"He belongs to the missing woman."

"I see." Beauvoir looked down at the smelly old thing, lying contentedly on the now-filthy rug. "I'm sorry we have to put that search on hold."

"Actually, we don't. Or at least I don't. If it's all right with you, I'd like to speak to her father in Ste.-Agathe, before the roads are closed. Do you mind if I take Agent Cloutier with me?"

"No, of course not. You don't need to ask, *patron*," said Beauvoir.

"But I do." Gamache smiled.

"Mind if I come, too?" asked Lacoste. "Seems I'm free for the afternoon."

"That would be great," said Gamache. Not only did he value her judgment and company, but he knew that she was a mentor to Agent Cloutier.

Isabelle Lacoste had been a young woman when, to everyone's surprise, he'd chosen her for homicide. That hadn't been all that many years ago.

Now her hair was prematurely graying and there were lines at her forehead and from her mouth. Caused by stress. And pain. She walked with a limp and a cane, still recovering from near-fatal injuries almost a year earlier.

He'd often wondered if he'd really done her, done Jean-Guy, done any of them such a favor by recruiting them into homicide. But they were adults, he told himself, and could make their own decisions.

And now one had decided to leave and one had decided to return.

As he waited for the elevator, with Isabelle and Fred, he looked out at Montréal. So much rain was sliding down the window, it looked as though the city was underwater.

Gamache put his hands behind his back, one gripping the other, and felt his core grow cold. And saw again the animation. Of much of Québec sliding into Vermont. Sent there by a flood of water and a fear of making the wrong decision.

"*All that most maddens and torments,*" he said.

"*Moby-Dick,*" said Lacoste. "Studied it at university."

"Right," said Gamache, turning to her. "I couldn't remember where it's from."

"But why remember it at all?"

"Just something someone in the meeting said."

"Well, that can't be good," said Isabelle Lacoste as they stepped into the elevator. "Hardly reassuring."

"*Non.*"

# CHAPTER ELEVEN

They pulled in to the driveway of the neat bungalow in the center of Ste.-Agathe forty minutes later.

As they stood on the driveway, they could see that ice still covered the lake. But it was heaved up here and there. Ice-fishing cabins had been abandoned, and there was a huge fissure through the middle of the hockey rink twenty feet off shore.

Lac des Sables was breaking up. It had obviously hit swiftly. Taking the villagers by surprise.

Even from there they could hear the bangs. Booms. As new cracks formed in the thick ice.

The thaw was moving north. More swiftly than imagined. More swiftly, certainly, than hoped.

Gamache put his hands in his pockets and brought his shoulders up against the wind.

They were in the Laurentian Mountains, and it was considerably colder. What had been coming down as rain farther south was turning to ice pellets here. And soon, he thought, freezing rain.

They'd have to be quick about this if they hoped to make it back home.

Chief Inspector Gamache brought out his phone and called in the report of the ice breakup. He rang off just as a man appeared at the door.

Homer Godin had clearly been waiting for them. He came out of his house, but he stopped short and brought his hand to his face.

"Fred," he said.

On seeing Monsieur Godin, Fred slithered out of the car. The man dropped to his knees to embrace the old dog.

Then Godin got up and wiped his face as he turned to Gamache and put out his hand.

"Thank you, thank you for coming. I'm Vivienne's father."

Not, Gamache noticed, Monsieur Godin. Not Homer. But Vivienne's father. That was his identity now. And, perhaps, had been since his only child's birth.

"Armand Gamache. We spoke on the phone."

"Yes. I stayed here, as you suggested. But she hasn't called." Monsieur Godin searched Gamache's face for reassurance. That she would.

But Armand Gamache was silent.

Homer looked down. At the dog. His shoulders rose and fell. And there was a gasp. A sob. His hands covered his face, and through the fingers came the muffled words.

"This's all my fault."

"No, no, that's not true, Homer," said Lysette Cloutier, reaching out to touch his arm.

But he didn't seem to notice. Then he finally dropped his hands, and wiped his face with his sleeve.

"I'm sorry. I'm better now." He pulled himself up, rigid. Then noticed the third person.

Gamache introduced Superintendent Lacoste.

"Thank you for coming. Thank you, thank you," said Godin, composed. Of stone and wishful thinking.

He was in his late fifties, maybe early sixties. Gray stubble was beginning to form a beard. There were dark circles under his eyes, which were weary and bloodshot. And moist.

Homer Godin was tall, solidly built. A man clearly used to physical labor. He spoke with the broad country accent of someone who'd left school early to work on the land.

Lacoste knew this man. Not personally, but her own grandfather was just such a Québécois. Still vigorous at ninety-one, he liked nothing better than getting into the forest, even in winter, and chopping wood.

"I thought you couldn't come," Godin said, turning to Gamache. "That there were more important things—"

He stopped here. Unable to go on.

"There's nothing more important to us, Monsieur Godin," said Gamache, "than finding your daughter. There is, though, that state of emergency I mentioned. We are, for now, the only ones assigned to the search."

Godin looked at the three of them, with new eyes. An accountant. A woman with a cane. A man covered in mud and smelling like—

"You're not needed?"

"*Non.*"

With some surprise Gamache realized he had become part of the refuse he'd spent his career salvaging.

But that didn't mean he was useless. Just, maybe, repurposed.

"Come inside, out of the weather," said Godin. "I'm sure this's nothing. I'm sure Vivienne's off with girlfriends, having fun, and I'm worrying for nothing. She'll call soon."

He searched their faces. Trying to find some reason to hope that what he'd just said could possibly be true. A patient in a doctor's office, self-diagnosing the lump as a cyst. The confusion as exhaustion. The numbness as a pinched nerve.

The missing daughter on holiday. Soon to call. Full of apologies.

Gamache recognized the natural, and probably necessary, delusion. That allowed parents, children, spouses, to go on. At least temporarily.

"I'm sure that's true," said Cloutier, as they followed Homer through the neat house and into the kitchen.

But Vivienne's father was watching Gamache.

"What do you think has happened to her?" Homer asked, sitting at the kitchen table.

Gamache, taking a seat across from Homer, could hear the fear creeping back into his voice. The dread. A frost quake, approaching.

"We don't know. We've just come from her home—"

"That was never her home. This's her home."

And it felt like a home. Smelled like a home. It was modest in size, comfortable and welcoming, with slightly worn furniture. A La-Z-Boy was close to the woodstove, positioned perfectly to see the television.

One chair. This was a man who not only lived alone but didn't often have company.

Fred lay on the floor, his head on Monsieur Godin's feet.

"Has he done something to her?"

Again the eyes were pleading with Gamache for reassurance. But there was, in them, more desperation than conviction.

"We don't know," said Cloutier. "We—"

"That bastard's done something, hasn't he."

It was a statement now, not a question.

"Why do you say that, sir?" asked Gamache.

"Because she'd have called me. I know my Vivienne. She'd know I was worried. She'd never—"

He stopped and looked down. Breathing heavily from the strain of carrying such terror.

Gamache watched as Vivienne's father groped his way forward. Into a terrible new world. Stumbling over shards of words he dared not say. Falling into emotions he dared not admit. Picking himself up. Moving forward.

Walking that tightrope of needing to push for action while not yet admitting the reason.

"Is there someplace you think she could have gone?" asked Gamache.

"I've called all her old friends. No one's seen her. They haven't even heard from her in a long time."

"How about friends she made since moving away?"

"If she had any, she never mentioned them. But I haven't seen her for a while myself."

"Why not?"

"He wouldn't let her come here, and I knew I wasn't welcome there. I tried a few times, but he wouldn't even let me on the porch. Said some terrible things."

"Like what?"

Homer paused, clearly unhappy with the question—and the answer. "That Vivienne didn't want to see me. That she hated me. That I was a terrible father."

He hung his head, his mouth falling open. After an excruciating few seconds, a thin line of spittle dropped from his parted lips.

His huge hands were trembling in his lap, and his breath came in short, sharp inhales and exhales. Panting. Like a wild animal in pain.

Lysette Cloutier reached out toward him, but Gamache put his hand on her arm and stopped her.

The man needed his space. His illusion of privacy.

Having seen more than his share of grief, Gamache knew that Vivienne's father must be allowed to cry, without well-meaning people trying to stop it. An act that looked like mercy but was more about their own extreme discomfort than any comfort they could offer him.

"He wasn't wrong," said Godin at last, his voice squeezing through his throat. "I wasn't a good father."

"What do you mean?" Gamache asked. "You said something similar when we arrived. You said it was all your fault."

"Did I? I meant that I should've said something. Done something. Way back even when they got engaged. I knew he was trouble. But I didn't want her to think, after her mother died, that I was jealous or anything. And I wasn't even sure if that's why I hated Tracey so much. It was confusing. But I could see, I could just see, that he wasn't good for her. But I never thought"—he paused to take some more breaths—"he'd hurt her. Not at first, anyway. Not like this."

"Hurt her in what way?" asked Gamache.

Though they knew, they needed to hear what Vivienne's father also knew.

Homer's mouth moved, trying to form the words. But no sound would come out. Finally he just stared at Gamache. Begging him not to make him say it.

Cloutier went to speak, but Lacoste stopped her.

And still they waited.

"He beat her."

The words came from Vivienne's father like blood from an open vein. Quiet. Almost belying the cost of it.

He continued to stare at Gamache. Pleading now. Not for understanding, because it seemed Godin himself didn't understand. How he could have suspected his precious child was being beaten and not stopped it.

He was pleading for help. To say what needed to be said. To admit the inexcusable. The inconceivable.

That he suspected his little girl was being hurt but had failed to stop it. Failed her.

"Do you have children?" he asked Gamache.

"Two. A son and a daughter."

"I'm guessing she'd be about Vivienne's age."

"*Oui*. Her name's Annie."

"You?" Homer asked Lacoste.

"Two as well. Son and daughter."

Homer nodded.

Lacoste watched this man. Was it possible to really put herself in his place? Inside the nightmare?

"He kept her away from me," said Homer, speaking now to Lacoste. "The few times I was able to see her in the past year, she was thin. There were bruises." He held his arms. "I begged her to leave him. To come to me, but she wouldn't."

"Why not?" asked Isabelle Lacoste.

"I don't know." He looked down at Fred, dropping his hand to stroke the sleeping dog.

"You tried," said Lysette. "There's nothing more you could've done."

"Oh, there was something I could've done." He looked at Gamache. "What would you have done? If your Annie . . ."

"When was the last time you saw Vivienne?" he asked, deflecting the question.

Godin smiled a little. "Not going to answer that, are you? Probably smart. But sometimes ya just gotta be stupid, you know? If I'd killed the shit, she'd be here today instead of you."

"But you would not be," said Gamache.

"Do you think I care?" said Godin. "I'd trade my life for hers like that." He snapped his fingers.

"When, Monsieur Godin?" Gamache repeated.

"I saw her just before Christmas. I went down to drop off presents. I'd even bought one for him. Oh, God." He stared at Gamache in disbelief. "I was so afraid of losing her I was willing to"—he fought to control himself again—"suck up to him. What was I thinking? Oh, God. She didn't invite me in. I think he was there. So I just left. That was the last time—"

Lysette Cloutier reached out, and this time Gamache didn't stop her. She put her hand on Homer's forearm and left it there.

"But you did hear from her again," said Gamache.

"Yes. She called on Saturday morning."

Godin seemed confused now. Could it have been so recently? Just two days ago? Time made no sense anymore. Days, dates, they were meaningless and would be for the rest of his life. There would only be before Vivienne disappeared and after.

A firm line drawn against which all else would be measured. Until the day he died.

"What did she say?"

"She told me she was pregnant and was finally going to leave him. I was so happy I could barely speak. I said I'd come and get her, but she told me not to. She needed to pick the time. When it was safe. When he was gone or passed out. She told me she'd be here sometime that night or maybe Sunday morning. She made me promise not to come. So I just waited." There was a long, long exhale. "I should've gone to get her. Why didn't I?"

But there was no answer, and Gamache was not going to give this dignified man some drivel.

They sat silently, staring at each other. Vivienne's father and Annie's father.

"It's my fault," Homer whispered.

"*Non, monsieur.* This isn't your doing."

But Gamache knew that no matter what he said, Godin would spend the rest of his life in an endless loop. Skidding along the same ground. Going back over and over and over the last conversation. And what he did or did not do. What he could have done, what he should have done.

*As I would*, thought Gamache.

"You said you called all her old friends," Gamache continued, "but do you know if she had a more recent friend? Someone special?"

If Godin caught his meaning, he chose to ignore it.

"No. No one."

And Gamache was forced to be more blunt.

"Carl Tracey says she had a—"

"I know what Tracey says," the man erupted. "He's trying to make her sound like some sort of . . . some sort of . . ." He couldn't bring himself to utter the word. "Vivienne wasn't like that. She never would, would she?"

He appealed to Cloutier, who managed not to respond.

Godin looked down at his hands, gripped so tightly on the edge of the table that the entire thing rattled. Like a visitation from the other side.

He brought himself under control, though his knuckles remained white.

"Besides," he said, his voice strained, "how would she meet anyone? He barely let her off the property."

"We have to ask," said Gamache. "If she did have a lover, she might've gone to him. Or he might be the one who—"

"She didn't."

"Though you say you hadn't seen her in a while. She might have—"

"She didn't," he all but shouted. "I know her. Look, why're you wasting time? If something's happened to Vivienne, we all know who did it. If you won't make him tell, I will."

"That wouldn't be wise, Monsieur Godin," said Gamache, getting to his feet.

"Really? Really?" demanded Godin, also getting up and turning to face Gamache. "And what would you call 'wise'? Was what I did on Saturday wise? Doing nothing? Maybe it's time to do something stupid."

There was silence.

"Imagine your Annie was pregnant. I want you to imagine that."

"Monsieur Godin—"

"Now imagine her missing. Them missing."

Despite himself, Gamache felt tugged into that world. Just for an instant, he crossed the line. To where the unimaginable happened. Where monsters lived. Where Vivienne's father now lived.

"You're right, *monsieur*. You have to act now. But confronting Carl Tracey won't get you anywhere. He won't tell you anything, and he'll just have you arrested. It would only make it worse."

Now Godin almost laughed. Almost.

"It can't get worse. And to be clear, Chief Inspector, I don't plan on confronting him. I plan on beating him until he tells me where Vivienne is. And then I'll beat him to death."

Gamache regarded Godin and knew he was serious. He made a decision.

"Come with us now. I live in the area. You can stay with my wife and me. We'll organize a search for Vivienne. You can help us. Will you do that?"

"Stay with you?" Homer asked. "Are you serious?"

It was, not surprisingly, exactly the same question Lacoste wanted to ask. Was he serious?

"Yes."

"Give me two minutes. I'll pack a bag."

Homer ran from the kitchen and along the corridor, the small home practically shaking with the force of his feet.

"Was that wise?" asked Lacoste, looking down the now-empty hallway. "You're taking him to within a few kilometers of the man he wants to kill."

"He'd have gone there himself, probably as soon as we left. This way we have some control. I can watch over him."

"I know him," said Cloutier. "If he says he'll kill Tracey, he means it. You can't watch him twenty-four hours a day."

"And what would you have us do, Agent Cloutier? Leave him?"

She thought and finally shook her head.

"*Non,*" said Gamache. "This isn't the best solution, I agree, but it's the only one I can think of right now. And we're running out of time." He looked out the window, where ice pellets were slapping against the panes. "Maybe Monsieur Godin's right. Sometimes we have to do something stupid."

It did not seem to Isabelle Lacoste a great addition to the Sûreté motto.

*Service, integrity, justice, and, occasionally, stupidity.*

# CHAPTER TWELVE

~

C lara Morrow stood in her studio, her dog, Leo, at her side. Her shoulders were drooping from exhaustion as she wondered which, if any, paintings she'd rescue, should the evacuation order come.

Would she take the miniatures? Were they worth saving? Had they earned their place on the ark? Two days ago she thought so. Now she wasn't so sure.

And with the water rising, decisions had to be made.

They'd run out of sandbags two hours earlier. Then villagers had begun bringing pillowcases and feed bags, garbage bags. Anything that could hold sand.

And then they'd run out of sand.

And then they'd run out of light.

And then they'd run out of steam.

And still the rain kept coming. Changing to ice pellets, then freezing rain, then back to rain.

It had stopped for half an hour, giving them hope that maybe . . .

And then it started to snow.

But still the villagers were reluctant to leave the wall they'd built. Four bags high. Two bags thick. Running a hundred meters on either shore of the Bella Bella. From Jane Neal's back garden, along Clara's garden, to the bridge. Then it continued behind Monsieur Béliveau's general store, Sarah's Boulangerie, the bistro, and Myrna's bookstore.

And ten meters beyond that, to the bend in the river.

It had been a herculean task. But as they finally dragged themselves back to their homes, for hot showers and dry clothes, each villager suspected that it was not enough. That the Bella Bella would rise up in the night and overwhelm Three Pines.

And there was nothing more they could do to stop it.

Ruth had stayed on the stone bridge, with Rosa. Like a droopy sentinel. Unwilling to leave her post. Staring at the river that had been her friend.

Until Clara and Myrna, Reine-Marie and Sarah the baker had coaxed her off. It wasn't fine words that did it, or fine food, or even the bottle of fine scotch that Myrna had brought with her.

It was Reine-Marie pointing out that Rosa was getting cold.

It was finally love that drew Ruth away from the river.

As the women accompanied the old poet back to her home, a car had appeared on the hill.

"Armand," said Reine-Marie.

"He's not alone," said Clara.

"Is it numbnuts?" asked Ruth.

"No, Jean-Guy's staying in Montréal," said Reine-Marie.

She'd long since given up trying to stop Ruth from calling her son-in-law "numbnuts." And even he'd begun answering to it.

The car stopped in front of the Gamache home, and two men and a dog got out.


Homer Godin looked around.

All he could see through the sleet and darkness was a ring of lights that seemed to hang in midair. He knew they came from homes, but those were invisible.

They'd stopped in Montréal and dropped Lysette and that superintendent woman at Sûreté headquarters.

Homer had sat in the outer office, listening, while Gamache met with a fellow named Jean-Guy something.

The young fellow was obviously another cop. Senior, it seemed. Gamache's equal? At times it seemed so. His superior? At times it seemed so. His subordinate? At times it seemed so.

They'd discussed the flooding. It was far worse than Homer had realized.

"Have they dynamited the jams on the St. Lawrence?" Gamache asked.

"Not yet."

"What're they waiting for?" asked Gamache.

"A decision, I guess. The Corps of Military Engineers is pushing for it, but the Deputy Premier seems afraid it'll set off a panic."

Gamache took a deep breath and let out a long exhale. "*Bon.* I'm almost afraid to ask, but . . . the dams?"

*The dams?* thought Homer. *What dams?*

And then he realized what dams they were talking about. The huge hydroelectric dams in James Bay. He leaned his head around the doorway and asked, "Are they in trouble?"

And for one brief moment, his personal catastrophe was replaced by the collective disaster that was threatening.

"*Non,*" said the younger man. But Homer Godin recognized a lie when he heard it.

It was said in the same grim tone Vivienne used every time he'd asked if Tracey was hurting her.

*Non.*

The two continued to talk, but now in tones that suggested much more than just colleagues. These men were friends.

"Keep in touch," said Gamache, at the door.

"You too. Good luck, *patron.*" Then this Jean-Guy Someone turned to Homer. "I promise, once the crisis is past, we'll do everything we can to find your daughter. In the meantime Chief Inspector Gamache will help. He's the best."

Godin looked at Gamache and couldn't help but think if he was the best, why weren't they using him in this emergency? Why send him away?

Homer couldn't help himself. He grabbed the younger man's arm. "I need more. Help me, please. Help."

"We're doing all we can. I'm sorry."

And now Homer Godin stood in the bleak village. In the mud. In the half rain, half snow, and while he couldn't see much, he could hear a great deal.

He looked toward the sound. The river. That was in full flood. And he thought of his daughter. Disappearing into the night. Disappearing into the flood.

Then he looked past the lights. Somewhere in the darkness, not all that far away, was Carl Tracey.

Homer wasn't sure how, but he'd get to him.

Lysette Cloutier poured herself another glass of wine and returned to the sofa.

She was at home now, having volunteered to help with the emergency measures but told she wasn't needed.

She was both very annoyed and very relieved. Mostly she was very worried.

Lysette hadn't been completely honest with Chief Inspector Gamache and Superintendent Lacoste about her relationship with Homer, such as it was. But also her relationship with Vivienne. Such as it was.

She wasn't sure why, but it had seemed important not to tell them that she was Vivienne's godmother. Perhaps because she was a god-awful godmother. Not having had one herself, Lysette had no idea what was expected. Except for her to take Vivienne, should anything happen to her parents, Kathy and Homer.

But beyond that?

The only other thing she could remember from the baptism was being told she needed to act as Viv's guardian. To guard her. To keep the child safe.

"Well," she mumbled. "Fucked that one up."

After taking a long gulp, perhaps even a guzzle, of wine, she pulled her laptop onto her lap and logged in. Agent Cloutier had been told to find out everything she could about Carl Tracey. Might as well start.

She was prepared to have to do a fairly deep dive into government records but had decided, as a lark, to just put his name into a Google search.

She sat there, openmouthed, when up came a website.

"Can't be."

Clicking on it, she looked at the photo of the man. Definitely Tracey. Surrounded by his pottery.

"Shit," she said, and clicked on more links. To exhibitions he'd had. To a buying link. To a brief bio that mentioned his wife, Vivienne, and their dog, Fred.

Like most of the stuff on the Web, it was bullshit. The life people wanted people to see. The neat front yard, not the squalor behind the front door.

She snapped the laptop closed in disgust and, putting it on the floor, she lay back and grabbed the TV remote. But then she looked down at the slender rectangle sitting on the floor below her. And she got to wondering.

How did a man without internet have a website?

Isabelle Lacoste ignored the phone call from Lysette Cloutier.

It was her strict policy to leave work behind, at least until the kids were fed and in bed. Unless the call was from Monsieur Gamache or Jean-Guy.

Besides, she was on leave.

It was only after the third attempt that Isabelle picked up.

"*Oui, allô?*"

"I'm so sorry to disturb you, *patron*." The voice was just the tiniest bit off. Not slurred. If anything, the words were too well enunciated. Too precise.

"What can I do for you?"

"Carl Tracey has a web page." And then came a sound between a laugh and a snort.

"Yes."

"But he doesn't have internet. He also has an Instagram account. That's active. So how does he do it?"

Now Lacoste's mind was engaged. How did he do it? There was only one answer—

"He has a webmaster," said Cloutier. "Some woman named Pauline. She must manage it all for him. Post for him."

"Okay," said Lacoste, sitting at her own laptop and putting in Carl Tracey's name.

"Dinner," her husband called.

"Be right there."

"You're coming here?" asked Cloutier with alarm, looking at the almost empty wine bottle and empty bag of chips.

"No, I was speaking to my husband." Putting her hand over the receiver, she called, "Start without me." Then she returned to Cloutier. "Is there anything incriminating on the sites?"

"Not that I can see, but there might be a private Instagram account that they use, just the two of them."

"That no one else can see? That's possible?"

"Yup."

"How would we know?"

"We wouldn't, unless we asked and she told us."

"And to get access to the private account?" asked Lacoste. By now she'd found the public Instagram account. It was pretty standard, clearly meant for marketing his pottery.

"Need to be invited."

"Why would they have a private account?" Lacoste asked.

"Dunno." Then Cloutier thought. "Private messages. That's why."

She sounded both triumphant and a little surprised she'd managed that answer.

"Things they don't want public," said Lacoste.

Cloutier sang, "Someone's trying to hide their privates." Then she definitely snorted.

Lacoste looked at the phone. She'd mentored the older woman since she'd been transferred, kicking and screaming, from accounting into homicide. Never once had the accountant snorted. Or even made a joke. She'd barely smiled.

She's drunk, Lacoste knew. Now, why would Lysette Cloutier get drunk?

"Are you all right?"

"Just fine." Now Cloutier sounded insulted. "I thought you'd be pleased about this."

Now she sounded hurt and a little irritated.

"I am. Look, it's been a long, difficult day. You've done well. Leave it and start fresh in the morning. And for God's sake, don't contact this woman, right? We don't want Tracey to know we're interested in his private Instagram. Right?"

"Right."

Lysette Cloutier hung up but did not take that advice.

She should have.

Clara put on the outdoor lights at the back of her home.

On warm summer evenings, she and her friends would sit in the garden having drinks and dinner. The lights were placed to illuminate the perennial beds of delphiniums and phlox and old garden roses.

Beds that had been first planted more than a century ago.

But on this cold April evening, Clara had climbed the ladder and repositioned the lights so that they pointed into the night, to where her garden met the river.

Now the lights illuminated an expanse of mud and the wall of sandbags.

"Floodlights," said Gabri, standing beside Myrna in the kitchen and staring out the window.

They'd gathered in Clara's home, partly out of habit, partly out of a need to be together, partly because it was the best vantage point to monitor the Bella Bella and still be protected.

And privately out of fear that this would be the last time.

The neighbors put the food they'd brought onto the kitchen island, buffet style. And now they gathered around the window, to see if they could see anything.

But Clara herself had left them and gone back to the doorway into her studio, where Reine-Marie joined her.

"You okay?"

"I'm well in body," said Clara. "But considerably rumpled up in spirit."

Reine-Marie laughed. Easily recognizing the lines from the Anne of Green Gables books she, her daughter, and now her granddaughters loved so much.

She put her arm through Clara's. "Fortunately, you're among kindred spirits."

Clara squeezed her hand and continued to stare into the studio.

"What're you thinking?" Reine-Marie asked.

"I'm thinking that if we need to leave, I can't take all my paintings. So which do I choose, if any?"

"If any?"

Clara turned to look at her. "Are they crap?"

"Why would you say that?"

"You know why."

"You haven't let those comments get into your head, have you? Those people are ignorant—"

"It was the *New York Times*. And *Art World*. Thank God the *Oddly Report* hasn't said anything."

"The what?" asked Ruth, who'd sensed pain and had gone over to bask in and, with luck, magnify it. "The *Oddly Report*? What's that?"

"The one major art journal that's never reviewed my work. Wouldn't you know it? It's the biggest, the most prestigious. Most people just call it *Odd*."

"And obviously the smartest," said Ruth.

"Now I'm glad they've ignored me," said Clara, snapping off the lights.

But, having reexamined the miniatures, she was both heartened and confused. They were, she felt, actually very good. Exceptional, even. Why couldn't others see what she saw?

She joined her friends, crowded around the kitchen window, while Ruth limped into the living room and stood behind the one person not watching the Bella Bella.

Homer Godin was staring out a window in the other direction. Into the forest.

Ruth's reflection, like an apparition, hovered in the window just over his shoulder. The rain coursed down both their faces.

"She's out there somewhere." Homer's words fogged the windowpane. He didn't turn around, but his eyes in the reflection met Ruth's. "Please. Can you help me?"

In the background, the CBC was broadcasting continuous updates on the flooding.

Reports were coming in from all over Ontario, Québec, the Maritimes, while Vivienne's father stared at Rosa's mother.

She reached out and touched his arm.

Homer closed his eyes tight. "Oh, please. Help."


Armand checked the wall of sandbags.

Floodlights had been set up on either side of the river. One pointing upriver, the other pointing down. So that the villagers could see what was happening. From where he stood, he could also see the lights in Clara's back garden.

The rain mixed with snow was teeming down, and he hunched deeper into his coat as a gust of wind lashed water into his face.

Every half hour since getting back, he went out to check the height of the river. It was, Ruth had made clear, his assignment. The least he could do.

"You don't think you can just swan in here and relax by the fire after we spent all day building the goddamned wall?" said Ruth.

Rosa, in her arms, bristled. She didn't like swans.

"Clearly the Sûreté doesn't think you're much use, or you wouldn't be back here. And don't get me started on what they're saying on Twitter, the dumb-asses. Not that I disagree."

"Ruth!" said Reine-Marie.

"What? It's the truth."

"*All truth with malice in it,*" said Armand.

"But still the truth," said Ruth.

Reine-Marie walked Armand to the door. "That was from *Moby-Dick,* wasn't it?"

Rosa turned and looked at Ruth, who whispered reassuringly, "Dick. Not duck."

"Yes," said Armand. "Someone quoted from the book today. Now it's lodged in my mind."

"Well, there's a coincidence," Ruth said to Clara. "You were talking about it, too."

"What were you hearing? I was talking about my art, not a book."

"You were talking about your critics, and the big one that got away," said Ruth. "Your white whale."

Armand went to put on his heavy rubber boots, then realized he'd grabbed the wrong pair. Looking around, he noticed they all had much the same boots, all bought at Monsieur Béliveau's general store.

"Don't let Homer out of your sight," he said to Reine-Marie as he did up his coat. "And whatever happens, make sure he doesn't get any car keys."

"You don't want him bolting," said Reine-Marie.

He nodded. "Bolting" was one way of putting it.

As he trudged through the mud, head bent into the sleet, Armand heard splashing behind him and turned to see Olivier running toward him.

The slender man was bundled up so that he would be unrecognizable, except to someone who knew him well.

"Thought you could use some help," said Olivier, above the roar of the water.

"To look at a river?"

"Okay, some company." On seeing the expression on Armand's face, Olivier amended that. "Okay, it was time to do dishes."

Armand laughed. Knowing that in fact Olivier had come out into the frigid night to offer help. In case.

*"Merci."*

At the wall, Armand put his arm out to Olivier. "Hold my hand."

"This is so sudden," said Olivier. "But not unexpected."

"Silly man," said Armand with a grunt of laughter. "Just hold on so I don't fall in."

With Olivier gripping his hand and sleeve, Gamache climbed over the wall and leaned out. Clicking on his flashlight as he did.

He saw that while there was certainly ice and debris in the swiftly moving river, it was at least moving.

They checked several other spots downriver.

At the last stop, Armand took longer. And leaned farther.

"Okay, that's enough," yelled Olivier. "I'm losing my grip."

"Another moment." The floodlights didn't reach this far, so Armand shone his flashlight on the frothing water.

"What?" asked Olivier, the strain of holding on apparent in his voice.

"There's some buildup beginning. In the bend in the river. I can see ice and some tree limbs."

He stayed there another few seconds. Trying to see more clearly. Though the sleet was hitting his face and he had to blink away the moisture.

"Better come back. Now." The strain in Olivier's voice was apparent, and Armand could feel his grip slipping.

He climbed back over the sturdy wall of sandbags. His brow furrowed in thought.

Wiping the rain from his eyes, he looked upriver. Past the stone bridge. Past Clara's home. Past St. Thomas's Church, lit so that even through the rain he could see the three stained-glass boys, trudging forever through the mud of some far-off foreign field.

"We need Billy Williams," he yelled above the river.

"Why?"

"The Bella Bella's about to break her banks. The sandbags will hold for a little while, but there's too much water coming down, and ice is backing up at the bend."

"What can Billy do? Break it up?"

Gamache looked upriver again, remembering the donkeys in the field and the sound of the Bella Bella behind them.

"He can dig a trench."

It was an oddity of Armand's relationship with Billy that they had a strangely close connection and yet Armand could not understand a word the man said. Granted, Billy Williams had a thick backcountry English accent, though Gamache managed to understand everyone else.

Despite this, Billy remained for Armand both a cipher and a confidant.

Olivier had run back to Clara's home and brought Billy out with him. Now the three stood next to the Bella Bella.

"How can I help?" Billy asked.

All Armand heard was a series of guttural sounds ending in an upward inflection. He looked at Olivier, who translated.

Armand told him what he wanted. Billy considered.

"For God's sake, hurry up and tell us," said Olivier, his teeth chattering in the cold.

"I'll need my backhoe," said Billy, pointing to the piece of machinery he'd used earlier in the day to move the piles of sand. "But it's heavy. It won't make it up the hills in this mud. The place you're suggesting is kilometers away."

Olivier translated again.

"I was afraid of that," said Armand. After all, he'd had an experience with a hill earlier in the day.

Billy made some more noises and gestures.

"When?" asked Olivier.

More sounds from Billy.

"Will it work?" asked Olivier.

Billy thought, then nodded. "Yurt."

That Armand got. "It's possible, then?"

"But you'll have to wait until the temperature drops and the ground hardens," said Olivier. "He figures it'll be sometime after midnight."

Armand looked over to the river. Then at his watch. It was almost 10:00 p.m.

"Do we have that long?" Olivier asked.

"I don't know," said Armand.

They went back inside and reported what they'd found as they toweled off their faces and hair, then stuck their hands out to the fire.

The others listened in silence. There was nothing to say and nothing to do, except wait.

Jean-Guy called from Montréal and reported that they'd decided to blow the ice dams on the St. Lawrence. "They'll issue a public warning and close the bridges while it's being done."

"Good. Let me know if it works."

"I will."

Armand lowered his voice. "And the dams?"

"No word. No mention of them now, even on the secure channels."

Gamache took a deep breath and said a silent prayer.

"How's it going there?" Jean-Guy asked.

"We've designated St. Thomas's as an evacuation center. Most of the residents have been moved up there, but some are staying behind."

"You speaking to numbnuts?" came a familiar voice in the background.

"Do witches float?" asked Jean-Guy.

"I believe they do," said Armand.

"Shame."

"I see he's staying where it's safe and warm," said Ruth. "I'd expect nothing less. Or more."

"Bitch," muttered Jean-Guy.

"Bastard," said Ruth. "Oh, and tell him to give my love to my godson. And tell Honoré I have a few more words for him to learn, and a special hand signal."

When Ruth moved on, Armand told Jean-Guy their plans for the Bella Bella.

There was a pause. "That's still two hours away, at best. Will the sandbags hold?"

"Hard to tell."

Armand exhaled, and Jean-Guy could hear the strain.

"Annie and Honoré are safe here, and I'm just sitting at HQ with my thumb up my—"

"Got it."

"I'm coming down to help"—he glanced at the clock—"if I can get off-island before they close the bridges. See you soon."

"But—"

But the line was dead.

"Jean-Guy's coming down to help," he reported to the others.

"Dumb-ass," said Ruth.

But Armand could see relief in the ancient face, illuminated by the flames from the log fire.


"I'm sorry sir, you'll have to go back. We've closed the bridge."

Beauvoir flashed his credentials, and the officer stepped aside and waved him through, alerting agents along the span to let this vehicle pass.

Just as he made it over, Beauvoir heard a huge explosion. He winced and instinctively ducked, even though he knew what it was. In the rearview mirror, he saw a plume of snow and ice shoot into the air.

A few minutes later, some distance down the autoroute, he heard another, more muffled explosion.

The ice was packed in tight, the St. Lawrence beginning to flood. If this didn't work . . .

As he drove, he monitored the secure Sûreté channels, while dynamite went off in a ring around the island and across Québec.

At least Annie and Honoré were safe on high ground. And he'd return to them by dawn. Even if he had to swim across the St. Lawrence to get there.

# CHAPTER THIRTEEN

It had been decided by Ruth, apparently in consultation with a duck and a bottle of scotch, that sentries would be placed on the bridge to sound the alarm should the Rivière Bella Bella break through the sandbags.

Reine-Marie and Armand chose to take the first shift.

At the door Ruth made sure their heavy raincoats were well fastened. "You have your whistle, in case something happens?"

"I do," said Reine-Marie.

"And your *Boys' Big Book of Flooding*?"

"Always," said Armand.

"Then we'll be fine," said the old poet.

"Fucked up," said Gabri.

"Insecure," said Olivier.

"Neurotic," said Clara.

"And egotistical, yeah, yeah," said Ruth. "Now, no necking, you two, and be home by midnight."

"Yes, Mom."

As the rain and ice pellets hit her face, Reine-Marie called to Armand, "Heck of a date."

Inside, a discussion had begun around the fireplace. What to take, if an evacuation order was given.

"I'd take Gabri," said Olivier.

"I'd take the espresso machine," said Gabri. "And some croissants."

At the bridge they stood, backs to the wind, shoulders hunched, hoods raised. Reine-Marie put on her flashlight and pointed it into the Bella Bella.

"It's rising," she shouted.

"*Oui.*"

"I'd take my Jehane Benoît cookbook," said Myrna. "The photo album. The Lalique vase. That hand-knotted Indian rug—"

"Hold on," said Gabri. "Do you have a moving van? Can we use some of it? I'd take my grandfather's Victorian sofa."

"Oh, no you don't," said Olivier. "The only good thing about a flood wiping out our entire lives is that it'd take that monstrosity with it."

Armand and Reine-Marie walked over the stone bridge. And back again. Over and back. Pausing every couple of minutes to switch on the powerful flashlight and check the level of the Rivière Bella Bella.

Then continue on.

Like guards on a lonely frontier.

Back and forth. Back and forth.

Armand could barely hear his own thoughts for the sound of the water rushing below and the ice pellets hitting his coat.

What he thought about, as he walked back and forth, back and forth, was Vivienne. Out there somewhere. And Vivienne's father. And Annie.

He tried to keep their daughter out of it, knowing how dangerous it was to personalize investigations. But perhaps his resistance was lowered by the cold, by the competing stresses, by incipient exhaustion, but he couldn't seem to stop putting himself in Monsieur Godin's place.

Suppose Annie were missing? And everyone he turned to for help, while nice, didn't actually help? If he pleaded with them, begged them, and all they did was smile and offer soup?

It would be a nightmare. He'd be mad with worry.

Pausing again at the top of the bridge, he took Reine-Marie's hand. Suddenly feeling the need for comfort.

The water in the beams of light was frothing, foaming. Like something rabid. It scudded along the lip of the shoreline. Rising faster than they'd expected. The jam, just a little way downriver, out of Three Pines, must be getting worse.

And then.

Armand heard a low hum, almost a moan, from Reine-Marie. As they watched, the Bella Bella broke up and over her banks.

It was now racing along the bottom of the sandbags.

"They'll hold," she said. "There's a long way to go before the river reaches us."

"*Oui.*"

Though they both knew that the problem wasn't necessarily the height of the river but the force of it. The danger wasn't that the water would cascade over the wall but that it would knock it down.

They'd built it two bags thick. So it shouldn't.

But then, the Bella Bella should never have gotten this high.

A lot of things were happening that shouldn't.

Just ask Homer Godin, who was living the great "should not be happening."

Reine-Marie lifted her eyes and through the sleet saw the lights of St. Thomas's Church on the hill. Where volunteers were making sure the children were sleeping soundly and not afraid. They were setting up more cots and organizing food, fresh water, generators, and composting toilets. Should the worst happen.

Then she shifted her gaze to the woods.

"Where is she, Armand?"

"I don't know."

"Is she—"

"I don't know."

"But you suspect. Have you spoken to the husband?"

"This afternoon. He's a piece of work. Sûreté's been called to their home more than once. Alcoholic. Maybe drugs."

"Abusive?"

"*Oui.*"

A buildup of trouble that had broken its banks, thought Reine-Marie. And the young woman was taken at the flood.

"She's pregnant?"

"*Oui.*"

"How could someone—"

But there was no use finishing the question. And there was no answer.

They continued to pace. Back and forth. Back and forth.

Still the question rankled.

How could someone . . . ?

"Can you make him tell you?" Reine-Marie shouted above the torrent.

"Short of putting a gun to his head or beating it out of him, no."

In her silence, he knew what she was feeling, if not thinking.

Maybe, just this once . . .

Maybe in some cases it was justified. Maybe torture. Maybe beatings. Maybe even murder was justified. Sometimes.

"Situational ethics?" he asked.

"Don't be smug," Reine-Marie said. "We all have them. Even me. Even you."

She was right, of course.

It was the asp at the breast of any decent cop. Any military leader. Any politician.

Any mother or father.

Any human.

Maybe. Just this once . . .


"I'd take Ruth," said Olivier.

"Thank you," said the old poet.

"Because she's a witch and would float?" asked Clara.

"Of course," said Olivier. "We could cling to her."

"I'd rather drown," said Gabri.

They turned to Billy.

"I think you'd know what I'd take," he said.

"Your tractor?" asked Myrna.

"So that's how you're doing it," Lysette Cloutier muttered as she stared at the IP address. "You shit."

Over the fifteen years she'd worked in accounting for the Sûreté, Lysette had rarely used foul language. And rarely had she heard it.

But in homicide she'd heard, and discovered within herself, a whole new vocabulary. It was, she thought, a form of verbal violence to counter the horrific things they saw every day.

Instead of lashing out physically, they lashed out verbally.

And yet, she thought as she put more commands into her laptop, she'd rarely heard Chief Inspector Gamache swear. She tried to think if she'd ever heard him.

Maybe that's why he was in charge. What was it he'd said to that Cameron? The population had a right to expect that people with a gun and a badge would also have self-control.

Maybe he had greater control over himself than most.

But what was he controlling? And what would happen if it ever broke free?

Bob Cameron sat in his car. The sleet had stopped. The skies were clearing. The temperature dropping.

His windshield was frosting over, but he could still see stars, the Milky Way. And that single light in the house.

In the bedroom.

Was Tracey lying on the bed, on top of that comforter with its bright pink and green flowers that Vivienne's mother had left her in her will?

Was he drinking himself stupid?

Stupider.

Was that even a word?

Or was he packing? Planning to run away.

125

Cameron hoped so. That's what he'd been waiting for. Hoping for. Expecting.

*Come on. Come on, you shit. Get in that truck of yours and just try it.*

Cameron had been reassigned from the effort to find Vivienne Godin to setting up emergency shelters. Sent home to rest, he'd come here instead.

Tracey was a weak man, Cameron knew. The sort who'd try to run.

*And then what would I do?*

But he knew the answer to that. He'd pull Tracey over. Tell him to get out of the vehicle.

And he'd do what he should have done weeks ago.

He looked at his watch. It was almost 1:00 a.m. He should go home. His wife might be wondering. But he couldn't. Not quite yet.

*Come on, you dumb-ass. Come on out. Come to me.*

Billy Williams stood on the road out of town. He held a long, gnarled stick, and as Reine-Marie and Armand watched, he drove it into the mud. As he'd done every twenty minutes for the past couple of hours.

He was testing to see how far the stick would sink in, but also, it seemed by his cocked head, listening for some sound from the earth. Some permission.

The sleet had stopped an hour earlier, and the temperature had plummeted. Exactly what they needed.

Maybe now . . .

"Well?" asked Reine-Marie, just as Armand noticed a glow on the hill above them.

Headlights. That could be only one person. Jean-Guy had arrived.

Billy spoke.

"Thank the Lord," said Reine-Marie, turning to Armand. "Billy says it's frozen."

# CHAPTER FOURTEEN

They stood on the frozen field, a few kilometers upriver of Three Pines, and watched as Billy's backhoe dug into the banks of the Bella Bella.

The strong beam from the light on the front of his cab illuminated the ice and muck and stones as the shovel dug in.

Reine-Marie held her phone in her mittened hand. They had, away from the forests and on the clear, crisp night, a fragile signal. That came and went. But was at least there. For now.

Jean-Guy was beside the river, and Armand stood on the running board, guiding the digging of the trench. While Reine-Marie listened for reports back from Three Pines.

They'd left Clara and Myrna on the bridge. The river was now up to the second sandbag.

Ruth was in Clara's cottage with her landline. Reporting back.

"River's still rising," Ruth shouted into the phone. Partly to be heard over the roar of the river and partly because she always shouted into a phone.

"Did you see that?" Myrna shouted into Clara's ear.

*Damn her*, thought Clara, who was busy trying to pretend she hadn't seen anything.

But Myrna rarely looked away from some awful truth. Preferring to know rather than to live in blissful, if dangerous ignorance. It was one of her worst qualities.

"They've shifted." Myrna turned and yelled across to Ruth. "Tell them to hurry. They've shifted."

"What's that?"

"They've shifted!"

"Well, you're pretty shitty, too!"

Gabri, standing beside Ruth in the kitchen, grabbed the phone. "Here, give me that. Reine-Marie? The sandbags are beginning to shift."

"*Merde.*"


"Hey! Hey!"

They turned and saw a flashlight approaching.

"Keep digging," Armand yelled into Billy's ear, then jumped off the backhoe.

"What're you doing? This's my land," came a man's voice.

Armand gestured to Reine-Marie to stay where she was and walked toward the light and the shout. "Sûreté. Who are you?"

But he knew the answer to that. Because he knew whose land they were on.

Jean-Guy left the river and joined Armand. The man was still twenty paces away. And held a flashlight in one hand and something else in the other.

"He's got a gun," said Jean-Guy, his sharp eyes not leaving the man slipping and stumbling toward them.

"*Oui,*" said Armand, and took a step in front of Reine-Marie. "A .22. Hunting rifle. Saw it earlier, in the search. He has a permit."

"Fuck," muttered Jean-Guy, shaking his head.

A .22. Small-gauge. But it could still do damage. To a gopher. A fox. A human.

"This's private property," Tracey shouted. "Get off."

They were downwind of him and could smell the whiskey. The donkeys had been put in the barn overnight, so it was just humans now, in the field.

"Monsieur Tracey, it's Armand Gamache. We met earlier today."

"I don't care who you are. You're on my land." Tracey stopped ten paces away and raised his rifle. "Get off."

"Armand?" said Reine-Marie, stepping forward.

"It's all right," he said, and put his arm out to gently move her behind him.

Obviously, she thought, his idea of "all right" and hers were very different.

"What's happening?" came Gabri's tinny voice down the phone. "Reine-Marie?"

"Drop the gun," commanded Beauvoir.

"Gun?" came the tinny voice. "Hello?"

"Get off my goddamned land," yelled Tracey. The rifle still raised.

Billy had stopped digging. Armand turned to him and shouted, "Whatever happens, keep digging."

"Yurz."

The machine began again, and Tracey stepped forward, slipping slightly on the snow and mud.

The danger, Gamache could now see, wasn't just that he'd fire the rifle on purpose but that he'd slip and it would go off accidentally.

"I said stop," yelled Tracey.

"And I said drop the gun," said Beauvoir, stepping directly in front of Armand. Directly in front of the gun.

"Oh, my God," shouted Armand, and waved toward the river.

Reine-Marie, alarmed, turned.

As did Tracey.

The only one who didn't was Beauvoir, who was expecting Gamache to do something like this. Divert, just for a moment, Tracey's attention.

Jean-Guy's hand shot out and wrenched the rifle from his grip.

When Tracey lunged for it, Beauvoir pivoted and knocked him to the ground.

Gamache bent down and lifted the drunken man to his feet.

"We're diverting the river," he explained. "To stop the—"

"You have no right. This's private land," Tracey shouted. With a yank, he twisted away from Gamache and ran toward the backhoe, waving and shouting, "*Arrêt! Arrêt!* Stop."

But, of course, Billy did not.

He hadn't seen that Beauvoir had disarmed him. As far as Billy knew, a man with a rifle was running toward him. And might very well shoot.

But Billy didn't care. Myrna was down there. The bags were shifting. And only he could stop it.

He pushed the shovel in deeper and dragged it forward into the field just as Gamache caught up with Tracey and, grabbing him around the waist, hauled the man around and away.

With a gush, the Bella Bella began pouring into the field.

"Hello?" came a tinny voice.

There was no deluding herself any longer.

The wall was coming down.

It was time to leave, Clara knew. Not just the bridge but her home. The village. Time to abandon Three Pines to fate.

Myrna and Clara quickly made their way off the bridge, half walking, half running.

The last of the villagers had to get out of Clara's home, out of Three Pines, and up to the church.

From there they would witness the destruction.

"Wait," said Clara, grabbing Myrna's arm.

Every particle of Myrna's being was straining forward. Telling her to flee. Now.

But she stopped. And waited, for a moment. Because Clara had.

Too afraid to even speak, she stared at the circle from Clara's flashlight. It rested, trembling, on the now-askew sandbags. Some had fallen, some were preparing to slide away, pushed by the force of the water.

She had to make sure.

"Oh, shit," she heard herself whisper.

Armand was physically holding Carl Tracey around the abdomen, while the man kicked and squirmed.

Jean-Guy hurried over to help contain him, but just as he arrived, Tracey slowly stopped thrashing, and a moment later he was standing still, clasped against Gamache's body.

130

Both men were staring.

"Stop!" This time it was Gamache who was shouting at Billy.

The floodlight on the top of the backhoe was pointing at the bucket of debris Billy had just dropped onto the field, next to the water rushing out of the Bella Bella.

"What's that?" asked Reine-Marie, taking a step closer.

Beauvoir saw then why Gamache had stopped the digging. Why Tracey had stopped fighting. And why he'd been so hysterical to stop the digging.

"What's that?" Gabri shouted at Clara and Myrna. He tried to keep the panic out of his voice. "What're you saying?"

The two women were waving their arms and yelling something about the river. If he had to guess, and it seemed he might have to, whatever they were shouting was not good news.

Billy went to dismount his machine, but Armand waved him to stay where he was. And told Reine-Marie the same thing.

Then he and Jean-Guy slowly approached the trench.

"Armand, Gabri's saying something. Something's happened."

"What?" yelled Billy from the cab of the machine.

"What?" yelled Gabri again, completely forgetting he had Reine-Marie on the line.

"What?" came the tinny voice.

"The water level's going down!"

Gabri and Reine-Marie heard it at the same moment. Clara's shout. And then Reine-Marie heard shouts of joy. Even Ruth was cheering. At least she thought that cackling was a cheer.

"The water level's dropping!" Reine-Marie reported. "It's worked. It's dropping."

Billy gave a whoop. But while both Armand and Jean-Guy looked over, Armand smiling with relief and Jean-Guy nodding, they quickly looked away.

In the harsh beam from Billy's backhoe, something pink was lying in the muck.

Armand knelt and reached out.

It was a bright pink duffel bag. With a name tag. A single embossed letter.

V.

# CHAPTER FIFTEEN

———

W hat've you done with her?" Gamache demanded.

"Nothing. I've done nothing. Maybe it isn't hers."

"It's hers," said Gamache. "It's Vivienne's, and you know it."

Tracey recognized it. But Gamache also recognized something. The look on Carl Tracey's face. He'd seen it before, when a piece of damning evidence, thought hidden, was found.

It was the unmistakable look of dread.

While he stayed with Tracey and the duffel bag, Beauvoir went to the river and was walking the banks. Shining his flashlight, to see if he could see something else. Someone else.

As he walked, Beauvoir's heart thudded in his chest, in his wrists, at his temples, and in his throat. His skin tingled. His face, in the cold, was flushed.

He'd spent much of his adult life looking for bodies, at bodies. What was out there didn't scare him.

What frightened him was what was in there. Inside himself. What dark thing had been aroused, awoken, when he realized he was in the presence of someone who'd almost certainly thrown his wife and unborn child into a freezing river. To die.

It was all Jean-Guy Beauvoir could do not to turn around. March back to Tracey. Tell Armand and Reine-Marie and Billy to look away while he forced Tracey to a kneeling position, took out his gun. Placed it at the base of the monster's skull. And fired.

Jean-Guy paced. Pointing the flashlight this way and that. Trying to settle his mind and focus on the job at hand.

What he saw were shards of ice, rocks, roots uprooted. Debris. Rushing water. But no Vivienne.

At Beauvoir's request, Billy had turned his backhoe so that its light faced the river.

From the cab, Billy Williams watched Jean-Guy pace. He knew torment when he saw it.

Then he looked over at Armand. Standing right up against Carl Tracey. Not side by side but facing him, in an act of extreme and ghastly intimacy.

Billy Williams knew that what he was witnessing was also an act of love. Not for Tracey, of course, but for Jean-Guy.

Armand had sent the younger man away to, on the surface, do the worst job. To look for the body of a young woman and her unborn child. But in reality, Armand was saving Jean-Guy. From himself.

Gamache was standing that close to Carl Tracey so that Beauvoir didn't have to.

When Tracey backed up, Gamache moved forward. Not letting the weaselly man step away. Get away. Gamache was at least two inches taller, twenty pounds heavier, and twenty-five years older than Tracey.

He had the advantage of height, weight, control, and sobriety.

But Tracey had the greater advantage of knowledge. He knew where Vivienne was.

Gamache's boots thucked in the mud as he stepped even closer to Tracey.

"Tell us," Gamache repeated, his eyes not leaving Tracey's. "Where's Vivienne?"

"I don't know. She went away," said Tracey. "Ran away with some guy she was—"

"Enough," said Gamache. "What did you do with her?" Then he modulated his tone. Corralling, with difficulty, his anger. His voice, when he spoke again, was unnaturally reasonable. Coaxing a brute to do one decent thing. "Tell us, Carl. Let us give her some rest."

Behind them, the Bella Bella ran off into the mucky field. The night air was crackling with cold and outrage.

"I have no idea where she is. Maybe she got drunk and fell into the river. Or maybe whoever got her pregnant tossed her in."

Out of the corner of his eye, Armand saw Reine-Marie take a step closer. Her hand gripped the phone, as though it were a baseball bat.

Somehow this vile man had managed to stir up in Reine-Marie an outrage that bordered on violence.

Gamache's own breath, through his nostrils, came out in long, warm puffs. Like a bull longing to charge.

He barely registered that behind him, Billy Williams was speaking.

"There's no sign of her," called Beauvoir. "Billy says he thinks the duffel bag came from farther upriver."

"There's an old logging road about a kilometer from here." Billy waved behind him. "A bridge goes over the Bella Bella. It's been closed for a while now, but hunters sometimes use it in the fall."

Jean-Guy translated what was said.

Gamache turned and looked at the .22 leaning against the backhoe. A hunting rifle.

"Can you show us?" he asked.

"Yurz."

"What about the bag?" Reine-Marie asked.

"We'll take it with us," said Gamache.

"You can't," said Tracey.

"Then we'll open it here," said Beauvoir.

Gamache asked Reine-Marie to use her phone to record the search of Vivienne's bag while Billy took his place beside Tracey.

"No," said Tracey. "Stop. It doesn't belong to you. It's on my property. It belongs to me."

"It belongs to your wife," said Beauvoir, unzipping it.

The duffel bag contained all the things you'd expect someone to pack who was going away for a few days. T-shirts, a pair of jeans. Some shorts. Pajamas. Underwear. Toiletries.

"What are these?" Gamache held up a bottle of pills and read off the label, "Mifegymiso."

When the others shook their heads, Gamache held them out for Tracey to see.

"How should I know? Probably some street drug she picked up, the—"

"Enough." Beauvoir got to his feet and took a step toward Tracey.

"Jean-Guy," snapped Gamache.

The cold, the exhaustion, the find, the growing certainty of what had happened to this young woman and who'd made it happen, were all fraying their nerves.

Beauvoir glared at Tracey but managed to contain himself.

"We're done," said Gamache, zipping the duffel bag shut. "We'll take this with us and give you a receipt."

"I don't want a receipt. I want the bag."

"You're coming with us," said Beauvoir, and shoved him toward the car as they all trudged across the field. Leaving the backhoe to sink further into the mire.

When they reached the car, Beauvoir placed the duffel bag in the trunk, and Gamache, having removed the bullets, put the .22 back there, too.

Tracey stood beside the car.

"Get in," said Gamache.

When Beauvoir went to get in beside him, Gamache held out the keys.

"Why don't you drive? Can you get in the front seat?" he asked Reine-Marie, who'd stopped recording and slipped the phone into her pocket.

Gamache and Billy got into the backseat, with Tracey between them.

"She isn't dead, you know. She's messing with you all. Trying to get me into trouble. I bet she threw that fucking bag into the river herself. You wait. When she shows up, after a bender with some guy, I'll be suing your ass."

"Let's hope," said Gamache.

Beauvoir drove while Billy pointed the way to the old logging road.

They came to little more than a break in the trees. Turning in, Beauvoir felt the tires begin to sink. "We have to walk from here."

The five of them followed the flashlight beams down the narrow lane through the trees.

The limbs of the trees loomed overhead, a tunnel of dead branches. Their flashlights created shadows so macabre that even Beauvoir, not given to fantasy, felt his skin crawl. This was how horror films began. Or ended.

And then it got worse.

Beauvoir's stronger beam landed on something up ahead. Blocking the way. A car.

"Stay here," Gamache said to the others while he and Jean-Guy approached.

It was Vivienne's.

Gamache nodded to Beauvoir, who carefully walked around to the other side and shone his light through the rear window while Gamache looked in the front.

Nothing.

Opening the driver's door, careful not to touch too much, Gamache played his light over the seat. The wheel. The footwells. There were assorted wrappers, some change. It smelled of stale cigarette smoke. He checked the ashtray and found stubs.

The same brand Tracey smoked.

There was a smear of blood on the steering wheel and another in the shift. The hair on the back of Gamache's neck was standing on end. Something awful had happened here.

He pulled a lever and popped the trunk.

"Nothing," Beauvoir reported.

Gamache closed the car door, and both investigators made for the wooden bridge.

"Don't worry," shouted Tracey. "It's safe."

"No it's not," called Billy. "It's probably rotten."

Beauvoir reached out and stopped Gamache, who was just about to step on the wooden boards. Armand had heard Billy but hadn't understood.

Beauvoir turned and glared at Tracey, who was smiling.

"Worth a try," Tracey said, his eyes cold. Calculating.

Reine-Marie took a step away from this creature while Beauvoir wondered if all five of them would make it out of the woods.

From the safety of solid ground, Gamache and Beauvoir shone their beams along the old logging bridge. Then stopped. The two circles of light converged on a single spot.

A section of wooden handrail was missing. The side opened up to thin air.

Gamache pointed his beam down. Into the drop-off. Twenty feet below, maybe more, was the churning river. Grabbing, dragging, swallowing all that it could.

They played their lights over both shores, but there was nothing. Then Beauvoir's beam stopped.

"Wait, I think I see something."

Gamache swung his flashlight over to the far shore.

"What is it?" called Reine-Marie. "Have you found something?"

"No, it's nothing," said Beauvoir, relieved. "Just branches. They looked like a body for a moment."

He moved his flashlight away. "We can't search the bridge or shoreline right now. Too dangerous. It'll have to wait 'til morning."

But Gamache's light hadn't moved. In the beam, he saw what Beauvoir had seen. Tree branches, bobbing slightly in the current. Nothing more.

He could see why Beauvoir would mistake—

Opening his mouth, Gamache took a sharp breath, almost a gasp.

"What is it?" asked Beauvoir. "Do you see something?"

Once more he swung his light over, to join Gamache's, until the two became one bright spot.

Beauvoir looked more closely at the clump of debris on the opposite bank. But still saw nothing. Certainly not anything that would explain the expression on his father-in-law's face.

It was one of surprise. Shock, even.

"Vivienne's not here," Gamache said, then looked at Beauvoir. "But I think I know where she is."

# CHAPTER SIXTEEN

~

T he two men ran along the path, the river on one side, the forest on the other.

Jean-Guy skidded once and went down on one knee in the mud. Armand grabbed his jacket and hauled him to his feet.

And then they continued on. Their flashlights bobbing wildly ahead of them, illuminating trees, path, rocks, river.

They didn't have far to go. Just to the bend in the river.

When they'd arrived back in Three Pines, they'd taken Carl Tracey to the bistro, where they found Olivier and Gabri, now that the danger of flooding had passed.

"Keep him here," Gamache had instructed them. "Billy will stay with you. Homer?"

"At your place," Olivier said. "Clara and Myrna took him there hoping he'd get some sleep. They're staying with him."

"What time is it?" asked Reine-Marie.

"Two thirty," said Gabri.

"That late?"

"That early," he said. "The wee hours, as Ruth calls it."

"Where is she, by the way?"

"She went home. Had to wee."

Reine-Marie glanced at Tracey. He was in the far corner, where he'd been placed by Jean-Guy. Far away from the warmth and soft light of the fireplace.

Then she turned to Armand. "I'll make sure Homer doesn't come over here. You go."

And Armand and Jean-Guy did.

Even though both men knew there was no need to rush, still they ran. Down the path. Beside the wall of sandbags. They ran behind the general store, the boulangerie, past the back of the bistro and the bookstore. The Bella Bella on one side, forest on the other.

And then they were there.

Gamache was panting and holding his flashlight out in front of him with both hands, like a gun. Aiming the beam, steadying it as he stood beside Beauvoir.

Their lights, pointed in the same direction, merged.

And then they saw it. Her.

Gamache had been there earlier, when he and Olivier had checked the river levels.

They hadn't come quite this far, but still, he'd seen it then as he'd leaned out. Olivier holding on to him.

The growing dam.

He'd noted the pale tree limbs and leaves bobbing up and down in the current. Trapped in the broken ice and debris that was forming.

He'd hesitated, trying to get a closer look. But Olivier's grip had been slipping, and he was pulled away.

Now he was back. And he saw, in the bright circle of light, his mistake.

At the logging bridge, Beauvoir had momentarily taken trees for a body. And in that moment, Armand Gamache realized he'd done the same thing, only in reverse.

He'd mistaken a body for trees.

Now he looked once again at the tangle of ice and tree limbs. Debris and detritus picked up by the Rivière Bella Bella as it rushed down from the mountains.

Here was Vivienne Godin.

This is where she'd come to rest.

Her dark hair, like leaves, floated on the surface, moving with the current. Her pale arms and legs. Limbs. Now so clearly human.

Armand Gamache crossed himself, just as Beauvoir shoved his flashlight into Gamache's hands.

"What're you doing?"

"What does it look like?" Beauvoir stripped off his coat. "I'm going to get her."

"You can't." Gamache placed himself between Beauvoir and the Bella Bella and reached out. "Stop."

But Beauvoir wasn't listening to reason. He looked at the bobbing head. At the arms.

And he saw Annie.

"Step aside," he said to Gamache.

"*Non.*"

"Step aside. That's an order."

"*Non.*"

Jean-Guy then did something he'd not have thought possible twenty-four hours earlier. An hour earlier. A moment earlier.

He shoved his father-in-law. Who dropped the flashlights and took a step back, partly from the force of it, partly from the shock of it.

"Get out of my way," Jean-Guy yelled, desperate to get to the young woman. As he hoped someone would try to save Annie, if . . .

This time Gamache saw him coming and wrapped his arms around Jean-Guy. Gripping him in a bear hug so tight that Jean-Guy could smell the slight scent of sandalwood and feel Armand's heart thudding against his own.

"It's too late," Armand said, directly into Jean-Guy's ear.

But still he struggled. Finally the fight went out of him. And he sagged in Gamache's arms.

"She's gone," Armand whispered, his own eyes screwed shut.

"She's pregnant," sobbed Jean-Guy.

"Yes. I know."

"Annie. Annie's pregnant. Almost three months."

Armand's eyes opened. And he heard a sob.

One. Single. Burst of emotion. Which might have been Jean-Guy's. Or his own. Or maybe it came from the Bella Bella as the river cried out.

And then he realized where it had come from.

Releasing Jean-Guy, he turned and looked up the path. In the darkness there was a greater darkness. A large figure, a father figure, outlined against the trees, standing silent. Rigid.

Then Vivienne's father started forward. One. Step. At a time. Picking up speed. Until he was running down the path.

"Homer, stop!" shouted Gamache.

But Vivienne's father didn't. Couldn't.

He made not a sound but ran straight for the river.

Gamache and Beauvoir just had time to step between Homer Godin and the water. But they might as well have been made of paper. Homer plowed right through them, running straight into the Bella Bella. Wading in. Breaking through the thin ice at the shore, he fought his way forward. To get to his little girl.

Gamache and Beauvoir plunged in after him.

The water was so cold their eyes watered, and their breath came in gasps. But on they lurched, toward the man thrashing through the current ahead of them.

The water churned and frothed as Godin, his arms flailing wildly, knocked them off.

He fought ferociously. Screaming now. Wailing. Baying.

Sobbing.

Gamache got an elbow in the head and was knocked backward, submerged. So cold was the water that his chest locked and he couldn't breathe, even when arms pulled him to the surface.

It was Jean-Guy. Armand stared at him for a moment, then managed, with a great whoop, to get air back into his lungs.

Then it was back to Godin. Who, after what seemed like hours, finally tired of dragging them with him. Like some great whale, harpooned, he slowed. Slowed. Sobbing.

Then stopped. It took both of them to drag Vivienne's father back to shore.

But Homer Godin wasn't finished yet. Once again he tried to break free, but this time they were ready for him. And he had little fight left in him.

"Stop," said Beauvoir softly.

And he did.

"Vivienne?"

"I'm sorry," Armand said.

Homer looked out into the river. "Please," he whispered. "I need to get her."

"We will," said Beauvoir. His teeth were chattering, and he was finding it difficult to form words.

He looked over at Gamache, whose lips were purple and trembling in the cold.

They were all on the verge of exposure. With Homer Godin also suffering from shock, it was a potentially fatal combination.

"Not you," said Homer, his voice shaky. "Me. I have to help her. I can get to her. Let me try."

"The water's too cold. You'll drown," said Gamache through chattering teeth.

"Does it matter?"

"It matters."

But Armand understood. He'd try, too. He'd fight, too. He'd run back into that freezing water, too. If . . .

Homer turned away from him, to once again face the river. And his daughter in the middle of it. Bobbing gently up and down in the current. Her body knocking against the ice.

A small sound escaped the large man.

Only then did Armand notice a figure standing farther down the path, toward the village. Even at a distance. Even in the dark. He knew who it was.

He walked toward her.

"I'm sorry," said Reine-Marie. "I tried to stop him, but he ran out of the house so fast. He must've been watching from the bedroom window and seen you come here."

Armand bent his face close to hers. "Your face. It's bruised."

"Is it?"

"Did he hit you?"

"Not on purpose. He didn't know what he was doing. I reached for his arm to try to stop him—"

Armand brought one shaking finger to within a millimeter of the bruise on Reine-Marie's cheekbone, below her eye. It was swollen, and swelling further.

Gamache could feel himself begin to tremble uncontrollably. It came in waves, sending shudders through his body.

It was, he recognized, the beginning of hypothermia. And outrage.

"My God, Armand, you're soaked. You need to get warm." She looked down the path and only then noticed that Jean-Guy and Homer were also dripping wet. Homer was standing on the shore of the Bella Bella, staring. She followed his eyes. "Is that . . . ?"

"*Oui.*"

# CHAPTER SEVENTEEN

⁓

The water cascaded over Armand's body as he showered. Over his head, over his upturned face. He opened his mouth and shut his eyes. And felt his body finally getting warm.

But then, unbidden, a sudden panic took him.

He was back in the water. Submerged. But this time Jean-Guy wasn't there. No one was there, to reach down and save him.

His eyes flew open, and he dropped his head, away from the water. Reaching out, he leaned against the wet tiles of the shower.

As he breathed, he knew his momentary terror was just a tiny part of what Vivienne must have gone through.

The horror of those final moments. Breaking through the railing. Hanging in midair. Nothing between the bridge and the water to stop her fall.

And then she fell.

Hitting the freezing-cold water. The breath knocked out of her. The shock. The bitter Bella Bella closing over her. And then she breached. Breaking the surface. Mouth open, fighting for air.

The struggle to keep head, mouth, nose above the water. To take a breath. Turning, tumbling, thrashing in the current. Hitting rocks and branches.

The terror. The tumult. The desperate struggle. Growing less and less desperate as the cold and the battering began to win.

And finally the knowing.

Both hands on the tiles, his head hanging down, warm water hitting his back, Armand gasped for breath. And watched the water swirl around the drain.

*Annie's pregnant. Annie's pregnant*, he repeated, following the words to the surface. And trying not to allow the rest of that thought to seep in. But still, it was there.

*And so was Vivienne.*

He opened his eyes and finished his shower.

Then went downstairs, to face Vivienne's father.


Homer and Jean-Guy were in the kitchen, in front of the wood-stove, wrapped in Hudson's Bay blankets. Mugs of strong tea in their hands.

Armand kissed Reine-Marie, softly, on her bruised cheek. "You okay?" he whispered.

The bruise wasn't as bad as he feared, more a glancing blow. But a blow nonetheless.

"I am."

Armand looked at her, closely, to make sure she was telling the truth. Then he turned his attention to the others.

Jean-Guy had stopped trembling.

Homer had not.

As soon as they'd returned to the house, they'd called the Sûreté divers and a Scene of Crime squad from homicide. But with the state of emergency across the province, they were told it could take some hours. Not before morning, for sure.

After letting Isabelle Lacoste and Agent Cloutier know what had happened and asking them to come down, they'd split up.

Jean-Guy had grabbed a shower first, while Armand helped Homer to strip off his wet clothing and get into his own shower. He stayed with the man, who'd sunk into silence, until the shower was over and Homer was in warm, dry clothes.

Armand stayed with him in the kitchen until Jean-Guy returned.

While he knew it wasn't Homer's fault, and it would almost certainly never happen again, he was damned if he'd leave Reine-Marie alone with Homer. Mad with grief, Vivienne's father was capable of almost anything.

Certainly, Armand knew, capable of murder. Though that was aimed at only one person.

After his own shower, Armand returned to the kitchen and caught Jean-Guy's eye. Both men turned to Reine-Marie.

"What?" she asked.

"Jean-Guy has something that might make you feel better," said Armand quietly.

"Can you come with me?" Jean-Guy stood up.

After a brief, baffled, glance at Armand, Reine-Marie followed her son-in-law out of the kitchen.

Fred had put his large head on Homer's slippered feet, and Henri did the same with Armand. Little Gracie was curled up on a blanket close to the fire.

The only sound was the slight rattle of the old windows as the night tried to get in. Not, perhaps, realizing it was already dark in there.

A few minutes later, Reine-Marie and Jean-Guy returned.

She was flushed, and her eyes were moist. And when she met Armand's, his, too, began to burn. She brought her hands to her mouth, and he embraced her.

"I just spoke to Annie. A baby," she whispered, words meant only for Armand.

Homer did not need to know that they were living his dream, while he lived their nightmare.

Excusing himself now, Armand went into his study and, picking up his phone, tapped in a familiar number.

"I'm sorry," he heard the polite young receptionist say, "but Chief Superintendent Toussaint can't take your call right now."

"Tell her it's Armand Gamache."

There was a pause. "She knows."

Now it was his turn to pause. *"Merci."*

Then he called the senior RCMP commissioner who'd been in the meeting the day before.

"Armand, what is it?" He sounded weary.

"I wanted an update on the flooding."

"Did you call Toussaint?"

"I tried."

Again there was a pause. Gamache could feel the embarrassment down the line.

"It's a hectic time," the officer said.

"*Oui.* Can you tell me what's happening?"

"The dynamiting on the St. Lawrence worked, but it looks like a temporary reprieve. The thaw's moving north."

"The dams?"

"Holding. Barely. The pressure's building. And they still can't decide whether or not to open the floodgates."

"Go on." Gamache, who knew the man well, could hear the hesitation.

"I've consulted with the armed forces engineer and Hydro-Québec. We're not waiting for approval. Hydro's going to open the gates."

Gamache took a deep breath. "You know that what you're doing could be considered insubordination."

"You think? Well, you're the expert, I guess," the Mountie said with a laugh. He sounded drained. "Once the floodgates are open, we'll pull the machinery from all but the most vulnerable dams and move it south. The corps of engineers will then begin digging trenches along rivers that're threatening communities. More insubordination. I don't think they're going to let us play together anymore, Armand. You're a bad influence."

Gamache gave a small sound of amusement. It was all he could muster.

"Armand?"

"*Oui?*"

"Be careful of Toussaint."

"She's doing well," Gamache said. "These are difficult decisions. She'll grow into the job."

"But what job? She has political aspirations."

"Nothing wrong with that."

"Except she's using her position in the Sûreté not as a responsibility but as a tool, a springboard. Surely that was obvious in the meeting. She needs to distance herself from you. Distinguish herself from you."

"Your point being?"

"With this flood, with our decision to follow your suggestion and not waiting for her approval, she'll be gunning for you."

"Not literally, I hope."

But there was silence down the line. Both remembering when that was exactly what senior officers had done to each other, literally. In the time "before."

"*Non.* But she's no friend of yours. You have the support and loyalty of the rank and file, Armand. She doesn't."

"Give her time."

"Have you been following the social-media posts? About you?"

"A bit."

"Where do you think some of that information's coming from?"

"Are you kidding?" said Gamache. "You think Madeleine Toussaint is leaking it?"

There was silence.

"You're wrong," said Gamache.

"How can you be loyal to her, Armand, when it's so clearly not mutual?"

"Does it have to be mutual? She's a decent person, who stepped up. She's earned my loyalty. And she'll grow into a great leader. I know that. Otherwise I'd never have suggested her for Chief Superintendent."

"There was no one left," said the Mountie, his exasperation growing. "Everyone else was either wounded or tainted by your actions. Even if you hadn't recommended her, Toussaint was the only one standing. Look"—there was a heaved sigh down the line—"I hope I'm wrong. Just be careful. You've gotta know, once she gets wind of what we're doing, she'll blame you, even if we're successful."

"God willing we are. That's all that matters."

"*Inshallah.*"

"*B'ezrat HaShem,*" said Gamache. "We'll worry about the rest later. Good luck. Let me know."

"I will, my friend. Anything I can do?"

Armand looked toward the kitchen. "Do you have any divers you can spare?"

"Huh?"

As the RCMP divers reached the body, Beauvoir heard a sharp intake of breath and prepared to grab hold of Vivienne's father, if necessary.

But it wasn't.

Homer Godin stood on the shore. Face rigid. Body at attention.

Only when the team turned Vivienne over did he move. But not forward, as they expected and were prepared for.

Vivienne's father sank, slowly, slowly to his knees. Then slowly, slowly he folded over. His head in the muck. His hands clutching the ground. The big man curled himself around his heart.

As Vivienne Godin approached the shore, her father lifted his head, sensing more than seeing her close by. Then he raised his body. Sitting back on his heels. And, with the help of Gamache and Beauvoir, he struggled to his feet.

They kept their hands under Homer's arms. Supporting him. Holding him upright.

Homer was swaying, openmouthed. Eyes glazed. As Vivienne was lifted onto a stretcher.

Dr. Harris bent over the body. Glancing at Gamache and Beauvoir, she shook her head. Confirming what was painfully obvious.

"I need to see her," said her father.

Dr. Harris whispered to Gamache. "It isn't good. She's been in the water at least two days."

"We need an identification," said Beauvoir.

Lysette Cloutier, who'd just arrived, said, "I'll do it."

"Me," said Vivienne's father. "Me."

"I'll take you over," said Armand quietly. "But you must promise not to touch her. If we're going to get enough evidence to convict, no one but the investigators must touch Vivienne. Do you understand?"

Homer's heavy head bobbed up and down.

"Are you ready?" Armand asked.

He nodded again.

They escorted Vivienne's father to Vivienne's body.

He stared down at her. With the eyes of a man who'd reached the end of a long tunnel and realized there was no light there.

He gave one curt nod. And mouthed, "That's Vivienne." Then, with more effort, he said it out loud. "That's Vivienne."

He brought his hand up to his face, covering his mouth, in a grotesque imitation of Reine-Marie's joy just hours earlier.

Gamache looked down at the body.

Her blue eyes were open, not in fear but in that surprise they often saw in those suddenly, prematurely meeting Death. He wondered if Death had been just as surprised.

Gamache swiftly, expertly took in the condition of her body before meeting Beauvoir's eyes. And nodding.

"Come away." He spoke softly to Homer. "We'll let the officers do their job."

"No," said Homer. "I need to stay. With her. Until . . . Please. I won't make trouble. I promise."

He motioned toward a tree stump, and Gamache nodded. "Of course." Then turned to Cloutier. "Stay with him, please."

Gamache noticed then a uniformed agent walking down the path toward them.

"What're you doing here?" Gamache asked. "You're supposed to be guarding Carl Tracey."

"I was relieved."

"By whom?"

"Agent Cameron."

"He's there with Tracey? Alone?"

"Well, there're others. The owners of the bistro—"

"Come with me."


Through the windows of the bistro, Gamache could see Bob Cameron. He was standing within feet of Carl Tracey, who was crammed into a corner. His chair overturned at his feet.

Cameron held something in his right hand. Something black.

His gun?

No, Gamache took in quickly as he made for the door. Not a gun.

Too big. It was a fireplace poker. As lethal as a gun, if swung at a person's head.

And it looked, by his stance, that that was exactly what Cameron was preparing to do.

Tracey was raising his arms to protect himself.

Gamache opened the bistro door with a bang, and Cameron turned around.

"He's going to kill me," shouted Tracey. "Stop him."

"Shut up, you stupid shit."

"Cameron," snapped Gamache. "Step away. Now."

After a slight pause, Cameron threw the poker onto the floor in disgust. And stepped back.

"I wasn't going to hit him," he said. "I just wanted to scare him."

"Get over there," said Gamache, pointing to the far corner.

The former left tackle jerked toward Tracey, who squeezed tighter into the corner. Then Cameron marched away, shoving a table as he passed Gamache.

"What's happening?" asked Gabri, coming cautiously out of the swinging door between the bistro and the kitchen, followed by Olivier, who was holding up a frying pan.

"Nothing," said Cameron.

"Nothing?" demanded Tracey. "He was going to hit me with that." He pointed to the poker.

"Did you see anything?" Gamache asked Gabri and Olivier.

Both men shook their heads.

"He told us to go into the kitchen and stay there," said Olivier.

"He'd picked up the poker," said Gabri. "We didn't need to be told twice. I tried to call you, but of course your phone didn't work."

He held up the receiver, still clutched in his hand.

Gamache turned to the agent who'd accompanied him and gestured toward Tracey. "Watch him."

Then he led Cameron farther away from the others.

"What were you thinking?" he demanded.

"What're you saying?" demanded Tracey. "I have a right to know. He was going to kill me."

"Be quiet, please," said Gamache, and while his tone was polite, anyone who saw the man would not be fooled by the courtesy.

Even as he turned back to Cameron, Gamache admitted that what Tracey said might very well be true. It certainly looked like that.

But how things looked and how they really were, were often two very different things in a murder investigation.

He waited for an answer.

"I wanted to get a confession out of him," said Cameron. "I wanted to scare him, not beat him. I had my phone on, recording. I can show you."

"You recorded yourself threatening a suspect with a fireplace poker?" asked Gamache, incredulous. "You know that any confession you might've gotten would've been inadmissible, and the whole case thrown out."

"I would've erased the beginning," said Cameron.

Now Gamache stared, clearly dumbfounded. "You say that as though you expect me to go along with you. I warned you about this just hours ago, and now you do exactly the same thing?"

"Not the same. You warned me about hitting a suspect. I never laid a hand on him."

"Threatening a beating is still brutality," said Gamache. "If you were under my command, Agent Cameron, I'd relieve you of duty right now."

"I'm happy to leave." He took a step away.

"You'll leave when I tell you to. What're you even doing here? This isn't your assignment."

"You think my responsibility stops at the end of my shift? Does yours?"

"Don't question me, young man. This isn't about me, it's about your behavior—"

"Yeah, well, you're quite a role model. Sir." Cameron glared. "I've been following the Twitter feed about you. Have you?"

"I asked you a question. What're you doing here?"

"How can you lead, sir, if you don't have the support of the population? Wasn't that the whole point of your lecture to me? Trust? Looks like you've lost it. Have you lost it?"

And the inflection made it clear that Cameron was talking about more than trust.

"Answer my question now, Agent Cameron, or I'll charge you with interfering in a murder investigation."

Gamache knew exactly what Cameron was doing. He was trying to throw him off balance. Put him on the defensive. Get control of the narrative and take focus away from the real question.

Why was Agent Cameron there? Why was he threatening Tracey for a confession?

This spoke of more than a cop going off the rails. Emotionally het up about the horrific crime. It spoke, and smelled, of personal involvement.

"Tell me," said Gamache. "You know I'll find out."

And Cameron could see that was true. Here was a man determined to, trained to, born to find things out.

Chief Inspector Gamache, sharp intent in his eyes, did not seem like the slightly pathetic, definitely incompetent, occasionally dangerous man described in the tweets.

"I came because I care about Vivienne," said Cameron.

And there it was. Confirmation of something that had become obvious to Gamache.

But Bob Cameron didn't just care, he cared so deeply he no longer had control of his actions. Or judgment.

"I see." Gamache paused. Studying the man. "Were you having an affair?"

"No."

"The truth."

"No. I wanted to help her. I asked her to call me, to have a coffee together. To just talk. But she never did."

"Did you go to the house?"

Cameron lowered his head, no longer looking Gamache in the eye. "A few times. When I knew he wasn't there. When he was in the bar or in jail to sober up."

"You detained the husband, then went up and propositioned the wife?"

Cameron's face flushed, the scars turning white against the red. "It wasn't like that."

"I think it was," said Gamache. "And you just don't want to admit it. She wasn't interested, but you continued to harass her."

"I wasn't harassing her. She was afraid." Cameron shot a filthy look at the man across the bistro. "She wanted to leave him, I could tell. I was just trying to help her break away."

He lifted his head and met Gamache's eyes. "I love my wife. I have two children. But there was something about Vivienne. Something . . ." He stopped and thought. "Not innocent. Not even fragile. She seemed strong, but confused. Beaten down. I just wanted to help her."

Gamache looked at Cameron's face. Disfigured. And knew how deep the blows went. How deep the disfigurement went. And knew how much this man, while a boy, would have wanted someone to help him.

Motivations were rarely straightforward, as he knew all too well. And Gamache wondered how confused Cameron was, between helping Vivienne and helping himself.

Gamache considered the man, then nodded. "Stay where you are," he said, and walked across the bistro.

He had a duty to perform. No matter how ludicrous it seemed.

"Monsieur Tracey," said Gamache, squaring himself in front of the man.

"What?"

"I'm sorry to have to inform you—"

"So she is dead," said Tracey.

"Yes. I'm afraid so. Her body was found in the river, just outside the village. She was thrown off that bridge."

"Thrown? You make it sound like it was done on purpose."

"We think it was."

"Prove it."

"*Pardon?*"

"How do you know she was thrown? I think she jumped. Killed herself." His voice changed. "She was very depressed, you know. It sometimes happens to pregnant women. Hormones. She talked about killing herself for weeks. I did my best. Tried to comfort her. Begged her to get help." Tracey's voice had become wheedling. Rehearsing lines for a judge. "But she wouldn't. She was drinking too much. Then she just disappeared. I was distraught."

155

A long, long silence greeted that. While Tracey smiled, the others in the bistro stared.

Gamache tilted his head slightly. Then he nodded. Slightly.

Tracey, with the instincts of a rodent, stopped smiling. Had he had hackles, they would have gone up. And for good reason.

He'd goaded the wrong person.

"Your wife was pregnant," said Gamache. His voice quiet. Unnaturally calm. "The night she disappeared, she told you the child wasn't yours. You have a history of drunk and disorderly. Police have been called to your place more than once for domestic violence. Judges are smart. Juries are smart. What do you think they'll make of that?"

"I'll tell you what they'd make of it." His voice rose. "That I'm a shit husband, but not a killer. She was drunk and knocked up, and she left me. Try to prove otherwise."

"And you never asked who the father was?" demanded Gamache.

"I didn't care."

"You cared. You cared about how it looked to others. You cared about being made a fool of. We found blood in your living room and in her car. What did you do to her?"

Tracey was silent.

"What did you do, Carl?"

The others in the room stayed absolutely still. Frozen.

"I have a right to know who my wife was screwing, okay. I didn't do anything you wouldn't do. Anything any normal guy wouldn't do."

He looked around but met only disgust.

"So what did you do? Come on, Carl. Tell me."

"I gave her what for."

"You beat her."

"My drunk and knocked-up wife? She was leaving me to go to the father. What did she think was going to happen? It was her fault."

But something, besides the grotesque description, struck Gamache.

"Her father or 'the' father?" he asked. "What did she say? Who was she going to?"

"The father. Her father. What difference does it make? I took a bottle and went to my studio. Passed out. When I woke up next morning, she was gone. But she was alive when I left her."

156

Tracey's gaze shifted to something over Gamache's shoulder. Gamache turned.

Homer Godin was standing at the door.

Staring.

"I'm sorry, *patron*," said Agent Cloutier, coming through behind Godin. She was out of breath from running. "I was watching the coroner, and when I turned around, he was gone."

"Don't let him close to me," said Tracey, backing away. "He's crazy."

"Homer." Gamache held his hands out in front of him, as though approaching a wounded wild animal. Or an explosive.

It wasn't that Gamache was afraid of him. Or afraid if Godin burst forward, they wouldn't be able to stop him before he killed Tracey. They could and would. But . . .

*But would that really matter? Maybe, if I step aside . . . If I was a little slow to react . . .*

Gamache knew then what he was really afraid of. Himself.

*How would I feel . . . ?*

With effort, he shoved those thoughts away. To be replaced by a certainty.

They might stop him now, but they couldn't keep Homer Godin from Carl Tracey forever.

"You have your car here?" he asked Cameron while not taking his eyes off Godin, who wouldn't take his eyes off Tracey.

"*Oui.*"

"Good. I'm placing him under arrest. I want you to take him in."

"Yessir," said Cameron with enthusiasm, and turned toward Tracey, who backed up further.

"*Non,*" said Chief Inspector Gamache. "Not him. Him."

Even Tracey turned to Gamache with surprise.

The Chief Inspector was pointing at Homer.

"You mean Carl Tracey, sir," said Cameron.

"No. I mean him." He took a step closer to Vivienne's father and said, "Homer Godin, I'm placing you under arrest."

Godin's eyes remained on Tracey, then slowly refocused on Gamache.

"What did you say?"

"I'm arresting you."

"What for?" asked Agent Cloutier, going to stand beside Homer.

"For assault."

"I haven't done it yet. Give me a moment." Godin's voice was flat, his cold stare returning to Tracey. "And you can make it murder."

"I mean the assault on Madame Gamache. You punched her in the face."

"I did?"

"He what?" said Gabri.

"Take him in," said Gamache. Then, in front of everyone, Gamache did something he'd never done before. He apologized, even as he made the arrest. "*Désolé.*"

"I hit your wife?" asked Homer, more stunned by that than the arrest. "Is she all right?"

"She will be."

"Oh, God," sighed Homer. "What's happening?"

They walked out of the bistro. Homer Godin in custody. And Carl Tracey a free man.

# CHAPTER EIGHTEEN

—

The morning sun was just slanting over the trees as Clara and Myrna
stood on the edge of the village green and watched.

Ruth joined them, limping out of her home, clutching Rosa to her
chest.

"What's going on?"

"I think they found Vivienne," said Clara, pointing to the coroner's
car and then down the path along the river.

Ruth and Rosa shook their heads. "It's tragic. So young." Then Ruth's
eyes and voice sharpened. "What's he doing?"

"Looks like he's arresting Homer," said Myrna as they watched
Armand walk with Homer to the Sûreté car.

"He can't think—" Clara began.

"Jesus, even Clouseau can't be that stupid," said Ruth.

"Fuck, fuck, fuck," muttered the duck.

Just then Homer stopped and turned. As did Gamache. As did everyone else on the village green.

Vivienne Godin was being brought out of the woods. In a body bag.

The bistro door opened, and Carl Tracey stepped out. Into the fresh
air. And sunshine.

He saw the stretcher, took a deep breath, and said, "I wonder."

"What?" demanded Olivier, coming out behind him.

"I wonder if she was insured."

Staring silently at the long black bag as it was slid into the coroner's vehicle, Homer Godin crossed himself. As did Gabri and Olivier. Even Ruth, unseen by the others, made the familiar gesture.

After the coroner's vehicle drove away, Vivienne's father closed his eyes and tilted his head as far back as it would go. Exposing his throat to the Universe.

"Chief Inspector?" said Beauvoir as he came around the corner from the path along the river.

He indicated Homer, clearly in custody, by the car.

"I'll explain," said Gamache, then instructed Cameron to take Godin into the local detachment. "Don't book him. I'll be in to do the paperwork later. Make him comfortable, but don't let him out of your sight."

Cameron turned to Homer. "I'm sorry, sir. Would you mind?"

Homer got into the backseat without complaint.

As Cameron went to walk to the driver's side, Gamache stopped him.

"One moment, please. I have a question for you." He led Cameron a few feet from the car. "Was the child yours?"

Cameron's eyes widened. "No, of course not. I told you, nothing happened between Vivienne and me."

"You knew she was pregnant before we said anything. She told you. Is the child yours? Tell me the truth."

"I am. It's not mine. Couldn't be."

"I think you're lying. I think there's a lot you aren't telling us. I understand you're worried about your family. Your job. But you know it'll come out. Best if you tell us yourself."

"There's nothing to tell."

Gamache pressed his lips together and gave a single curt nod. "You're helping a murderer."

"How?"

"By muddying the waters. By leaving questions unanswered. Questions we have to now take precious time investigating."

"I have answered them."

"But not truthfully."

Gamache made a mental note to call the Alouettes organization and ask why they'd let Bob Cameron go. And why no other football team picked him up.

"May I go with him, sir?" Lysette Cloutier asked Chief Inspector Beauvoir.

He looked at her a moment. "Why?"

"Why? Because he's my friend. He's just lost his daughter."

Beauvoir nodded. "Is it possible, Agent Cloutier, that you're more than friends?"

"More . . . ? *Non.* I care about him, but his wife was the one who was my friend. My best friend. I was maid of honor at their wedding."

"When did she die?"

"Five years ago. Ovarian cancer."

"I'm sorry." He paused. "You've kept up a relationship with Monsieur Godin?"

"There is no relationship. Not in the way I think you mean. We're old friends, that's all." On seeing Beauvoir's skepticism, she pressed her lips together before nodding. "All right, you're right. But my relationship isn't with Homer, it's with Vivienne. She was my goddaughter."

She dropped her gaze and studied her muddy boots before lifting her head and looking him straight in the eyes. Perhaps, he thought, a little too straight.

"I should've told you sooner, but I was afraid."

"Of what?"

"That you'd think I was too close. That you'd take me off the case."

"You're right. I probably would've."

Cloutier shook her head. "I've screwed up everything. I promised Katherine I'd look after her daughter. Keep her safe. I made that promise at the baptism, and I made it again at her deathbed. I didn't do a good job of it, did I? But what I can do now is help catch her killer. That's all I want."

"And Homer Godin?"

"What about him?"

"More than professional interest?"

"Of course not."

"You took his hand."

"I was trying to comfort him. Haven't you ever held the hand of the mother, or father, of a murder victim? To console them?"

Beauvoir had to admit he never had.

He'd seen Chief Inspector Gamache do it.

And he himself had reached out, come within inches of that brute sorrow, but something stopped him every time.

They were different men, with different strengths. And maybe, he thought, that was one of the many reasons he was leaving the Sûreté. Heading to Paris. He knew, deep down, that there was a level, deep down, he could never reach as an investigator.

While Jean-Guy Beauvoir explored the tangible, what could be touched, Armand Gamache explored what was felt. He went into that chaotic territory. Hunting. Searching. Tracking. Immersing himself in emotions until he found one so rancid it led to a killer.

Beauvoir stopped at the door. Gamache went through it.

Which wasn't to say Beauvoir was insensitive to feelings. Watching Agent Cloutier, he'd picked up on hers.

There was something between her and Homer Godin, he was sure of it. Though he doubted Godin knew that. He wondered if Cloutier had even admitted it to herself.

"May I go with them, sir?" she asked again.

Beauvoir looked over at Homer. As though the day wasn't bad enough, now he found himself alone in the back of a police car. While the man who killed his daughter was standing in the sunshine.

"Go."

He might not be able to hold Homer's hand, but he could offer comfort in other ways.


Clara, Myrna, and Ruth stepped back as the cop car passed them.

Ruth shook her head and looked over at Gamache and Beauvoir, conferring on the village green.

"Shouldn't there be a third Stooge?" Just then another car arrived. "Never mind. Spoke too soon."

Isabelle Lacoste got out and walked, limping slightly, over to her two colleagues.

"Was that Monsieur Godin in the back of the patrol car?" Lacoste asked. "Is he under arrest?"

Gamache explained to both of them what he'd done, and why.

"I know Reine-Marie won't press charges. It was an accident. But maybe we can hold him long enough to collect evidence."

"Against Tracey, *oui*," said Beauvoir, glancing over his shoulder at the man lounging, like a reptile, in the early April sun.

He turned to Lacoste and Gamache. "Walk with me, please."

Isabelle raised her brows in amusement and wondered if Gamache recognized those words. It was something he'd often said to them during murder investigations.

Now they fell into step and waited for Beauvoir to speak.

"What do you think?" he said.

"This one might be difficult," said Lacoste. "Proving she was murdered."

"Is it possible she wasn't?" asked Gamache.

Beauvoir considered, glancing over at Tracey, then back to his two colleagues. "Possible, I suppose, but I don't believe it was an accident, or suicide. Do you?"

"Not for a moment," said Lacoste.

Gamache nodded. It was murder. He knew that. What he didn't know was whether they could prove it.

"Did you know that Agent Cloutier was Vivienne Godin's godmother?" Beauvoir asked.

"Huh," said Gamache. "Why didn't she tell us that before?"

"Says she was afraid of being taken off the case. But I'm not convinced. Why keep that a secret unless there's more there?"

Gamache then told them about Bob Cameron.

"*Merde*," said Beauvoir. "He was having an affair with her?"

"Denies it," said Gamache.

"You don't believe him?" asked Lacoste.

"I don't."

"You think he might've killed Vivienne?" Beauvoir couldn't keep the skepticism out of his voice.

"I think he and Vivienne were much more involved than he admits. And where there're secrets—"

"There's fire. What do you think happened?"

"I think one possible scenario is that they arranged to meet on that side road by the bridge. Where they wouldn't be seen. If she told him then that the child was his and that she'd left Tracey to be with him—"

"Is he married?" Lacoste asked.

"*Oui.* With two children."

"You think in a moment of madness he pushed her off the bridge," she said.

"Or just pushed her away and she fell against the railing. I've seen him play. He's strong. And it's the sort of instinctive move a left tackle makes." Gamache mimicked the pushing motion. "It wouldn't take much for Vivienne to break through the railing and fall."

"And he just left?" asked Lacoste.

"Once she was in the water, he couldn't save her even if he wanted to." Once again, and just for an instant, Gamache felt himself submerged in the bitterly cold water. Unable to breathe.

"And now he's too afraid to admit anything," said Beauvoir. "Still, do you think that's what happened?"

It didn't take Gamache long to answer that. "*Non.*"

"We all know who did this," said Lacoste.

"*Bon,*" said Gamache, and turned to continue walking, but when he realized Beauvoir had not joined him, he stopped and returned.

"There's something I'd like to ask you," said Jean-Guy.

"*Oui?*"

Reine-Marie had walked around the village green and joined Olivier and Gabri outside the bistro.

"Jesus, he did hit you, didn't he?" said Gabri, looking at the bruise on her face. "You okay?"

"Nothing Honoré hasn't done, also by accident." She touched her bruised cheekbone lightly. "I put frozen peas on it."

They brought her up to speed on what had happened, and as they talked, she took another few steps away from Carl Tracey, who was sitting at a table on the *terrasse*. Drinking a beer. At eight in the morning.

"Does that remind you of anything?" Olivier asked.

"A clown in a sewer?" Gabri suggested.

"No, not him. Them." Olivier gestured toward the three Sûreté officers on the village green.

Reine-Marie cocked her head, staring. And then she gave a short puff of amusement and recognition.

Isabelle. Jean-Guy. Armand.

Three colleagues.

Three friends. A trinity. Sturdy. Eternal. Together.

"Three Pines," she said.

"Three Stooges," said Ruth as she walked by and entered the bistro.


"I know I assigned this to you, that you're the lead investigator, but do you mind if I take over?" Before Gamache could answer, Beauvoir held up his hand. "I know it's a lot to ask."

"You have a perfect right to assume command of any investigation. May I ask why?"

"This will probably be my last case with the Sûreté. With any police force. This's the one I want to go out on."

When Gamache didn't answer, Beauvoir asked, "What is it?"

"Have you thought that maybe this isn't the one you want as your final case?"

"What do you mean?"

"We're pretty sure we know who did it."

"More than 'pretty sure,' I'd say. Tracey all but admits it."

"He admits he beat Vivienne, not that he threw her off the bridge. He keeps insisting it was suicide, and we're going to have a helluva problem proving it wasn't at least an accident. And, as you said, even if we can prove it's murder, it might be extremely difficult to convict the man."

"We've had more difficult cases," said Lacoste.

"True."

"Are you reluctant to give it up? Because of Annie? I've seen how much you sympathize with Godin. More than usual."

Armand smiled and nodded. "It's true. This one's gotten under my skin. And yes, because of Annie. I'm trying not to, but the truth is, I find myself asking how I'd feel, if . . . And even more since you told us Annie's pregnant."

"Pregnant?" asked Lacoste. When Jean-Guy nodded, she gave him a quick embrace. *"Félicitations."*

*"Merci."*

"I think you feel the same way," said Gamache. "About Vivienne and Annie."

"Not really."

Gamache stared at his son-in-law, frankly and openly amazed. "I beg your pardon?"

"This is a terrible case, absolutely. But I haven't personalized it."

There was silence as Gamache watched him. And then spoke.

"You almost killed yourself trying to get to her body," he pointed out. "I've seen you desperate to stop a murderer, but I've never seen you take it so personally."

"I'm not." Then he relented. "Okay, maybe a little. It's hard not to. But I have my feelings well under control. Don't worry."

Isabelle Lacoste looked from one to the other. Both, she knew, were personalizing this. Far more than she'd ever seen. Far more than was healthy.

If they weren't worried, she was.

*"Bon,"* said Gamache. "I'm happy to hand over the case. May I act as your second-in-command, *patron*?"

"For the first time?"

"And, with luck, the last."

Beauvoir gave a small laugh and put out his hand. "Welcome aboard. I'll try to go easy on you, son. Just don't screw up."

"You inspire me already, Chief Inspector."

"Now, isn't it your nap time?"

"You might want to consider grabbing some sleep yourself," said Gamache. "Long day behind us and long day ahead."

"Work still to be done. I need to set up an incident room."

"I'm sure your second-in-command can do that."

"You're my second-in-command."

Gamache gave a short grunt of laughter and clapped Beauvoir on the arm. "Well, good luck."

But as he walked away, Armand's smile faded. Replaced by a slight frown.

He called his RCMP colleague as soon as he got back home.

It rang. And rang. Finally clicking over to voice mail.

Gamache looked at his watch. The sun had been up for slightly over an hour.

The floodgates at the mighty dams had been open for slightly under an hour.

What was happening up there?

He left a message, then went upstairs, suspecting he wouldn't be able to sleep. But the moment his head hit the cool, fresh pillow, he was out.

Reine-Marie, also exhausted, had joined him, and in their sleep they moved to the middle until their warm bodies touched.

Beauvoir and Lacoste walked past the thick wall of sandbags, pausing to consider them.

"Came close," she said, pointing to the ones that had been pushed over by the force of the river.

Beauvoir grunted.

How close they all were, without knowing it, to disaster. All the time.

They walked over the stone bridge to the old brick train station. It had seen its share of reunions. And partings. Its share of tears. And shouts of joy.

Even he, fairly immune to fantasy, could feel that every time he entered the familiar building.

It had also seen its share of murder investigations, having been used in the past by Chief Inspector Gamache as temporary headquarters for the homicide unit.

Now Chief Inspector Beauvoir directed his team to set up shop.

Abandoned decades earlier by the railway, the building was now home to the Three Pines Volunteer Fire Department, overseen by its chief, Ruth Zardo, who glared down at them from the official photo, taken when she'd been given the Governor General's Award for poetry.

"*I didn't feel the aimed word hit,*" Beauvoir said, looking up at the embittered old poet. "*And go in like a soft bullet.*"

> *I didn't feel the smashed flesh*
> *closing over it like water*
> *over a thrown stone.*

"What was that, *patron*?" asked one of the agents.

"Nothing."

"Sounded like poetry," she said with some alarm.

"Keep working." Beauvoir caught Isabelle Lacoste's eye and saw amusement there. And recognition.

*My God*, he thought. *I'm turning into Gamache.*

But while he feigned alarm, what he actually felt was a sort of contentment. That on his last case he should finally turn into his mentor.

He stood still amid the activity and let the evidence come to him. But what came to him was an image. Clear as day. Young and pregnant Vivienne Godin, breaking through the railing. Arms out. The duffel bag, her worldly possessions, falling with her.

Her blue eyes wide, as realization hit.

And then the water. Cold as ice. Closing over her.

*. . . like water over a thrown stone.*

How would I feel if it was Annie . . .

Armand was right, of course. He was struggling to separate the two women.

> *Does my twisting body spell out Grace?*
> *I hurt, therefore I am.*
> *Faith, Charity, and Hope*
> *are three dead angels*
> *falling like meteors—*

"Always cheerful, eh, you old witch," muttered Jean-Guy as he gave one last glance up at Ruth before turning to examine the sodden items at his feet.

They'd found Vivienne's purse in the tangle of the dam. Its contents were spread out on the sanitized plastic sheet on the floor, alongside the things from the duffel bag.

An agent described each item for the recording as it was removed. Tagged. Cataloged. Photographed. Swabbed. Examined.

Private items transformed, like black magic, into public property.

Finally the entire contents were spread out.

From the purse they'd taken a wallet, with a hundred and ten dollars and change. Driver's license. A bank card but no credit card. Some paper, too wet to read, the water having turned it into pulp. Some mints. A Bic lighter but no cigarettes. What looked like house keys and car keys.

"Nothing unusual," said Lacoste. But something had caught her eye. Taken from the duffel bag.

Wearing gloves, she picked up the pill bottle and sounded out the label. "Mifegymiso. I don't know it."

"I do," said one of the agents, looking over. "It's an abortion pill."

"You mean the morning-after pill?" asked Beauvoir.

"No, that's different. That's for the day after sex, to stop insemination from going further. This's for pregnancies in the first few months. To terminate them."

"I didn't know there was such a thing," said Beauvoir. "Legal?"

"Yessir."

"What do you think?" he asked Lacoste as they stared down at the collection of items.

"I think it's strange that Vivienne Godin was beyond three months pregnant and she takes abortion pills with her. I'm assuming they won't work this far into a pregnancy. If she had the pills, why not use them earlier?"

"Maybe she thought they would work," said Beauvoir. "Maybe she was waiting to see how the father would react, and if it went badly, she'd take them."

"This isn't prescription," said Lacoste. "There's no doctor or pharmacy on the label. Not even her name."

"Black market," said Beauvoir.

"Seems so. If they're legal, why go onto the black market?"

"And why would she tell her husband that the baby wasn't his, even if it was true? She must've known how he'd react. Why not just get out while she could?" said Beauvoir.

Tracey, goddamn him, had said the same thing. That Vivienne knew what he'd do. That he'd hit her. Beat her. Though surely she never thought he'd kill her.

"Maybe she didn't tell him," said Lacoste. "We only have Tracey's word for that."

Beauvoir was considering. "Then why would he say it? He gave us a motive. He's clever enough to know that."

"He told the Chief that they were drunk," said Lacoste. "Maybe she didn't mean to tell him but it just came out. Maybe it wasn't even true."

Beauvoir nodded. He, more than most, understood the corrosive effect of booze. How it stole judgment and inhibitions until things were said and done that could never be unsaid. Undone. Alcohol stole dignity and friends and family and livelihoods before finally taking the life.

Alcohol was a thief. And often a murderer.

"She wanted to hurt him before she left," said Lacoste.

"She couldn't match him physically, but she could hurt him with words."

*The aimed word . . . like a soft bullet*, thought Beauvoir, glancing up at the photo of Ruth scrutinizing them.

"Sober Vivienne probably knew better, but drunk . . . ?" said Beauvoir. "The toxicology report will tell us more."

"There's something else," said Lacoste. "The clothes she packed don't make sense."

"Why not?"

"Where're the sweaters? The heavy shirts? The socks?"

"There're shirts and jeans."

"Summer weight. It's freezing out. Why take those?"

"Maybe she planned to go south. Florida."

"Maybe," said Lacoste.

"Or . . . ?"

"Or maybe she packed in a hurry. Just grabbing things. Or—"

"Maybe she didn't pack the bag," said Beauvoir. "Maybe he did."

Lacoste nodded. "To make it look like she'd gone away. No woman in her right mind would take those clothes in early April."

"The problem we're going to have," he said, "is proving that Tracey packed the bag. Even if we find his DNA and fingerprints on the items, his defense would argue they were there because they lived together."

"*Oui*," said Lacoste. "But if his prints are on that"—she pointed to the pill bottle—"we might have something. I think he tossed it in not knowing what it was."

"Not exactly a smoking gun," said Beauvoir, but he could feel hope rising, if not faith and charity. This might be the first nail.

Lysette Cloutier sat in the Sûreté detachment. She'd chosen a desk with direct line of sight into the cells. Where she could watch Homer.

The sandwiches and coffee she'd taken in were untouched.

Lysette had stayed with him for a while, but he seemed lost in his own world. Oblivious to her presence. Even, she felt, a little annoyed by it.

He clearly wanted just to be left alone.

If she couldn't comfort him, there was one thing she could do.

Glancing around, making sure she wasn't being watched, she went online. Found Carl Tracey's Instagram feed. And typed.

Reviewing it, going over each word. Changing one, adjusting another. Until it was just right.

Then she hit send and tapped the pen on the desk, waiting for a reply.

# CHAPTER NINETEEN

⌒

**@NouveauGalerie:** Hello **@CarlTracey** Love your ceramic pieces. Am a gallery owner looking for exciting new talent. Can we meet?

The phone woke Armand with a start. He was instantly alert and grabbed it before it could wake up Reine-Marie.

"*Oui, allô?*"

"Sorry to disturb you," said Beauvoir.

"Not at all," said Armand, rubbing his hand across his face and feeling the stubble. "You have news?"

"The search warrant has come through."

"Excellent. I'll meet you at the car in . . ." He checked the bedside clock. It was 9:40 in the morning. He'd been asleep for just over an hour, but felt refreshed. "Twenty minutes."

Armand quickly and quietly showered and shaved, not wanting to wake up Reine-Marie, though he did check and make sure she was okay.

The bruise now spread across the left side of her face, but there was little swelling. Still, it hurt him to see it.

She roused and opened her eyes, giving a start on seeing his face so close to hers.

"Everything all right?" she mumbled, still half asleep.

"I'm just going out. You okay? That must hurt."

He reached out but didn't touch it. Not wanting to add to the pain he knew she must be feeling.

"Well, I now have a much better idea, *mon coeur*, what you've gone through."

"Me? Oh, no," he said with a smile. "Anytime a fist comes even close, I drop to the ground and play dead. Let Jean-Guy sort it out."

"Belly up, feet and hands to the ceiling, like a bug. Yes, I've seen that. You also do it when Ruth enters a room."

"I'll get you a Tylenol," he said, smiling, and returned a minute later with a couple of pills and a glass of water. She was sitting up in bed now, and he sat beside her.

They talked about Annie and Jean-Guy's news. A brother or sister for Honoré. Another grandchild for them. Yet one, neither said but both knew, who would grow up a continent away.

"There's something I need to tell you." He did up his tie as he spoke. "I arrested Homer Godin."

"Yes, I know. You think he killed his daughter?"

"No, but I need to keep him from Tracey. I charged him with assault. For that."

He pointed to her face.

"But—" she began, bringing her own hand to her face.

"I know. I won't follow through. I just needed to get him off the streets, so he won't go after Tracey."

"So this might've been a good thing." She touched the bruise.

"*Non*." He kissed her before getting up. "Jean-Guy's waiting for me."

"What will you do without him, Armand?"

He opened his mouth, but there was no answer.

"I'm sorry," she said. "I shouldn't have asked."

"No. It's good to talk about it. Jean-Guy reminded me it's less than two weeks away."

It wasn't, of course, just losing Beauvoir as a colleague and friend, it was losing Annie and Honoré. And now the new baby. With their son, Daniel, and his wife and two daughters already in Paris, it meant they had no children or grandchildren close by.

But, for Reine-Marie, the dread went deeper. Something she'd never admitted to Armand. For many years she'd felt that as long as Jean-Guy was close by, he'd protect Armand.

They were meant to be together. Had been, in her opinion, for many lifetimes. As colleagues, as father and son. As brothers. As long as they were together, both would be safe.

Once downstairs, Armand flicked on the television to cable news and placed a call.

As Radio Canada interviewed an increasingly agitated Deputy Premier about the terrible flooding, Armand waited for the phone to be answered.

The phone rang, as the politician tried to explain that it could have been worse.

The phone rang, as the journalist tried to explain that it was pretty damn catastrophic for those towns that were underwater.

Both, Gamache knew, were right.

The graphic on the screen showed where work was under way to divert floodwaters upriver.

The phone rang. And rang. Then clicked over to voice mail.

The RCMP commissioner wasn't answering. Or couldn't answer.

Armand hung up. And decided that no news was good news. There was nothing he could do about it now, anyway.

He grabbed his coat and joined Beauvoir and Lacoste.

"Knock, knock," said Myrna.

"Who's there?" asked Clara, not looking up.

"Me."

"Me who?"

"No, this isn't a knock-knock joke," Myrna said, entering the studio. "I just didn't want to startle you. We were supposed to meet at the bistro for breakfast, weren't we?"

"Sorry. I lost track of time."

Myrna sat on the low sofa, her considerable derriere hitting the concrete floor, as it always did. She groaned, more in annoyance than pain. Would she never learn?

From her vantage point, essentially on the floor, Myrna could see that Clara was staring at a series of miniatures on her easel.

"I've been sitting here trying to decide if the tweeters are right," Clara explained. "If these're shit."

"I believe we call those people twats, and no, they're not right. And you think that's bad, you should see what they're saying about Armand's return to the Sûreté. Madman with a gun. At least you only have a paintbrush. How much damage can you do?"

"You'd be surprised, apparently."

Myrna brought out her phone. "Listen to this."

"I don't want to hear it."

*"Strange, intense, feverish,"* Myrna read.

"Is that about me or Armand?"

"It's about van Gogh. Here's another. *The museum could have saved a good chunk by getting the plan and having the thing run off by the janitors with rollers.* That was a review of an early Barnett Newman. I looked it up. One of his paintings just sold for eighty-four million."

"Dollars?"

"Dog biscuits."

At that, Leo got to his feet, tail wagging. Myrna dug into her pocket and brought one out before returning to her phone. *"He's a madman, desperate for conquest."*

"Picasso?"

"Gamache."

Clara made a retching sound. "Just shit. Lies."

"So if you know the tweets are wrong about Armand, why don't you know they're wrong about you and your art?"

"Because one's objective and one's subjective," said Clara. "The record proves that Armand didn't do any of what he's accused of. And what he did do was to save greater pain. He's been investigated, exhaustively, and cleared. But what I do"—Clara returned her gaze to the easel—"is open to interpretation. I had an email from my gallery in Montréal. A few collectors are asking about returning the paintings they bought, some from years ago. They're concerned that the value has fallen through. That I'm not a real artist at all but . . . what did one tweet call me? A poseur."

Actually, thought Myrna, that was one of the more polite descriptions she'd seen.

"Those are just mean people."

"Just because it's mean doesn't make it wrong," said Clara, tilting her head this way and that. Examining her works on the easel.

"*All truth with malice in it,*" said Myrna.

"What did you say?"

"Just a quote, from *Moby-Dick*," said Myrna. "Something Armand said yesterday."

"You think there's truth in those tweets?"

"No, no, I didn't mean that." Myrna's arms were pinwheeling as she tried to back up the conversation. "There's no truth in them. Believe me. Just malice."

But Clara was shaking her head. Her confidence shaken.

"Come on over for lunch later," said Myrna, lugging herself off the sofa with a groan. "You need to get out of the studio. And out of your own head."

"Or someplace lower?" asked Clara.

"All truth . . ." said Myrna, and heard her friend laugh. "You know, *Moby-Dick* was also savaged when it first came out. Now it's considered one of the great novels of all time."

Clara didn't answer. She'd gone back to staring at the miniatures on her easel.

Myrna almost pointed out that what had happened to Vivienne Godin, what her father was living, was a tragedy. What Clara was going through was a setback. Nothing more.

But she didn't. Myrna understood how damaging it was to compare pain. To dismiss hurt just because it wasn't the worst.

As she walked back across the bright village green, her feet squelching in the soft turf, Myrna thought about those miniatures Clara had painted.

Perhaps, she admitted to herself privately as she walked past the wall of sandbags, not Clara's best work.

# CHAPTER TWENTY

—

@CarlTracey: Cannot meet you now @NouveauGalerie. What exactly do you want?

Agent Cloutier smiled. Had she been an angler, she'd have recognized a nibble on the bait.

She was also amused, and reassured, by the cautious, even terse, response.

But mostly it was the speed of the response that grabbed her attention.

This was Carl Tracey's Instagram account, but it was not Carl Tracey she was communicating with. He had no cell phone. And no cell phone coverage.

"Best not to discuss business publicly," she typed, having already composed this response in her head. "Do you have a private account?"

Her phone was ringing the *Bonanza* theme, and she answered it but continued to stare at the screen. Trying not to see the amused looks of the other Sûreté agents in the open room.

"Cloutier," she said.

"It's Beauvoir. The search warrant's come through. Meet us at the Tracey place."

"On my way, *patron*."

But still she stared at the screen, and then, just as she was about to shut it down, a single word appeared.

"*No.*"

Far from being disappointed, Cloutier smiled. It was the response she'd expected. Hoped for.

A normal potter, approached by a gallery about representing them, would be falling all over themselves to invite them into the private address. To talk business. But Carl Tracey or Pauline Vachon or whoever Cloutier was communicating with, was not.

Now, why was that?

Only one answer. They didn't want anyone else to see what was on the private account. Posts. Photographs.

She had them in her sights now. It would just take a little time. A little teasing. A tastier bait. But she'd get there. She'd get them.

With effort, she didn't type the response she'd already formulated. Let them stew.

Before leaving, she checked on Homer.

"Do you need anything?"

There was no answer. He was staring straight ahead.

She wondered what he was seeing, though she could guess. The image he would see for the rest of his life.

"We're searching the home. I'm heading there now. We'll get him."

That penetrated, at least a little. Homer turned to her and smiled weakly.

"*Merci*, Lysette."

Her fingers were around the bars, and he reached out and touched her hand.

It took most of the day to go over the Tracey property.

Where the earlier search was for Vivienne, today they were looking for her killer. And the evidence to convict him.

It had been decided that Lacoste would stay behind in the incident room, to coordinate the information as it came in and assign agents as necessary.

Beauvoir dropped Gamache off at the Tracey house, while he himself continued to the dirt road and the car. And the bridge.

His team had been there for hours, calling in engineers to first secure the bridge so they could walk on it safely.

While one crew did that, another went over the car.

"Tell me what you know."

"There're smears of blood on the outer and inner door handles, the steering wheel, the gearshift, a small smear on the trunk handle, and a drop on the backseat."

"A drop, not a smear?"

"Exactly." The agent showed Beauvoir. It had the telltale splatter of blood that had formed a drop, then hit. Maybe from a bleeding nose or lip.

"Prints?" Beauvoir asked.

"From at least three different people. There're butts in the cigarette holder. We've bagged them, and we've taken dirt samples from the tires, of course. To see if we can work out where she's been recently."

"Tire tracks?"

"None. The rain washed everything away, including boot prints."

"Damn," said Beauvoir, looking around.

"Chief," said an agent standing by the bridge. "We're ready."

"Chief?"

"*Oui?*" Gamache turned to see Agent Cloutier at the door to the living room.

"There's something curious in the bedroom," she said. "Something different from when we were here yesterday."

He followed her through the rambling old farmhouse to the bedroom and saw immediately what Agent Cloutier meant.

When he was last there, the room was a mess. Now it was tidy. Not, perhaps, ready for a photo shoot in *Country Living*, but far neater than it had been.

He brought out his phone.

"There's no reception, sir," said the inspector in charge.

"*Merci,*" he said, and continued to scroll until he found what he was looking for. The photographs he'd downloaded the day before, from the first search of the Tracey home.

"Here's what this room looked like yesterday when we came looking for Vivienne Godin."

He turned the phone so that the inspector could see. The photo was taken from exactly the place where they now stood.

It showed a room in disarray. Clothing scattered on the floor and draped on a chair. Bed unmade and sheets dirty. Though not bloody. Which wasn't to say traces of blood weren't there. Just unnoticeable except by people trained to find them.

"Get Monsieur Tracey up here, please," said Gamache, and Cloutier hurried away.

"We've looked, *patron*, and we can't find any clothes that obviously belonged to Madame Godin."

They heard footsteps on the stairs, and Tracey appeared.

"What do you want?"

"What did you do with your wife's belongings?" asked Gamache.

"Well, she didn't need them anymore."

"How did you know? You haven't been back here since her body was found. Which means you got rid of her things before you knew she was dead. Unless you did know."

"All I knew is that she'd left me and I was pissed off. Before I went to bed last night, I took all her shit and burned it in the kiln."

"I'll get Scene of Crime to check the kiln," said Cloutier, and left.

"You cleaned the place with bleach?" The inspector held up a swab.

"What can I say? Place was a shithole." He turned to Gamache. "You saw it. What did you think?"

When Gamache didn't answer, Tracey sneered. "I live in a pigsty and you judge. I clean it up and you judge. Well, fuck you. I'm finally free to live the way I want."

They were, Gamache recognized, the words of either an extremely well-balanced person who didn't care what others thought. Or a psychopath. Who didn't care what others thought.

"Why in the world do you care what others think?" demanded Ruth as they sat in the bistro, in front of the warm fire.

"Because I'm human and live in the world," said Clara. "With other humans."

Part of her felt that Ruth was probably right. She shouldn't care. But she also felt there was a criticism there, that Ruth was implying she was weak or needy. For caring.

"People are canceling their orders for my works," said Clara.

"So?"

"So this's my life, my career. My livelihood."

"What do you need money for, anyway?" asked Ruth. "We live in a tiny village. We buy clothes from the general store, barter turnips for milk, and the booze is free."

"Not free," said Olivier, pouring her another shot of what looked like scotch but was actually cold tea.

There was a suspicion Ruth knew about the substitution but played along. Because, as with so much else in her life, she didn't really care.

As she watched Ruth, Clara remembered that in the past few hours someone had gone onto Twitter and defended her.

*You ignorant turd. Clara's works are genius.* #MorrowGenius

If it wasn't Ruth, it was someone doing a damn fine imitation of the foulmouthed poet.

Those tweets were trending. Not because, Clara realized, they were insightful defenses of her creations but because the tweets were in themselves a form of genius.

There was now a Twitter account from someone calling themselves @ignorantturd.

"You're far too needy," said Ruth, watching as Rosa dipped her beak into the glass of cold tea.

The duck raised her head and muttered, Fuck, fuck, fuck. Apparently realizing it wasn't really scotch.

"And you," said Clara, "are an ignorant turd."

There was a hush as everyone else around the fireplace braced for impact. But Ruth, after a moment, just chuckled.


"I'll do it," said Beauvoir, putting out his hand.

"I think I should, sir," said the young agent. "I'm trained."

And once again Chief Inspector Beauvoir found himself facing what had become a familiar decision tree.

In fact, since becoming head of homicide, he'd faced a veritable forest of comments like that. Testing his authority and certainly questioning his competence.

Once again, he stood at the verbal crossroads.

Should he reply, "Give me the testing kit, you stupid shit. How do you think I got to be Chief Inspector? By sitting on my thumbs?"

Or should he say, with a patient smile, "That's all right, I do know what I'm doing. But I appreciate your concern."

As Gamache might have answered. Had indeed answered many times, sometimes in response to Agent Beauvoir's own somewhat insulting comments.

When asked about it one night, years into their relationship, Armand had explained, with a laugh.

"After I'd said something especially patronizing to my first chief, he just looked at me and said, 'Before speaking, Agent Gamache, you might want to ask yourself three questions.'"

"Not the ones that lead to wisdom," said Beauvoir, who'd heard them before.

"*Non*. Those are statements, these are questions. Are you paying attention?"

"What?"

They'd been sitting on the front porch of the Gamaches' home, in the height of summer. An iced tea beside Beauvoir, a beer beside Gamache.

As he spoke, the Chief Inspector raised a finger, counting the questions.

"Is it true? Is it kind? Does it need to be said?"

"You're kidding, right?" said Jean-Guy, shifting in his seat to look at Armand. "That might work in our private lives, but with other cops? You'd be laughed out of the room."

"You don't necessarily say them out loud," explained the Chief.

Which was true. Beauvoir had never heard Gamache run through those questions, but he had heard, more often than not, a patient and constructive reply.

"Civility," Armand had said. "How can we expect it if we don't give it? Besides, when we do get angry, people pay more attention. Otherwise it's just white noise."

*Is it true? Is it kind? Does it need to be said?*

Beauvoir, with effort, ran through the questions as he stood on the bridge, looking at the young agent.

Then he heard himself say, "That's all right. I do know what I'm doing. But thank you."

*You stupid little shit.*

Yes, it did need to be said, but maybe not out loud.

Though he did now wonder what Gamache had chosen not to say out loud.

Beauvoir took the harness from the agent and attached it, expertly, to himself, then put his hand out for the evidence kit.

"I'll go out first. If it's safe, you can join me. One at a time. *D'accord?*"

"*Oui, patron,*" said the agents.

Turning around to face the rickety old bridge, Beauvoir took a breath and whispered to himself, *Don't pee, don't pee, don't pee.*

# CHAPTER TWENTY-ONE

﹏

How can they let that murderer back in the Sûreté?
#losingallrespect

@dumbass: Do you mean self-respect?

They dropped Agent Cloutier at the local detachment and headed through the bright spring day, into the morgue.

Gamache had insisted on driving when he saw how exhausted Jean-Guy was.

Beside him, Jean-Guy's lids were heavy, and he fought to keep his eyes open in the warm car as it moved smoothly along the autoroute.

"I couldn't be happier for Annie and you," said Armand. "Your family is growing."

"As is yours."

As an only child, growing up without parents, Armand had always yearned for a large family. For brothers and sisters. For aunts and uncles. It was an abstract, though potent, wish.

And now, in his late fifties, he had it. Children. Grandchildren. Sons and daughters. Of the flesh and of the heart. Those he'd held in his arms and those comrades-in-arms whose lives he held in his hands.

His family.

"When's the baby due?"

"October."

"Boy or girl? Do you know?"

"We do." Jean-Guy smiled at his father-in-law. "But you're not going to get it out of me. Annie and I want to keep that to ourselves."

"Fair enough. Have you chosen a name?"

Jean-Guy laughed. "You're not really very good at this interrogation thing, are you?"

"I'm hoping to learn from you, *patron*."

Beauvoir smiled, and Gamache fell silent. Knowing if he did, Jean-Guy would lose the battle and let himself drift off to sleep.

He'd told Beauvoir about the search of the Tracey home. Then Beauvoir had reported on their preliminary findings at the bridge.

Now Gamache, in the silence as Jean-Guy slept, went back over that conversation.

"We lifted three sets of fresh prints off the interior of the car," Beauvoir had said. "Probably Vivienne's and Tracey's. But the third?"

"Can we prove that she wasn't alone? That someone was on the bridge with her?"

"No. That's a problem. The heavy rain washed away all foot and tire prints."

"Shame." Gamache thought for a moment. "But we still think she either met someone there. Something happened, and she went off the bridge. Or—"

"Or Tracey followed her there and killed her."

"But if he wanted her dead, why wait until she left?" mused Gamache, keeping his eyes on the highway. "He struck me as someone who doesn't plan ahead. I can imagine him lashing out and killing her that night, in their home, either on purpose or in a fit of rage, but to follow her?"

"He told you he left her in the living room and went into his studio and drank, right?"

"*Oui.*"

"Maybe he worked himself into a rage. Getting angrier and angrier the more he thought about Vivienne and another man. He sees her leave and decides to follow her, thinking she's meeting her lover."

Gamache nodded. That, he could see.

"He'd confront them. Do you think there really was a lover?" Beauvoir asked, then yawned.

"Must have been," said Gamache. "At least in your scenario. Otherwise why would she drive to the bridge?"

"Okay, she goes to meet a lover, but then wouldn't Tracey kill him, too?"

"Maybe he did. But I doubt it," Gamache said. "Like all abusers and bullies, Tracey's a coward. He wouldn't attack someone who could fight back."

"So if he did follow Vivienne, he found her alone on the bridge. Waiting. And threw her in."

"What did you find there?"

"I discovered I don't like rotten bridges over rivers in flood."

"Ahhh," said Gamache. "Most helpful. Anything else?"

"Wouldn't take much to break through the railing. It was broken from the inside out and looks recent. I think there's little doubt that's where Vivienne fell."

"Any actual proof?"

"Not yet. We're testing the wood for fibers and blood. We've removed the section where she broke through so technicians can take a closer look in the lab. Then there's the duffel bag," said Beauvoir. "Lacoste pointed out that most of the clothes are for summer."

"Huh," said Gamache. "That's strange."

"Not the only strange thing. You know those pills in the bag?"

"Yes."

"They're abortion pills."

"They're what?" Gamache glanced over quickly before returning his eyes to the road.

"Medication to end an early pregnancy. Looks like she got them on the black market."

"I wonder how far along she was," said Gamache.

It looked to both of them as though she was beyond what could be called an early pregnancy. But the coroner would tell them.

"Isabelle doesn't think she packed the bag, and neither do I," said Jean-Guy, yawning again. Between the heat of the car and the gentle hum of the engine, Jean-Guy could feel himself losing the fight to stay alert. To even stay awake.

"You think Tracey packed the bag," said Gamache.

"Yes. I think it was a simple mess of a murder. You found blood in the living room. And we found blood in the car. Tracey admits beating her. I think either he killed her in the home, beat her to death, drove her to the bridge, and threw her over, wanting to make it look like suicide or an accident, or he took her there while she was still alive and threw her off."

"I don't think he beat her to death in the house. There wasn't enough blood. And if she was still alive, why would she get into the car with him?"

"Yes, that's a problem. She wouldn't. Not voluntarily, anyway."

"So the most likely explanation is that he knocked her unconscious, drove her there, and threw her off the bridge," said Gamache. "Hoping, like you said, it would look like an accident or suicide. He packed the duffel bag, grabbing things at random, and threw it in after her. But people don't pack for suicide. If that's what he wanted us to believe, he made a mistake."

"There's another problem," said Beauvoir. "The blood smears are on the driver's side. It looks like she was hurt, but conscious enough to drive."

"So she took herself there," said Gamache, considering. "And there's no physical evidence of anyone else on that bridge with her."

"Not yet. You think he didn't do it?"

"Tracey? Oh, he did it. It's just a matter of understanding the evidence. And getting enough to convict."

He glanced over at his companion. Jean-Guy's eyes were just about closed.

Within a minute of Gamache's falling silent, Jean-Guy had fallen asleep.

By the time they pulled in to the morgue, Gamache had been over that conversation a few times but was no closer to a solution.


When Agent Cloutier returned to the local detachment, she found a very different Homer Godin than the man she'd left.

"How come I'm in here and he's free?" he demanded. "Let me out."

"I can't."

"Of course you can. You're a goddamned cop."

Lysette paled. Not used to being spoken to that way. And certainly not by Homer. She stared into those angry eyes and knew in her rational mind that it wasn't Homer speaking. It was grief.

But though her brain told her that, her heart still recoiled.

She saw Homer now in a different light. Not as a man but as a father. Not having children herself, she hadn't quite appreciated the depth of his feeling for his daughter. Now she knew what her friend Kathy had been talking about. That bond between father and daughter. It was almost cliché and, in some cases, mythic.

Kathy had long complained, but Lysette, as much as she loved her friend, could understand why Vivienne would be drawn to her father and not her mother.

Kathy was not demonstrative. She was efficient. Kept a clean and tidy and orderly home. But Homer brought the joy into it. As Vivienne brought joy into his life.

It was a perfect little ecosystem. But it left Kathy on the outside looking in.

As soon as Vivienne had been born, her father had become simply skin stretched over his love for his daughter.

But now she was gone. And there was nothing holding him together.

Except hatred.

Chief Inspector Gamache had seen that before anyone else. He knew, perhaps because of his love for his own daughter, what a person in that position could do. Would do.

Unless they were locked up.

Though Agent Lysette Cloutier did just wonder if it would really be such a bad thing, if she opened the cell door.

Homer would murder Carl Tracey, of course. But he'd almost certainly be given as light a sentence as the justice system allowed.

He would not be held criminally responsible. And he would clearly not be a menace to society. Just to one man.

She would also be arrested and tried, for letting him out. But at least Homer would know what she was willing to do for him.

The other agents in the room, including Agent Cameron, looked at her as she returned to her desk and brought up the Instagram account.

*Do they suspect what I'm considering doing?*

Did it matter?

Lysette Cloutier looked down at her computer and saw, again, the curt *No* on the screen. Now a few hours old. She typed in her own reply.

> **@NouveauGalerie:** *Sorry. Busy with buyers. No worries. Lots of other promising ceramicists. I'm sure you have other options. Good luck to you.*

Within two minutes there was a reply. Again, terse. But enough. It contained an invitation to join Carl Tracey's private Instagram account.

# CHAPTER TWENTY-TWO

⌐

@NouveauGalerie: Thanks for the access. Looked at your
work. Ceramic pieces promising, but not right for the gallery.
Good luck @CarlTracey.

@SeriousCollector: Rethinking the Morrow portrait I bought.
Three old women laughing. Weaker than I first thought. Sorta
superficial.

Holy shit. Check out this video. #GamacheSux

There was, Gamache knew, an unmistakable smell about a morgue.
Not the sickly aroma of rot. He could pick that up from a distance after years of approaching corpses. And killers.

No. The morgue smelled of extreme, almost severe cleanliness.

It turned his stomach.

As the door swung open, sterile air met him, and he braced himself.

But Armand Gamache knew the slight sick feeling in the pit of his stomach this time went beyond the smell. Went beyond, even, the gnawing thought that this could be Annie on the metal slab.

Only once before in his career had he felt this particular sensation.

It was doubt. Not that they could find the killer. He was pretty sure they'd already done that. But that they could convict him.

That other time, his first year as head of homicide, he had indeed failed. And a killer had gone free.

And now he looked down at the body of Vivienne Godin. Saw her bruises. Saw the incision on her belly.

And felt that wave of nausea. That fear that whoever did this would walk free.

"What do you have?" Jean-Guy Beauvoir asked Dr. Harris.

"As you can see, the body is badly damaged. Some trauma clearly postmortem, but some done while she was alive."

"She was beaten," said Beauvoir.

"Well—"

"Well, what?" he snapped, then put up his hands in apology. "*Désolé.*"

"It's okay. I feel it, too. This's a particularly nasty case. The problem is, I can't say for sure which injuries, if any, were done in a beating just before she died and which ones were caused by being battered in the river while still alive. There're some obviously older bruises." Dr. Harris pointed to some yellow and greenish blotches on Vivienne's arms and legs. "But these"—the coroner pointed to other marks on Vivienne's body—"are harder to explain."

"They're fresh," said Gamache.

"*Oui.* But what made them? A person? Or rocks and tree limbs? She'd have been tossed around in the floodwaters. That could've done a lot, even all of the damage we see."

They looked down at Vivienne's naked, battered body.

"The fetus?" asked Gamache. "How far along?"

"I'd say she'd be about twenty weeks."

"She?" said Beauvoir. "A baby girl?"

Jean-Guy paled and looked across the body. To his father-in-law. And Armand knew then.

Annie and Jean-Guy were having a daughter. A baby girl.

"Yes."

If Dr. Harris noticed this moment between the two men, she chose not to say anything.

"What I can say for sure is that she was alive when she went into the river. There's water in her lungs."

"If questioned on the stand," said Gamache, giving Jean-Guy a moment to compose himself, "what would you say about the bruising?"

She considered the body again. "Some of her wounds could have happened before she went into the water, but most have signs of battering

194

consistent with being hit by rocks. It's a sort of tumbling action as a body's swept along."

"You say most of the wounds are consistent with battering in the water," said Beauvoir, recovered. "But not all?"

"There are two bruises that're harder to explain." She pointed to Vivienne's upper chest, just below the collarbone.

Beauvoir and Gamache leaned closer.

At first it looked like one large blue mark spreading across her chest. But, looking closer, they could see other marks. Like something trapped below the surface. One on either side.

Armand put on his glasses and leaned closer still. "What do you think made them?"

"At a guess?" Dr. Harris raised her hands, palms toward them. Then thrust forward.

"She was shoved," said Beauvoir. He looked at Gamache, who nodded.

"*Oui.*" She put her hands over the bruises. "You can see that the hands are quite big."

"Could you say for sure those marks were made by a person and not by debris?" Gamache asked.

Dr. Harris sighed. "I've been struggling with that. I'm not sure I could swear to it. What I can say is that the chances of two identical bruises happening while she was being tossed about in the river are astronomical. These"—she looked back down at Vivienne—"were done at the same time, by the same thing. The only explanation I have is that she was pushed, violently."

"Intentionally."

"Maybe in a fit of rage, but yes, whoever did this wanted to shove her back. Hard."

"Can you measure those bruises?" Gamache asked.

"To give you the size of the hand? I could, but it wouldn't be very accurate. There's weeping of the blood around the edges. Again, any defense will argue, quite rightly, that the hand could've been smaller. Besides, a lot of people have hands that big."

Tracey's hands, Gamache knew, were not large. But as the hands of a potter, they'd be powerful.

And he could think of one person related to the case whose hands were very big.

Bob Cameron.

Left tackle's hands. And what did a left tackle do? He pushed and shoved. Violently. Perhaps, at this stage, instinctively. When threatened.

"Any idea how long she's been dead?" asked Beauvoir.

"Two, maybe three days. The water was cold, so that has to be taken into account. This is Tuesday? I'd say she went into the river on Saturday night, maybe at a stretch early Sunday morning."

Gamache was nodding. Thinking. And finally asked the question Jean-Guy Beauvoir did not seem willing to ask.

"Is there any evidence, any proof, that she was murdered?"

Sharon Harris paused before answering. "I'm sorry. I looked. Hard. But I can't find anything. It could've been suicide. It could've been an accident. I think she was murdered. I think that she was hit so hard in the chest she fell off the bridge. But as for absolute proof?"

She raised her hands. No.

"And the blood work?" Beauvoir asked.

"Very preliminary. None of the more detailed results yet, but I can tell you that she'd been drinking."

"She was drunk?" asked Beauvoir.

"No, but she'd had a few ounces of alcohol shortly before her death. No sign of drugs. But if there're just traces, that won't show up until I get the detailed report. I've put a rush on it, and we should have something by later this afternoon."

"Can you ask them to check for this?" Beauvoir brought out the pill bottle in its sterile baggie.

Dr. Harris examined it while Gamache walked back to Vivienne's body.

He looked down at her, at the wounds caused by the river. By the fall. By her husband. And by the coroner. Who'd cut into this young woman in an effort to find out who'd caused the other wounds.

He picked up her hand, to tuck it next to her body and draw the sheet over her.

The hand was, as he expected, cold. It would have shocked him to the core had Vivienne's hand been warm.

He held it for a moment and realized he was, unconsciously, trying to comfort her. He noticed then that there was a gash on her palm.

"Doctor, what's this? It looks like a defensive wound."

"Not from a knife," she said, joining him. "Too jagged."

"Could it have been caused by reaching out for the railing," Gamache asked. "And having it break?"

Dr. Harris lifted up Vivienne's hand to take a closer look.

Then, stepping away from the body, Dr. Harris stood straight and lifted both hands in front of her.

Anyone would have thought she was being threatened by the two Sûreté officers.

Her face was intent. Her body rigid in feigned alarm. Then she leaned away from them and reached behind her. With her right hand.

"What height is the railing?"

"Ninety-eight centimeters," said Beauvoir.

Dr. Harris adjusted her hand to just over three feet off the floor. Then she nodded and walked over to her desk.

Doing quick calculations of Vivienne Godin's height. The height of the railing. The angle of the cut on her hand and the likely trajectory of her body. The coroner then returned to the metal slab.

"What's the thickness of the handrail?"

Beauvoir needed to consult his notes for that and gave the dimension to her.

Harris measured the wound and reexamined it closely.

"Still no splinters, but I'll do a microscopic examination. There might be something wedged into the flesh. It looks likely that it was caused when she fell and not when she was in the water."

"How can you tell that?" asked Beauvoir, stepping closer.

"Because the cut starts here"—Harris pointed to just above Vivienne's wrist, where the palm began—"and tears up to her middle finger. It would be unlikely a cut like this would be made when a person was going headfirst down the river. Her hands would be out in front of her, if possible, and a cut would go from fingers down, not wrist up."

"You think it was made when she was going backward, not forward," said Gamache, also moving closer. He put his glasses back on.

"I do."

"So Vivienne was pushed backward while on the bridge," said Beauvoir, and when Dr. Harris didn't contradict him, he went on. "She reached for the railing"—he also mimicked the action—"to stop herself, and it broke."

There was what felt like an eternal silence while the two Sûreté officers stared at the coroner. And the careful coroner considered.

"Probably."

"Yes." Beauvoir clenched both fists in excitement, knowing what that would mean to their investigation.

"Probably," said Gamache, more cautious. "But not definitive?"

"No. It's likely that's what happened. I could testify to it. But the defense could argue that it was caused in the water. That her body was twisting around so it was at times going backward down the river, and that's when the cut was made. It would be difficult, but just possible. I'd have to testify to that, too."

"What do you need to be sure?" asked Gamache.

"What we don't have. A splinter that matches the wood from the railing." Then she paused. "You say it was rotten?"

"*Oui*," said Beauvoir. Perking up. Noticing the slight shift in her tone. "Very."

"Do you have a sample?"

"We've removed that whole section. It's in the lab."

"Good. Have them test for spores. For algae. For microscopic traces of organisms. Lots of things make their home in rotting wood. And flesh. I'll take samples from the cut and test as well. It's possible not everything was flushed out. We'll see if what's found on the wood matches what's in the cut."

"And if it does, that would place her on that bridge," said Gamache. "Going backward through the railing. It would prove the wound wasn't made after she went into the water."

"Yes. Absolutely."

"But," said Gamache.

"But," said Beauvoir, looking at him. Knowing what he was thinking and coming to the same conclusion.

"But what?" asked Dr. Harris.

Gamache nodded to Beauvoir, inviting the lead investigator to explain.

"A clever defense would still argue that she might've tripped. She was drinking, after all. She might've just lost her balance and fallen backward. Or she might've been leaning against the rail and it broke."

"That I can refute," said the coroner. "By the angle of the cut, she was at least two feet from it when she reached back and fell—"

"Or was pushed," said Beauvoir.

"—against it. And yes, she was trying to save herself. So you can rule out suicide at least."

Gamache exhaled.

It was far from the first time he'd stood over the corpse of a woman who'd been punched and kicked, belittled and shamed and pushed to the end of her rope. And beyond.

Vivienne Godin, it seemed, had reached the end and had made a choice that cold and dark April night. She'd chosen life. For herself and her baby girl.

*Le beau risque*. The great risk. The beautiful risk. To climb out of the hole and start again.

Like Annie and Jean-Guy, heading to Paris with their young and growing family. Away from the dangers here. To start fresh.

But while they could escape, Vivienne could not.

Once again, Gamache felt the tightening in his stomach.


Isabelle Lacoste stood in the doorway of the Cowansville detachment, leaning on her cane. And looked around the open room.

"She's over there," said the receptionist, waving toward Agent Cloutier, working at her laptop.

"*Merci.*"

But the receptionist had already left.

Heads turned as she limped through the room. There was about her an air of ease and confidence. This stranger who belonged.

Then, one by one, they realized this was no stranger. Though most had never met Superintendent Lacoste, they knew her by reputation. Knew what she'd done. And what had, as a result, been done to her. The cane being only the most visible sign.

"Superintendent," said one young agent, getting up to stand at his desk.

"*Bonjour*," said Lacoste, not bothering to correct him and explain she was on leave. Though the rank still held.

"Agent Cloutier," said Lacoste as she approached the desk.

Lysette Cloutier gave a start and looked up into the familiar face. Then she quickly stood up, smiling.

"*Patron*. I didn't expect to see you. I thought you'd be with the Chief Inspector. Sssss."

Lacoste laughed. With more than one, the grammar became problematic.

"I've struck out on my own," she said. "Are you free?"

"For sure. Do you need my help?"

"You seem to be working on something."

"I traced the IP address for Carl Tracey's website. It's through a local server, and the billing address is a home here in Cowansville, registered in the tax rolls to the same woman I told you about last night. Pauline Vachon."

Lacoste was slightly surprised Lysette Cloutier could remember anything from their call the night before.

"So that confirms it," she said, taking a seat. "And we have an address. Well done."

The website was on Cloutier's laptop, and Lacoste scrolled through. It showed a man bending over a wheel, intent on the lump of clay he was forming. Down the sides of the page, there were photographs of different works.

"Huh," said Lacoste. "Quite nice."

"Yes. He's talented." Cloutier would give him that. "Then I went onto the Instagram account and looked around. Not particularly interesting. Just what they want us to see."

"Yes," said Lacoste, cautious now. "We talked about this, too, last night. I told you not to do anything else. We don't want to alert them that the police are interested in any possible private account."

"Right, well, we're in."

"In where? In what?"

"Their private Instagram account." Cloutier was beaming.

Lacoste was not.

"What've you done?"

"I asked if we could communicate privately, and she gave me access."

"To a cop?"

"Well, not exactly. Like you said, we didn't want her erasing anything that could be evidence, so I pretended I was someone else."

"Who?"

Now Lysette Cloutier clicked again, and another website came up. An art gallery in Old Montréal called NouveauGalerie. Specializing in modern Québécois art.

It was a slick, minimalist site. Very cool.

"Who're they?" Lacoste asked.

"They're me. I created it."

"Wait a minute," said Lacoste, trying to keep up. "You're pretending to be this NouveauGalerie?"

"*Oui*. I showed interest in his work, asked to speak privately. After refusing a few times, this Pauline finally give me access to their private Instagram account."

"Why would she do that?"

"So we can discuss business," said Cloutier. Her tone said that must be obvious.

"Why wouldn't she just pick up the phone?"

"Phone? Young people don't talk on phones. Everything's done through texts and social media. And with the private Instagram account, she can show galleries—me—" said Cloutier with a smile, "works in progress. Things they might not want public yet. Besides, she's trying to pretend she's Carl Tracey. God knows, you don't want that asshole talking to galleries."

"Got it," said Lacoste. "So private Instagram it is."

Where anyone could take on a false identity. And often did.

Lacoste didn't know whether to be pleased with the brilliance of this or angry that Cloutier had disobeyed orders.

Before she made up her mind, Cloutier said, "Look at this." She clicked again. "Voilà."

Up came photographs and posts. Private messages between Carl Tracey and Pauline Vachon. Just the two. No one else, it seemed, had access to the private account.

Except, now, NouveauGalerie.

And one thing was immediately obvious.

"They're lovers," said Lacoste.

"*Oui.*"

"Can you zoom in on this picture, please," said Lacoste, leaning closer.

It was a selfie Pauline Vachon had taken. She was lying on a sofa in a very suggestive pose.

"There. And there," said Lacoste, reaching out and moving the image until it showed a close-up of the woman's bare arm.

Bruises.

"Goddamn," said Cloutier, with disgust and, Lacoste thought, a touch of triumph.

"What're they saying to each other?" Lacoste asked.

"I've just gotten in. Haven't gotten to their messages yet."

Just then Lacoste's phone vibrated, and she read the email.

It was from an agent back at headquarters, reporting on the phone messages into and out of the Tracey home for the past few weeks. There weren't many. They'd all be checked, but what Lacoste scanned down to were the ones for that Saturday.

None had come in, and just two numbers were called from the house that day. One of them repeatedly.

"Is either of these Pauline Vachon's number?"

"*Non.* But it is a Cowansville exchange," said Cloutier. "I can look it up. That other one is to her father. That's Homer's number."

Lacoste nodded. And realized Cloutier must know it well.

While Cloutier looked up the second number, Lacoste called Beauvoir.

"*Oui, allô.*"

"The phone records from the Tracey place have come in," she said, without preamble. "It shows the call to Vivienne's father, like he said, on Saturday morning. But someone in that house called another number, repeatedly, early Saturday evening. Most of the calls lasted only seconds."

"Where to?"

"A local number. Agent Cloutier's checking now."

Beauvoir stayed on the line and could hear the clicking of computer keys. Then silence. Before he heard Agent Cloutier's voice.

"The number belongs to a Gerald Bertrand."

Jean-Guy put his hand over the phone and relayed the information to Gamache.

"The lover?" Beauvoir said.

"Could be," said Gamache.

"We'll find out," said Lacoste, rising with the help of her cane.

After hanging up, Beauvoir returned to the coroner.

"Have you done a DNA test on the fetus?"

"I have. The results will be in with the rest of the tests, later today."

"About the medication that was found in her duffel bag—"

"Mifegymiso. Yes."

"It's an abortion pill, right?"

"Yes."

"Does that mean she was trying to end her pregnancy?"

"It's unclear. It's only legal in Canada up to ten weeks, and she was further along than that. I'll test for both in her blood, but I can tell you there were no signs of an imminent miscarriage."

"Meaning what?"

"Meaning I doubt she took the pill. And you know that this bottle"—she held it up—"wasn't from a prescription, right? It's almost certainly black market."

"Yes."

"I have a question for you," said Gamache.

"*Oui*," said Dr. Harris.

"Is Mifegymiso free?"

"If prescribed by a doctor, yes."

"So if it's both legal and free, why would anyone pay for it on the black market?"

"Well, I guess if she was twenty weeks along, no doctor would prescribe it," said the coroner.

"Possible," said Gamache.

"But you don't think so," said Beauvoir.

"I'm wondering if Vivienne got those pills," said Gamache. "Or if Tracey did."

"Why would he do that?" asked Dr. Harris.

"He would," said Beauvoir, "if he knew the baby wasn't his and wanted her to abort. Probably without her knowing."

"Which would mean he knew all that long before Saturday," said Gamache. "But if he knew what the drug was for and he packed her duffel bag, why put them in?"

"Maybe to confuse us," said Beauvoir.

"Well," said Gamache, and raised his brows. It was working . . .

"Or maybe—"

Dr. Harris watched as the two investigators discussed possibilities and probabilities.

She'd worked with them for years. Seen their relationship blossom and wither. Seen it through all its spasms, incarnations, hoops, and dips. The ruptures and the mendings.

Things are strongest where they're broken.

Gamache had said that, quietly, once. Years ago. In the cathedral in Québec City, at the funerals for four of his agents, killed in a raid. He'd whispered it to himself as he knelt, head bowed, during one of the silent prayers. Not realizing, perhaps, that anyone other than God was listening.

And God knew, as did Sharon Harris, that the relationship between Gamache and Beauvoir had been shattered, more than once. But it had survived to this day, stronger than ever.

She listened, and marveled, and envied this bond.

She also noticed that in each scenario they knew exactly who the murderer was. Which was a good start.

"Or," said Gamache, "Vivienne did pack the bag, intending to leave her husband. She put the pills in because she was still undecided about the baby."

"At more than three months out? Why would she decide to end the pregnancy now? I think protecting the baby was the reason she left him. Vivienne wanted to start a new life, with the child."

"The problem is, we can't always get clean away," said Dr. Harris. "Not when we're running from our demons."

She knew. She was surrounded by their work every day.

Gamache nodded and caught Beauvoir's eye.

They'd spent decades tracking the creatures. Into dark alleys. Into homes. Deep into lives. Often in the guise of friends, lovers, caring colleagues. Sometimes complete strangers. Sometimes they were of people's own making.

Vivienne's demon had found her on that bridge.

Though Gamache had never really doubted it, now, thanks to that long, jagged cut on her hand and the ghostly bruises, he was sure. Vivienne had been murdered.

And, what was more, he could put a face and a name to this particular demon.

Now they had to prove it.

# CHAPTER TWENTY-THREE

—

@CarlTracey: @NouveauGalerie, We have other more recent work. Would that help?

@NouveauGalerie: No. @CarlTracey, Moving on. But thank you.

In the car on the way over to Gerald Bertrand's place, Isabelle Lacoste read the Instagram exchange between Pauline Vachon, pretending to be the artist, and Agent Cloutier, pretending to be the gallery owner.

It was true, she thought. Nothing, and no one, on social media was as they seemed.

Still, it looked as though Cloutier had been masterful in her manipulation. Turning Tracey down. Forcing Vachon to almost beg NouveauGalerie for attention.

Stringing Vachon along. Until she got exactly what she wanted.

When they pulled in to Gerald Bertrand's driveway, Lacoste put away her phone and rang the bell.

"Gerald Bertrand?"

"*Oui?*"

"My name is Isabelle Lacoste. I'm with the Sûreté du Québec. This is Agent Cloutier. May we come in?"

The man was young, perhaps early twenties. With the burly arms and torso of a fellow who did manual labor. There was about him a sort of cologne of testosterone.

His dark beard was bushy but groomed and his hair styled shorter to his head. His brown eyes were clear and bright, and he held, in his sturdy arms, an infant.

For an instant, Isabelle Lacoste forgot she was married. With two children. She hoped her mouth hadn't dropped open, but she was pretty sure her eyes had widened.

Beside her, Lysette Cloutier was smiling. Grinning, really. Having lost both her heart and apparently her mind.

"The Sûreté? What's this about?" he asked.

"We need to speak with you about a homicide."

"A murder? Here?"

He looked out the door and held his baby closer to his body, instinctively protecting her.

Cloutier swallowed whatever drool had pooled in her mouth.

"No, not right here," said Lacoste, who'd recovered most of her wits. "May we come in?"

"Yes, sorry."

He stepped back, and after removing their dirty boots, they followed him into the kitchen of the modest home.

He lived in a subdivision of Cowansville, in a cluster of bungalows exactly the same.

"Can you tell us about your relationship with Vivienne Godin?" Lacoste asked as she took the chair he'd indicated, the best one in the room, and leaned her cane against the arm.

Monsieur Bertrand had taken them to the back of the house, past the small front room normally used as a formal living room, but in this home it held workout equipment.

The kitchen opened to a sitting area with a sofa, two chairs, and a huge television on which cartoons were playing. A card table doubled as a dining table, though Lacoste doubted there'd been many, if any, dinner parties there.

Dishes were piled in the sink, and a near-empty baby bottle was on the counter.

The place was messy, but not, Lacoste could see, dirty.

"Don't tell my sister," he said as he muted the sound.

"I'm afraid I can't promise that," said Lacoste. "It's very serious. We might have to talk with her, too."

"Really? Well, I can tell you now that she doesn't approve."

"Few would."

"It's not really that bad, is it?"

It was about here that Isabelle Lacoste began to suspect they were discussing two different things.

"What isn't?" she asked.

"Television. Vendredi likes Babar, so I put it on when Pam isn't around."

"Vendredi?" asked Cloutier.

"She was born on a Friday."

"Pam's your sister?" asked Cloutier.

"*Oui.*"

"So this isn't your child?" asked Agent Cloutier.

"No." He smiled. "I look after her whenever I can. I'm off work right now. Construction season'll start again in a couple of weeks." He looked at the little girl and grinned at her, and she grinned back. "Gotta spend as much time with Dee as I can."

The agents exchanged looks. Both thinking much the same thing. That he was adorable. And maybe a murderer.

But would a mother, a sister, trust her baby to a man, a brother, capable of murder? A sibling would probably know, would have seen some of that darkness, that menace, as they grew up.

But maybe he hadn't intended to kill his lover. Maybe it was a terrible accident and he was afraid to come forward. If he was afraid to tell his sister about an animated elephant, how would he feel about admitting to murder?

Superintendent Lacoste repositioned herself so she was facing him directly.

"Your relationship, sir. With Vivienne Godin."

His brow dropped in concentration as he bobbed his niece, gently, on his knee.

"I'm sorry, I don't think I know her. Is she the one who was killed?"

They watched him closely, but neither agent could see any distress, beyond a normal human reaction when hearing that a stranger was dead.

"Please just answer the question," said Lacoste.

Despite the fact Agent Cloutier was clearly the elder of the two and should have been the more senior, Gerald Bertrand understood innately that the young woman with the old eyes and cane was in charge.

"I have. I don't know her. Why do you think I do?"

"Think a little harder," said Lacoste.

"I don't know what to tell you," said Bertrand, looking from one to the other.

Then another thought occurred to Lacoste. Maybe it wasn't Vivienne who called.

"How about Carl Tracey?"

"What about him?"

"Do you know him?"

"No. Never heard of him either. What's this about? Why do you think I know these people?"

"Because either Vivienne or Carl called you on Saturday. Repeatedly."

"Oh, *merde*. That was her? Some woman kept calling. The first time I tried to tell her she had the wrong number, but she seemed really upset. I'm not sure she was listening. She called back, and I tried again, but after that I just ignored the calls. She left a couple of messages—"

"Can we listen to them?" asked Cloutier.

"I erased them."

*Of course you did*, thought Cloutier. What else would a guilty person do?

But then she rethought that.

What else would an innocent person do? She did the same thing with messages from wrong numbers.

She was beginning to see how quickly something completely normal could suddenly seem sinister, if you chose to see it that way.

"May we have a look around?" Lacoste asked.

Gerald Bertrand looked surprised but nodded.

"Do you have a girlfriend?" she asked as they surveyed the small home. It was very messy and very masculine. A man-child lived here, alone. It was furnished with pieces that looked like they'd come from friends or family or a dumpster. Some hockey trophies. A pile of skis and skates and hunting gear was in the basement.

There were a few photos, of Gerald with mates, with teams, with his family. But none of him with Vivienne.

"Who's this?" Lacoste looked at a photo among many on the fridge.

"Old girlfriend. We broke up a couple of months ago."

"You keep her picture up?"

He shrugged. "I forgot it was there."

It showed the two young people in bathing suits at the lake, faces smashed together for a selfie. Beaming.

"Do you own a gun?"

"A hunting rifle, yes. I have a license."

He showed them the weapon, safely locked up, with ammunition locked in a separate room. He produced from his wallet the license.

Lacoste inspected the rifle. Clean. Well maintained.

"Where do you hunt?"

"Wherever my buddies want to go, but mostly up north. The Abitibi. But haven't been for a while. Not since Vendredi was born."

"Why not?"

"Lost my taste for killing things, I guess."

"Where were you on Saturday afternoon and evening?" asked Lacoste.

"You're kidding, right?"

But it was clear by her expression that she was not.

Bertrand thought for a moment. "I was looking after Dee until about six, when my sister finished work and came over to get her, and then some buddies dropped by and we watched the game."

"Which game?"

"The hockey game." He seemed shocked she needed to ask. "Canadiens and Leafs. Terrible game."

He was right. Lacoste had watched it with her husband and kids. The Leafs won.

"May I have their names, please. Your friends," said Cloutier, bringing out her notebook.

"You're going to talk to them?" he asked.

"Yes."

"But they'll think I had something to do with this."

"Names, please."

Gerald Bertrand hesitated and, in doing so, moved up the suspect list. Carl Tracey still held the top spot and would be hard to tumble, but this anxious man was closing in.

He gave them some names and phone numbers.

"Please don't get in touch with them, Monsieur Bertrand," said Cloutier. "We can easily check up on your calls."

By now Bertrand was sheet-white. He hugged the baby to him as though she were the one threatened.

Superintendent Lacoste considered the child.

No bruising. No sign at all of anything other than comfort and happiness.

This man might have been a threat to Vivienne Godin, but Lacoste was assured he was no threat to the baby.

"*Merci, monsieur,*" said Lacoste, giving him her card as they walked to the door. "We're probably going to ask you for fingerprints and a blood sample—"

"Come on," he said, clearly upset now. "Why? I had nothing to do with whatever happened. I don't even know these people."

"Then your prints and DNA will clear you," said Lacoste.

Cloutier opened the door, and they stepped out.

"Did you know she was pregnant?" asked Lacoste.

"I didn't know her," he said, his voice plaintive. Then he paused, and his muscular shoulders sagged a bit. "She was pregnant?"

"Yes."

"And someone killed her?"

"Yes."

"The baby . . . ?"

"Died, too."

He covered Vendredi's ears and said, "Goddamned fucking shit of a fucking horrible world."

Then he uncovered his niece's ears and kissed her. Gently.

"That's either a really great guy," said Cloutier, putting the car in gear, "or a monster."

Lysette Cloutier never dreamed, while working in accounting, that it could be so difficult to tell the two apart. But it was.

As Beauvoir and Gamache slid into the booth at the café in Cowansville, Gamache's phone rang. It was from the RCMP.

"Excuse me." He slid back out and went outside to take the call.

"Armand?" came the familiar voice, shouting over a familiar noise. "Sorry, meant to get to you sooner, but I wanted to see it for myself."

"Are you in a helicopter?"

"*Oui*. Over the La Grande-3 dam."

One of the oldest, Gamache knew. If any dam was going to—

"We've opened the spillways," the RCMP officer shouted above the rotors.

"And?" Gamache shouted back.

Inside the café, Beauvoir could hear Gamache's voice through the window and saw him hunkered over, a hand covering his other ear, straining to hear whoever was on the other end.

"It seems to be working. Will let you know about the others." Gamache heard him give muffled instructions to the pilot. "Call you back."

"And the diversions farther south? Are they being dug?" Gamache shouted into the phone, but the connection had been broken.

Gamache hung up and exhaled. Closing his eyes for a moment. It just might work.

"What was that about?" Jean-Guy asked when he returned, but there was no chance for an answer.

Someone was walking toward them.

"Thank you for coming, Simone," said Gamache, as the elegant woman in her early forties approached their booth. "I'm not sure you've met Chief Inspector Beauvoir. He's the head of homicide for the Sûreté. Jean-Guy, this's Simone Fleury. She's on the board of the Réseau de Violence Conjugale du Québec and runs the local women's shelters. We've sat on several committees together."

"Committees." Madame Fleury made a dismissive, almost rude noise. She looked at Beauvoir's outstretched hand, ignored it, and sat down.

"Nothing's changed. Women are beaten, women are killed. That's why we're here, isn't it?"

"*Oui*," said Beauvoir, dropping his hand and sitting down next to Gamache.

"I see you're back at work, Armand." Her voice was abrupt. There was a tone of displeasure and impatience. "Not everyone seems pleased."

"I'm sure the vast majority are thrilled I'm back," he said with a smile.

"They're just too busy to mention it on Twitter, I suppose," she said. "Though you do have one defender. A dumb-ass."

Beauvoir looked at her with surprise. But Gamache just gave a small grunt of laughter. What Madame Fleury said next confirmed Beauvoir's suspicions about her.

"Let's get on with it." She looked at her watch. "I have a hair appointment, then a luncheon."

Rich. Bored. The kids gone, husband busy making more money. A do-gooder.

Simone Fleury regarded Beauvoir.

A bundle of coiled energy she found repulsive. Here was a young guy promoted beyond his competence. Just beginning to develop a paunch. Probably going to seed, she thought.

He was good-looking, clean, well groomed, but Madame Fleury had trained herself to look beyond what could be seen.

Probably went home and whaled on his wife when the Habs lost. Or after he'd had a few. Or just because.

Simone Fleury did not like cops. She tolerated Gamache. Barely.

"What can you tell us about Vivienne Godin?" Beauvoir asked, placing the photo of her on the table so that the blank-faced young woman was looking up at them.

"Tea, please," said Madame Fleury to the waitress.

Beauvoir ordered one as well, while Gamache took a coffee.

The waitress had looked Madame Fleury in the eye as she ordered. Brief enough, meaningless enough. Except she hadn't made eye contact with either Beauvoir or Gamache.

"I've seen that," said Madame Fleury, pushing the photograph back across the table to Beauvoir. "You sent it to me, Armand. I asked around. She didn't show up at any of the shelters, and if she called, she didn't use her own name. Most don't."

"So she could've called but didn't give her name."

"Isn't that what I just said? We get twenty-six thousand calls a year." She let that sink in and was gratified to see the look of surprise on Beauvoir's handsome face. "Most never give their name. Most never show up."

"Why not?"

"Most women, when they call for help, don't want to leave the relationship. They just want the beating, that beating, to end."

It was, Gamache knew, exactly what Cameron described with Vivienne.

"But they must know there'll be another," said Beauvoir. "Why—"

"Don't," Madame Fleury snapped. "Don't you dare ask why they don't leave. Don't you dare judge these women for staying."

"But it's a legitimate question, isn't it?" He looked from Madame Fleury to Gamache.

"There's an implied criticism," said Madame Fleury. "That these women are weak or stupid."

"I never said that."

"No, but you think that. Why don't they leave? Because they've been conditioned to believe it's their fault. Because they've been isolated. They have no money and no support. Because they have a shred of hope or delusion. Because they actually love the guy. Because they're stuck. Because they're terrified. And for good reason. Because it's all they know and all they think they deserve. Because they believe there's nothing better out there. You can see it in her face. That dazed look. As telling as bruises."

She jutted her slender hand toward the photo on the table. The picture had been taken before Vivienne was married, but Gamache didn't bother to correct her.

"That's why the law was changed," he said instead. "With Madame Fleury's help. So that when police show up, they can use their discretion and arrest the abuser. The woman doesn't have to be the one to lay charges."

"Yeah, right," said Madame Fleury. "But how often does that actually happen? Goddamned cops. You need 'sufficient information.' I think that's the phrase, right?"

"You know it is," said Gamache.

"Did she call the cops?" asked Madame Fleury, looking from one to the other.

"She did," said Beauvoir. "Charges were never laid."

"Insufficient information," said Madame Fleury. "How long before she was killed was that?"

"First time? Thirteen months. There were other calls after that, but no arrest."

"And then he kills her."

She looked from Beauvoir to Gamache. Neither of whom disagreed.

"*Alors*," said Madame Fleury, raising her manicured hands. "All we can do is provide a safe place for those who do break free."

"Would they know where to go, though?" asked Beauvoir.

The location of shelters was closely guarded. For good reason.

"We don't advertise the location of shelters, if that's what you mean."

It clearly was not what Beauvoir meant. He was coming to deeply dislike this woman, who had a knack for taking what he said and exaggerating it, twisting it, into something ridiculous.

"If they want help, we arrange to meet them," she continued. "And bring them to a shelter."

"But still," said Beauvoir, "must be hard in a small community to keep that secret. Neighbors and all."

"It is. How did she die?"

"Pushed off a bridge into a river in flood. She either drowned or was battered against the rocks. She was pregnant."

Simone Fleury raised her head so that she was looking down her long nose at Beauvoir.

He realized he was being brutal. Stating the facts as though they were just words. Matching her own matter-of-fact tone. Beside him, he heard Gamache take a deep breath of disapproval.

He pulled himself back in. "It's a terrible thing."

There was a pause, until through those thin lips came one word: "Yes."

She turned to Gamache. "Her husband, of course, otherwise I wouldn't be here."

"He's a suspect, *oui*."

"If you have any trouble convicting him, just send him over to the shelter. We'll take care of him."

"*Merci*," said Gamache. "We might have trouble."

Barely under her breath, as she squeezed her tea bag, Madame Fleury muttered, "Cops."

"If an abuser does show up at a shelter," said Beauvoir, "what do you do?"

"Invite him in for tea and petits fours. What do you think we do?"

*Is it true, is it kind, does it need to be said?* Beauvoir held his tongue. Barely.

"You call the cops," he finally said, through his own thin lips.

"Yeah, right. And wait the twenty minutes until they move their fat asses?"

"That's not true," said Gamache.

"Okay, that might be true, but not fast enough. Never fast enough when the guy's pounding on the door."

"So what do you do?" Beauvoir persisted.

"We take care of it."

"How? Do you have a gun?"

"Are you kidding? Do I look crazy?"

Gamache cleared his throat in a warning to Beauvoir not to answer that.

"Believe me," Madame Fleury continued, "those of us who managed to escape won't put up with that bullshit ever again. No one gets through the front door. No one touches any of those women. Never. Ever."

"Us?" asked Beauvoir. "You?"

"You don't think I do this out of the goodness of my heart?"

Beauvoir did not think that.

"Listen, Chief." She almost spit the word out. "Doctors go home and beat their wives. Lawyers. Cops. There's a huge instance of abuse from cops." She glared at him in what he realized, with some shock, was a warning. Maybe even an accusation.

"My father was a judge," she continued, "and inside our big old house in our respectable neighborhood, he beat us kids. And worse. I married a banker at eighteen, to get away, and guess what? He beat me, too. Then he'd bring me flowers and jewelry and he'd cry. He'd sob and say how sorry he was. And that he'd be a better husband. He'd never do it again. And you know what?" Her eyes opened wide as she stared at Beauvoir. "I believed him. Because I wanted to. Because I had to. I put on the beautiful silk scarf he brought me, to hide the bruises, and went to the country club for lunch."

She let that sink in.

"Without realizing it, we go to what's familiar. When I finally told my best friend, she didn't believe me. No one did. They didn't want to know. There was only one shelter here at the time. Overflowing. But they took me in and gave me a mattress on the floor. I slept on it for three months. First time in my life I felt safe. You know why it's safe? Not because the cops protect us but because we look after ourselves. We make sure it is."

"'We' the workers?"

"'We' every woman there. You asked if we have a weapon? We do. And you gave it to us, with every blow. Every bruise. Every broken bone. It's the toy at the bottom of the cereal box." She clunked her mug down on the table so hard that tea shot out the top and other patrons looked over.

"Rage," said Beauvoir.

"Baseball bats," said Madame Fleury. "Next time you see a group of women in a park practicing their swings, you think about that."

She wiped up the spilled tea with a thin paper napkin, then pointed to the words Gamache had just written in his notebook. "What you just wrote is true, but no excuse. Cycle of abuse. My husband was beaten by his father. He saw his mother hit. But he was an adult when he hit me, and responsible for his own actions. They all are. After a beating they feel horrible and buy presents and promise to be better men, but they don't change. They don't grow up. They remain out-of-control children in a man's body."

"Simone," said Gamache, "a bag was found on the side of the river with some of her belongings in it, but it was a strange assortment. Summer clothing. Medication she probably didn't need anymore."

"So?"

"We're wondering if she packed it herself."

Madame Fleury considered. "Might've, in a panic. Some women leave suddenly, just take off. But most have thought about it for a while. They have a bag packed and hidden, ready to grab. I had one packed for almost a year before I got up the courage to leave."

Beauvoir tried to imagine Simone Fleury as a frightened young woman. But then, he knew that few people would look at him and imagine the wreckage he'd crawled out of, not all that long ago.

Madame Fleury glanced at her watch. "I'm leaving. My hairdresser doesn't like it when I'm late. If you need anything else, you know how to reach me."

And leave she did. Armand did not offer her his hand, and she did not offer him hers.

But Beauvoir did. As a sort of peace offering.

Simone Fleury looked at it and walked away.

"She thinks every man's an abuser," said Beauvoir, dropping his hand to his side. "That's unfair."

"She was beaten by two men she trusted. That's unfair. She works with abused women every day. She's surrounded by it. It's incredible she can even bring herself to look at us, never mind talk to us in anything close to a civil manner." Gamache nodded toward Beauvoir's hand, which was at his side, his fingers relaxed into a loose fist. "What would you do if a weapon were thrust at you?"

Beauvoir looked down. He saw a hand. One that wrote notes, and chopped vegetables, and bathed his son. But Madame Fleury saw something else.

Twenty-six thousand calls a year, he thought.

As they stepped into the sunshine and the unseasonably warm April day, Beauvoir instinctively scanned the faces and realized with some amazement why he always did that.

He was unconsciously looking for danger. Always. He saw potential threats everywhere. In everyone. In the elderly man across the way, with that bag. In the kids laughing and shoving each other. In the SUV heading a little too quickly down the main street.

Suppose . . .

It had become second nature. Hardwired into him.

Jean-Guy Beauvoir knew that every person had a killer inside them.

And Madame Fleury knew that every man had an abuser inside of him.

Both were unfair. But such was their experience. And conditioning.

That was one of the many reasons he had to leave. Had to escape the Sûreté and get far, far away. From a world filled with threats. He longed to see a kinder world.

He realized it might be too late. Too much damage might've already been done. But Jean-Guy Beauvoir had to try to break free.

As they walked by the window of the café, he glanced in and saw the young waitress clearing their mugs and picking up the money they'd left.

She looked at him and quickly dropped her eyes.

Jean-Guy Beauvoir returned his gaze to the road ahead. Scanning it.

# CHAPTER TWENTY-FOUR

@MyrnaLanders: I love @ClaraMorrow works. They're genius.

@ClaraMorrow: Thanks @MyrnaLanders, but you sent this to me privately. Did you mean to? I'm sitting with you in the bistro. Oh, oh. Here comes Ruth. Look busy!

@MyrnaLanders: #ClaraSucks *Merde.*

@ClaraMorrow: @MyrnaLanders That one you put out on the public twitter feed. You just agreed with everyone who says my art is shit.

@MyrnaLanders: #ClaraSucks Did I? Fuck

@ClaraMorrow: @MyrnaLanders Please stop.

The incident room in Three Pines was filled with the aroma of wet socks, sweat, cilantro, and lime.

Olivier and Gabri moved aside the firefighting equipment and set out the ginger-garlic chicken soup, sandwiches, and drinks.

Along with the senior officers, there were the more junior agents. Cloutier and the big guy. Cameron. They suspected he'd eat lots.

"Any news on the flooding?" Isabelle Lacoste asked.

"Here?" asked Olivier. "The Bella Bella's gone down. Thank God."

"Across the province," said Isabelle.

"Only what we see on the news," said Gabri. "You probably know more than we do."

"Maybe not," she said. "We've been busy."

"Well, according to CBC, they're digging huge trenches to divert some rivers," said Gabri. "That must've been where you got the idea from, Armand."

"Good," said Gamache, and exhaled. "Good news."

"Did you see the Deputy Premier in the scrum when that reporter asked about it?" said Olivier.

Gabri and Olivier reenacted, with some exaggeration, Gamache suspected, the Deputy Premier's face as it went from bafflement to anger to confidence when he was told it seemed to be working.

"And then, just as he'd said he was in the meeting where it'd been decided to dig, another journalist asked about the angry farmers whose fields were now flooded," said Gabri.

His face fell into an expression somehow combining annoyance and obsequiousness.

"Poor man," said Olivier, putting linen napkins on the table. Beauvoir watched all this and wondered if they'd pull a candelabra out of the hamper next. "Can't win."

While food was being organized, Gamache picked up a landline and went into the storage room. No need for the others to hear this call.

"Alouette Organization," came the cheery voice.

"The general manager, please."

"I'm afraid he's in a meeting. Can I take a message?"

"If you could ask him to step out for a moment, this won't take long."

Gamache explained who he was, and a minute or so later the phone was picked up.

They talked for less than a minute. When Gamache hung up, he thought for a moment, then returned to the table.

Olivier and Gabri had left, and now, as they ate, the Sûreté officers compared notes.

"So this Gerald Bertrand denies knowing Vivienne Godin," said Beauvoir.

"*Oui.*" Lacoste picked up an egg salad sandwich on a fresh baguette, spiked with just a little curry, poached raisins, and arugula. "He says it was a wrong number. Says she was slurring her words and upset. Probably drunk."

Beauvoir casually reached out and took the peanut butter, honey, and banana sandwich on crusty white bread after noticing Cloutier also eyeing it.

"Not drunk," said Gamache. "Beaten. The coroner's report says she'd had a few ounces, but not intoxication level." He passed around hard copies of the preliminary report. "The slurring was probably from being hit."

He put down his sandwich.

"Nothing more from Dr. Harris?" asked Lacoste after quickly scanning the coroner's report.

Beauvoir checked the emails again and shook his head. "Nothing. What else did you find?"

"Gerald Bertrand's alibi checks out," said Agent Cloutier. "His friends confirm they were over at his place watching the hockey game on Saturday night. They arrived just before seven. None of them knew anything about Bertrand having an affair with Vivienne Godin. In fact, none had even heard of her."

"The other thing is the baby," said Lacoste. "He was looking after his niece until six on Saturday night. Not much time to meet Vivienne on the bridge and get home before his friends arrived."

"You don't think it was him, do you?" said Beauvoir, sitting back in his chair and taking a large bite of the sandwich.

"No," admitted Lacoste. "I think logistically it would've been tough, but I also believe he's telling the truth. I saw him with his niece. He likes kids. I think if his lover had told him she was pregnant, he might not have been thrilled, but he wouldn't have killed her and the baby."

Gamache looked at Beauvoir to continue the questioning but saw he was struggling to chew the sandwich, his mouth apparently glued almost shut.

"So the other possibility is that he was telling the truth," said Gamache, picking up the mantle. "He didn't know her. Which means Vivienne was calling the wrong number. But over and over?"

"Looks like it."

"I wonder who she was trying to call?" he said. "They were made in a cluster, right? At six fifteen."

"Starting then. There were four calls over ten minutes. All to Bertrand's number."

"Strange to have called the same wrong number over and over," said Gamache. "Once, maybe, if you hit the wrong button. We've all done it. But to make the same mistake over and over? Even if disoriented you'd think she'd hit different numbers."

"What do you think it means?" asked Lacoste.

Once again Gamache looked at Beauvoir, who was now regretting not the sandwich itself but taking such a huge bite. Jean-Guy chewed more vigorously and gestured to Gamache to continue.

"I think," he said, "that Vivienne was given a number to call but had written it down wrong. So while she was dialing correctly, she didn't realize she was calling the wrong number. Was there a piece of paper found on her body, with a number?"

"No," said Lacoste. "In her wallet we found paper, but it was wet through. Disintegrated."

"Nothing legible?"

"No."

"But that explains why she kept making the same mistake," said Cloutier, nodding. "She wrote it down wrong and didn't realize that. So who did she think she was calling?"

"I'm not willing to give up on Bertrand yet," said Beauvoir, finally swallowing. "What you say is true. She can't have made exactly the same mistake over and over. So maybe it wasn't a mistake at all. She meant to call Bertrand and did. We have no idea what she actually said to him. Someone met her on that bridge, and she'd have had to arrange it. I think he's lying. I'll put an agent on his place."

"There is something else," said Lacoste. "Something Agent Cloutier here discovered."

She turned, like a proud parent, to the older woman.

This was the accountant's moment to shine. Lysette Cloutier gathered her notes.

"Vivienne Godin might be having an affair, but her husband certainly was."

"How do you know?" asked Beauvoir.

"The internet," said Cloutier.

"Wikipedia?" asked Beauvoir, half joking, half dreading the answer.

"*Non*," laughed Cloutier. "Google."

Beauvoir opened his mouth, but Lacoste jumped in. "Let her explain."

"Since Tracey doesn't have internet at home," said Cloutier, "but does have a website and a social-media presence, it seemed pretty obvious someone was doing it for him, so I tracked down the IP address and found her. I then went onto his public Instagram account and convinced her to give me access to their private account."

"How did you do that?" asked Beauvoir.

"I set up a dummy website and Instagram account. NouveauGalerie. Said I was a gallery owner looking for new artists. I needed to communicate in private and to see more of Carl Tracey's work."

"So she gave you access to their private account, not knowing who you were?" said Gamache.

"Smart," said Beauvoir.

"*Merci.*" She smiled and looked at Isabelle Lacoste, who nodded encouragement. "This's what I found."

She turned her laptop around for Beauvoir and Gamache to see the photos of Tracey and Vachon together. It was obvious they were lovers.

They scrolled through the pictures and read the private messages between Carl Tracey and Pauline Vachon.

"Look at this one," said Cloutier. "*She's a drunken slut. You deserve better.* That's from Pauline. Pretty clear."

"Of an affair," said Gamache. "Maybe. But murder?"

"Look here, *patron*," said Lacoste. "On the day of the murder."

Both Beauvoir and Gamache leaned closer to the laptop as she found the posts sent Saturday around midday.

*Stuff's in the bag. Everything's ready. Will be done tonight. I promise.* That from Carl Tracey.

And Pauline Vachon's reply: *Finally. Good luck. Don't mess it up.*

Beauvoir sat back and exhaled. "*I promise.* Jesus. So this Vachon was in on it."

"More than that," said Lacoste. "I think it was her idea."

"Well, her encouragement anyway," said Gamache.

"Enough to charge her with being an accomplice," said Beauvoir.

"Is it enough to arrest him for murder?" asked Cloutier.

"I doubt it," said Lacoste, and she turned to Beauvoir. "What do you think?"

"I think it's turning into a very strong circumstantial case. And that might be the best we can do. Any jury would be able to follow this evidence directly to Tracey. The admitted abuse, these photos and posts clearly showing he was having an affair, the fact, admitted here, that he packed her bag." He stopped to think. "That might explain the summer clothes. He just took things at random or maybe took things he knew Vivienne wouldn't miss."

"To make it look like she'd decided to leave on her own," said Cloutier.

"Tracey even told this Pauline that it was happening that night," said Beauvoir. "Doesn't get more incriminating than that, the dumb shit. Well done, Cloutier."

"*Merci.*"

"Have you spoken to this Pauline Vachon?" asked Beauvoir.

"*Non,*" said Lacoste. "I wanted to see if there was more that Agent Cloutier could get out of her, posing as the gallery owner."

Beauvoir was nodding. Considering.

He used to kid Gamache when he'd find him at his desk, staring into space. The Chief would patiently explain that being still and doing nothing were two different things.

Now Beauvoir stared into space while his mind worked.

This was no time for a misstep. It seemed Pauline Vachon was key. If they could get her to turn on Tracey, testify against him, in exchange for a deal, they had their case.

"Is he okay?" Cloutier whispered to Lacoste, who couldn't suppress a smile.

"He's thinking."

"Looks like he has a headache."

"Let me tell you," said Beauvoir, slightly annoyed, "what I think might've happened that night."

As he spoke, the others saw clearly what he was describing.

"Suppose Tracey beat Vivienne, maybe into unconsciousness, then went to get piss drunk before finishing her off. He might've even thought she was already dead. While he was gone, she came to and made those calls to Bertrand. Pleading for help. Maybe telling him to meet her on the bridge. Tracey hears and sees an opportunity. Much better than putting her body in the woods. He decides to follow her, with the duffel bag he'd packed. Once there, he pushes her off. Vivienne reaches out to stop herself, making that deep cut in her palm from the rotten wood. Then Tracey tosses the bag in after her and leaves. The heavy rain washes away all the footprints and tire marks."

Done.

That was the scenario he'd take to the Crown Prosecutor when the time came. Unless something showed up to contradict it. Which he doubted.

"And Bertrand?" asked Lacoste.

"Doesn't show up." He nodded. It fit. "But let's keep digging. I want to go for premeditation. Those posts prove first-degree, but I want more."

He looked around the table.

Gamache nodded. He also wanted first-degree but felt somewhat comforted knowing if all else failed, they probably had enough circumstantial evidence right now to convict Tracey of manslaughter.

But still, a few things perplexed him.

"It's strange that Madame Vachon would let you see those private messages," he said, returning to the laptop. "Even if she didn't know you're with the Sûreté."

"She might've forgotten they were there," said Lacoste. "And unless you knew they were planning a murder, you wouldn't guess from those posts. On the surface, they could be about anything."

"*Oui,*" said Gamache. "And that could be a problem."

"One thing I don't understand," said Beauvoir, leaning forward and putting his elbows on the table, "is how Tracey managed to send those messages if he doesn't have internet at home."

"You can log into an account from anywhere," said Cloutier. "He must've been in town and used someone else's device or an internet café. I'll see if I can track down where they originated."

Beauvoir paused to study the posts again.

*Stuff's in the bag. Everything's ready. Will be done tonight. I promise.*

"I don't want to blow this," said Beauvoir. "It needs to stick."

Lacoste was nodding. "It will."

"On another issue, I'd like to release Monsieur Godin," said Gamache.

"But," said Cloutier, "won't he—"

"Try to kill Tracey?" said Gamache. "Maybe. But I'm hoping we can convince him that an arrest is imminent. That putting Tracey through a trial and then in prison is far worse than killing him."

"Would you?" Cloutier asked. "Be convinced?"

Gamache stared at her. She turned beet red and stammered an apology.

"I'm sorry, sir, it's just that I know you have a daughter about Vivienne's age, and I thought—"

"Don't presume, Agent Cloutier," he said, his voice uncharacteristically hard. Showing Lacoste and Beauvoir, who knew him well, that while Cloutier's comment was inappropriate, she had indeed hit a nerve.

While they studied him, Gamache studied Agent Cloutier.

He realized that something about her made him wary. And he knew Jean-Guy felt the same way.

While it was obvious that his love for his own daughter had created an emotional frisson about this case, it was equally obvious that Lysette Cloutier cared very deeply for Homer Godin. Perhaps too deeply.

But did that matter?

And was it even true? Could her protectiveness toward him not be the natural instincts of a close friend?

That was one of the problems with being a homicide cop. Interpreting innocent, even admirable, acts as somehow suspicious. Once that started happening, it was hard to change the perception.

"I'd like you to come with me," he said to Cloutier. "You might be able to help calm Monsieur Godin. Talk sense into him."

"I'll try," she said. *"Merci."*

She seemed to think it was a peace offering, never dreaming this courteous senior officer might have other motives for asking her along.

"Is this all right with you?" Gamache asked Beauvoir.

"Can we talk?" Beauvoir jerked his head toward the window at the far end of the room, away from the others.

Gamache followed him, and despite himself he felt, if not annoyed, then perplexed, and he realized with some amusement that he'd asked Beauvoir out of consideration, not expecting he might actually disagree.

As they walked to the window, Beauvoir heard the Chief's footsteps. Familiar yet foreign. He was used to hearing them in front of him. Leading. Not behind, following.

This was not getting any easier, he realized. He'd certainly disagreed with Gamache in the past, sometimes arguing quite forcefully. But he'd always understood that the final word would be Gamache's. As would the responsibility.

But now it was his. He was in charge. The decisions, and responsibility, were his.

He turned and faced his mentor and father-in-law.

"Cloutier's right. Homer Godin's gonna try to kill Tracey. You know that. I think you're making a mistake."

He watched Gamache closely. And saw him nod.

"Would you rather we didn't release Monsieur Godin?"

Jean-Guy relaxed and realized Armand Gamache would not make this difficult. "I'd like to understand your reasoning."

Gamache considered Beauvoir for a moment. His protégé, now his boss.

He remembered the first time he'd seen the younger man. They met at the outpost where Agent Beauvoir had been assigned straight out of the academy. He'd been placed, by the station commander, in the basement evidence locker because none of the other agents liked working with the arrogant, cocky, disgruntled new guy.

Agent Beauvoir was composing his letter of resignation, in which he'd tell them, yet again, what he really thought of them, when the famed head of homicide for the Sûreté showed up to investigate a murder.

The station commander had assigned this difficult young agent to help the Chief Inspector, in hopes that he'd run afoul of either Gamache or the killer, and one or the other would rid them of the problem that was Jean-Guy Beauvoir.

Gamache had stared through the bars at the caged young man. Beauvoir had stared back.

And they'd recognized each other.

From lifetimes past. From battlegrounds past.

And on the spot, to the shock of everyone except himself, Chief Inspector Gamache had hired the unruly young agent. The human refuse no one else wanted. Eventually promoting him, several years later, to be his second-in-command.

And now this would be their final investigation together. As Jean-Guy broke free and Armand let him go.

It would be, if Gamache had anything to do with it, a successful end to a courageous career.

But they weren't over the finish line yet.

"Why would you even consider letting Monsieur Godin go," Beauvoir was saying, "before we've arrested Tracey? Knowing what he planned to do. Unless—"

Beauvoir stopped. Almost in time.

"Unless?" asked Gamache, and once again Jean-Guy could feel the natural authority of the man. It radiated off him. "You think I want him to kill Tracey?"

"*Non*, not at all. It's just . . . honestly?" said Jean-Guy. "Between us? I can understand how Homer feels. And obviously you do, too. If we couldn't convict Tracey, if he walked free, I'd be tempted to just step aside and let him do it."

Gamache tilted his head and stared at his son-in-law.

"Don't tell me that you wouldn't be tempted, too," said Beauvoir.

"Tempted, maybe. I honestly don't know what I'd do, Jean-Guy. But I hope to God not that."

"So why do you want to let him go now?"

"I'm worried that holding him any longer will just make things worse. My reason for detaining him was to give him a cooling-off period. When he couldn't do anything. But if it lasts much longer, instead of cooling off, his anger will heat up. I agree that letting him go is a risk, but so's keeping him in jail. Besides, it's just not right."

Beauvoir thought about it, glancing out the window at the Bella Bella and the sandbags lining the river. At the ones still standing and the ones fallen down.

So close to tragedy. It didn't really take much to tip the balance.

"Okay. Let him out. I'll have an agent watch his place and follow him if he leaves."

"You won't have to. I was thinking of inviting Monsieur Godin to stay with us. His things are already here. And that way I can keep an eye on him. Besides, he shouldn't be alone."

"Is that smart?"

"Probably not," said Gamache with a small laugh. "Is it my first choice? *Non*. But sometimes you have to do something stupid."

Beauvoir laughed. "I never thought I'd hear you say that. Sounds more like something I'd say."

"Guess you're rubbing off on me, *patron*." Gamache smiled, then it faded. "Am I my brother's keeper?"

"He's not your brother," said Jean-Guy.

"*Non*, that's true. And Vivienne isn't Annie. But still, I'd want someone to do this for me, to watch over me, if . . ."

If Annie . . . If Reine-Marie . . .

Beauvoir considered and realized that if anything happened to Annie. . . . To Honoré . . .

Someone would have to do the same for him.

"Agreed, *patron*," he said. "By the way, who were you talking to in the store room?"

"The Montreal Alouettes."

"What did they say about Cameron? Why'd they let him go?"

"Too many penalties. He was a good player but was costing them yards."

"Roughing?" asked Beauvoir.

"I'd have thought so, but no. Holding. Apparently it was almost a reflex of his, to grab hold of something and not let go. They couldn't break him of it."

As Gamache walked to the car, listening to Agent Cloutier go on excitedly about continuing to string Pauline Vachon along in hopes of getting more evidence, he felt some anxiety stir.

It wasn't the slight sour feeling he'd had in his gut earlier. The worry they wouldn't be able to nail Tracey. That was still there, but less and less as the evidence mounted and now threatened to bury Carl Tracey.

This was something else. A prickling at the back of his neck.

Something was wrong. A mistake had been made, or was about to be made.

"Who's that?" asked Myrna, nodding toward a car just arriving in Three Pines as Armand's vehicle left.

"Probably more Sûreté," said Clara. "They've set up in the old railway station again."

"Huh," said Myrna. "It's stopped in front of your house."

"Really?" said Clara, turning to take a closer look.

"Is that who you've been looking for?" Reine-Marie asked Ruth. The elderly poet had been glancing out the bistro window all morning.

Now Ruth was smiling as she, too, watched the car arrive.

"What've you done?" asked Myrna.

"You'll see." Ruth turned to Clara. "You might want to go say hello."

A young woman was just getting out of the car.

"Why?" asked Clara, not at all liking the satisfied expression on the old woman's face.

"*All that most maddens and torments,*" said Ruth. "*All that stirs up the lees of things. Moby-Dick.*"

"Have you stirred up the lees of things?" Myrna asked.

Ruth was so pleased with herself she was almost exploding with pleasure. It was not an attractive sight.

As they watched, the stranger knocked on Clara's door and, getting no answer, turned to look around.

And Clara recognized her. "Oh, God, Ruth. What've you done?"

"Your white whale," said Ruth, triumphant. "Thar she blows."

# CHAPTER TWENTY-FIVE

—

@CarlTracey: I've put up more pictures of Carl's work for you to see.

@NouveauGalerie: Who's this? I thought I was communicating with Tracey.

@CarlTracey: Pauline Vachon. Carl's partner.

@NouveauGalerie: Business or life partner?

@CarlTracey: Does it matter?

@CarlTracey: Hello?

@CarlTracey: Hello?

@CarlTracey: Both.

Gamache sat on the cot across from Homer Godin while Lysette Cloutier stood by the open door to the holding cell.

Homer looked sick. Gaunt. His eyes were bloodshot and puffy, his face blotched. Bright red in places, white, almost green, in others.

"We've come to release you," said Gamache. "If you promise not to do anything to Carl Tracey."

"Or yourself," said Cloutier.

Homer continued to stare at his large hands, hanging limp between his knees.

When he finally spoke, his voice was remote. "I can't promise."

"Then I can't release you," said Gamache. He leaned forward and dropped his voice even further, so that Homer had to also lean forward. Had to make some small effort.

Which he did.

"You can do this," Armand said softly.

"There's only one thing I want to do."

That sat between them. The silence stretching on. Until Homer finally broke it himself, lifting his eyes to Armand's.

"How'm I gonna go on?"

Armand placed his hand on Homer's. "You'll come stay with us. We'll keep you safe."

"Really?"

And for a moment, a split second, Armand saw a glimmer amid the gloom. And then it was gone.

"I can't come to your house."

"Why not?"

The two men were quiet for a moment before Homer spoke again.

"You've been kind. Your wife—" Homer lifted his hand to his own face. "I'm sorry. I didn't mean to . . ."

"I know. She knows. Are you worried about doing it again?"

Homer shook his head. "No. Never. But if I stay with you, I'll hurt you in other ways. When I kill Tracey, they'll blame you."


"And what's this?"

Dominica Oddly went to lift the corner of the canvas, but Clara stopped her.

"Something I'm working on."

"A portrait?"

"Sort of."

Clara's uninvited guest raised her brows in a way that would be comical, cartoonish, if it weren't so terrifying.

Ruth Zardo had somehow managed to convince the art critic for the online journal *Odd* to come from Brooklyn to Québec. To come into the countryside, to Three Pines. To come into Clara's home. Where Clara, against every instinct, had invited her into her studio.

Seemed courtesy beat good sense. Almost to death.

"Come," Dominica Oddly said after an all-too-cursory glance around.

She indicated the shabby sofa against the wall of Clara's studio. They sat side by side, the young woman turning her lithe body to Clara.

She was dressed in sort of harem pants, with combat boots and a T-shirt that read YES, HE'S A RACIST.

Clara doubted she'd passed thirty. Her hair was in long dreadlocks. Her face was unlined and unblemished. No piercings and, from what Clara could see, no tattoos. She didn't need those to prove she was cool. She just was. So cool that Clara felt goose bumps rise on her forearms.

To say Dominica Oddly was a rainmaker was to vastly underestimate her power. Clara knew that the woman sitting next to her didn't just make rain, she made the whole goddamned environment. She could cause the sun to shine on your career. Or a tsunami to sweep your life's work away.

She had an eye for the avant-garde, an ear for undercurrents, and, perhaps above all else, a savant's gift for social media.

Oddly had understood early that those platforms were the new "high ground." The place from which attacks could be launched. Territory could be captured. Where hearts were influenced and opinions made.

Her online journal, *Odd*, had millions of subscribers while still managing to position itself as underground, even subversive. Dominica Oddly was like some hipster oligarch.

Clara subscribed to *Odd*, and every morning over coffee she read Dominica's daily column.

Oddly's pithy, articulate, often cruel, always elegant prose both amused and appalled Clara, as the critic stripped away the artifice in the art world. Ruthlessly.

*All truth with malice in it.*

But, despite Clara's rise, Dominica Oddly had never reviewed her works. As far as Clara knew, Oddly had no idea she existed. She'd never met the woman and certainly had never seen her at one of her shows.

Every artist, every gallery owner, every agent, every collector scanned the horizon for Dominica Oddly.

And here she was. In Clara's studio. Amid half-finished canvases, empty yogurt containers. A banana peel lay flopped on the arm of the sofa. Clara shoved it off with her elbow, but not fast enough for the keen, and disconcertingly amused, eyes of the critic.

Ruth was right when she'd described this young woman as her white whale. The one she sought. The one she dreamed of landing.

But where Ahab was obsessed with vengeance, Clara was not. There was nothing to avenge. Clara really just wanted Oddly to notice her. To acknowledge her. Okay, and to love and laud her art.

Now that she had the critic's attention, Clara began to see something else. The size of the creature, and what would happen if it turned on her.

But it was too late. The white whale was in her home. In her studio. On the sofa kneading Leo's ears.

With her latest show taking so many hits, one from this woman would be enough to sink Clara Morrow.

"Cake?" she asked, and saw Dominica Oddly smile. It was a nice smile. A nice face.

It was the sort of look that happened just before you're eaten, Clara thought.


"I don't think you can stop me."

Annie's father had no doubt that Vivienne's father was right. He probably couldn't stop him.

Homer Godin would leave this jail cell and spend the rest of his life trying to kill the man he could not name.

And, once done, Homer would almost certainly then kill himself.

"Suppose you didn't."

"*Pardon?*"

"Suppose you didn't kill Tracey," Gamache repeated. "What would your life look like?"

The question, so simple, seemed to stump Godin. It was like asking him, Suppose you could fly. Suppose you became invisible. Suppose you didn't kill the man who just murdered your daughter.

He was asking Vivienne's father to consider the inconceivable.

"Think about it while I do the paperwork."

Chief Inspector Gamache got up and left, taking Cloutier with him and leaving Godin alone with thoughts that inevitably circled back to his daughter. He saw her face as she fell, backward. Off the bridge. Arms pinwheeling.

And then the splash.

He rammed shut his eyes until all he saw was darkness. Then Vivienne's face floated up, to hover just below the surface.

Accusing.


"It's in," said Isabelle Lacoste, grabbing a chair across from Beauvoir in the incident room.

No need to say what "it" was.

Beauvoir quickly clicked over to his email and opened the document from the coroner, with the attachment.

Both scanned it, then went back to the top and read more closely. Their faces, their expressions, almost exactly the same.

At first triumphant. And then perplexed.


"I do this because I love art. I love the whole world of art. Being around people who are creative and daring."

As she spoke, Dominica's face became almost luminous. Her voice, while deep, was also light, bright.

"I search the world for people who have a true muse and not just some insatiable hole in their soul they need to fill with fame and money. And when I find the real thing . . ."

Her entire face opened, in unguarded delight. An awe rarely seen in the cluttered world of ego and fear and greed that was the international art scene.

"I take aim at the poseurs and try to lift up those who create from their very being." Dominica's hand, clenched into a fist, thumped her breastbone and stayed there. "Those who are daring and brave and willing to be vulnerable. Like you."

"Me?" said Clara.

"Yes, you." Dominica laughed, and Clara almost tumbled forward into her arms, so magnetic was the woman. And so welcome the words.

"If you feel like that," said Clara, "why haven't you reviewed any of my shows?"


"Did you hear what he said? And you're still going to let him out?" asked Cloutier, following Gamache across the open room to Cameron's desk.

It didn't warrant a reply, so Gamache did not offer one.

Agent Cameron saw them coming and rose. "Sir."

"I'd like to start the paperwork to release Homer Godin."

"Yessir. I was expecting that, so I've filled it in."

Gamache scanned the page. No charges filed. As far as the law was concerned, Homer Godin was never in a jail cell. It had never happened.

As the officer who'd brought Godin in, Cameron would have to countersign the release.

"Can you redo this, please, but remove your name."

"But I was the—"

"I know." Gamache held his eyes. Unwavering. "Just do it."

Though confused, Cameron sat back down and redid the paperwork while Chief Inspector Gamache tore up the evidence that Agent Cameron had anything to do with releasing a man who'd vowed murder.

He then signed the new form so that his name, and his name alone, would be seen.

"Now," said Gamache, dropping the pen, "we'll let Monsieur Godin out in a few minutes. First, tell us what you've found out about Tracey's movements on Saturday."

"Turned out to be quite easy," said Cameron. "He was in Sherbrooke at an art-supply shop. Apparently that's where he gets most of his clay and other things he needs. His bank card shows a purchase there at eleven forty."

"Roughly the same time as the posts," said Cloutier.

"What did he buy?"

"A bag of clay, some glazes," said Cameron.

Gamache nodded. They'd found unopened clay wrapped in plastic and new pots of glaze in Tracey's studio.

"I've also been to the local pharmacist about the abortion drug. She has no account for Vivienne Godin or Carl Tracey and confirms that bottle is black-market."

"Why would Vivienne need to get it on the black market?" asked Cloutier. "She could get it for free, right?"

"With a prescription, *oui*," said Cameron. "If you don't have one—"

"Or you want to terminate a pregnancy too far along," said Gamache.

"—then you go on the black market to get the drug."

"Mail order?" asked Gamache, and said a quiet prayer.

"Many are, but the pharmacist didn't think so in this case. Buyers are beginning to realize that while pushers might not be the most reliable people, mail order is even worse. I know a few dealers. People we've dealt with in the past. Want to come?"

Gamache looked in the direction of the holding cell where Godin waited. The abortion drug could be one of the keys to the case against Tracey. If it turned out he was the one who'd bought it. It could strengthen their argument that he wanted to end the pregnancy, one way or the other.

"*Non*. There're other things I need to do. But let me know as soon as you have any information."

"*Oui, patron*," said Cameron, pushing back from his desk.

"Good." Gamache brought out his iPhone. "Give me your cell number."

Cameron did.

As Gamache was putting it in, his own phone vibrated with a call.

"*Excusez-moi*." He took a few steps away.

"Coroner's report is in," said Beauvoir. "They found spores in her hand. An exact match for the ones on the rotten wood."

Gamache exhaled. They'd just taken a big step closer to making an arrest.

"This proves she was on the bridge," said Beauvoir. "And she died trying to save herself."

"*Oui*. But we still need to place Tracey there. And prove it wasn't an accident."

"We're going over Tracey's clothes to see if we can find any of the microorganisms. The forensics team found something else, *patron*.

When they moved her car, they found boot prints. They'd been protected from the rain by the car."

"Are they a match for Tracey's boots?" asked Gamache.

"They're looking now."

"Good, good," said Gamache, his thoughts moving quickly ahead. Is it enough? Is it enough?

He made up his mind.

"I'm going to hold Godin for another couple of hours until you find out more. By then—"

"We might have enough to nail Tracey. I think it's time we brought Pauline Vachon in."

"Agreed."

"I've applied for a warrant to search her place while she's being questioned," said Beauvoir. "As soon as it comes through, I'll have her picked up. Isabelle will interview her at the station. She'd like Cloutier there. Any news from your end?"

"Agent Cameron has a lead on the abortion drug found in Vivienne's bag. Definitely black-market. I'm hoping we can get proof that Tracey bought it."

"About that," said Beauvoir. "We have news on the fetus."

Gamache listened, his eyes narrowing as he absorbed the information. When Beauvoir finished, Gamache simply said, *"Merci."*

"What is it, *patron*?" asked Cloutier, seeing his expression after he'd hung up.

Gamache paused for a moment, staring at the blank wall in front of him. His lips were pressed together in concentration. Then he clicked his device off and slipped it into his pocket.

"Superintendent Lacoste will be by in a few minutes," he said, striding back to the desk. "We're bringing in Pauline Vachon."

"But there's more I can get from her private Instagram account," said Cloutier. "I'm sure of it."

When he turned to her, she was surprised to see that the anxiety that had flitted across his face a few moments ago was gone, replaced by a smile.

"You've done a good job. It's only because of you we've found Madame Vachon and the pictures. And the damning messages. Chief

240

Inspector Beauvoir feels we have enough, and I agree with him. Now the job will be to turn her. Pay attention to Superintendent Lacoste. Learn from her. She'll lead the interrogation. You'll be there to support."

It wasn't lost on either Cloutier or Cameron that he'd said "interrogation." Not "interview."

They were almost there. They could see the finish line. It was just a matter now of dashing across it. Without falling.

"And Homer?"

"Let Monsieur Godin know he'll be released soon. Agent Cameron, I'll come with you after all. Chief Inspector Beauvoir will meet us there."

"*Oui, patron.*"

As they made for the door, Cameron reached behind him, to double-check that he had his gun. He knew he did, but best to be certain. Besides, touching it was a comfort.

But he noticed, as he followed Gamache, that the Chief Inspector was not carrying a weapon.

He wondered if he should say something. Remind him that drug dealers were dangerous. But then he remembered who this man was and what he'd seen. And what he'd done.

Chief Inspector Gamache did not need to be schooled. He was the principal.


Beauvoir stood at his desk in the incident room in Three Pines and checked his belt.

The gun, as always, was there.

He wondered if he'd feel naked going into work every day as a senior executive at the engineering firm in Paris without this accessory.

Jean-Guy Beauvoir quite liked the feel of it. The heft. The ability to just pull back his jacket and expose it. To see people's eyes widen.

The gun on his belt meant not simply safety but power. Though just lately, something odd had begun to happen.

It had felt heavier. More awkward. Less natural. The gun had begun to feel foreign.

Was this how it had started with Gamache? Surely as a young agent, as an inspector, even, he'd worn a gun? At what stage had he taken it off?

When does a cucumber become a pickle? It was the question Gamache sometimes asked when contemplating human behavior. And now Jean-Guy asked himself that.

When does change occur? Change that is irreversible.

At some point guns had become, for Armand Gamache, a necessary evil. But still, and undoubtedly, evil.

Gamache had knelt beside too many corpses. Had made too many.

Had reached behind him and pulled the weapon from its holster. Had swung it up, steadied his hand. Pointed. And Armand Gamache had fired. Into another human being.

Felt the recoil. Smelled the discharge. Seen the body drop. The person drop.

Someone's son, daughter, husband, father.

It was a terrible, terrible thing to have to do.

Seeing the bullet strike was almost as bad as feeling it hit, as Jean-Guy knew too well. Being lifted into the air by the impact. The shock. The pain. The terror.

That was almost as bad as seeing colleagues go down. Gunned down.

Seeing Gamache himself hit. Lifted off the ground. And collapse.

Jean-Guy Beauvoir pushed that image, that memory, away. Unable still to really face it. Face the fact he himself had done it once. Had seen Gamache through his sights and fired. Felt the report. Smelled the discharge.

Seen him rise and watched him fall.

It was the worst moment of Jean-Guy Beauvoir's life. And it had changed his life.

His hand now closed briefly over the holster, but instead of feeling the usual reassurance, he felt a wave of revulsion.

And he knew, in his gut, it was time to leave. He'd done his bit, done his best.

Time to take a job where the only weapon was his mind. Where there were no victims, only clients. And no suspects, only competitors. Where everyone who started the day with a heartbeat ended the day with one.

Or, if not, it wasn't his doing.

But he wasn't there yet. Soon. Just this one, last case. Jean-Guy Beauvoir just had to get across the finish line.

Instead of answering Clara's question, why she'd never reviewed her shows, Dominica Oddly had hauled herself out of the sofa and was wandering around the studio. Nodding as she took in the collection of stuff.

A jumble of old works. Failed and abandoned pieces sat beside finished and lauded portraits. There were stones and twisted tree roots. Feathers and sticks and assorted broken eggs, fallen from nests. It was as though Clara had left the door to her studio wide open and the wilderness had blown in.

Oddly took a deep breath and closed her eyes. The studio smelled of oil paint and turpentine and wet dog. And something else.

Clara had given up trying to look sophisticated and had rolled off the low sofa onto her hands and knees, and now she got to her feet with a grunt.

To Clara's horror, Oddly had stopped in front of a collection of dusty ceramic pieces. And was taking photographs.

"What do you call these?" she asked.

"Warrior Uteruses."

Oddly laughed. A deep, rich rumbling sound that filled the space with genuine amusement.

"Perfect. Have you shown them?"

"They're old. I did them maybe ten years ago," Clara explained. "Showed them once."

"And?"

"Not a success."

Oddly nodded, clearly not surprised. Then she turned back to Clara. "I've been to all your shows, you know. Privately."

She walked over to the small portrait lounging against the wall. The one of Ruth. The old woman glared back at the young woman, her whole being filled with rage and pain, with bitterness and disappointment. Ruth gripped her worn blue shawl at her scrawny throat and looked out at a world that had left her behind.

"I didn't get it at first," Dominica admitted, as though talking directly to the old woman. "Didn't see what others saw. All I saw were portraits done in a predictable, conventional style. Granted, the subjects were interesting, but that struck me as a sort of cheat. A shorthand to cover up for a lack of technique. A lack of depth."

Dominica Oddly turned away for a moment, to look at Clara, and then returned her gaze to the portrait.

"I had my review all written. Scathing. I especially hated her."

She lifted her chin toward Ruth. Who clearly hated her right back.

"But something stopped me from publishing it. I decided to reserve judgment. I went to all your other shows and slowly, slowly began to see."

"See what?"

"That I was wrong. But more than that. I saw why. When I looked at your portraits, I saw the work of a middle-class, middle-aged white woman, living in middle-of-nowhere Canada. Working in a traditional, conventional medium. I was prejudiced. I couldn't believe that you, Clara Morrow, could come out of nowhere and possibly rock the art establishment. But you have."

She turned back to Ruth.

"This's the woman who contacted me about your work, right? Who convinced me to come here, isn't it? This's the poet, Ruth Zardo?"

"Yes."

She nodded, her dreadlocks bouncing on her shoulders.

"*Who hurt you once, so far beyond repair?*" She muttered the words of Ruth's most famous poem, then looked at Clara. "You painted her as the Virgin Mary. The mother of God. Forgotten, bitter, filled with despair. Which would have been amazing enough. Without—" She reached up her hand and pointed. At a small white dot in the rheumy eye. "That."

It was the smallest hint of light. In a soul that had known much too much darkness.

"No fraud could do that. Once I saw that, I revisited all your other paintings and saw what you were really doing. You're subversive, my friend. A sort of artistic agent provocateur. Appearing to be one thing while actually being something else. Something quite extraordinary. Undermining all conventions. You don't just paint people, you capture them. Make them give you their emotions. Not just despair and hope but joy. Hatred. Jealousy. Love. Contentment. Rage. How you managed to capture belonging is beyond me, but you did. The Three Graces? I actually wept. I stood in front of it, all alone in the gallery, crying. I still don't know why it made me cry." She turned to Clara. "Do you?"

"I don't know," she said quietly. "But I think you do."

Dominica smiled and gave a single grunt of either laughter or recognition.

"I saw your latest exhibition," said Dominica. "In the cooperative collection of miniatures at the Brooklyn Art Space. Very generous of you, by the way, to agree to show with unknowns."

Clara closed her eyes briefly. This was it. Finally. She had what she wanted. Needed. Dominica Oddly would tell the art world, all the naysayers and trolls and shits who'd turned on her, that they were wrong. Clara Morrow was a force within the art community.

Clara Morrow would get her revenge.

"Thank you," she said. "You must know how important this is to me. You've seen all the horrible things people have said on social media. My own home gallery is threatening to drop me. People are saying I'm a . . . what did you just call it . . . ?"

"A poseur. A fraud."

"Yes. A fake. But a good review from you would change all that. Would stop all the attacks."

"I've seen what they're writing, yes."

Then a thought occurred to Clara. Dominica was, for all her confidence, still young. Maybe she's afraid that if she voices a dissenting opinion, she'll lose credibility.

"I have no problem telling it like it is," Oddly said, as though reading her thoughts. "Going against popular opinion. It's one of my favorite things to do."

"Then why haven't you posted? Why wait to defend me? Damage is being done."

"Because I don't disagree."

"Pardon?"

"Your miniatures are appalling, Clara. Trite. Predictable. A blunder."

She turned back to the Warrior Uteruses. "I admire an artist for trying something different," and then she looked at Clara again. "But your miniatures show not just a shocking lack of technique but an almost insulting lack of depth, of effort. They're cowardly."

Clara stood stock-still in her studio.

"I was about to publish the review when Ruth Zardo's invitation arrived. I decided to wait until I saw you. Until I had a chance to look you in the eye. And thank you personally for your previous work, and tell you how I feel about your latest. I think all those people posting are right. You're insulting those who once loved your work, who once supported you. You're insulting the art world. And, worst of all, you've squandered, cheapened your talent. Betrayed the gift you were given. And that's a travesty. No real artist would do that, could do that."

She brought a piece of paper out of her pocket. "Here."

As she held it out to Clara, she caught, again, that elusive scent. Below the oils, below the turpentine, the wet dog, the old bananas.

It was lemon. Not the sour smell but the fresh, sweet scent of lemon meringue pie.

Clara reached for the paper, even as she felt the thrashing and heard the crunch of bones.

# CHAPTER TWENTY-SIX

⌒

Catch this video. Sick. **#GamacheSux**

Heard Odd about to post review of Morrow stinkers. Finally.
**#ClaraMorrowSucks**

**@CarlTracey:** Carl, trying to reach you. What's happening?
Call me.

Information was coming in quickly now.

Sitting in his car on rue Principale in Cowansville, Jean-Guy Beauvoir scanned the messages from his agents.

Smiling, he clicked the phone closed and got out to join Gamache, who'd sent him the address and had just arrived himself outside the pizza joint.

"The boot prints match Tracey's," said Beauvoir without preamble.

"*Bon,*" said Gamache. "It's all coming together."

"They're in there," said Cameron, coming around the corner to join them.

He pointed to an old low-rise apartment building.

"Used to be a crack house, run by the mother of one of the kids. We busted her, but the kid now runs his own operation out of there. Not crack but black-market shit."

"Kid?" asked Gamache.

"Minor. Fifteen. Name's Toby."

There was a character in a book Beauvoir read to his son every night named Toby. A mischievous boy with a pet balloon.

Honoré found the adventures of Toby and his balloon hilarious.

Jean-Guy found them strangely moving, as the boy struggled mightily to protect his vulnerable friend. And no matter what happened, to never let go.

"He runs a gang of kids dealing mostly prescription meds, painkillers. But other stuff, too. We catch them, but they're on the street again in no time. Don't be fooled by their age."

"We aren't," said Beauvoir.

They followed Cameron into the building.

The place reeked of damp and mold and rot. The chipped concrete stairs were sticky.

They climbed up one flight, but just as Cameron stepped onto the landing, there was a sharp whistle and the sound of footsteps racing on the floor above.

"Shit," said Cameron, and ran up the stairs, taking them two at a time, followed by Gamache.

Beauvoir, though, seeing where this was going, ran downstairs, out the front door, and into the side alley, scanning for the back door.

There was a loud bang as a door flew open, and kids piled out of the basement.


Gamache and Cameron split up, chasing different kids down the hallways. Cameron cornered one in the stairwell leading to the roof.

"Where's Toby?"

"Dunno."

He frisked her and came away with packets of foil and a switchblade.

He cuffed her to the railing and moved on.


Gamache chased another kid into an apartment, where he tackled him, both of them falling onto one of the stained mattresses pushed together on the floor. Getting quickly to his feet, Gamache put the kid in a hold, patting him for weapons and scanning the room for other occupants. It was then he noticed pill bottles neatly arranged on shelves lining all four walls.

"Are you Toby?"

The boy was silent.

Gamache pulled a knife, a bottle of pills, and an ID from his pockets.

Not Toby.

"Where is he?"


Beauvoir grabbed hold of the collar of the largest kid as he tried to escape down the alley and swung him around. Not a he. A she. A girl about fifteen.

"Let her go," came a voice from above.

Beauvoir turned, still holding the girl, and saw a skinny kid on the fire escape. Pointing a gun.

"You a cop?" the kid asked. "Of course you are."

The girl yanked her jacket out of Beauvoir's grip and stepped away.

"Toby?" Beauvoir asked the kid holding the gun.

"Get his gun," said Toby.

The girl reached out, but Beauvoir backed away. "You don't want to do that."

"Give her your gun, old man," said Toby.

"Or what? You'll kill a cop?"

Beauvoir looked at the large girl standing in front of him. Her eyes were wide, round. She was stoned and afraid.

Then he looked at the kid on the fire escape and felt his heart leap in his chest.

He was not afraid. Not stoned.

His gray eyes were empty. Not cold. But not hot. Not glaring, not even threatening.

Chief Inspector Beauvoir had seen eyes like that, often. But only in the recently dead.

"I'm a minor," said Toby. "What're they gonna do to me?"

"You know what they'll do to you?" came a voice down the alley.

Toby immediately turned his gun on the older man walking toward them. His hands were out by his sides, his jacket was open to show he wasn't armed.

"If you kill a cop, if you even hurt one, they'll try you as an adult.

You're close enough, right? What're you?" Gamache turned his attention to the girl beside Beauvoir. "Fourteen. Fifteen."

"Almost fifteen," she said.

"Shut up, Daph," said Toby, not moving the gun from the newcomer.

"There's a third cop, you know, Daphne," said Gamache. "Is that your name?"

She gave a small nod.

"If your friend shoots Chief Inspector Beauvoir—" He saw the girl's eyes widen even further, though Toby did not react.

Gamache stopped where he was and addressed himself now to Toby. "That's right. Not just a cop, but Monsieur Beauvoir here is head of homicide for the Sûreté. If you shoot him, you'll have to shoot me, too. And our colleague will almost certainly then have to shoot you. Both."

He let that sit there before speaking again, this time to Daphne. "Do you want to see fifteen?"

"I'm fifteen," said Toby. "It's not so great."

"No," said Gamache. He'd also noticed the look, or lack of it, in the boy's eyes. "I don't suppose it is. And I'm sorry about that. But it can get better."

Just then Cameron rounded the corner, skidding in the slush as he tried to stop himself. Regaining his balance, he pulled out his gun. Pointing it at first one, then the other kid, finally settling on Toby on the fire escape.

"Put down your weapon, please," said Gamache. And to everyone's astonishment, it was clear he was talking to Cameron. "You might keep it at the ready. But just lower it."

"But—"

"Do it," said Beauvoir.

The girl Daphne had backed up and, quite sensibly, was now standing a few paces away from Chief Inspector Beauvoir.

But Daphne was not the problem. Nor was she the solution.

"We've come to ask you about a bottle of pills we found in a murder investigation," said Beauvoir. "Mifegymiso. It's an abortion drug."

"I know what it is. I know all the shit I sell."

"So you do sell it?" said Gamache. "But probably not a lot."

As he spoke, he moved a step closer to the fire escape but away from Beauvoir. Dragging Toby's attention, and his gun, toward him. Forcing Toby to choose between them. Making it more difficult for the boy to shoot both before Cameron could get off a shot.

"Stop," snapped Toby before glancing at Daphne. "I said get his gun."

To Beauvoir's dismay, he felt his gun removed from its holster. This was, he knew, another reason Gamache never wore one.

Because it could be taken. Used against him. Them. Anyone and everyone. Most guns used in crime were stolen from people who had them legally.

And here was one more on the street.

Gamache looked over his shoulder at Cameron, warning him not to react. Not to overreact.

Nothing had happened yet. Not really. Nothing that could not be undone. But once a trigger was pulled, there was no going back.

"We need to know who bought the drug from you," said Beauvoir. "That's all."

His own voice was steady, matter-of-fact. Trying not to betray the fear he felt. Trying not to flash back to what it was like. To feel the bullet strike. To be lifted— He stopped there and fought to harness his thoughts. "Then we'll leave."

Toby did what Beauvoir hoped he'd do. He turned his attention, and his gun, away from Gamache. And onto him.

What Toby could not see, what no one could see, was that Beauvoir's knees had begun to tremble. But his face remained placid. As though this were an everyday occurrence and nothing to worry about.

Cameron, watching this, his weapon lowered but ready to raise and shoot, felt he was looking into some parallel universe. Where people held reasonable conversations while pointing guns at each other. And were not terrified.

Because he was very afraid. And Cameron knew one thing, from his time on the gridiron and his time as a cop. People who were afraid often did very stupid things.

*Don't be the one. Don't be the one. Don't be the one to do something stupid. And please, please, don't let me be the one shot.*

Gamache was very still. Alert to any movement. Anything that could trigger the boy with the empty eyes. The only comfort, if it could be called that, was that Toby would almost certainly get off only one shot before Cameron took him down.

Still, by Gamache's calculations there seemed a better-than-average chance at least one of them would die in that alleyway.

He took another step away from Jean-Guy, forcing Toby's attention, and weapon, back onto him.

"Stop," said the boy. "Not another step. You think I won't shoot, you dumb fuck, but I will."

"I know you will, Toby," said Gamache. "But I hope you don't."

"We just want one thing," said Beauvoir. "The name of the person who bought the pills from you."

"You think I asked for his name? You're a fucking idiot."

*His*, thought both cops. *His* name.

So Vivienne hadn't bought the drug. A man had. Almost certainly Carl Tracey.

"Can you describe him?" Beauvoir asked. They had to be sure.

"Are you kidding? Look, the guys I sell to don't like it when I tell the cops on them."

"I can appreciate that," said Gamache. "My friends don't like it when I pass their address on to burglars."

Daphne laughed, but Toby did not. Though he did cock his head with interest at the old cop, with the gray hair and thoughtful eyes.

He held those eyes for a moment, sensing something else in them. There was menace, for sure. Here was a man who might be old but wasn't weak. And with a start, Toby recognized him.

He wasn't just a cop. The fucker had failed to say he'd been the head of the whole Sûreté. Toby knew that because he'd seen the video that morning, posted on Twitter and going viral.

Gamache noticed the change in the boy. Saw a look come into those eyes. It was venal. Feral. Triumphant.

*My God*, thought Gamache. *He's going to shoot me.*

He stared into the boy's eyes and thought of Reine-Marie. And silently apologized for what was about to happen.

But what did happen was unexpected. Toby relaxed. Just a little. But enough to get Gamache's heart going again.

"Okay, old man. He was Anglo. Not fat, but soft. I didn't like him. Didn't trust him."

"How many people do you trust?"

Toby gave one gruff laugh. But didn't answer.

"I think we have enough," said Beauvoir. "We're going to leave you now."

He slowly lowered his arms and held out his hand toward Daphne.

This was the moment.

"My gun, please."

Daphne looked up at Toby, who raised his gun slightly.

Seeing this, Cameron raised his slightly, before Gamache could signal him to stop.

Toby, alarmed, raised his gun more, until it was pointing at Beauvoir's head.

Jean-Guy was staring straight down the barrel.

Everyone froze.

This was, Jean-Guy knew, a bullet he would not feel.

"It's all right," said Gamache softly. "No one needs to get hurt. We're almost done."

He stopped talking. Allowing the tension to ease.

He saw Toby's gun lowered. Slightly.

It was a millimeter in the right direction. But they weren't out of it yet.

*Please*, Gamache begged. *Please don't let anyone come into the alley now. Please.*

The moments stretched on. Elongating.

Gamache wanted desperately to say more, to try to reason with the boy. But he knew it would be a mistake. If they were to avoid a bloodbath, the next move had to come from Toby.

"Go," said Toby.

"My gun," said Beauvoir. "You know I can't leave it behind."

"Do you want to die, man?" shouted Toby. "Get out, before I change my mind."

*Oh, for God's sake, what're you doing?* Cameron's mind screamed. *Let's go. Oh, please, let's go.*

And Jean-Guy Beauvoir wanted to. With every part of his being, he wanted to turn and walk away. Run away. Go back to Annie. Hold her tight. Smell the sweet, fresh scent of her. Hold Honoré in his arms. Get on a plane to Paris and never look back.

But he couldn't go. Couldn't let go. Not yet.

Instead he stood there, staring. Willing the boy to see what he saw. They held each other's eyes.

Finally Toby spoke. "I'm fucked, aren't I? If I shoot, he'll kill me. If you leave without the gun, you'll be back to get it. You have to. You'll find us and arrest us. Daph and me."

"That's true," said Beauvoir.

He gave Toby a small nod. Of admiration. Acknowledging the boy's logic. And clarity.

"So either I kill you all now. Or I give up."

*Oh, God,* thought Cameron. *Oh, God, here it comes.*

"*Oui,*" said Beauvoir. "That's about it. One you live. One you die."

Toby seemed to make up his mind. He braced.

It was slight and too subtle for Cameron to see. But Gamache could, and he knew what it meant. Every muscle tightened, even as he realized there was nothing he could do.

Toby was about to shoot. Jean-Guy.

"You know," said Beauvoir, his voice remaining conversational even as his knees threatened to give way. "I once faced exactly the same situation."

"Shut the fuck up."

"I'd reached the end. Couldn't go on. I didn't care anymore."

"Shut up."

"I thought about killing myself. But when it came down to it, I realized that what I really wanted was for the pain to stop. I didn't really want to die, but I didn't know how to live. How to go on."

There was silence then. Utter, almost suffocating silence. As the air was sucked out of the alley.

"What did you do?"

"I let go." Beauvoir closed his eyes. "I let go." Then he opened them again and met Toby's. "Sometimes we just have to let go. And trust.

There is a way back. Believe me." He smiled and opened his arms wide. "And look at the great place it brought me."

The words hung in the air of the void before the boy laughed.

Jean-Guy cocked his head. "Toby, I don't want to die. And I don't think you do either."

Toby closed his eyes, and while they could have moved, no one did.

Then, eyes still shut, Toby let go of his gun.

# CHAPTER TWENTY-SEVEN

—

@SûretéCrooked: I knew it! Cops killing kids.

@dumbass: You morons. That tape's doctored. Here's the real one.

@CommonGround: @SûretéCrooked Can't we all just get along?

@SûretéCrooked: @CommonGround Go fuck yourself.

Your name?" asked Superintendent Lacoste.

"Pauline Vachon."

"Your profession?"

"Web designer and manager."

"Do you know this man?" Isabelle Lacoste placed a photograph on the metal table in the interview room.

Lysette Cloutier sat off to the side. Watching closely.

Pauline Vachon was younger than she appeared in the Instagram pictures.

Her hair was clean and nicely done. Makeup carefully applied. She was pretty.

Her clothes were simple, almost elegant, thought Cloutier. Black slacks and a white blouse, with a bright red silk scarf.

Lacoste was also taking in Vachon's appearance. The makeup was cheap, clumping, and too heavily applied. The slacks were from a discount store, and the red scarf was rayon. Masquerading as silk. And hiding, Lacoste could see, a coffee stain on the white blouse.

Lysette Cloutier saw what she was meant to see. Isabelle Lacoste saw the truth.

Still, Lacoste knew that making the most of herself, on very little money, while holding together her own company at the age of twenty-one, was far from criminal. In fact, it was remarkable.

Pauline Vachon was a remarkable young woman. But she was also a nervous young woman. She clearly had not expected them to connect her to Tracey. And certainly not this quickly. And certainly not in any way that would lead her to be sitting in a Sûreté interview room.

Beneath Pauline's calm, helpful veneer, Lacoste could sense alarm. Barely suppressed. But suppressed. This was indeed a self-possessed young woman.

So why had she hooked up with the mess that was Carl Tracey? That was just one of many questions that came to mind.

Pauline sat upright in the interview room. Almost prim. And looked down at the photo on the metal table.

"Yes. He's one of my clients. Carl Tracey."

"And what do you do for him?"

"I set up his website and manage his social media."

"Which platforms?"

"Instagram mostly."

"Can you give us the address of his website and social-media accounts?"

Cloutier wrote it down, though, of course, she already knew it. Vachon did not volunteer the private account.

"Many followers?" Lacoste asked.

"Not really. I tried to tell him that you need to post a lot to get interest, but honestly, what can a potter post that could go viral? More pictures of a lump of clay on a wheel?"

Lacoste smiled. "I sympathize. Unreasonable clients. The worst."

Pauline relaxed a little. "He's not really that bad. He just doesn't understand."

"You post for him?"

She nodded.

"Why doesn't he do it himself?" asked Lacoste.

These were softball questions. Every interrogator had a particular technique. Hers was to set people at their ease. Have them lower their defenses.

"He's an artist. Not great at technical things. Besides, there's no internet at his place. Can you tell me what this's about?"

It interested Lacoste that it had taken this long for Pauline Vachon to ask. It was normally the first question out of anyone's mouth. But then, this young woman already knew the answer.

"Has something happened to Monsieur Tracey?"

She looked directly into Lacoste's eyes. Not blinking. Brown eyes all innocent with just the right touch of curiosity. Without, it would appear, guilt or guile.

"I'm afraid his wife has drowned, and we just have some questions."

"Oh, that's terrible." Pauline looked from Lacoste to Cloutier and back again.

"Yes," said Lacoste. "Did Monsieur Tracey ever talk about his wife?"

Vachon paused to gather her thoughts. To sort through the truth and lies and decide which to choose.

"A bit. He didn't seem happy. He said she drank. Was depressed. I felt sorry for him."

"Pauline," said Lacoste, leaning forward a little and dropping her voice so that it sounded as though she were about to confide in the young woman. "I really hope you don't mind, but I'm going to ask you some questions that might seem odd. Is that all right?"

"Sure. Of course." She looked at her watch. "I have an appointment in an hour—"

"Oh, this won't take that long. Don't worry," said Lacoste with a motherly smile, despite the fact there weren't that many years between them. It wasn't years but choices that separated these two women.

"How old was your mother when she had you?"

Both Vachon and Cloutier looked at her with surprise.

"You weren't kidding about the strange questions," said Pauline with a laugh. Though she was slightly guarded now. "She was sixteen."

"Young. Must've been difficult. And your grandmother? How old was she when she had your mother?"

"Do you really need to know this? What does this have to do with Carl's wife?"

Cloutier had the same question and just barely stopped herself from nodding agreement.

"I'm sorry," said Lacoste, and looked it. "I just need your help understanding some things about this community. How judgmental it can be of young women."

It was a vague answer but seemed to satisfy, mollify, Pauline.

"My grandmother was fifteen."

"And you're twenty-one?"

"Yes."

"How old were you when you first got pregnant?"

That hovered between the two women.

"Why—"

"Please, Pauline. It would help a lot."

Cloutier could see that Vachon realized she'd created a problem for herself. She'd offered to help, needed to appear willing to help. And these questions were not, on the surface, threatening or even, it must be admitted, pertinent.

But they were deeply invasive.

"I was sixteen."

"And what happened?"

"I had an abortion."

"The next time?"

Now Pauline shifted in her seat. "Why are you asking this? It's not illegal. It was all done by a doctor in a hospital."

"Yes, I know. But I also know that small towns can be supportive, but they can also be pretty awful. You get a reputation. . . . Nasty rumors spread. Rumors with just enough truth in them to do damage. People don't always like it when you're a success, do they?"

"Not always," Pauline said, lifting her chin slightly.

Isabelle Lacoste found herself admiring this young woman. Who refused to give in. She had guts. But did she have a conscience?

"*Non*," said Lacoste quietly. "They're not always as kind as we'd like. Especially painful when friends aren't happy for you. You're trying hard to get out, to make a career for yourself. To make a success of your business. Get a little money. And people are all, 'Oh, she's too good for us now,' just because you dress nicely and take some care. Right?"

Pauline nodded but was guarded. Though not as guarded as she should have been.

"Can I tell you something?" Lacoste lowered her voice. "Something no one else outside the police knows."

Pauline nodded, leaning forward.

"Vivienne was pregnant. That's why I'm asking. But we don't really know who the father was."

"Really? Got it," whispered Pauline. "Poor Carl."

"Yes. Poor Carl. Who can blame him for wanting out of that marriage?" Lacoste leaned back in her chair, her voice once again businesslike. "Now, the second time you were pregnant, another hospital procedure?"

"D and C, yes."

"And the third time?"

There was now, in Lacoste's tone, a slight edge. Not of judgment but of warning. Tell the truth.

"How did you end that pregnancy, Pauline?"


"I know who you are," said Toby, sitting at a desk in the station, not all that far from where Lacoste was interviewing Pauline.

"You're the cop everyone hates," said Daphne.

She was at the next desk over, also being booked.

Gamache smiled. "Not everyone, I hope."

"Everyone I know."

Gamache was not particularly surprised to hear that teens running a criminal operation might not be fans.

"I saw the video of you killing those kids," said Toby. "Brutal."

Cameron, the arresting officer, stopped typing on his computer. Jean-Guy Beauvoir, sitting nearby and going over messages, looked up.

And Armand Gamache tilted his head slightly, the smile fading. "What video?"

Toby laughed. "You haven't seen it? Posted about an hour ago. Gone viral. Funny that I watched it, then there you were."

Gamache drew his brows together. There was a video out there of him gunning down children? How could that be?

He turned to Jean-Guy, who still looked pale, after that confrontation in the alley. As they'd driven back, Gamache had noticed Beauvoir trembling, and quietly asked if he was okay.

"I didn't think I'd get out of there alive," Jean-Guy said, under his breath.

Gamache thought the same thing, but didn't say it. He still felt the acid burning his stomach.

"You'll be on the Champs-Élysées soon," he'd said. "In the sunshine."

"Not soon enough."

While Jean-Guy knew Paris wasn't immune to danger, it would at least be unlikely. There was a far better chance of returning home each day.

Now, on hearing what Toby said, Jean-Guy swung around to his laptop, hitting the keys.

*Sûreté, video, kids.*

*Gamache, video, shooting.*

"I coulda shot you, you know," said Toby. "Payback. For what you did."

"Why didn't you?"

Toby sat back and crossed his arms. "You weren't worth the bullet. And you sure aren't worth dying for. He'da killed me."

He nodded to Cameron, who was staring at the boy.

"You got that right," said Cameron.

Toby turned back to the older man. With the gray hair. And that nasty scar by his temple. That made him so recognizable.

The cop's face wasn't so much wrinkled as lined. From a great distance, from half a century away, he looked to the boy like a man broken and pieced back together.

Humpty Dumpty. Who'd had a great fall.

"*Patron,*" said Beauvoir from the other desk, breaking into Toby's thoughts.

His voice was hushed. Almost a whisper.


Annie was working from home in Montréal. Studying for the French law admission exams.

A friend from her firm in Montréal had sent a link. And a warning. But, of course, she had to look.

Clicking on it, she watched. Blood draining from her face.

Honoré, on her knee, was also watching. But she quickly took him away, placing him in his playpen. Then she returned to her laptop, approaching it warily.

The screen was paused on an image of her father.

Her eyes were wide. Her breathing shallow. She muted the sound and hit play.

Reine-Marie covered her mouth with her hand and closed her eyes. The bruise on her face forgotten, she now felt as though she'd been hit, hard, in the gut.

Then, opening them again, she asked Myrna to go back to the beginning.

"Are you sure?" Myrna asked.

They'd gone up to Myrna's loft over the bookstore, where the internet was most stable. Annie had sent the link. She knew that her mother would want to know. To be warned about what was out there.

In the few minutes it had taken the women to get upstairs, more and more messages had come in from friends who were alarmed and upset. Who wanted to warn both her and Armand.

Myrna and Clara were in the loft with her. As were Olivier and Gabri. Ruth was sitting beside her in front of the computer, her veined hand holding Reine-Marie's.

"Please," said Reine-Marie.

Myrna clicked, and the short video played again.

"Do you mind if we use your meeting room?" Beauvoir asked the station commander, who, on seeing him at her door, clicked her computer closed. And reddened. But not before Beauvoir had heard the telltale sound of muffled gunfire coming from her laptop.

"Not at all."

Beauvoir closed the door to the private office and placed his laptop on the table. Gamache stood beside him, staring at the frozen image on the screen. It was of himself, in flak jacket. Weapon out. And raised. Eyes sharp. Preparing to shoot.

"It's bad," said Beauvoir.

Gamache nodded. "Go on."

He stood straight and faced the screen. Much as he'd faced the boy on the fire escape earlier that day.

Beauvoir hit play.

The images were jerky but still fairly clear. It had been pieced together from old video, taken from the raid on the factory. They were images both Gamache and Beauvoir had seen before. Many taken from the cameras they themselves had worn.

But there were other images. Ones neither had ever seen. Video culled from God-knew-where on the internet. Of kids being gunned down. Many of them black kids. Clearly unarmed.

As Armand Gamache watched the screen, Beauvoir watched him.

Saw the narrowing of the eyes, the wincing at the terrible images.

The video had been edited to make it appear that Gamache was responsible for all of it.

The editing was rough. Not really designed to fool anyone. Except those who wanted to be fooled.

As Jean-Guy Beauvoir watched Gamache, he realized he'd never seen anyone actually gutted before. Until now.


Madeleine Toussaint sat at her desk with her second-in-command and watched the video.

Her email, her phone lines, had lit up. All guiding her to this travesty.

She watched it three or four times.

"What're you going to do?" her second-in-command asked. "There has to be a response. The Sûreté has to condemn—"

"I know what has to be done. Leave me." After a moment she added, "Please."

When alone, Chief Superintendent Toussaint got up and walked over to the wall map. It showed the current flooding. Of which there was a lot, and more to come.

But her eyes rested on the massive hydroelectric dams. Without her consent, without her knowledge, the floodgates had been opened.

And, more, the resources had been diverted south. Runoffs had been dug, were still being dug. River levels lowering. There was collateral damage, to farms and fields, but most farmers not only understood but had helped.

Toussaint accepted the congratulations from the Prime Minister for her handling of the situation. Smart enough not to acknowledge it hadn't been her doing.

She herself had still been considering the options when she'd been told there were no more options. The decision had been made. An irreversible action had been taken.

And she suspected by whom.

She looked across her vast office, at the image on the screen. Of the former occupant. Gunning down black teens. Some, she realized with horror, not even that old. She felt sick. Physically ill.

They could be her own son.

Yes, something had to be done about Gamache. Something more than what she'd already done.

Madeleine Toussaint sat back down and composed her response. Then, before she could regret it, she hit send.


Reine-Marie was sitting in Myrna's kitchen with a shot of scotch. Talking with Annie on the phone while the others huddled together. Conferring.

All except Ruth. Who'd returned to the computer. Drawn back, like a compass to magnetic north, to the unimaginable violence. Done to those children.

Done to Armand.

Reine-Marie, phone to her ear and listening to Annie vent, watched as Ruth clicked away on the keyboard. Her bony fingers thudding the keys as though punishing the computer for its complicity.

Then, with a final flourish, the old woman hit one last key and sat back. Smiling.

"Annie, I have to go," said Reine-Marie.

"I need to call Reine-Marie," said Armand, reaching for the phone.

"I'll call Annie."

Jean-Guy got through, but Armand did not. After trying home, then the bistro, he finally reached her at Myrna's.

"I saw it," said Reine-Marie before he'd even spoken. "Don't worry. No one believes it. It's crude."

"It's cruel," came a voice shouted in the background. "But I fixed it."

Ruth, Armand recognized. "How did she fix it?"

"Armand?"

It was Jean-Guy's voice. He had Annie on the line and was sitting once again at his laptop.

"Hold on," said Armand, and he turned to his son-in-law. "What is it?"

"Annie sent me a link. Just posted."

"The same one . . . ?" Armand began to ask as he walked around to the laptop.

But he stopped, walking. Talking. Breathing.

The image frozen on the screen was clearly from the same raid on the factory. But this was a different video. It was, he could see immediately, from the original recording. The true record of what had happened that day.

It was never meant to be made public. Never meant to be seen outside the Sûreté and the official inquiry. But the video had been leaked and posted years ago, in a violation so profound it had taken Gamache, Beauvoir, the families, years to get over.

Scenes had obviously been taken from it to create the bastardized video that had gone up that morning.

Armand now knew how Ruth had "fixed" it.

Thinking she was helping a friend, she'd reposted the original. In hopes of showing the truth.

What the old poet didn't realize, or had forgotten, was that social media was less about truth than perception. People believed what they chose to believe.

Neither did she appear to understand the damage she'd just done.

"I have to let you go," Armand said into the phone.

When he hung up, he looked briefly at the clear image on the screen, taking one deep breath after another. Trying to control his outrage.

Then, reaching for the phone, he said to Jean-Guy, "Can you give me a few minutes?"

Jean-Guy stepped toward the door, paused, then turned around. He knew what Armand was about to do. *"Non."*

*"Non?"*

"I'm staying with you." He sat down. There would be no argument.

Jean-Guy did not leave his side as Armand called the families of the officers who'd been slain that day. Whose deaths, like some horrific snuff film, were once again played out in public.

Armand placed call after call.

They were numbers he knew by heart, since he spoke to the mothers, fathers, husbands, and wives every week and visited the families whenever he was invited.

Now he called to warn them. To listen to their rage. To absorb, again, their agony.

When he'd finished, he asked Jean-Guy to leave him. Just for a couple of minutes.

And this time, Jean-Guy did.

When he was alone, Armand sat quietly, then dropped his face into his trembling hands.

*Things are strongest where they're broken*, the young voice reassured him. And Armand gasped with pain as he held the agent, no more than a boy, in his arms.

# CHAPTER TWENTY-EIGHT

—

$S$ ome abortion drug."

Those were Pauline Vachon's words. Too ashamed to go back to her doctor, she'd gone where desperate women had for centuries. Into a back alley.

But this time it wasn't some sadist with a coat hanger. It was a kid with a pharmacy.

"Mifegymiso?" Lacoste asked.

"Maybe. I dunno. I just took it, and it worked."

"Is that how Carl Tracey knew about it?"

There was silence. Except for the ticking of the old clock on the wall. As the reality of what they were really talking about hit Pauline.

"I was just trying to help a client. Nothing wrong with that."

Lacoste remained silent.

"His wife was pregnant," Vachon went on. "He said it probably wasn't his, that they hadn't had sex in months. So I told him about the drug."

"And where to get it."

"Yes."

"You knew he was going to give it to her, probably without her knowledge, and that was fine with you?"

"What he did with it was his business."

Lacoste struggled not to show her disgust. At Tracey. But also at this alarming young woman who didn't seem to see anything wrong with this.

"It didn't work," said Lacoste. "Vivienne was still pregnant when she died."

"She couldn't have been. This was last summer," said Vachon.

Isabelle Lacoste's mind raced.

It seemed they were talking about two different pregnancies. Carl Tracey had ended one with the abortion drug last summer. But now Vivienne was pregnant again.

Had she suspected what he'd done? Was that one of the reasons, perhaps the main reason, she'd decided to finally get out now? So the same thing didn't happen to this child?

"Well, she was," said Lacoste. "Pregnant. You didn't know?"

"I didn't know him all that well. He didn't tell me everything."

"You knew him well enough to set up an illegal drug buy. Well enough to help him abort the baby, without his wife's knowledge. Well enough to sleep with him."

Lacoste opened the file in front of her and removed the photographs, taken off the private feed. She placed them, one at a time, on the table.

Pauline was momentarily taken by surprise but then recovered herself. With speed rarely seen by Lacoste, she grasped the situation. And made a decision.

"I'm not exactly picky, am I?" said Pauline, smiling.

Lacoste realized she'd underestimated this young woman and how remarkable she really was.

This was strategic. Mix truth in with lies, so it became more and more difficult to tell them apart.

"It meant nothing," Pauline explained. "Might not've been the smartest thing I've done, having sex with a client, but hey, people've done worse."

"Like murder," said Lacoste.

There could be no more doubt about the relationship between Tracey and Vachon, and neither was there any doubt about the relationship between interviewer and interviewee. One was in charge, the other in trouble.

Pauline Vachon looked down at the photographs, her lips compressing. "How did you get these?"

"You've been corresponding with NouveauGalerie, I believe," said Lacoste.

"You?" said Vachon, looking first at Lacoste, then at Cloutier, who gave a curt nod.

The clotted makeup could not conceal the panic in her face.

Lacoste opened the file again and read, "*Stuff's in the bag. Everything's ready. Will be done tonight. I promise.* That was a message from Carl Tracey to you, around noon on the day Vivienne disappeared. And your reply?"

"Look, I had nothing to do with it."

"*Finally. Good luck. Don't mess it up.*" She looked up from the file. "But he did, didn't he? He messed it up royally. That's why you're here, Pauline."

The younger woman was flushed. But she tried one more twist to get off the hook.

"Those were about the clay Tracey was buying. He was going to do more pieces that night. I told him not to mess it up. He'd been promising some for weeks."

Lacoste got up. "I'll let you think about what you just said. Unless something happens in the next few minutes, like a meteor strikes, you'll be charged with the murder of Vivienne Godin."

She and Cloutier left the room. Leaving the file behind.

"We have her," said Lacoste, walking up to Beauvoir, who was standing outside the meeting room. "Pauline Vachon doesn't admit to being part of the murder—yet—but she will. I'm letting her stew for a few minutes. She was clearly shaken when she realized we'd seen the private account."

"You should've seen her face," said Cloutier.

Lacoste nodded. "She admits she used the abortion drug herself and was the one who told Carl Tracey how to get it on the black market."

How Lacoste got the young woman to admit to a third abortion, never mind buying the black-market drug, still amazed Cloutier. It had been a masterful combination of guile, of guesswork, of knowing when to push and when to make nice. Until Vachon had nowhere to go but the truth.

Cloutier was looking at Lacoste with something close to awe. But there was caution there as well. She did not want to make the same mistake as Vachon.

Whether by natural instinct or honed skills, Isabelle Lacoste had the power to see things people wanted to hide.

And they all had them, as Lysette Cloutier knew only too well.

But while Cloutier was focused on Lacoste, Lacoste was focused on Beauvoir.

"What is it?"

He told them about the video.

Before Lacoste could react, the door opened and Gamache stepped out. He was pale but composed.

Every agent in the open room looked over at him.

They'd all read the Twitter feed and seen the doctored video that was blowing up online. They had yet to see the real video that had just been posted.

"What can we do, *patron*?" Lacoste asked, going to him and touching his hand.

"There's nothing to be done. *Mais merci*, Isabelle. I've spoken to the families." His smile was tight and his voice brisk. "How did the interview go with Pauline Vachon?"

As they returned to the meeting room to talk privately, both Lacoste and Beauvoir noticed that Gamache's right hand was closed into a tight fist. But still it trembled.


They watched on the monitor as Pauline Vachon turned the folder around and went through the photographs and printouts.

Then she sat back in her chair. And stared at the far wall.

Seeing, Lacoste knew, all her work, all her dreams, dissolving.

Then Beauvoir closed the feed on his laptop and turned to Lacoste. "Tell us what happened."

When Lacoste finished, Beauvoir thought for a moment. "She'll crack."

"I'm not so sure," said Lacoste. "She's clever and she's tough. Makes me so angry. She really could've made something of her life. I still don't know why she'd hook up with Carl Tracey."

"She saw a shortcut," said Beauvoir.

"To what? An abusive relationship in a remote farmhouse? Not exactly Cinderella."

"She probably thought she was smarter, tougher than Vivienne Godin," said Beauvoir. "That she could control Tracey."

"We saw the bruises on her arms," said Cloutier. "She must know."

"Maybe she does. Maybe it's the cycle of abuse, right, *patron*?" said Beauvoir, and Gamache nodded.

Beauvoir and Lacoste exchanged glances but said nothing. They'd give him time, and space, to return to them.

Beauvoir sat forward, his voice all business. "The coroner's report came in. The fetus, a baby girl, was his."

"His who?" asked Lacoste, needing to be absolutely clear.

"Carl Tracey. The baby was his."

"You're kidding." It was, of course, rhetorical. Isabelle Lacoste sat back in her chair. What did this mean?

"Do you think Vivienne knew this and was messing with Carl when she told him it wasn't his?" she asked. "Or did Vivienne really believe the baby was someone else's?"

"We only have Tracey's word on it that she said anything," Beauvoir pointed out. "I think that's bullshit. Her father said she was desperate to get out as soon as she could, that day. Why would she provoke Tracey by saying anything?"

"What did Pauline Vachon say about the messages on the private Instagram?" Gamache asked, speaking for the first time in the meeting. "How did she explain them?"

"Said they were about clay he was buying."

Gamache frowned. "Smart. She's quick on her feet."

"She is that," agreed Lacoste. "This might not be as easy as we'd hoped."

"But she must know no one in their right mind would believe that," said Beauvoir. "Not after what happened."

"Do you get the impression she cares for Tracey?" Gamache asked.

"Not especially," said Lacoste. "I think she has sex with him for the same reason she has sex with so many other men. It's a form of self-loathing."

"What role do you think she has in all this?" Gamache asked.

"I don't know, but I can tell you she's involved. And she knows we know."

"What do you think would happen if you told her the baby was Tracey's?" Beauvoir asked.

Lacoste considered that.

"It'd be a surprise. A shock. Not because she loves Tracey, but it would prove to her that he lied about that. He can't be trusted."

"Exactly," said Beauvoir, sitting forward. "She's smart. She must realize that he'd blame the killing on her in a second if he was cornered."

"So we need to press that home," said Lacoste. "She must be thinking about it even now. This information about the fetus might be just that last shove we need."

"Give it another go, Isabelle," said Beauvoir. "Try to turn her. We have enough now to arrest him, but her testimony would secure a conviction."

Lacoste gave one curt nod. "Leave it to me."

"I'll apply for an arrest warrant for Tracey, but we'll wait to hear from you. Even if you can't turn her, we'll bring him in. He'll crack, even if she won't."

"She will," said Lacoste. "I'll make sure of it."

Clara Morrow dropped the printout onto the bistro table and sat down across from Dominica Oddly.

"Do you really think this?"

"I do."

"You say here"—she tapped the paper—"that I was once promising. Exceptional, even. But then I got lazy."

"Yes."

"But it's not true."

"No?" asked Oddly. "Are you sure?"

The critic had left Clara in her studio to read in private the review that had just gone public. She'd strolled across the village green, and, brushing slush off the bench, she sat, looking at the three pine trees that clearly gave the place its name. It seemed a little "on the nose" for Oddly. Too obvious. Three pines in Three Pines.

She'd have preferred if there were two pines. It would make the place more interesting. Give it a story. What happened to that third tree? Granted, not much of a story, but better than none.

As it was, this hidden little hamlet was pretty but banal. She could almost see the stone and brick and clapboard homes, the church on the hill and the forest behind, turning into a watercolor before her eyes. Something not quite real. Not quite of this world. Certainly not of the gritty, noisy, aggressive world she'd just left.

This was like a pretty painting by some elderly, marginally gifted artist.

Nice. Sweet. Predictable. Safe.

Oddly smiled as she thought of the residents peering through their curtains at the wild black woman in dreadlocks and combat boots sitting in the middle of their peaceful village. She must, she thought, scare them to death.

She'd spotted the bistro when she'd arrived, and now she made for it. Her boots, veterans of sidewalk garbage and dog shit, squelched on grass and mud.

She opened the door and was prepared to enter a space decorated with Grand-mère in mind. All lace and gingham. Stuffed with old snowshoes and spinning wheels and dusty twig baskets filled with dried flowers hanging from the rafters. Furnished with cheap imitation pine tables and uncomfortable chairs.

If Oddly knew one thing about Québec, it was that it was a cheap imitation of the real thing. France.

Instead what she found was a place both contemporary and somehow ageless. It seemed to straddle the centuries. Comfortable armchairs upholstered in fresh linens sat around an assortment of rugged old tables. Dark oak. Maple. Pine. Tables made from the forests that surrounded the village. They were scratched and dented and worn by a century or more of meals. Of drinks. Of companionship. And hardship.

The place settings, displayed in an old Welsh dresser, were white china with clean modern lines.

Oriental rugs, hand-tied, were scattered on the wide-plank floors. The walls were freshly plastered and painted a shade that contrasted nicely with the warm wood and stone.

She looked up.

Nothing hung from the sturdy beams.

The bistro smelled of rich coffee and subtle maple smoke from the fieldstone fireplaces at either end of the room.

It was a place of confidences. Of companionship. Where secrets were exchanged and yearnings admitted. Where children grew into adults, into seniors. Where homecomings were celebrated and lives celebrated by those left behind.

It was a place where both grandmother and granddaughter would feel at home.

"*Bonjour*," said a young woman coming from behind the long bar to greet her. "*Une table? C'est votre choix.*"

She smiled at Dominica, as though dreadlocked New York critics were their regular customers, and pointed to the near-empty room. It was midafternoon, between rushes.

The few other customers had glanced at her, then gone back to their conversations. Showing little interest and no fear.

"Ummm," said Oddly, not at all sure what the young woman had said.

"Oh, sorry. English. Sit anywhere you like. The fireplace has just come open. I'll clean the table for you."

The young woman spoke in slightly accented English. As Oddly followed her to the large armchair by the fire, she thought she might have to do something rare for her.

Reconsider her opinion.

This was no France wannabe. This was genuine Québec. With its own history, etched into flesh and bone, into stone and wood. Into the cushions of the armchairs and sofas, retaining the impressions of warm bodies who'd sat there before her. Eating, talking, commiserating, laughing. For generations.

This was no imitation, but the real thing.

By the time Clara found her, Dominica had enjoyed a glass of red wine and a delicious buttery Riopelle de l'Isle. A cheese made on a tiny Québec island, and named after one of her favorite artists. Jean-Paul Riopelle. Dominica hadn't realized that the abstract expressionist painter came from Québec. And lived, worked, and died on a small island.

She smeared the cheese on a baguette fresh from the bakery next door, and looked at the village, framed by the mullioned windows.

She was wondering how much homes around the village green cost, and if any of her subscribers would notice, or care, if she decamped to Canada.

Though, looking at Clara Morrow's face, she knew one person who might not be pleased.


Vivienne's father closed his eyes and, bringing his hand to his heart, made a sound.

Gamache, sitting across from him, watched closely. It wasn't clear if Homer was sighing or moaning. Whether he was relieved or having a heart attack.

Armand noticed that the hand over his heart was crunched into a fist. But not tight. Not in pain. At least not physical pain. His heart, under attack for days, might just, with the news of the imminent arrest of Carl Tracey, finally be fighting back.

"I know you're not messing with me, Armand, but I need to hear it again. You're arresting him. For what he did."

"Yes. I'll be going with Chief Inspector Beauvoir. We'll be bringing him in probably within the hour. You're free to go, but, Homer"—it was the first time he'd used the man's first name to his face—"I'd like Agent Cloutier to drive you back to Three Pines."

"To get my things."

"No. To stay with us. Just for a few days. You shouldn't be alone."

"No. I want to go home. I need to be with . . ." He made a vague gesture. "Alone."

Armand knew he'd feel the same way, if Annie . . . If Reine-Marie . . . If Daniel . . .

It was instinctive. A badly wounded animal, crawling off alone. To lick wounds. Or, if they proved too deep, to die.

Gamache had seen it more than once. People died from grief.

Carl Tracey had killed the daughter. Gamache was damned if he'd let him kill the father, too.

"You don't have to be social, but you shouldn't be alone." Armand leaned forward and touched Homer's hand, lightly, and whispered, "Please."

He saw Agent Cloutier bristle a bit. Perhaps annoyed that it was not she who was comforting Homer.

But that's why Gamache had asked her to drive Homer down to Three Pines, so that Homer would have the company of someone he knew and trusted. Someone he felt comfortable with. It might even be the bonding experience they both needed.

"I can leave your place whenever I want?" Homer asked. "And go home?"

"Yes, of course," said Armand. "Lysette will stay with you until I get there."

That served several purposes. It kept Homer company, kept him there, and kept Reine-Marie safe. Armand doubted Homer would lash out again, but he wasn't going to take that chance.

"You're going to arrest him?"

It was the third time Homer had asked and the third time Armand had said yes. And he was happy to say it all day and into the night.

Yes. Yes. Carl Tracey would face a judge and jury for what he did to Vivienne. Carl Tracey would spend the rest of his life in prison.

"And he'll be convicted. You promise?"

Gamache hesitated for a moment. "There's one more piece of evidence that will seal it. Someone's testimony."

Godin's eyes widened in surprise. "Someone was there? They saw what happened?"

"No. There're no actual witnesses. Though there rarely are. A case is built from evidence. And we have plenty. But this last piece would guarantee a conviction."

"You promise?"

Annie's father stood up and put out his hand to Vivienne's father. "I promise."

Homer took it, then leaned forward very slowly. As did Armand. Until their foreheads touched.

They stayed there for the briefest of moments, eyes closed.

Then Homer pulled back and caught his breath, wiping his face with his sleeve.

"Sorry. Out of Kleenex."

"Here," said Lysette, offering a box she'd plucked from a nearby desk.

Homer took it without really noticing who was attached to the offering. "*Merci.*"

"Ready?" asked Armand.

Homer blew his nose, then stooped to pick up all the balled-up tissues he'd dropped on the floor.

"Leave them," said Armand.

But the large man would not, could not, leave a mess for someone else to clean up.

# CHAPTER TWENTY-NINE

⌒

Jean-Guy Beauvoir sat behind the wheel of the unmarked car.

By tradition, the senior officer rode in the passenger seat. But Beauvoir could not bring himself to do that while Gamache was in the vehicle. Except that once, when he was too exhausted to drive.

Now they sat side by side. As they had for years. Watching the home of a murder suspect. Waiting for word from Lacoste. Waiting to give the word to go.

"What do you mean you're staying the night?" demanded Clara.

"Sorry, but my flight from Burlington to New York was canceled," Dominica Oddly said.

What she didn't say was that she herself had canceled it. And spoken to the big gay guy about a room at their bed-and-breakfast. Or, as he insisted on calling it, bed-and-brunch.

If their B&B looked like their bistro and tasted like the bakery, she really might never leave. She did not tell Clara that. The woman already looked like her hair was on fire.

"Can't you stay over in Burlington?" asked Clara, her voice rising. "Close to the airport?"

"Too late," said Gabri, dropping a key into Dominica's hand. "She's booked in. The Basquiat Suite."

"Since when do you name your rooms?" Clara all but hissed at him.

"Since she showed up," said Gabri, unapologetically. "And if you're not careful, we'll call the public bathroom the Toilette Clara Morrow."

"You know what she's just posted online about my works," said Clara, watching as Ruth and Myrna joined the critic at the bistro fireplace.

Reine-Marie had gone home, feeling the need for a long shower after watching those vile videos.

Gabri turned to face Clara, his expression no longer a little goofy. "I do. And now you have twenty-four hours you didn't have before to change her mind."

"She won't change her mind."

They walked over to the bar, and while Clara helped herself to a licorice pipe from the jar, Gabri poured her a red wine.

"You don't know that." He smiled and touched her hand. "People do change. Minds change. I know you know that."

Clara turned and glared at Dominica Oddly, now laughing and chatting with her best friend and her mentor. In her seat. By the fireplace.

She felt the bile grow. Felt the subtle demonisms of thought take hold.


Lysette had tried to engage Homer in casual conversation. But, understandably, the only thing he was interested in hearing about was their investigation.

Lysette wasn't really sure how much to tell him but suspected he would not pass any of it along. And it would be public knowledge anyway, as soon as Tracey was arraigned.

Besides, she was desperate to connect with him. To let him know the important role she'd played in having Tracey arrested.

To let him know she wasn't just on his side but by his side.

In the twenty-minute drive from Cowansville to Three Pines, she'd been debating how much to reveal. Not just about the case against Tracey but about herself.

About her feelings.

It was just dumb luck that Chief Inspector Gamache had given her this time alone with Homer. He couldn't possibly know what it meant to her. But now she needed to actually use it.

They were getting closer and closer to Three Pines.

Now was the time.

But what should she say? She couldn't just blurt out, "I love you."

Or could she? Maybe he needed to hear it. Especially now. To know someone loved him. Deeply.

Just before cresting the hill that would take them down into Three Pines, she reached over and placed her hand on top of his.

He didn't pull away.

As they arrived at the Gamache home, just before putting the car in park, she squeezed.

And he, she was pretty sure, squeezed back.


Jean-Guy checked his phone again. It was instinctive.

There were, as he already knew from the last time he checked, no bars. No reception. Which was why he'd chosen a car with a radio connecting them to the station.

Now he stared at the handset. While beside him, Gamache stared out the window. Into the twilight. Through the trees to the lonely home and the single light at a single window.

Jean-Guy checked his phone again.


"That's not true."

"It is. The coroner just confirmed it. That baby was Carl's." Lacoste leaned forward. "A little girl. His daughter. Kinda makes you wonder, doesn't it, Pauline?"

Pauline was silent, but Lacoste could see her mind whirring.

Superintendent Lacoste had another question for Pauline Vachon.

"Where were you on Saturday afternoon and evening?"


Homer knelt and put his face against the smelly old dog, rubbing him, mumbling to him, before standing back up.

"Armand called to say you were coming," said Reine-Marie, standing at the door as Henri and Gracie ran out to greet the new arrivals. "I'm glad."

She was freshly showered and had put on slacks and a soft sweater. She turned to Agent Cloutier. "I have soup and sandwiches in the kitchen. You must be hungry."

She was. "Yes, please. *Merci.*"

As they entered the home, Homer stepped closer to Reine-Marie, looking at her face. Then he shook his head.

"I did that," he said, pointing to the bruise. "I can't believe it. I'm so sorry. I don't know what came over me."

"I do," she said. "And I think you showed amazing restraint. I shouldn't have tried to stop you. I'd have ripped the head off anyone who tried to stop me."

If it had been Annie dragged from the river. Or Daniel. Or Armand. She'd have done far worse to anyone standing between her and them.

"Your room is waiting for you. Would you like to freshen up, then meet us in the kitchen?"

He nodded, and the two women watched as he slowly climbed the stairs. Followed, slowly, by Fred.

"Homer?" said Lysette, not sure what to do.

"I'll be fine, Lysette."

Even something as small as hearing him say her name thrilled her.


"Chief Inspector, this is Cameron."

Beauvoir snatched the mouthpiece off its cradle and pressed the button. "*Oui.*"

Gamache turned to watch, holding Beauvoir's eyes.

"We have the warrant for Tracey's arrest."

Beauvoir exhaled. They had it.

But he wanted more.

"Is Superintendent Lacoste still in the interview room?"

"Yes."

"Tell her to call as soon as she comes out." He went to replace the handset, but Gamache stopped him.

"I have an idea."

"Hold on, Cameron," said Beauvoir, and clicked the handset off while Gamache explained.

Beauvoir nodded approval, then clicked the handset back on. "Still there, Cameron?"

"*Oui, patron.*"

"This is what I want you to do."

Agent Cameron knocked on the door, then entered.

Lacoste glanced at him with some annoyance. It was unusual to be interrupted in the middle of what was proving a difficult interrogation.

Pauline Vachon was holding unexpectedly firm.

She would not admit that Tracey planned to kill his wife and that that's what the posts were about.

Cameron bent down and whispered in her ear, then left.

Lacoste smiled and turned back to Vachon, who was watching her with feigned boredom. But after a few seconds of silence, Vachon's brows lowered.

"What?" she demanded.

"I probably shouldn't tell you this, but an arrest warrant has just been issued for Carl Tracey. For the murder of Vivienne Godin. Chief Inspector Beauvoir is bringing him in. He'll be here in half an hour."

Lacoste got up and, collecting the papers, closed the file.

"Can I go now?"

"Not quite yet. I want to hear what Monsieur Tracey has to say. Then you can go."

She walked to the door. And stopped when she heard that one word. That beautiful word.

"Wait."

The radio crackled, and Jean-Guy reached for it so quickly it bobbled out of his hand.

He juggled it for a moment before finally grasping it.

"Beauvoir."

"We have him," said Isabelle Lacoste. "Pauline Vachon just admitted they'd discussed killing Vivienne. That Tracey planned to do it."

"She'll sign the statement? Testify against him?"

"Yes."

They knocked on the door.

By now it was dark. Not even the porch light was on. Though there was still the one light on. Upstairs.

They knocked again. Still no answer.

Beauvoir turned to the two uniformed Sûreté agents and signaled them to go around back. Then he and Gamache exchanged glances.

Beauvoir turned the handle of the front door. It was unlocked. He swung it open.

"Tracey? Carl Tracey?" Beauvoir called. "Sûreté. We have a warrant for your arrest."

He walked in, slowly, carefully, with Gamache right beside him. Both seasoned officers scanned the room. Looking for a killer.

They found him passed out, drunk, on the bed. In a puddle of his own vomit.

# CHAPTER THIRTY

~

The arraignment was held the next morning, in Superior Court at the Palais de justice in Montréal.

Once he'd sobered up, Carl Tracey had been given a shower and a change of clothes. He spent the night at the Cowansville detachment, where he'd been booked for murder.

From there, early in the morning, he'd been driven to a cell in the Montréal courthouse.

Chief Inspectors Beauvoir and Gamache met there first thing and interviewed him, with his court-appointed lawyer present. Predictably, his lawyer told him not to say anything. Equally predictably, Tracey couldn't help but talk.

After Tracey claimed he had nothing to do with Vivienne's death, Beauvoir presented him with Pauline Vachon's statement.

"She says you talked about killing your wife—"

Tracey snorted. "Who doesn't say that every now and then?"

"I don't," said Chief Inspector Beauvoir.

"You will."

Beauvoir knew he shouldn't let this man get up his nose, but Tracey was firmly lodged there. That smug, weaselly look. From a man who'd just killed his wife and unborn child.

"You know nothing—" Beauvoir began.

"Chief Inspector," said Gamache, a warning in his voice.

Carl Tracey turned to Gamache. "I wouldn't kill my own wife. Too obvious. But someone else's . . . That was your wife in that village, right? Looks like you and I have something in common. That bruise on her face?"

Gamache grew very still, very quiet. Then he turned back to Beauvoir, who was staring, dumbfounded by what Tracey just said.

The lawyer ended the session there.

Beauvoir and Gamache walked down the hallway. Finally Gamache spoke.

"He'll confess."

"You think?"

"*Oui*. He's a foolish, weak man. If he doesn't actually mean to confess, he'll incriminate himself with his bravado. He'll hang himself."

"If only."

Gamache glanced at Beauvoir but said nothing.

They stood as the judge took her seat.

The prosecutor, with Chief Inspector Beauvoir beside him, was on one side of the courtroom. Tracey and his lawyer on the other.

Gamache and Agent Cloutier sat immediately behind the prosecution desk, with Homer Godin between them. Behind them sat Simone Fleury with at least twenty other women.

Young. Middle-aged. Elderly. Stony-faced.

Valkyries. Warrior Fates. Magnificent and terrifying.

Gamache caught Madame Fleury's eye. She nodded.

The seats behind Tracey were empty.

Barry Zalmanowitz, a prosecutor they knew well, had been given the case. He was feeling confident enough to kid Gamache when the Sûreté officers showed up at his office.

"I see you're trending, Armand. Of course, I knew the video was faked. You're not that good a shot."

He smiled. Obviously trying, with a spectacular lack of success, to lighten the mood.

Seeing the grim look on Chief Inspector Gamache's face and the anger on Beauvoir's, the prosecutor dropped his voice and added,

"I also saw the real thing. I can't believe it was posted again. I'm sorry. I hope they find out who did that. Someone calling themselves 'dumbass.'"

"We have an idea," said Beauvoir.

He'd stayed away from Three Pines, not wanting to see Ruth. Not wanting to say things that could never be taken back. He knew that the elderly woman actually meant well. But in true Ruth fashion, she'd managed to inflict a wound.

And this one went deep.

Before the proceedings started, Beauvoir had pulled Vivienne's father aside and said, "This won't take long. The judge will ask Tracey how he pleads—"

"What will he say?"

"We think his plea will be not guilty."

Beauvoir waited for the outburst, but there was none. Monsieur Godin, in the past twelve hours, had managed to harness his emotions. Though Beauvoir could see it was a struggle.

Gamache had prepared the man the night before, as much as possible, for what would happen.

Carl Tracey would be led in. He'd sit at a distance from them, but Godin would certainly see him.

"Will you be able to control yourself?" Gamache had asked.

"I think so."

Gamache had paused before speaking again. "If you don't think you can, then you shouldn't go. If there's an outburst, you'll be thrown out, or even arrested. You'll do yourself and the case no favors."

Homer had glanced into the fire, mesmerized by the liquid flames. It was just the two of them now, and Fred the dog.

They'd had dinner in the kitchen with Reine-Marie and Lysette Cloutier. It was a simple meal of lentil soup and thick-cut fresh bread, warm from the oven, and cheese.

Homer managed a few spoonsful and finished off one piece of bread, with melted butter.

Now they sat alone in the restful room, with coffee and a plate of untouched chocolate chip cookies. Reine-Marie had gone to bed. Henri and Gracie trailing along behind her. Agent Cloutier had driven back to Montréal.

"I'll control myself," said Homer.

Gamache studied the man. And nodded. He wasn't completely convinced Godin would do it, or that it was even possible. But he also knew there was no way to prevent Vivienne's father from being there when Carl Tracey was arraigned for Vivienne's murder.

Homer had to face his daughter's killer.

They talked into the night. About Vivienne. About her mother. About everything except what had happened.

Finally, at just after two in the morning, Godin fell silent. After a few minutes, he got up.

"I think I'm ready for bed." He looked at Armand. "I've never had a brother. Not even a close man friend. Know a lotta guys, but we never really talk. Now I wonder why not." He paused and gathered himself before speaking again. "This has helped."

"I'm glad."

Gamache slept lightly, listening for the sound of restless footsteps. But finally Homer had to be woken from a deep sleep at six thirty.

"There's coffee and breakfast, if you'd like," Armand had said after poking his head in the door and seeing a groggy Homer. "Then we need to drive in."

And now they sat in the courtroom. The early April, late-morning sun struggling through the grimy windows.

Homer ran his hands, shaking a little, through his short gray hair and then jerked when there was a sound off to their left. A door opening.

He reached out and grabbed Armand's arm as a passenger on a suddenly doomed aircraft would reach for the person in the next seat.

Gamache turned with him, as did everyone else, and watched as Carl Tracey, in handcuffs, was led in.

Homer rose to his feet and stood stock-still, face immobile, hands clenched at his sides. Eyes fastened on his former son-in-law. Willing Tracey, daring him, to look in his direction.

But Tracey did not.

Homer stared, in a pose so contained, so dignified, so stoic it both amazed Gamache and bruised his heart.

Armand had also gotten to his feet, to stand with Homer. And now the others joined them, as the bailiff announced, "Silence. All rise, please. The Superior Court is now in session, the Honorable Caroline Pelletier presiding."

The judge, in long black robes, entered. With a signal, everyone in the courtroom sat back down. Except Godin.

"Homer," whispered Gamache, getting back up and touching, slightly tugging, his arm. The man, roused from a sort of trance, sat.

But continued to glare at Tracey.

The rustling stopped as Judge Pelletier got herself organized. And then there was silence. One that went on. And on.

Gamache's face revealed nothing, but he grew wary. Alert. This protracted pause was unusual.

He knew the judge. She was strict. No-nonsense. Not chummy or clubby. She brooked no informality and no bending of the rules or the interpretation of the law.

She was, in his opinion, a great jurist.

But now she was looking down at her papers, shuffling them a bit, instead of doing what she should have been doing, which was to have the charges read and ask the defendant how he pleads.

It was rote. Routine. Something they went through all the time. Clear, simple.

Tracey would be remanded for trial. Led away. And that would be it.

Except . . .

Out of the corner of his eye, Gamache could see Beauvoir stirring. The prosecuting attorney was staring intently at the judge.

Beauvoir turned in his seat and mouthed, "What's up?"

Something was up. Something was wrong.


Judge Caroline Pelletier looked out at the courtroom.

Her heart sank when she saw the women ranged behind Chief Inspector Gamache.

291

She knew who they were and why they were there.

She intentionally skimmed past the man beside Monsieur Gamache. She assumed it was the victim's father.

Judge Pelletier did not want to catch his eye.

Instead her gaze moved to the defense table and rested on the man sitting next to his lawyer.

The defendant, Carl Tracey.

Judge Pelletier had been up most of the night, going over and over the file. The evidence.

She knew it was folly, and ethically wrong, to prejudge. But judges were, after all, human. And some cases were just obvious.

There was very little doubt in her mind who had killed Vivienne Godin. Nor was there much doubt about the outcome of the day.

Still, to be sure, she'd called up colleagues and asked opinions.

Then asked more colleagues, judges across the country, and collected more opinions.

She'd even phoned her old, now retired, law prof and gone through the case against Carl Tracey.

All, save one, said the same thing.

And now it was her turn to say it.


"There is, I'm afraid, a poisonous tree in this case."

Jean-Guy Beauvoir stared at the judge in amazement, then turned to the prosecutor. Zalmanowitz's mouth had fallen open. Beauvoir swiveled to look at Gamache, whose eyes were wide, his mouth also slightly open.

"It goes back to the very beginning," said Judge Pelletier, her voice almost a monotone. "Even before Vivienne Godin's body was found."

"What's she saying?" asked Homer, his voice below normal conversation, but above a whisper. "What does this mean?" He could tell, a child could tell, that something unexpected had just happened. Something bad. "What's a poisonous tree?"

"In a minute," whispered Gamache, glancing briefly at Homer before returning his attention to the judge.

"When Vivienne Godin's overnight bag was found on the shores of the river—" Judge Pelletier turned to Beauvoir. "You did not have a warrant, I believe, to go onto that private property."

Beauvoir shot to his feet. "No, Your Honor, we didn't. But it was an emergency. The river was in flood, and it needed to be diverted. The law allows us to enter private property in an emergency. We don't need a warrant to rescue people from a fire, for example."

"True, but in going onto private property you didn't just create a runoff for the flood. You discovered the victim's duffel bag. Did you open it?"

"We did."

Judge Pelletier nodded. "*Oui*. That's what it says here." She placed her hand on the papers in front of her. "There's video evidence of that, too, which has been submitted. Your written statement says that upon opening it and examining the contents, you realized it belonged to the missing woman, which led you to the bridge, which led you to her body—"

"What's happening?" Godin whispered, more urgently.

"Just listen," said Gamache, keeping his voice low, calm, reasonable. He reached over and touched the man's arm, feeling it so tense it might snap.

His own body was taut. He could see where this was going, though he barely believed it.

A poisonous tree? Surely not.

He'd become hyperaware of his surroundings. The world was bright and in sharp focus. Sounds were magnified. The smallest movement noted. Every word, every inflection absorbed.

It was the way he became when under attack. For this felt like an attack. Like someone had just tossed a grenade into the courtroom.

And there was nothing he could do to stop it from going off.

Off to the side, at the defense desk, he could see the court-appointed lawyer equally surprised. But unlike the prosecution, who was looking at the judge as though he'd been hit in the face, the defense was smiling.

Zalmanowitz, the prosecuting attorney, got to his feet. "If it pleases the court, there's case law covering this. Where officers go onto private property to stop a crime being committed and in the course of that come across another crime—"

"True." The judge stopped him there with an upraised hand. Predicting just this objection. "But no crime was being committed. A river was flooding. It was an act of nature. A violent one, potentially dangerous, granted. I have no doubt that the actions of the officers saved property if not lives. It was the right thing to do. Except when they found the duffel bag, they should have immediately applied for a warrant, before removing it. And certainly before opening it."

Beauvoir, in near panic, looked once again at Gamache.

Gamache himself was shocked. Never had he heard such a severe, such a narrow interpretation of the law. He immediately scribbled on a piece of paper and handed it to the prosecution, who read it and said, "Your Honor, a life was at stake. As you said, Madame Godin had not yet been found. She could have been hurt, or kidnapped. They needed to search the overnight bag, to determine if it was hers and if it could lead them to her. Which it did."

"And that might have been justified," said the judge. "Had they not been on the defendant's private property. Let me ask you this: Did the officers get Mr. Tracey's permission before opening the bag?"

The prosecution turned to Beauvoir, who had gone so pale his lips were almost white. He thought and thought, glancing at Gamache once.

Beauvoir was not pausing to remember, Gamache knew. He remembered perfectly well, as did Gamache. Carl Tracey shouting at them not to open the duffel bag. That it was none of their business.

No. Jean-Guy Beauvoir was pausing to decide whether or not to tell the truth.

Judge Pelletier was giving them a potential out. A way to cut down the poisonous tree. Whose roots and branches and fruit looked to infect so much of their case against Tracey.

"While not formally sworn in, Chief Inspector," the judge said, "you are presumed under oath."

She could see his thoughts, his struggle. And it seemed clear to Gamache that she sympathized. This was not giving Judge Pelletier any pleasure. But it was, according to her lights, the law.

Before Beauvoir could answer, the defense got to his feet. "Your Honor, my client tells me he told them—" Tracey grabbed his arm, and the lawyer bent down to listen to his client, then straightened up. "He begged them not to open the bag. But they did, anyway."

"I see," said the judge. "Just out of interest's sake, why didn't he want the police to open the bag? If it could have helped them find his wife, which, presumably, he wanted."

That was met with silence. It was a very good question.

Both Gamache and Beauvoir would have been amused by Tracey's bringing this scrutiny on himself had they themselves not been so appalled by what was happening.

The lawyer consulted his client, then turned to the judge. "He says he believed his wife was alive and that the bag contained things she wouldn't want strangers to see. Like underwear."

"Oh, for Christ's sake," burst out of Homer. "You're not . . . You can't . . . This's . . ."

"Homer," said Gamache, turning to him, but Godin was already on his feet.

Gamache also rose and faced Homer, who was glaring at Tracey with all the violence a look could contain. Then Gamache turned to the judge.

"Please, Your Honor," he said.

"For you, Monsieur Gamache, I will give you a moment to settle him. I'm assuming that is the young woman's father?"

"He is, and thank you." Gamache turned back to Homer. "Do you need to leave? Look at me." He stood between Homer and Tracey, breaking Homer's line of sight. Forcing Homer to focus on him. "You need to hold it together." Gamache was speaking so quietly that no one else could hear. And so forcefully that Godin would not just hear but listen. "Or you need to leave. Do you understand?"

Godin nodded.

"Do you want to stay?"

Godin nodded.

"And you'll control yourself, no matter what happens?"

"What is happening, Armand?" The man's voice now sounded almost like that of a child.

"I don't know, but losing control will only make it worse. You understand?"

"You promised. You promised it would be okay."

"Please," said Gamache. "Just sit down."

Homer sat, and Gamache turned to the judge and gave a nod that was almost a small bow. *"Merci."*

The judge looked tired, strained. Even, Gamache thought, a little sad. Which did not bode well.

She turned back to Beauvoir. "You still haven't answered my question, Chief Inspector."

Beauvoir got back to his feet. "No, Your Honor, we didn't ask, and the defendant did not give us permission to open the bag."

"I see." She gestured to him to sit back down.

As he did, he glanced at Gamache, who nodded approval. A lie would make this even worse. Besides, there was the video Reine-Marie had taken at his request.

"The opening of the bag is, in my opinion, a poisonous tree," said Judge Pelletier, "and everything that stems from that act is its fruit and therefore tainted and inadmissible."

The prosecutor leaped up. "I object!" Speaking more forcefully than was perhaps wise.

"Noted," said Judge Pelletier.

"Are we in trouble?" Agent Cloutier leaned across Homer to whisper to Gamache.

"We're all right. We have Pauline Vachon's signed statement. That didn't stem from the discovery of the duffel bag."

"Right. Good."

"Now," said Judge Pelletier, no longer looking up at them. "On to the other issue."

The world seemed to stop for Gamache.

Other issue?

He could feel, almost hear, his heart throbbing. Everything, everyone else seemed to recede, except the judge. He was completely, totally, focused, and when she next spoke, it was as though her words were deposited directly, and uniquely, into his head.

"The statement by Madame Vachon. I've considered this and consulted colleagues across the country, many of whom are beginning to form judgments on the issue of social media and boundaries."

"What's she saying?" hissed Beauvoir. "My God, she's not . . ."

But he couldn't continue. Couldn't conceive that—

"The boundaries of a person's house are clear," said the judge. "The property line. The front door. A warrant is needed to cross. A warrant is needed to tap into a phone and listen to private conversations, to read private emails. But the very notion, even the name, of social media confuses issues of trespass. How can something social, public, be trespassed? There are limits, of course. Laws against hate speech. Pornography. But even those are unclear, blurry. When is social media private and when is it public? Pauline Vachon and her relationship to Carl Tracey were discovered after a Sûreté officer tricked Madame Vachon into giving her access to her private Instagram account."

Agent Cloutier's eyes opened wide. "What . . . ?"

"Oh, my God," whispered Beauvoir.

"Armand?" said Homer. "What's this?"

The judge had not raised her head. Would not look their way. And appeared to be reading now from notes.

"There's not much jurisprudence on this as yet, but the vast majority of jurists I consulted agreed that in posing as NouveauGalerie, it was the equivalent of a robber posing as an electrician to gain access to a private residence. Under false pretenses. With the intent to compromise the occupant."

The prosecution shot to his feet. "I object. That isn't the correct analogy."

"And what is?"

"Undercover operations," snapped Zalmanowitz. "A police officer posing as someone they are not in order to gain evidence in a criminal case."

"Yes, I did consider that," said Judge Pelletier. "Except there was as yet no reason to suspect Madame Vachon of anything criminal. Monsieur Tracey, perhaps, but as soon as Agent Cloutier realized she was corresponding with this Pauline Vachon, she should have disengaged.

Instead she tricked Madame Vachon into giving her access to an account that led to not just evidence of an affair but to those incriminating posts."

Judge Pelletier turned to Carl Tracey. With her voice flat, she began to speak.

Armand Gamache held his breath.

*Don't do it. Don't do it.*

"Monsieur Tracey, I am having the charges against you dropped. You're free to go."

"No!"

Godin shot to his feet, as did Gamache.

He reached for Homer and braced himself but was still propelled backward as Vivienne's father exploded forward. Toward Tracey.

There was sudden mayhem as chairs and benches were knocked over. Guards ran to yank the judge off the dais and into the back room.

People fell over, and others joined the fight to stop an inconsolable, uncontainable father.

Gamache felt his feet go out from under him and fell backward, dragging Homer down with him. They landed in a pile on the marble floor.

There was an eerie silence. Then the squealing of overturned chairs being shoved aside as arms and legs reassembled themselves into individual people.

There were moans and groans. Orders issued by guards and cops.

Beauvoir, who'd leaped over the railing to try to stop Homer, now rolled off the man's back. And tried to get air back into his own lungs.

"Armand?" he gasped.

"Okay. You?"

"*Oui.*"

Gamache freed his legs and, scrambling to his knees, bent over Homer's inert body. So still was the man that Gamache felt for a pulse, then laid down, his cheek on the cold marble floor. Face-to-face. Their noses almost touching.

"Homer?"

His eyes were closed, and Armand noticed blood on the floor. "Get an ambulance."

A court officer ran to make the call.

Beauvoir was keeping the guards away, explaining the man wasn't armed. Wasn't a danger.

Homer's eyes fluttered, then opened. And focused on Armand.

"You promised," he whispered.

# CHAPTER THIRTY-ONE

~

Vivienne's father was taken by ambulance to the Hôtel-Dieu hospital.

Gamache had wanted to go with him but sent Cloutier and Cameron instead.

It had been Bob Cameron who'd finally brought Godin down. He'd come into the courtroom late, standing unnoticed at the back, as the judge had given her reasoning and conclusion.

And when Homer had burst forward, Cameron had instantly seen what was happening. And what needed to be done.

The left tackle did what he'd been trained to do.

He'd run into the fray, diving at the last minute, using his body to sweep Godin's legs out from under him. And, in so doing, also tackling Gamache. And Beauvoir. And Cloutier. And anyone else hanging on to Vivienne's father.

"Give me a few minutes," Zalmanowitz, the prosecutor, said to the Sûreté officers once the ambulance had left and order had been restored. "I'll speak to the judge. Then we can talk."

Judge Pelletier had decided not to charge Monsieur Godin. Clearly sympathizing with the man. The father.

"*Merde, merde, merde,*" muttered Beauvoir.

"*Merde,*" added Lacoste.

She'd been in another interview, to possibly take over command of Public Security, when word had reached her about what had happened in the courthouse.

301

She'd hurried over, and now the three of them walked along the slushy cobblestoned streets outside the courthouse. In need of fresh air and to try to clear their heads.

"A shitshow. What the fuck was that?" Beauvoir stopped, took a deep breath, closed his eyes, then opened them again. "Sorry. But really. What the fuck was that?"

They circled the building in Old Montréal. Feeling the sun on their hot faces. And the fresh air in their lungs.

They spoke a little, mostly curses from Beauvoir. Gamache, who had said almost nothing since the judge's pronouncement, let them vent. While he walked and considered.

Then they all fell silent, lost in their own thoughts. The same thoughts.

Partly about what had gone wrong, mostly how to fix it.

Beauvoir's phone buzzed. A text from Zalmanowitz. As terse as the man.

*Meet me in my office.*

The three Sûreté officers were around the back of the building, but Gamache knew the way in, past the trash and recycling bins. After he'd pressed the button and stared into the camera, the door was unlocked. It helped that Gamache knew the guards by name and they knew him. After decades of trials. And tribulations.

Beauvoir and Lacoste followed Gamache along grimy, ill-lit corridors. Taking the service elevator, they finally emerged into the gleaming marble hallway. The public face, hiding the smelly, dark underbelly of justice.

"Well, that was a clusterfuck of a decision," said Zalmanowitz, not bothering to get up or even look up from his laptop, as they entered. "I spoke to Judge Pelletier, who walked me through it."

"And?" asked Beauvoir.

"And we'll appeal, of course," said the prosecutor.

"Will we win?"

"Hard to say."

"Try."

Now Zalmanowitz gave them his complete attention, turning from his screen. "Honestly? I doubt it. As much as we hate the decision, Judge

302

Pelletier did her due diligence, even canvassing jurists across the country—"

"But a poisonous tree?" interrupted Beauvoir. "Come on."

"I know. I can't explain her interpretation. Well, I can. But it's an incredibly narrow view of the law."

He rubbed his eyes and sighed. Then, looking up, he smiled weakly. "You know what they say about lawyers—"

Gamache gave Beauvoir a warning glance.

"—that we're like children in the dark, imagining all the monsters."

It was, Gamache knew, a pretty apt description of his job, too.

"Seems I missed one," said the lawyer. "Two, really."

"We all did," said Beauvoir.

Zalmanowitz nodded his thanks for sharing the blame. "Judge Pelletier had latitude. It could have gone the other way, and I think she genuinely struggled with it. Especially since, as she privately told me, our case was a lock—"

Beauvoir's hands slammed down on the wooden arms of his chair, and he growled, "Jesus."

Getting up, he paced the room, trying to blow off the pent-up frustration. The others let him pace until he'd regained control of himself.

Sitting back down, he didn't apologize. But he did look directly at Zalmanowitz and say, "Someone needs to make sure Tracey gets what's coming to him."

"We're trying."

"Try harder."

"Look, you're the ones who opened that duffel bag," he said, his voice rising, his frustration getting away from him with every word. "Who let an inexperienced agent loose to goose-step around in that Instagram account—"

Zalmanowitz stopped himself, with effort. Putting his hands out in front of him as though to protect them from his wrath.

He sat back in his chair. Which bounced with the force of his body.

Staring at Gamache, he saw that while the Chief Inspector's tone had been civil so far, and his face calm, his jaw muscles were clamped tight.

This was not a relaxed man. This was a man who was simply better at containing his emotions.

"I'm sorry." Zalmanowitz took a deep breath and looked at the three investigators. "This isn't your fault."

"Of course it is," snapped Beauvoir. "I fucked up."

"So did I," said Gamache. "I'm the one who actually opened the duffel bag."

"And I let Agent Cloutier pursue the Instagram account. Even encouraged her," said Lacoste, shaking her head.

"None of us looks good in this," Zalmanowitz admitted. "I'm the lawyer, the prosecutor. I should've seen that there might be a problem. But I didn't."

Now he rubbed his face with his hands. Trying to erase his expression of defeat.

"That is true. This's mostly your fault," said Beauvoir, and when the prosecutor looked at him, Beauvoir smiled. And Zalmanowitz gave one gruff laugh.

Truce.

"As I said, I'll file an appeal," said the prosecutor. "But that'll take months to be heard. The poisonous tree is the most damaging ruling. It's just unfortunate that so much stems from something so early on. It affects almost every bit of evidence."

"'Unfortunate' isn't the word," said Lacoste.

Zalmanowitz nodded. "Her decision on the poisonous tree sits right on the boundary, which is why no other judge will overturn her ruling. And you'd better note it, because it'll become case law from now on. And affect all other searches. But"—now he leaned forward, arms on his desk—"the more gnarly decision, by her own private admission, concerns the social-media issue."

"The Instagram account," said Lacoste, pulling her chair closer to the desk.

"Exactly. Judge Pelletier's right, of course, that courts are struggling to figure out the laws around social media. The government's working on legislation, but it's controversial and sensitive, and you know how politicians love those two things."

He waited for their laugh of appreciation. Instead all he got were three glum stares.

"If this judgment stands," he went on, "it'll redefine boundaries."

"But it's not right," said Beauvoir. "It ties our hands when it comes to social-media accounts. It pretty much locks us out and lets people do anything they want."

"As they can in the privacy of their own homes," said Zalmanowitz. "That's the analogy she's using. As Pierre Elliott Trudeau said when he was Prime Minister, the government has no place in the bedrooms of the nation."

"But there are limits," said Gamache. "Assault, child pornography, murder. Just because people do it in the privacy of their homes doesn't mean they're beyond the reach of law. But I also know we aren't solving anything by going over and over this. A decision was reached. You'll appeal. In the meantime, Carl Tracey is free. Do we have other evidence, untainted, that can be used?"

"Vivienne called her father that day, to say she was finally leaving Tracey," said Beauvoir. "That sure suggests she was afraid."

"There's the evidence of Agent Cameron, who responded to Vivienne's 911 calls," said Lacoste. "It was clear there was abuse."

"But not clear enough for him to actually bring Tracey in. He didn't feel it met the 'reasonable suspicion' test. Besides, abuse isn't murder. What else do we have?"

"There's that young man, what's his name," said Beauvoir. "The one she called over and over the day she was killed."

"Gerald Bertrand," said Lacoste. "He claims it was a wrong number."

"And you believe him?" asked Zalmanowitz.

"Yes, I think I do. We checked him out, and there's absolutely nothing connecting him to Vivienne or Tracey. I think she wrote the number down wrong."

"What number was she calling again?" asked Gamache.

Lacoste gave it to him.

"I don't understand why, if she was so afraid, she didn't ask her father to come get her," said Zalmanowitz.

"He offered," said Gamache. "But she said it was too dangerous, that she had to choose her time carefully."

"So she feared for her life?" said Zalmanowitz. "She told her father that?"

Gamache considered, remembering that first conversation with

Godin, in his home in Ste.-Agathe. "Not specifically. I think she was afraid and let him know that, but not for her life. I think if she'd told him that, Monsieur Godin would have definitely gone to get her. He didn't want to make it worse or trigger any violence. So he stayed home."

"That poor man," said Zalmanowitz. "How do you live with yourself?"

There was no answering that.

"So," said Zalmanowitz after a pause. "Vivienne was obviously afraid of her husband."

"*Oui*. Afraid of what he'd do if he knew she was leaving—"

"But wait a minute." Zalmanowitz raised his hand to stop Gamache. "According to the girlfriend, Pauline Vachon, Tracey wanted to get rid of her. Wouldn't her leaving solve the problem, and then they wouldn't have to kill her? Why not just let her go? He didn't really have to kill her."

"He might not have realized she planned to leave," said Beauvoir. "He says she told him, but does that really seem likely?"

It did not.

"So you think he killed her without knowing she was leaving anyway?" asked Zalmanowitz.

"Even if he knew, Tracey still had a motive," said Gamache. "He admitted to me he had no intention of giving half the home to her. Or to support the child."

He told them about his exchange in the kitchen when Tracey admitted that Vivienne's leaving and taking half the farm with her was a pretty good motive.

"So there's your answer," said Beauvoir. "Tracey's violent. Drunk. He planned to kill her, and he did. The fact she was going to leave anyway only drove him more crazy."

"And the bag?" asked Zalmanowitz. "How did it get into the river? Who packed it?"

"We think Tracey did," said Beauvoir. "Based on strange things in the bag and the private message to Vachon."

"*Stuff's in the bag*," Lacoste read from her notes. "*Everything's ready. Will be done tonight. I promise.*"

Zalmanowitz sighed. "Damning. And completely inadmissible. But what I don't get is if she did plan to leave, like she told her father, why didn't she pack the bag? Oh, never mind." He flung himself back in the chair again and threw up his hands. "It's all academic. The duffel bag is out of bounds. It's as though the bag never existed."

"*Non*," said Beauvoir. "It's as though we didn't find it. But it happened. And now we need to find another way to get him."

They looked at him. Beauvoir had climbed out of his outrage, more determined than ever. Far from defeated.

They'd get Carl Tracey. Somehow.

The prosecutor leaned forward again, drew his notepad toward him, and picked up a pen.

"Right. What we can use is Carl Tracey's first statement to you," the prosecutor said to Gamache. "That was before the bag or the body was found."

"And we have the first interview with Homer Godin, when Vivienne was still missing," said Beauvoir. "And we have the phone records that led us to Gerald Bertrand."

They went back over and over those conversations.

Tracey saying Vivienne was drunk and abusive.

Tracey claiming she was having affairs.

That she told him the baby wasn't his and that she was leaving him. That she'd gone off with some lover.

Tracey admitting to hitting her that Saturday night. And then going into his studio with a bottle, getting wasted, and passing out. When he woke up, she was gone.

"Okay," said Zalmanowitz. "That's his version of what happened. We know it's all bullshit. How did he seem to you, Armand, when you first spoke to him?"

Gamache thought back. It seemed months ago now, not mere days. "Belligerent. Violent."

He described the pitchfork and the shouts to get off the property.

"Not very cooperative," said Zalmanowitz. "The one good moment from a shitty day was the judge asking Tracey why he didn't want you to open the duffel bag, if he was so worried about his wife. It's a good question. A telling question. It must eat her up to have to release him. But you know, something's bothering me. After meeting Tracey and hearing more about him, I can understand him killing someone. What I don't understand is the method."

"How so?" asked Gamache.

"Wouldn't you expect this fellow to do something stupid and brutal?"

"Throwing his pregnant wife off a bridge to be battered and drowned in a freezing river isn't brutal enough for you?" asked Lacoste.

Zalmanowitz regarded her. "No. It's not. Given his history, I'd have expected something simpler. More hands-on. Beating her to death. Shooting her. Hitting her with a shovel and burying her. Why throw her off a bridge half a kilometer away?"

"Maybe it was Pauline Vachon's idea," said Lacoste. "She seems smart."

"No messages to support that it was her idea?"

"Where she suggests throwing Vivienne off the bridge?" asked Lacoste. "Yes, but we decided not to show you."

For one brief moment, Zalmanowitz believed her, then lowered his brows.

"Of course there weren't," said Lacoste. "They must've come up with the plan when they were together. We've canvassed the neighbors. A few saw him entering her place last week. She says that was for business."

"Right," said the prosecutor. "And even if there were explicit posts, describing it in detail, we couldn't use them, thanks to Nouveau-Galerie and that agent."

"It wasn't her fault," Lacoste repeated. "Like I said, she ran it by me and I approved. Encouraged her, even. So lay off her."

"Okay, sorry, you're right," said Zalmanowitz. "Back to the bridge. How did Tracey even get Vivienne there?"

"The coroner thinks the most likely explanation is that he beat her senseless at home, put her in the car, and drove her to the bridge," said Beauvoir. "Her blood on the car handle and steering wheel might've come from her blood on his hands."

"But that doesn't explain his boot prints," said the prosecutor. "How would they get under the car if he drove her there?"

"Made when he was scouting the place, maybe," said Beauvoir. "We don't really know the details. And probably never will. Another possibility is that part of what Tracey said is true. Vivienne arranged to meet her lover on the bridge. Tracey overheard and got there first."

"Okay," said Lacoste. "But then, what happened to the lover? And when did she call him? There were only five calls out of the house that day. Four to what we think is a wrong number and one to her father."

"You said you believed Bertrand when he said he didn't know her," said Gamache. "Is it possible you were wrong?"

Lacoste considered. "It's always possible."

Gamache nodded, even as he recognized it for what it was. Desperation. But sometimes that uncovered something useful.

And they had precious little left to them except desperation.

"All right, let's walk through it," said the prosecutor. "Vivienne is afraid. She calls her father, telling him she's leaving her husband but has to choose her time. That evening Tracey beats her senseless, and then, either thinking she's dead or trying to work up the courage to finally kill her, he goes into his studio and gets drunk."

"Then Vivienne regains consciousness and calls Bertrand, her lover," said Beauvoir. "Begging for help. Telling him to meet her on the bridge. But this Bertrand fellow doesn't show up. She was a fling to him, nothing more. He sure didn't want to get involved with a pregnant woman running from a dangerous husband."

"Vivienne gets in the car and drives herself there," said the prosecutor. "Bertrand doesn't show, but Tracey does. He's waiting for her. He throws her off the bridge and tosses the bag in. The one he'd already packed, according to the posts."

"There is another possibility," said Gamache. They turned to him, and he sat forward. "That Bertrand did show up."

"Go on," said Zalmanowitz.

"Suppose Tracey didn't pack the bag, but Vivienne did. Suppose she called Bertrand, telling him to meet her on the bridge."

"Why there?" asked the prosecutor.

"Maybe that's where they always met," said Gamache. "She shows up and waits for him."

As he spoke, the cold, dark April evening appeared before them. Vivienne Godin, bruised from Tracey's latest and last beating, stands on the bridge. Bertrand's headlights appear down the disused dirt road. Little more than a path.

He gets out, and she tells him she's pregnant. Maybe even that the baby is his. She might have even believed it.

Tells him she's leaving her abusive husband and needs his help.

And then Bertrand snaps. Sees his frat-boy life changing completely. In panic, he pushes her backward. Into the railing. It breaks, and, to his horror, she falls.

Beauvoir, Lacoste, Zalmanowitz sat in silence, once again imagining Vivienne's face as she hung in the air between the bridge and the water. Then disappeared.

"To cover his tracks, he throws her bag in after her," said Beauvoir.

"Or maybe she had it in her hand or over her shoulder," said Lacoste. "And it went in with her."

"But what about Tracey's boot prints under Vivienne's car?" asked Zalmanowitz.

"Maybe they weren't Tracey's," said Gamache. "It's a pretty common boot. Monsieur Béliveau even sells it in his general store in Three Pines. And it's a standard size for a man. Ten."

"Are you seriously suggesting that Carl Tracey did not kill his wife?" asked Zalmanowitz. "But that this Gerald Bertrand did?"

"*Non*," admitted Gamache. "I'm just following possibilities. Things any defense would throw out there. I have no doubt that Tracey is the murderer, but there are questions."

Zalmanowitz was quiet, lost in thought, then looked at Gamache again. "Was he afraid?"

"I'm sorry?"

"Tracey. When you first went there to interview him about his missing wife. You said he was belligerent. But did he seem nervous? Afraid?"

Gamache thought, then shook his head. "No. Nor did he seem concerned that his wife was missing, as any normal husband would be."

"Or any husband smart enough to pretend," said Lacoste.

"We're just running in place," said Zalmanowitz. "Going back over crumbs and trying to assemble a banquet. The only thing we know for sure, besides that Vivienne was killed, is that she called her father that morning, then made four calls to what might, or might not, be a wrong number. Shit."

He threw down his pen. "All of this could've been avoided if she'd just asked her father to come get her. He's clearly the sort who could hold his own in a fight and would move heaven and earth to rescue her. And he sure wouldn't shy away from beating the shit out of her abusive husband. We saw that today."

As Zalmanowitz spoke, he continued to look at Gamache.

"He reminds me a bit of you, Armand. You have a daughter about Vivienne's age, don't you?"

"Annie, *oui*."

"What would you do if you knew her husband was abusing her?"

Armand raised his brows at Jean-Guy. Barry Zalmanowitz had obviously forgotten, or didn't know, that they were married.

"I think it's best if I didn't answer that." Then he grew serious. "What I can tell you is that Homer Godin confronted Tracey several times, but when it came down to it, Vivienne always intervened and denied abuse. It's not clear if she was trying to protect her husband or her father. Or, most likely, was afraid of another beating. Eventually Tracey isolated her, as abusers often do, refusing to allow Homer to visit. Refusing to allow Vivienne to visit him."

"In his statement, Tracey says it was Vivienne who didn't want to see her father," said Zalmanowitz.

"That's clearly a lie," said Beauvoir.

"Obviously, but there's no one except Homer to contradict him," said Zalmanowitz. "And unfortunately, any statement by him could be seen as colored by animus."

"There is Lysette Cloutier," said Lacoste.

"Who?" asked Zalmanowitz. "Her name sounds familiar."

"It would. She's the Sûreté agent who posed as NouveauGalerie," said Lacoste. "She's an old friend of the Godin family. It's because of her that we got onto Vivienne being missing. Homer had asked for her help."

"They're friends?" asked Zalmanowitz.

"She was best friends with Homer's late wife," Lacoste explained. "They stayed in touch."

"And she's Vivienne's godmother," said Gamache. "There seem to be feelings there, between Agent Cloutier and Monsieur Godin. At least on Cloutier's part. It's unclear how Homer feels."

"Hmmm," said Zalmanowitz. "Might be worth seeing if she can add anything."

"I think if she could've added something, she would've," said Lacoste. "But I'll ask."

Again they all recognized it for what it was. Desperation.

"Any word from the hospital on Godin's condition?" Zalmanowitz asked.

"There's no concussion," said Gamache. "They're releasing him soon."

"Good about the concussion thing, but now what? You know he'll try to—"

"Yes, we know," said Beauvoir with a sigh. That seemed to be the only thing they did know. "I've put an agent on Tracey. To protect him."

He actually felt his stomach sour as he said it. But he also remembered what Tracey had said in the interview room while looking directly at Gamache.

"There's a restraining order on Godin, is that right?" asked Beauvoir. "Keeping him away from Tracey."

"Yes," said Zalmanowitz. "It was issued after that fracas in the courtroom."

"I'd like one put on Carl Tracey as well," said Beauvoir. "Keeping him a distance from Godin and from Three Pines."

"Three Pines? Your village, Armand?" Zalmanowitz had been taking notes. Now he looked up at the man.

"*Oui*," said Gamache. "I doubt he was serious, but he threatened my wife."

"Really? Jesus, he is stupid. Is it enough to arrest him?"

"*Non*. It was vague," said Gamache.

"He said he wouldn't kill his own wife, but someone else's . . ." said Beauvoir, using the same upward inflection Tracey had used. "He was looking at Monsieur Gamache as he spoke."

"I see. I'll apply for a restraining order against Tracey." Zalmanowitz made a note. "But we all know if someone really wants to do harm, a piece of paper won't stop them."

*But a baseball bat . . .* thought Gamache.

"I take it Godin will be returning home?" said Zalmanowitz.

"I've asked the agents to bring him back to Three Pines," said Gamache. "He can stay with us."

"And if he doesn't want to? You can't force him, Armand," said Zalmanowitz.

"Since when was it against the law to imprison another human being?" asked Armand. "Oh, wait. I do remember something from my training."

Lacoste laughed, and Zalmanowitz smiled.

"Okay, I get it. You know what you're doing. But you can't keep him there, even with his consent, forever. He'll want to leave eventually. And I doubt time will blunt his desire to kill the man who killed his daughter."

"I doubt it, too," said Gamache. He took a deep breath, then sighed. "I'd hate to have to arrest him for that."

"And I'd hate to have to prosecute him," said Zalmanowitz.

"What would he get?" asked Beauvoir. "Out of interest's sake."

The prosecutor thought about that. "He'd be charged with murder. His defense would probably say that he was not criminally responsible. Diminished capacity, brought on by extreme grief. If they're smart, his lawyers will try the case in front of a jury. He'd be convicted, probably of manslaughter, but wouldn't serve much time. A year, probably less. Maybe time served."

"That's not so bad," said Beauvoir.

Gamache was staring at him. He wasn't considering taking the protection away from Tracey? Leaving the path clear for Godin to kill the man.

Surely Jean-Guy's last act as head of homicide would not be as an accessory to a homicide.

They'd have to talk.

Chief Inspector Beauvoir looked at Lacoste, then over to Gamache. And finally back to the prosecutor.

"We don't have enough evidence, untainted by the poisonous tree or the social-media fiasco, to convict Tracey. Do we."

"No," said Zalmanowitz. "Not even close. Unless you can find something else, we're screwed."

"And Carl Tracey gets away with murder," said Lacoste.

Beauvoir got up, and the others rose. "*Merci*. I'm sorry about this."

"So'm I. I'll put in the appeals. Even Judge Pelletier asked me to. She feels awful about it. I think she's more than half hoping she'll be overturned."

He walked them to the door and shook their hands. When it came to Gamache, he leaned in and whispered, "I'm sorry about the videos. Shitty day. I don't know if dumbass has done you a favor or not. Releasing the real video."

"I know the answer to that," said Gamache.

Zalmanowitz nodded. "There is one more thing, Armand."

"*Oui?*"

"Did you steal Tracey's dog?"

Now both Beauvoir and Lacoste turned and stared, first at the prosecutor, then at Gamache.

"I took Fred, yes. But I paid Tracey for him."

"Apparently not enough. He wants the dog back. He's filed a complaint."

"You stole the dog?" Beauvoir asked. "I thought he came with Homer."

"No. He was Vivienne's dog. Tracey was going to shoot him, so I took him. And I'm not giving him back."

On this day of blurred boundaries, one clear line had to be drawn, and it seemed to have been drawn at the dog. They couldn't save Vivienne, they might not even be able to save Homer. But they could save Fred.

Barry Zalmanowitz stared at Gamache, then nodded. "I'll take care of it. Don't worry."

"*Merci.*"

Now the prosecutor watched as the three of them, Gamache flanked by the two younger officers, walked down the corridor.

And he remembered the images on the real video. Gamache, amid ferocious gunfire, dragging a critically wounded Beauvoir to safety. Stanching the wound. Then having to leave him there and head back into the battle.

Then, later in the tape, Isabelle Lacoste was seen kneeling beside Gamache, holding his bloody hand as he lay, apparently dying, on the factory floor. Shot in the head and chest.

Now the three of them walked down the corridor, their feet echoing along a bright marble hall that hid so much stench below.

And while the prosecutor didn't envy Armand Gamache anything about what was happening, with the case and with the social-media attacks, he did envy him this.

He watched until the three of them walked out the huge double doors and disappeared into the crisp April day.


Once hit by the cold air, Beauvoir, as though slapped awake from a reverie, began to talk.

"I'm not going out like this."

"What do you suggest we do?" asked Lacoste.

"We head back to the incident room in Three Pines and go over the evidence we can use. Again and again. Until we find something we missed. There has to be something else there. Isabelle, I know you're still officially on leave, but—

"I have an overnight bag in the car, all ready to go," she said with a grin. "Old habits, right, *patron*?"

Gamache smiled. Old habits. Always being prepared to head out at a moment's notice.

"I have to get back to headquarters," she said. "I'll meet you down in Three Pines when I've finished."

Gamache and Beauvoir paused by their cars.

"How're you going to keep Homer at your place?"

"Helps that he won't have his own car, and I'll ask the others to stay with him."

"He'll walk there if he has to, Armand."

"*Oui*," said Gamache. "But he needs help, and I don't know what else to do, Jean-Guy. Do you?"

He was genuinely asking. But Jean-Guy Beauvoir had no answer.

As he drove down the familiar highway, Chief Inspector Beauvoir hoped and prayed they'd find something they'd overlooked.

Something.

Anything.

# CHAPTER THIRTY-TWO

⁓

Gamache was in his car, following Beauvoir and talking with Reine-Marie on the phone, explaining, or trying to explain, what had happened in court.

"Homer?" she asked. "How is he?"

Armand paused, unsure how to answer that.

Out of his mind with grief and pain and rage?

Incensed that a system that called itself "just" would allow his daughter's murderer to go free? On a technicality. Or two.

Inconsolable? Working out how to punish Carl Tracey himself?

Instead Armand gave the only answer he knew for sure. "There's no concussion. He can go home. But do you mind—"

"If he stays with us? Of course not. But—"

"Will we be able to keep him from Tracey?" said Armand. "I don't know. Can you hold on for a moment?"

Agent Cloutier was calling.

"Chief Inspector? We have a problem." She was whispering, urgency in her voice.

"What is it?"

"We're still at the hospital. They're just releasing him, but he won't come back to your place."

"He wants to go home?"

"Yes, but mostly he says . . ." Her voice faltered.

"Go on." Though Gamache suspected he knew what she was about to say.

"He says he never wants to lay eyes on you again."

"I see." Gamache took a breath.

He did see. It wasn't just that Tracey had walked free. That somehow the investigators had screwed up. It was that he'd broken his promise to Homer.

"Give him the phone, please."

There was a pause. "He won't take it."

"Then hold it up to his ear."

He knew he had seconds to get through to the man. Only one word, two at most, before Homer would pull away. He had one shot. And he took it.

"Fred."

Pause. Pause.

There was a rustling of the phone, some muffled conversation, then Cloutier's voice. "He'll come. But just to get the dog. He won't stay."

"Tell him I'm asking for one night. Just one. Then he can take Fred and go."

There was more muffled conversation.

*Come on. Come on.*

Finally, Cloutier's voice. "One night, *patron.*"

*"Bon."*

It was something. Twenty-four hours he didn't have before.

"I'll be in the incident room," said Gamache. "Let me know when you get to Three Pines."

*"D'accord, patron."*

He hung up and went back to Reine-Marie. And explained what had just happened.

"And you? Are you all right?" she asked.

How could he answer that?

"Never mind," she said. "I know. Come home soon."

"We're not far. Should be there in—"

"What is it, Armand?"


In the car ahead of him, Jean-Guy had put on the brakes and swerved, taking a dirt road off to the right.

They were almost at Three Pines. But now Jean-Guy was heading away from the village. At speed. Recklessly bumping along the washboard road.

The agent guarding Tracey had just reported that instead of going straight home, as he'd been advised to do after being discharged, Tracey had headed to his local bar.

To celebrate.

"What do you want me to do, *patron*?" the agent asked. "Should I go in?"

"No, stay where you are. I'm coming to you."

Jean-Guy knew he shouldn't, but still he did. He turned the car and now was gunning it toward Carl Tracey.

Beauvoir pulled in to the parking lot of the dive bar and parked beside the very well-marked Sûreté vehicle.

Normally, when doing surveillance, they wanted to be discreet.

But Beauvoir had specifically asked for a vehicle with "Sûreté du Québec" clearly marked. "In neon if possible," he'd said. "And I want the agent in uniform."

Tracey needed to be in no doubt that he was being not just guarded but watched.

As Beauvoir walked toward the bar, his hands flexed into tight fists, then opened. Then closed again. Into weapons.

Jean-Guy knew this was a mistake. The issue wasn't whether he was about to step into a pile of something soft and smelly. That much was obvious. The only question was, how big would it be? How deep would he go?

And could he stop himself before . . . ?

Chief Inspector Beauvoir walked right past the agent sitting in the car and said only two words.

"Stay here."

He heard a car pull in to the parking lot. As he reached the door to the bar, his hand on the knob, he heard the familiar voice behind him.

"Jean-Guy."

But for one of the few times in his life, Beauvoir chose to ignore Gamache.

"Stay here," said Chief Inspector Gamache as he strode by the agent who was beginning to get out of the car.

She stayed.

Beauvoir stepped into the bar.

It was dark. Smelled of stale cigarettes and fresh urine and flat beer.

A television was on, showing an *Andy Griffith* rerun. Opie had questions for his father. Again. But the answers were drowned out by the burst of laughter from a group of grubby men at the bar.

Four of them, Beauvoir saw immediately. No, five.

Two bottles of rye on the bar. Beer bottles clasped in hands, the men turned and squinted into the unexpected and unwanted light through the open door before it swung shut.

"Who the fuck are you?" one of them demanded.

Beauvoir didn't answer. He just stood there. Staring.

At Carl Tracey.

"Wait a minute," said Tracey. "A little respect, please. This's Chief Inspector Beauvoir. The guy who arrested me. Come to apologize?"

That brought more laughter.

Beauvoir did not react. Did not speak. Did not move.

Tracey lifted his beer. "Come on in. Jean-Guy, isn't it? Now that it's over, we can be friends. No hard feelings. Beer?"

He held the drink out toward Beauvoir, who could smell the musky, familiar aroma.

Gamache had stopped at the door. Through the dirt-smeared window, he was just able to make out the occupants of the bar.

Every cell in his body was straining forward. Demanding that he go in. To rescue Jean-Guy, from himself.

He was pretty sure, judging by the look on Beauvoir's face, that the head of homicide for the Sûreté du Québec was about to beat the crap out of Carl Tracey.

Maybe worse. Maybe he wouldn't stop at the crap.

But still, Gamache stopped himself. And he wondered why.

Then the thought appeared. Was it possible he wanted Beauvoir to do it?

Jean-Guy Beauvoir stood ten paces from Carl Tracey.

He stared but didn't move. Didn't speak. Didn't react at all.

Even when Tracey stepped toward him, goaded on by his drinking buddies, Jean-Guy's face remained completely impassive. A mask.

Gamache's expression changed. He was still watchful, vigilant. Prepared. His hand on the door. But now there was a very small smile. Of surprise and recognition.

Still, he remained prepared to act.

Watching Tracey laughing, Beauvoir felt himself almost overcome with rage.

But still he stood. Still.

"Come on," Tracey shouted, holding his beer by the neck and swaying slightly. "You're not joining in the celebrations."

But the men behind Tracey were growing uneasy in the face of this relentlessly still man at the door.

A couple continued to shout encouragement, but their voices were thinning. Their enthusiasm waning.

Carl Tracey was right up against Beauvoir now. But Beauvoir didn't react.

"Why're you here?" shouted Tracey. "I'm going to file a complaint. This's harassment."

Beauvoir's silence. His blank stare. Were driving Carl Tracey mad. And his friends away.

Gamache's smile had disappeared, and he prepared to enter the bar. Enough was enough.

Tracey staggered back.

His drinking buddies moved away and watched as he tripped and fell to the floor. Spilling his beer.

As silently as he'd entered, Chief Inspector Beauvoir left. Leaving behind four drunks staring down at the man wallowing on the floor. Tracey's eyes lifted, and for a split second Beauvoir thought he saw sadness there. Sorrow.

And then Carl Tracey threw up.

Once outside, Jean-Guy closed his eyes and, turning his face to the sky, took a long, long breath of the fresh, pine-scented air.

When he opened them, he saw Armand Gamache standing right in front of him. Staring.

Then Gamache's eyes crinkled at the corners. Wordlessly, because there was nothing to say, Gamache walked him back to his car, pausing for Beauvoir to speak to the agent.

"I'm going to get another officer here. I want one of you to stay in the vehicle and the other to stand outside the bar. Look through the window at Carl Tracey. So that he can see you. Whatever happens, don't engage him. If he comes to you, don't react. Only if he physically attacks you."

"So you want me to just stare at him, *patron*?"

"Yes. And when he leaves, follow him. Always keeping a distance. But I want him to see you. Understand? If he goes into a shop, stand outside and stare. If he meets someone, stop and—"

"Continue to stare?"

"*Oui.*"

"Why?"

Beauvoir bristled slightly. Not liking being questioned. But he knew his orders were unconventional in the extreme.

"This's a man who understand threats and violence. But this?"

"But what is 'this'?" the young agent persisted.

"A conscience."

"Huh?"

Chief Inspector Beauvoir recognized the expression on the agent's face. It was exactly the same look he'd given Gamache. For years. When the Chief Inspector had said, or ordered, something unconventional. Or downright odd.

That blank stare, colored slightly by concern that the senior officer had lost his mind.

Beauvoir now smiled. In the same way Gamache had smiled at him. For years.

While he could have simply left it at that, he wanted the agent to understand. And to never be afraid to question the orders of a superior.

As Gamache had patiently explained things to Beauvoir. For years.

"Your job is to protect the man, but you will also act as a sort of external conscience for a man who obviously doesn't have one."

He could see it dawning on her. And she, too, smiled. "Got it. I'll be the ghost of his dead wife."

"*Oui*. That's a good way of looking at it."

For a brief moment the agent considered asking if she could take a selfie with Chief Inspector Beauvoir and Chief Inspector Gamache.

But wisely decided against it.

As they walked to their cars, Armand Gamache placed a hand on Jean-Guy's back.

"Well done."

"It was close," said Jean-Guy, leaning toward him and lowering his voice. "You have no idea how much I wanted to—"

"I know."

Jean-Guy grunted. "Yes. You do." He looked behind him. "It won't change anything. This . . ." He waved toward the agent now standing outside the bar. Staring. ". . . won't make him confess. Not to murder."

"No. But it might make that young agent realize there're other weapons at our disposal besides our guns."

Gamache tapped his temple.

"Honestly? I suspect she thinks it's more . . ." Beauvoir raised his finger to his own temple and twirled it in a circle. "Thank God I told her I'm Chief Inspector Gamache."

Now Armand did laugh. "I am going to miss you, old son."

"And I'm going to miss you, too, sir. But I won't miss this."

He gazed at the fresh young agent standing straight and tall, twenty feet away from the cruddy bar.

Staring.

At a man Chief Inspector Beauvoir, as lead investigator, had let get away with murder.

Jean-Guy did not need anyone staring at him to know that it would be a long time, if ever, before his own conscience was clear.

# CHAPTER THIRTY-THREE

⁓

They spent the balance of the day in the incident room going back over all the evidence. Over and over.

Starting with what little was still admissible, then moving on to what they knew to be true but couldn't use.

Homer Godin returned to Three Pines, and according to Reine-Marie, after quietly walking Fred around the village green and being offered and declining food, he went into his room and closed the door.

Agent Cloutier stayed in the house, checking on him every now and then, to make sure. . . .

As Armand talked to Reine-Marie on the phone, he looked through what had once been the ticket window. He could see the bridge over the Rivière Bella Bella, the sandbags still in place. And beyond that, his home on the far side of the village green.

Between him and his home was a stranger, sitting on the bench.

"Who's that?" he asked Reine-Marie.

"Dominica Oddly."

Reine-Marie explained who she was and why she was there.

Gamache grimaced. Seemed Clara was having a day to rival his own. Both thanks, in no small part, to Ruth.

He turned and looked up at the photo of the old poet, glaring down at him.

When he hung up, Armand rubbed his eyes. Then, putting his reading glasses back on, he returned to the statements. Trying to find something.

Anything.

Isabelle Lacoste arrived. She barely had her coat off when Jean-Guy handed her a bunch of files.

"Here. You take these."

They divvied up the evidence, the interviews. Going over one another's work. Fresh eyes on old evidence. Looking for something overlooked.

"I'd like to speak to Monsieur Bertrand," said Gamache, getting up.

It still struck Gamache as unlikely that Vivienne would call this man again and again on the day she died, and its being a wrong number.

Surely she knew him. Surely he's lying.

"So do I," said Beauvoir, putting on his coat.

Gerald Bertrand was cordial. Young. Attractive. Holding his baby niece in his arms. He was apparently eager to help, but with nothing helpful to add.

Gamache tried. This way. That. He prodded, looking for holes. For chinks. For hairline fractures in Bertrand's story. In his demeanor. But found nothing.

They came away just as convinced as Lacoste. Bertrand was telling the truth. He did not know Vivienne. Or Tracey.

"Tracey lied, of course," said Beauvoir. "Vivienne didn't have a lover."

"At least," said Gamache, "not this lover."

Still, Vivienne Godin had spent the last few minutes of her life doing one thing.

Reaching out to one person.

But who was it? Who did a desperate, terrified woman call for help?

Not her father—he was too far away, thought Gamache. Was she trying Cameron?

But there was someone else in the picture. Someone who'd been in Vivienne's life, all her life. Her godmother. Who was, after all, a woman and a cop.

On the way back, they stopped at Pauline Vachon's place. Her signed statement had implicated Carl Tracey, but not herself. Now the investigators wanted the whole truth.

"Did I want her gone?" Pauline said. "Yes, for sure."

"Why?"

"So I could have Carl."

"You don't seem to even like him," said Beauvoir.

"I did at first. I like older men." She leered at Gamache.

"And after that?"

"Well, there'd be money, right? If she divorced him, he'd lose money, probably lose the house. But if she died . . ."

"Yes?"

"Well, there'd be an inheritance. There's always money when someone dies."

"Not always," said Beauvoir.

Jesus, he thought. Vivienne was killed for money she didn't have?

"Why didn't you tell the other investigators this?" he asked.

"What? That there might be a reason I'd want her dead? Let's guess. . . ."

"Then why tell us now?" asked Beauvoir.

"Well, it doesn't matter now. My lawyer says you can't touch me. Besides, Carl did it, not me."

Gamache considered her so closely she began to fidget.

"I'm not going to confess, you know," she said. "So you might as well leave."

She got up, and they followed her to the front door. As she held it open, Gamache tried one more time.

"Tell us what happened that day, Pauline. For her father's sake. For yours. Get it off your chest."

"Oh, you're interested in my chest, are you?" she said, in a way that was so artless it made her seem very young. "And as for her father . . ." She made a rude, dismissive noise. "Have you asked yourself why she'd marry a shithead like Carl Tracey?"

"You were going to marry him."

"I was going to live with him."

"Until the money ran out?" asked Beauvoir.

"Fuck you. This's none of your business. Now, get out."

"He lied to you. And he killed his wife," said Gamache. "We saw the photos. Those bruises on your arms."

327

"I like it rough." Again she leered at Gamache, who just stared back. In a way that made her uncomfortable. Not because it was sexual but because it was a look she couldn't remember ever seeing before. It took her a moment to put a word to it.

Concerned. This man was concerned for her.

But she knew it was a lie. An act. No one had cared before. Why would this stranger?

"No happy person," he said quietly, "no healthy person, seeks out pain. Be careful."

"Yeah, well, what the fuck do you care?"

And the door slammed shut in his face.

"Well, that was a waste of time," said Beauvoir. "But had to be done."

As they walked to the car, Gamache thought about the look on Pauline Vachon's face. That leer. Meant to be seductive, but there was, at its core, something cruel. Definitely something calculating. Though, just for a moment . . . And then it was gone.


"Homer?"

The voice of the elderly woman penetrated the closed door as Homer lay on the bed, staring at the ceiling. Working out how . . . Fortunately, there was no thought of trying to get away with it. No need.

He didn't answer.

"It's Ruth Zardo. We met at Clara's home the other night. I know you're there and can hear me. There's something I want to say to you."

What he heard then was a very soft murmur. It sounded like *fuck, fuck*.

He sat up in bed but didn't open the door. He had no desire for company.

Undaunted, Ruth said her piece, then left.


"There," said Isabelle Lacoste, dropping a pair of boots at Beauvoir's feet with a thud.

"Been shoe shopping?" he asked, picking them up.

He'd left Gamache at his home and returned to the incident room. Now he held the boots at arm's length, examining them.

They were olive green. Rubber. Lined with felt. And came up to the knees.

"A going-away gift for Paris?" he asked. "Too kind, my little cabbage."

"More of that and you'll find them up your ass."

"Should the new head of organized crime be talking like that?" He smiled at her. "Congratulations. I've heard from other senior officers that you accepted the job."

"Not quite yet," she said. "Have to talk to my family. And you do know I won't actually be heading up a crime family, right?"

"*Merde*, I thought we'd be getting free appliances for life."

"Silly man. Free cheese, maybe." She took a seat at her desk. "About the boots, I got them from Monsieur Béliveau's general store. The Chief was right. According to Monsieur Béliveau, those're the most common boot he sells. Everyone has a pair."

"And why wouldn't they? Very stylish." Beauvoir dropped them to the floor. "Same ones as Tracey has, right?"

"Right. Same boots that made the print under Vivienne's car. Same size. Ten. Even Chief Inspector Gamache has a pair."

"Are you suggesting he's a suspect?"

"Yes, yes I am," she said with a patient smile. "You know what I'm saying."

Jean-Guy did know. He picked up the boots again and examined them.

She was right, of course.

They were exactly like the ones that had made the boot prints under Vivienne's car. Like the ones they'd found in Tracey's home and used for evidence. Evidence now deemed poisonous fruit.

And, apparently, like the footwear everyone in rural Québec owned.

"I put them on," Lacoste said, "and walked around in the snow and mud. Took pictures of the prints I made. The strange thing is, while those're size-ten men's, my feet are size seven."

"Women's."

"Thank you. Yes. But because the rubber sole is so thick and the treads so deeply stamped, my boot prints look exactly like the ones under the car."

"Exactly?" He turned the boots over. The treads were made from tough rubber, designed to insulate and grip. And not to wear down. So that the tread of a five-year-old boot would not be much different, if at all, from that of a brand-new one.

"I sent the pictures to the lab, and they'll analyze them, but I couldn't see a difference."

"So—"

"So anyone could've made those boot prints under her car. A man, a woman—a child, even, I suppose."

"This isn't getting us closer to Tracey," he said. "In fact, you're making the defense's case, if a case was still needed."

"I know," she said.

It didn't have to have been a large man on that bridge. It could have been a smaller woman. And now that Beauvoir thought about it, the coroner had said that those handprints on Vivienne's chest, bruises made in a shove, probably were made by a large man.

But—

The coroner also pointed out that bruises bleed. Spread internally. Dr. Harris had left the possibility open that they, too, could have been made by a smaller woman.

"Pauline Vachon?" he asked.

Lacoste nodded.


Lysette Cloutier got to her feet when Chief Inspector Gamache entered the kitchen.

Homer and Reine-Marie sat in front of the woodstove, a pot of tea and some shortbread cookies on a tray on the hassock between them.

Fred lay on the rug at Homer's feet, barely raising his head to look at the man who'd just come in.

Henri and Gracie had run to the door to greet him and now chased each other into the kitchen, getting between Armand's legs, almost tripping him up. But he was used to it.

Homer stared down at his large hands, which gripped each other tightly.

Then he got up slowly and turned to Armand. There was a bandage on the left side of his head, above his temple, where he'd hit the floor of the courtroom, knocking himself out. He had a black eye and bruising into his hairline.

His face, as he faced Armand, was impassive. A mask.

He just stood. And stared. And stared.

And then, silently, he moved. Brushing past Armand.

"Homer?" said Armand.

But the man had left the warm kitchen. There was a whistle from the living room. Fred lifted his head, struggled to his feet, and followed the sound.

"Please stay here," said Armand to the others.

Homer was on the front porch with the old dog.

It was five in the afternoon, and the shadows were long. The temperature was dropping with the sun.

Woodsmoke rose from the homes, slightly scenting the chilly early-evening air.

Armand held the door open, and, at a nod, out shot Henri, followed by Gracie, who was looking, and behaving, more and more like a chipmunk every day.

They caught up with Homer and Fred, who were walking with a measured pace along the edge of the village green. Neither in nor out of the circle.

Lights were on in homes around Three Pines, and Armand could see the glow from the old railway station across the still-swollen river and knew that Jean-Guy and Isabelle were in there, working to solve a crime that seemed to be getting away from them.

Then he turned to the grizzled man, walking through the twilight.

"I'm sorry," he said as he fell in beside Homer, keeping slow pace with him.

But Homer didn't reply. Just stared ahead, at the hills and forests growing darker and darker around them.

At the path into the woods, which followed the Rivière Bella Bella and went to the place where Vivienne was found, Homer stopped. It was now little more than a slightly darker opening in a dark forest.

Then he turned and looked in the opposite direction. Upriver. Where Vivienne had first gone into the water. Where she'd last been alive.

His breath came out in warm, soft puffs. Joining, mingling with Armand's.

"What do you want from me, Armand?"

"Nothing."

"That's not true. I can see it in your eyes." He turned to face him. "What is it? Forgiveness? You want me to say it's okay that you messed up? That I now have to do what you couldn't? Get justice for my little girl."

Armand was quiet. And he thought maybe Homer was right.

He wanted to be absolved of his guilt.

Vivienne's father was quiet for a long time, his eyes returning to the river. Before he finally spoke.

"Is it possible some things can't be forgiven? They're just too terrible? Abuse? Murder?" He looked at Armand. "Could you?"

"Forgive murder?" asked Armand. He thought about it. He was being asked to consider the murder not of a stranger but of his wife. His child. His grandchild. Could he forgive? Sincerely. "It would take years and a huge amount of work. And help. And still . . ."

"Yes?"

"I hope I'd get there—"

"But?"

"But I think it would take a better person than I am," admitted Armand.

Homer deserved the truth. And there it was. Could he forgive? In his heart, in his soul? Armand was far from sure.

"Would it help if whoever did it was genuinely sorry?" asked Homer. He searched Armand's eyes.

"Yeeesss, I think it would."

Homer nodded. "I wonder if Vivienne believed it."

"You think Tracey said he was sorry?"

Armand doubted that Tracey would ever have apologized, but maybe he had. Abusers often did. They begged forgiveness. Declared their love.

They brought flowers and gifts, and through a flood of tears they promised to never, ever do it again.

And maybe they were even sincere. Until the next time.

"You don't have to forgive him," said Armand. "You don't have to forgive me. But for your own sake, for your own sanity, you do need to give up this obsession with revenge."

"Have you given up?"

"Trying to get Tracey? *Non.*"

"Then why should I? Does your badge give you more of a duty to Vivienne than I have, as her father?" He let that sit there for a moment before going on. "That old woman came to your house to see me this afternoon. I didn't let her into my room. Didn't want to see anyone. But she said something anyway, through the door."

"What old lady?"

"I think she's a poet."

Armand tensed. Had Ruth done to Homer what she'd done to Clara? To himself? In trying to help, had she made things worse?

"What did she say?" Armand braced.

"Something from St. Francis. Something he said to a woman who'd lost her child in a river." Homer closed his eyes. "*Clare, Clare, do not despair. Between the bridge and the water, I was there.*"

# CHAPTER THIRTY-FOUR

*N*on, nothing new," Jean-Guy reported over the phone to Gamache, who was calling from his study at home. "The warrant we applied for a couple days ago to look into Vivienne's bank accounts should come through soon. We'll see if Pauline Vachon was dreaming or if there really is something there."

"That number Vivienne was calling is still bothering me," said Gamache. "If it wasn't Bertrand's, then whose? Is there anyone related to the case with a number close to it?"

"I've checked that," said Beauvoir. "Nothing."

Gamache smiled. He should have known Beauvoir would be on top of that.

"You must be hungry," he said. "Clara's invited us over for an easy dinner. Let's take a break."

Beauvoir sighed and looked over at Lacoste.

She'd taken her regular room at the B&B but hadn't yet dropped her bag there.

"Dinner at Clara's?" he called across the room.

"Sounds great." But she didn't look up.

They were chasing their tails, and they knew it. A break would do them good.

"We'll meet you there," he said into the phone. "Another half hour."

Jean-Guy picked up the statements again. And started reading. Again.

Gamache hung up and turned to Agent Cloutier.

They were alone in his study.

Homer was in the kitchen with Fred, as Reine-Marie prepared a squash, pear, and blue cheese soup to take to Clara's. Homer seemed to find her company restful.

Cloutier, on the other hand, clearly did not feel the same way about Monsieur Gamache's company.

"Tell me about Vivienne."

"Vivienne?"

"Yes. You must've known her well."

"I suppose so. To be honest, I wasn't the best godmother. I never had one, so I had no idea what was expected, except that if anything happened to Kathy and Homer, I was to take her."

"What was she like?"

Lysette thought about it. "Shy. A little hard to get to know. Bit of a homebody. She was a beautiful girl. You can see that in the pictures."

Gamache nodded. "Was she nice?"

"I suppose."

But there was reservation there.

"Go on."

"No, it's just that Kath found her difficult at times. I guess most mothers and daughters fight sometimes."

"Do you mean fight? Or argue?" Gamache asked.

"Argue," said Cloutier. "You don't think Kathy actually hit her?"

Gamache raised his hands. "I have no idea what happened in that home. That's why I'm asking you."

"They argued. Quite a lot. But just words, nothing more. Like I said, that's natural, isn't it? Between mother and daughter. I sure did with my mother."

Gamache nodded, remembering the foot stomping and dramatics from Annie and Reine-Marie's narrowed eyes and tightly clamped jaw. Trying not to say something mean that she didn't really mean.

Though Annie had no such qualms or restraint.

But now Annie and her mother were very close. Annie was a mother herself. He suspected that helped. With another child on the way. A girl.

Like Vivienne—

He brought his mind back to the job at hand.

"In what way did she find Vivienne difficult?"

"I actually don't think it was Vivienne's fault." Lysette dropped her voice. "I think Kath was a little jealous of her."

"Why?"

"Vivienne and her father were always close. From the moment she was born. Homer adored both his girls, as he called them. But there was a bond between him and Viv. Fathers and daughters, I suppose."

"Yes," said Gamache. Annie. Annie. Healthy and happy. And alive. And leaving . . .

"It was hard on Kathy. She didn't help herself, though. The more jealous she got, the angrier and more demanding she got. It just pushed Vivienne even further away."

"And toward her father."

"*Oui.*"

A self-fulfilling prophecy, thought Gamache. How often we made our worst fears come true, by behaving as though they already were.

"He took her to soccer practice," said Cloutier. "Coached her hockey team. When she was a child, he'd read to her at bedtime. Babar. Tin-tin. I've never seen a daughter more loved by a father, or a father more adored. I felt bad for Kathy. To be honest, I was never sure if she was jealous of Vivienne or Homer. But I do know that Vivienne left home as soon as she could."

"Pushed out by her mother?"

Lysette nodded. "And then Kathy died. It makes this even worse for Homer. Not having Kathy here to turn to."

"Was it a happy marriage?"

Lysette thought. Finally nodding. "It got better once Vivienne was out of the house."

"When we visited Pauline Vachon this afternoon, she said if Vivienne died, Carl would come into money. We're checking out accounts and insurance, of course, but do you know if Vivienne had any money of her own?"

"Vivienne? I don't think so."

"Did her mother leave her anything in her will?"

"No. She left some jewelry and a comforter that came from her grandmother, but no money. I was a liquidator. She didn't have much, and what she had, she left to Homer. Do you mind my asking why you want to know all this? We know who killed her—we just have to get him."

"We have to regroup," Gamache explained. "And part of that is getting to know Vivienne better. Is it likely she was having an affair?"

"I know what Tracey said, but I can't see that happening. She always seemed more a loner, really."

"Did you like her?"

Cloutier frowned. "What little I saw, yes. I guess."

It was not exactly a ringing endorsement. But then, Gamache suspected that Cloutier's opinions were affected, perhaps even infected, by what her friend Kathy had said. It was all too easy, Gamache knew, to believe the worst of others.

He thought for a moment. "Why do you think she married Carl Tracey?"

Cloutier considered. "Small community. Not much choice. She probably thought he was the best she could do. Maybe he wasn't so bad at first. I don't really know."

Gamache nodded.

Could there have been love there once? Or was Vivienne punishing her parents? Look what you made me do. Or was it a childish attempt to make her father jealous?

Everyone made mistakes. Gamache had made his fair share, especially when young. Annie had married and divorced before finding Jean-Guy. As had Jean-Guy, before finding Annie.

Vivienne's mistake just happened to be far worse than she could have planned or imagined.

They'd come to the end of what Agent Cloutier could tell him about Vivienne. Though there was one more thing.

"Did she like dogs?"

"*Pardon?*"

"Dogs. Did she like them?"

"Well, yeah. Loved them. Look at Fred. She rescued him as a puppy. Found him hurt on the road. He's been with her a lot longer than Carl."

"*Merci,*" he said.

# CHAPTER THIRTY-FIVE

～

"Chief Inspector and Madame Gamache, this," said Clara, with a slightly manic flourish, as though producing the dinner guest out of thin air, "is the famous art critic Dominica Oddly."

Ta-da.

Then poof, Clara disappeared.

"Madame Oddly," said Armand, shaking her hand.

"Chief Inspector?" said the critic.

"Armand."

"Of the Sûreté? Sounds like some old Nelson Eddy/Jeanette Mac-Donald movie. *Gamache of the Sûreté.*"

Armand smiled. "That was the Mounties. No horse, I'm afraid."

"And yet quite a lot of horseshit," said Ruth, joining them.

Dominica's eyes flickered to the duck in Ruth's arms, then back up to the elderly woman's face. Choosing to ignore the fowl, she said, "I didn't mention before that I like your poetry."

"Thank you. Her name's Rosa."

Fuck, fuck, fuck, said Rosa.

"Poetry," Reine-Marie whispered in Ruth's ear. "Not poultry."

"Oh." She turned back to Dominica, looking her up and down. "Are you related to the maid?"

Reine-Marie dropped her eyes, and Armand gazed around as though he'd never met the old woman before.

"Maid?" asked Dominica.

When Ruth began to point toward Myrna, who was talking with Clara by the fireplace, Reine-Marie jumped in. "How could you possibly know about Nelson Eddy?"

"I love classic cinema," explained Dominica. "When the art form was just beginning."

"And you'd consider *Rose-Marie* a classic?" asked Ruth. "I suspected you had no taste. That's why I thought you'd like Clara's art."

Dominica laughed. "But I like your poetry. And your poultry."

"An aberration. The exception that proves the rule."

"Not a rule," the critic pointed out. "An opinion."

Dominica Oddly hadn't yet decided if the people who chose to live in this small Canadian hamlet were wonderful and creative or simply inbred.

"Beer?" asked Gabri, bringing a bottle over to Dominica. She'd left the group and was looking around.

"Thank you. Is the duck okay? She looks strange."

"Oh, the duck's okay. It's the fuck who's strange."

Dominica laughed. "But a great poet."

"And Clara's a great artist."

To that, Dominica just raised her bottle. "Thanks for the beer."

Across the room, Clara was trying to keep the smile on her face and the bile down as she watched the young woman, who'd just destroyed her career and was now drinking her beer and eating her food. She wouldn't be surprised if she found this young woman sleeping in her bed.

The wolf, not at her door but in her home. In her life. And tearing it apart. With a smile.


Jean-Guy and Isabelle joined them in time for dinner.

Jean-Guy had spied Ruth and began walking toward her when Armand headed him off.

"Don't."

"But she needs to be told," said Jean-Guy, watching the old poet swig scotch and talk with the critic, who seemed fascinated by her.

"Told what?"

"That the video she posted has hurt people. You. The families." He paused. "Me. That she had no business doing that."

"She did it out of kindness. She thought she was protecting me."

"That doesn't change anything. She should never have done it."

"I agree. But it's done now. Let it go, Jean-Guy."

Still, as Jean-Guy passed Ruth, he whispered, "Dumb-ass."

"Numbnuts," she replied with a laugh. Clearly not understanding his message.

Armand was tired and wouldn't normally have accepted Clara's invitation. But he knew that Homer didn't want to see him. Didn't even want to know he was in the same house. And he'd promised the man time alone. This was one promise he could keep.

So they'd come here and left Homer and Lysette to have dinner by themselves.

Everyone at Clara's had heard what had happened in court that day, though only Ruth had asked about it. If asking how they'd managed to make a clown-car disaster out of a sure thing was a sincere query.

Beauvoir seethed. Gamache remained quiet. Only Isabelle responded. She reached out and held the old woman's veined hand and whispered, "Shut the fuck up."

It delighted Ruth, who laughed. And, for once, did as she was told.

After dinner, while Armand and Reine-Marie cleared the table and Gabri made coffee, Jean-Guy took Dominica aside for a quiet word.

"Pottery?" Dominica asked when she and Beauvoir were far enough away from the others. She was clearly surprised this cop wanted to talk about ceramics of all things.

She launched into a discourse on the history of ceramic artworks, some of which survived beyond the peoples and cultures that made them. Some of which he even found interesting.

"What about in modern art?" asked Jean-Guy.

"What about it?"

"Can a person make a living from doing pottery stuff?"

She studied the man in front of her. Having grown up in the Bronx to an activist mother, Dominica found that she was wary, even privately afraid, of cops. She'd seen her brothers, her friends, her lovers harassed too often to see cops as anything other than threats.

She'd had very little respect for them and almost no contact with them socially. They lived on different continents and came from different tribes.

Gabri had told her about the murder of the young woman and what had happened in court that morning.

This officer had been involved. In charge. And now they were making small talk about pottery, over after-dinner drinks.

Though watching this cop, his intensity, Dominica Oddly began to suspect this was not actually small talk.

"Are you thinking of making a career change?" she asked, and was relieved to see him smile.

"Not to the art world. Way too dangerous."

"Yes. I've heard the critics can be brutal."

"It's the artists who scare me." Then his smile faded. "Ceramics," he reminded her. "Pottery. Much of a market?"

"For art pottery? Not the kind we eat off of?"

"*Oui.*"

She considered. "There's always a market at the high end. But you have to be very, very good. And very, very lucky. Lucie Rie, for instance. Highly collectible. Modern, but inspired by ancient Roman pottery. Grayson Perry in the UK is huge. Won the Turner Prize for his ceramics. Elisabeth Kley is a New York artist. Festive yet—"

"How about this?"

He brought out his phone and clicked on Photos.

Dominica Oddly felt a spike of annoyance. She wasn't used to being interrupted. Most people were in awe of her and hung on every word.

But she realized they were not, in all probability, actually talking about pottery. They were discussing murder.

She leaned in.

Up came a picture of a vase. Then a bowl. Then another piece. One after another appeared. She asked him to stop scrolling as she examined a few. Enlarging them.

"Huh," she finally said, looking up. "Whose is it?"

"A fellow named Carl Tracey. Ever heard of him?"

"No." She stepped back and examined his face. "Is he the one who killed the girl?"

"We think so, yes. What do you think?"

"What do you think?" Clara asked.

She'd taken some of her friends into her studio, to show them copies of the miniatures that had been savaged by the critics. Including, and especially, the critic in her living room.

"Not bad at all," said Gabri.

Clara felt her heart squeeze and a sort of panic wash over her. She was expecting an immediate and passionate, "They're brilliant! She's wrong!"

Not this muted reply.

She looked over at Reine-Marie, whose head was tilted, as though maybe that would help. There was a strained look on her face, like a child with the beginnings of indigestion.

"These are the ones that didn't make the cut, right? The ones you were less happy with?" Reine-Marie asked, barely meeting Clara's eyes.

"Yes," she said. She lied.

The tiny oils on the easel in her studio were almost exact replicas of the series she'd sent to the collective show in New York.

The critics, the other artists, even the gallery owners could all be dismissed. The crap on social media certainly could be. Or if not outright dismissed, at least explained.

Jealousy. Nothing more.

But now her own friends, her cheering section, were tilting their heads, squinting their eyes, and offering faint praise.

*Damn*, thought Clara. *Damn*.

That Oddly woman had poisoned the well. Turned even her most ardent supporters against her. Or, at least, against her art. Which was almost the same thing, so deeply intertwined were the woman and her creations. An attack on one felt like an attack on the other.

She felt her world sinking, and Clara Morrow was far from certain she could keep her head above the swiftly rising tide of opinion.

Ruth put a thin, veined hand on Armand's. "You did your best, you know."

He looked down at her hand, then into her rheumy eyes.

"But he got away. Thanks in large part to me."

"Not on purpose."

"Does it matter?"

"You're a cop, doesn't intent always matter? If you didn't intend to hurt . . ."

He wondered if this was Ruth's way of apologizing for posting that video. Knowing now the pain she'd caused.

"That could be true," he said. "But Vivienne is dead, and her killer is free."

"Not for long. Homer's going to kill the man who killed his daughter, isn't he?"

"He's going to try."

"Will you stop him?"

"I'll try."

"In a halfhearted way?"

Armand turned to her in surprise. "No. With all my heart."

"Why?"

She looked at him with genuine curiosity. As did the duck. But then, ducks were often curious.

Why would he stop Homer?

"Because it's not for us to be judge, jury, and executioner."

"Yeah, yeah, yeah. Cliché. And in the real world, when the system fails?"

"Then we have to look somewhere else for a solution."

"You mean revenge."

"For some, yes."

"And others?"

"You know the answer to that."

"You mean giving up? Just"—she waved her hand—"letting it go and getting on with life?"

"I mean grabbing hold of something other than rage and revenge. You came over to the house this afternoon."

"Yes," said Ruth. "What of it?"

"You said something to Homer."

"So?"

"I think that's why you visited him. To offer Homer that option, a way out. If not to forgiveness, perhaps to peace. It was a quote from St. Francis, to a woman who'd lost her child in a river. The thing is, I looked it up, or tried, and couldn't find it anywhere."

"Meaning?"

"Meaning, does it exist?"

"Does it matter? Isn't the power in the belief and not the proof?" She looked at him, hard. "Wouldn't you want to believe, Armand? If it had been Annie?"

In the silence that followed, he met her eyes.

"*Clare, Clare,*" she said, her voice shaky and her eyes steady, "*do not despair. Between the bridge and the water, I was there.*"


"Does she always carry the duck around?" Dominica Oddly asked Reine-Marie as they left to walk home.

The cold April night air seeped past Dominica's light coat and into her bones. She wrapped her arms around herself.

"Always," said Reine-Marie. "Would you leave your child behind?"

"Child . . . ?" Dominica began to dismiss the statement but then heard Rosa muttering and saw the resemblance between mother and duck.

They took a few steps in silence before Reine-Marie spoke again.

"You do know how much your review hurt Clara, don't you?"

"It was brutal," said Olivier.

"I was just telling the truth."

"*All truth with malice in it,*" said Ruth.

"But it's still the truth."

"Maybe," said Reine-Marie. "But you need to also own the malice."

Jean-Guy dropped back to where Armand and Isabelle were walking, a few paces behind the others.

Isabelle was tired, and her limp was more pronounced.

"I asked her"—Jean-Guy indicated Dominica Oddly—"about Tracey's pottery. She said it was quite good. Showed actual promise."

"Jesus," said Isabelle, "don't tell Clara that. Her head'll explode."

"I was thinking that might be another motive," said Jean-Guy. "To kill Vivienne."

"How?" asked Isabelle.

"If Tracey knew he was about to be a success?" said Jean-Guy. "He sure wouldn't want to share it with Vivienne."

"But isn't 'success' relative? Even successful ceramicists couldn't make much money, could they?" asked Isabelle.

"They can make hundreds of thousands, even millions, if they become collectible," said Jean-Guy, as though he knew that from experience.

"Does she think Tracey's likely to be that successful?" asked Armand.

"Not sure. She said it's possible. Takes a lot of luck, of course."

"I wonder," said Isabelle, then lapsed into silence.

"Wonder what?"

"If a scandal could be considered luck."

"A scandal like being a murder suspect. Shit." Beauvoir broke away and jogged up to Dominica Oddly. "I have a question for you."

"Yes?"

"If an up-and-coming artist is accused of murder, then let go on a technicality, what would that do to his career?"

"Are you kidding?" she asked. Staring at him. "You're not seriously thinking—"

"The question. Please answer it."

They'd stopped, and now Armand and Isabelle joined them.

Dominica Oddly thought about it, but not for long. "He wouldn't be the first artist to benefit from something like that. The cult of celebrity can be pretty perverse. Just look at—"

"Tracey," Jean-Guy reminded her, before the lecture began. "Would getting away with murder help him?"

She nodded. "Probably. But how would he know he'd get away with it?"

"Maybe it didn't matter," said Isabelle.

"Would matter to him," said Oddly. "His art might start selling for tens of thousands, or more, but what good would it do him if he's executed?"

"We don't actually kill prisoners in Canada," said Lacoste.

"Are you sure?" asked Oddly.

"What're you thinking?" Gamache asked Lacoste.

"Who would benefit," she whispered to Gamache and Beauvoir, "if Vivienne was murdered and her suddenly famous artist husband was convicted?"

"Pauline Vachon," said Beauvoir. "You think she's that clever?"

"You met her, what do you think?"

Myrna and Billy helped Clara clean up, though most of it had already been done by the others.

"You okay?" Myrna asked her friend.

"Just fine."

"Pour yourself a vat of wine, cut a huge slice of chocolate cake, sit by the fire, and know you're loved. You and your art. Okay?"

"Okay."

"I'll walk you home," said Billy as they put on their coats to leave.

"That's all right. It's not far."

"I know. I'd like to." He put on his gloves and hat and was glad Myrna couldn't see his face.

"Billy—" Myrna began as they walked along the road.

"Don't say it. Please."

If only he hadn't allowed himself to imagine their lives together. What might have been. The quiet nights. Reading. Cooking. Having friends over. Meals in the bistro. Together.

Growing old. Together.

He left her at her door, then got in his truck and drove home. Alone.

Clara took Myrna's advice, as she almost always did.

*It helps*, she thought, as she cut herself a huge wedge of cake and carried it into the living room, *to have a wise friend. Who can bake.*

As she sat in front of the fireplace with Leo, Clara tried to clear her mind. But found it cluttered with Dominica Oddly. And that review.

Leo placed his magnificent head on her lap, and they both stared into the roiling fire.

"I've been thinking about Tracey and his pottery," said Isabelle.

"Yes?" said Beauvoir.

They'd walked over to Gabri and Olivier's bed-and-breakfast, where Isabelle had "her" room. With its familiar four-poster bed and eiderdown comforter, the fireplace laid and ready to be lit. The armchair in front of it. With a carafe of tawny port, a glass, and a small box of her favorite chocolates.

While Dominica Oddly had gone upstairs to work, Isabelle had deposited her bag in her room and returned to the living room of the B&B to join the others.

And work.

"Isn't that just a little bit of a stretch?" asked Isabelle. "To think Tracey killed his wife so that his art would be noticed? Besides, he's not smart enough to think that far ahead. I doubt he even knows what he's having for lunch most days."

"Tracey couldn't plan it," Jean-Guy agreed as he poked the fire, then grabbed a chocolate chip cookie off the tray on the sideboard and joined the others. "But like we said, Pauline Vachon might."

Isabelle nodded. "I can see her planning it. But really, would she kill Vivienne on the off chance it would give Tracey's career a boost? Seems a pretty drastic marketing tool. I don't believe it."

"It obviously wouldn't be the only motive," said Beauvoir. "There're lots of reasons she'd want Vivienne dead. She'd get Tracey, for one. And any inheritance, real or imagined, coming his way as Vivienne's husband. And if his pottery did hit, she'd be right there to collect. If there's a scandal, like a murdered wife, to help it along, so much the better."

Up until now, Gamache had preferred to listen as the two investigators tossed around ideas. Taking in what they were saying. Letting his mind both focus and be free. Now he got up from the comfortable armchair.

"Excuse me," he said, bringing out his phone. "I just need to check something."

He stepped over to the window, where the wavering signal was strongest, and returned a couple of minutes later. His face grim.

Dominica checked her site. The review of Clara's art was up and getting good notice. Lots of hits. Lots of shares. The new item she'd just posted was also beginning to trend.

Not yet tired, she Googled around, and then, bored, she typed in "Jean-Guy Beauvoir."

A few items came up, including a commendation. There was a photo of this Chief Inspector Gamache, giving him a medal. But the line under the photo identified him as Chief Superintendent Gamache. The head of the Sûreté du Québec.

Curious, she put in "Armand Gamache. Sûreté."

Lifting her brows at the number of stories, she scrolled down. The photographs, clearly taken over the course of a long career, showed a man aging. From dark, wavy hair to gray. From smooth-faced to lines, growing deeper and deeper with each passing story.

And then that scar appeared. At his temple. The first time was in a photo of him in dress uniform. Grim-faced, with a cane. In a funeral procession.

But there was one constant. His eyes. Intelligent and thoughtful. And even kindly.

It was disconcerting. In a cop.

There was a link to a recently posted video, with half a million views already.

Dominica Oddly sat in her quiet room, in the quiet village, and watched, horrified, as the quiet man with the kindly eyes shot a succession of young, mostly black, kids.

She recognized that the video had been hacked together. And knew it was probably bullshit, but she found herself sucked in. Probably because she was predisposed to believe that's what cops did.

Did that explain his demotion? Is this how the good folk of Canada react to mass murder? A wrist slap?

Then another video came up. Also newly posted. With almost the same number of hits.

Her eye, trained to see the manipulation of images, realized this was the real thing. Uncut. Unedited. Raw. The parent of the previous, perverse video. The place from which those images had been culled, to create a false, but compelling, narrative. Of a man, a cop, out of control.

But this second video showed something very different. A commander in complete control. Leading a raid on a factory. Against what were clearly heavily armed gunmen.

In shaky but clear images, she watched Sûreté agents, including the three people she'd just met over a civilized dinner, advance through the gunfire.

Jean-Guy. Isabelle. Armand.

"Christ," she whispered as she watched last rites hurriedly given by one agent to another.

As hoarse last words were placed by one dying officer into another.

She watched as Jean-Guy fell, hit in the abdomen, and Armand dragged him to safety, kneeling over him to stanch his wound. Then he headed back into the battle. But before he did, Chief Inspector Gamache bent down and, for all the world to see, kissed the frightened young man on the forehead and whispered, "I love you."

Words they both must have believed would be the last Jean-Guy Beauvoir would ever hear.

Minutes later, Isabelle was holding Armand's hand as blood ran from the wounds at his temple and chest, and he whispered to her, barely audible, words he must've thought would be his last.

"Reine-Marie."

Dominica Oddly was shocked by the violence, and even more shocked by the tenderness.

She snapped her laptop shut. And for the first time felt real revulsion for social media.

That would cut, twist, put a lie to the truth.

That would nail decent people to posts.

And then she remembered what she'd just done.

"What is it?" asked Jean-Guy.

Armand turned his phone around for them to see.

There, beneath the title, "All Truth with Malice in It," was the story of a man in the remote Québec countryside. An undiscovered but important ceramic artist. Who also happened to be, allegedly, a murderer.

"*Merde*," said Jean-Guy as he read.

"How'd you know?" Isabelle asked Gamache.

"If you're given a lead, don't you follow it? She's a critic, but she's also a journalist and an entrepreneur. And a good one. We handed her a great story. What else was she going to do with it?"

"Be a decent human being?" suggested Isabelle. "Respect Homer Godin's pain and not promote a murderer."

"I handed it to her," said Jean-Guy.

"We all did," said Armand.

"It's disgusting, but it won't harm the case," said Isabelle.

"What case?" demanded Jean-Guy. "And what'll Homer make of this? It's not enough that that asshole Tracey killed his daughter, now he's profiting from it. Thanks to us."

"He might not see it," said Isabelle. "Why would he?"

"Why would we see the video?" said Jean-Guy. "Because people sent us the link."

"There's something else," said Gamache, looking at the two of them. "Something I should have thought about earlier. Vivienne's dog."

"Fred?" asked Jean-Guy. "That's what you're thinking about?"

"Exactly," said Armand. "Ruth told Dominica that she never leaves Rosa behind. And we'd never move and leave Henri and Gracie. So why didn't Vivienne take Fred with her to the bridge? Agent Cloutier told me Vivienne rescued him as a puppy and adored him."

"Maybe she couldn't take him with her," said Isabelle. "Maybe she was going someplace where a dog wasn't allowed."

Armand was shaking his head. "She'd never leave him with Carl. She must've known what he'd do to Fred."

"So what're you saying?" asked Jean-Guy.

"I don't know," said Armand slowly.

As they walked back to the Gamache house, Armand and Jean-Guy noticed that the light was out in Homer's room. But Reine-Marie was still awake.

Reading in bed and waiting for him, Armand knew.

"Long day," said Reine-Marie when he finally got into bed. "Bad day."

"*Oui.*" No use denying it.

Though the walls of the old home were thick, Armand could still hear Jean-Guy's voice. He couldn't make out the exact words, nor did he try. But he knew that he was speaking to Annie. Telling her about the long, bad day. Not hiding anything.

After a few minutes, there was silence, except for Reine-Marie's steady, deep breathing.

The minutes ticked by. Armand found he couldn't settle. It was midnight. Then 1:10 a.m. Then 1:35.

Tick, tock. Tick, tock.

At 2:07 he heard a sound. Movement. Footsteps in the hall outside their room. Then down the stairs.

Armand got up. The room was chilly as the fresh spring air drifted through the open window. The curtains billowing slightly.

Slipping his phone into the pocket of his dressing gown, he stepped out into the hallway. Going carefully, slowly, to the stairs, he looked down and saw Homer by the front door. His coat and boots on.

Homer knelt and said something to Fred, who'd followed him there. Then, kissing the dog on the forehead, he left. Leaving Fred to stare at a closed door.

Armand raced down the stairs, taking them two at a time. Throwing on his outdoor clothes and grabbing the flashlight, he, too, slipped out.

It was a clear, cold night. Below freezing. The moon was full, and he didn't need to turn on his flashlight.

Still, it took him a moment to make out Homer, up ahead. Walking up the hill out of Three Pines. His feet crunching on the frozen ground.

Armand followed. This was it, he knew. And he also knew he'd almost missed it. Had he been asleep, Homer would have left unnoticed. And walked those kilometers to Tracey's home unhindered.

At the top of the hill, Homer stopped. Getting his bearings, Armand suspected. He, too, stopped.

He wanted to give Homer a chance to change his mind. He felt he owed it to the man.

Homer took a few steps forward, then hesitated again. And finally made up his mind.

Turning left, he climbed the steps to the front door of St. Thomas's chapel. And entered.


Armand sat at the back, in the very last pew. While Homer sat at the front.

If he knew Armand was there, he didn't show it.

Homer didn't kneel. Didn't cross himself. He just sat there, staring at the stained glass.

Armand wondered if Homer was thinking of St. Francis. Thinking that there was another way forward.

As the minutes ticked by, into an hour, Armand's mind wandered. Not to a prayer but to Dominica Oddly's piece on Carl Tracey.

And the now familiar refrain.

He sat there, and in the quietude he turned the case around. In the calm, he saw what had eluded him before.

Armand rose to his feet, then slowly sat back down as the import of it struck him.

Until all he knew to be fact was revealed as fiction.

Until the givens were gone and another story emerged from the cold, dark depths of this murder.

*All truth with malice in it.*

# CHAPTER THIRTY-SIX

⁓

I saw a light down here," said a groggy Jean-Guy. "How long have you been up?"

"A little while," said Armand, gazing over his reading glasses.

He'd left the church an hour earlier, with Homer, who'd finally turned around and, looking at Armand without surprise, said that he was ready to go home. To bed.

The two men had walked in silence back to the Gamaches' place, and from there Armand had gone to the old railway station. He picked up files and laptops and, returning home, settled into the living room.

Where he could see if Homer tried to leave again.

When Jean-Guy came down, he found Armand in front of the lit fireplace with a mug of coffee, reading.

Armand was unshaven. His hair messed. But his eyes were bright and alert. No sign of fatigue.

Outside, clouds had once again rolled in and brought with them snow. Again. Huge soft flakes, as though the clouds themselves were breaking up and drifting down in pieces.

"Can you call Isabelle?"

"It's five twenty. In the morning. It's still dark out."

But Armand just looked at him as though none of that mattered.

And it didn't, Jean-Guy realized.

"What's up?" he asked as he walked into the study and dialed the familiar number.

"I'll tell you when Isabelle gets here."

As he waited for the line to engage, Jean-Guy looked across the village green, past the three tall trees. And noticed that theirs wasn't the only light in Three Pines.

"*Oui, allô*," said Isabelle, instantly awake.


Clara sat on the stool in her studio. Stale chocolate crumbs and icing in her hair. Leo at her feet.

The miniatures on the easel in front of her.

Suppose, her drunken mind had allowed the traitor thought in. Suppose . . .


"Suppose," Gamache began as they sat with their coffees around the warm wood fire, "we were wrong."

Isabelle had arrived, looking more than a little scruffy herself, but at least fully dressed.

Jean-Guy had also showered and dressed while they waited for Isabelle. Armand stayed in the living room, not wanting to risk Homer sneaking out.

"What do you mean?" she asked, putting her mug of coffee down and leaning closer. "Wrong about what?"

"Just suppose," Gamache said, "Carl Tracey was telling the truth."

Jean-Guy's eyes narrowed. "How much wine did you have last night?"

Gamache ran his hand through his hair, but instead of smoothing it down, he just managed to make it stand up even more. Far from looking comical, he looked deadly serious.

Armand Gamache might hold a rank equal to or even below their own, for now. But both knew he was in fact their superior. Always would be. And had earned the right to be heard. If not agreed with.

So now, they supposed . . .

Gamache remained quiet, watching their faces. Seeing the concentration and the skepticism. Seeing them try to imagine the inconceivable. What it might look like if Carl Tracey had been telling the truth.

Isabelle was the first to put into words what Jean-Guy could not. "But that would mean Tracey didn't kill his wife?"

"Perhaps. I don't know. What I do know is that we're stuck. There seems no way to convict him."

"So we try to convict someone else?" asked Jean-Guy. At the look of surprise on Gamache's face, he backtracked. "*Désolé.* I didn't mean you were suggesting we arrest an innocent person, just . . . I can't quite get my head around what you're saying. And why."

"There're enough things in this case that we can't explain," said Gamache. "Why Vivienne left her dog behind. Why was she on that bridge at all? Why would Carl Tracey kill her there and not at home? Who was she calling in the last hour of her life?"

"Why she didn't want her father to come get her when he offered earlier in the day," said Isabelle.

"All last night a phrase kept repeating itself. Dominica Oddly even used it as the title of her piece on Tracey."

*"All truth with malice in it,"* said Beauvoir. "It's a quote, right? Where's it from? Not 'The Wreck of the Hesperus,' I hope."

"As a matter of fact," said Gamache, clearing his throat in advance of a recitation.

He smiled slightly as Jean-Guy's eyes widened and he recoiled from what promised to be an onslaught of poetry. It was a familiar bit of mutual self-mockery.

Dear God, thought Isabelle. How're they going to live without each other?

*"Non,"* she said, smiling at this set piece. "It's from *Moby-Dick.*"

"You were thinking about a fish?" asked Jean-Guy.

"About human nature," said Armand. "About obsession. About allowing rancor to cloud judgment. About what happens when we see the malice but fail to see the truth. We were all appalled by what happened to Vivienne. Even before she was found, we more than suspected that her drunken, abusive husband had done something to her. I thought that myself. I had absolutely no doubt that if something had happened to Vivienne, her husband did it."

"It wasn't a wild guess," said Isabelle. "Experience points to him. The statements of others, including a local Sûreté cop, point to him. Her father. Even Agent Cloutier."

"Yes, that's true," said Gamache.

359

He leaned forward. Trying to get them to see what he saw.

"And that's the point. It was all so obvious, we never even considered anything, anyone else. Not seriously, anyway. I'm not saying Tracey didn't murder Vivienne. I am saying we owe it to her to look at all possibilities. Including that he was telling the truth."

"That's what you've been doing all night?" asked Beauvoir, looking at the papers scattered on the coffee table and sofa.

"Yes." Gamache sorted through them until he found Tracey's statements.

"I'll call in Cloutier and Cameron," said Beauvoir. "We'll need their help to go back over all this. Again."

It was impossible to miss the exasperation in his voice. This was, Beauvoir knew, a waste of time. They should be concentrating on nailing Tracey, not looking elsewhere.

But then he wondered if that wasn't exactly what Chief Inspector Gamache was doing. Trying to get Tracey. Sometimes, sometimes, if you didn't look directly at a thing, something caught your attention. Out of the corner of your eye.

When Beauvoir looked at Gamache, as he did now, he saw a man who would easily, even in a bathrobe, perhaps especially in a bathrobe, pass as a college professor. A decent and thoughtful man. Who loved sitting by the fire, or in his garden, or in the bistro with a book. He loved good food and poetry and friends. He loved his wife and children and grandchildren. And Armand Gamache loathed violence.

But out of the corner of his eye, Jean-Guy Beauvoir saw cunning. A man who was calculating. Shrewd. Ruthless at times.

And determined. He would stop at nothing to catch a murderer. To catch Tracey.

"Why don't you look over these." Gamache handed over Tracey's statements. "I'll call Cameron and Cloutier."

"But before you do . . ." Beauvoir looked him up and down, and Gamache smiled.

"Good point."

He left Beauvoir and Lacoste by the fireplace. With their coffees. Reading.

As he mounted the stairs, Gamache looked back at Jean-Guy. He saw a man carefully held together. Taut. Intense. Nervous energy simmering close to the surface. Curt at times. Fierce in a fight. A man who blew off tension by happily smashing opponents into the boards in his hockey games.

But out of the corner of his eye, Armand Gamache saw kindness. Loyalty. A deep, almost inconceivable capacity for love.

Jean-Guy Beauvoir would stop at nothing to catch a killer. This killer.

"Oh, shit," said Clara.

She was sober now. She felt she'd never been more sober.

Getting up from the easel, she had a shower, put on clean clothes, made a pot of strong coffee, and took a mug over to her kitchen window.

It was dawn. But barely light. Huge flakes only April could produce were falling. Plump with moisture, they hit the ground and melted. But not all. Some stayed behind.

A thin layer of white covered the grass, the road. It clung to the three huge pines. The cars and bench.

It should have been beautiful, except that by April most yearned to look out and see green. Not winter, clinging on.

Clara returned to her studio, but instead of going in, she snapped off the light and closed the door.

Then, needing fresh air, she took Leo for a walk. Their feet making dark tracks in the bright snow.

While Isabelle and Jean-Guy read over the files, Armand showered, shaved, and changed into slacks and shirt and tie. Quietly. So as not to awaken Reine-Marie.

Gray light and a cool breeze were now coming through the windows.

Before going downstairs, he looked in on Homer, to make sure he was all right and to see if Fred was hungry and eager to go out. Homer was asleep, and Fred just lifted his head, then lowered his gray muzzle to his paws.

Armand returned with food and water bowls, which he placed on the floor, then softly closed the door.

When he returned to the living room, he looked up the numbers for Agents Cameron and Cloutier in the Sûreté files. He reached for the phone, but that was as far as he got.

"When you're ready, *patron*."

Jean-Guy's voice broke into Armand's thoughts. Broke his concentration. His hand still resting on the phone, Armand looked over and saw Jean-Guy and Isabelle staring at him. Waiting for him.

*"Alors,"* said Jean-Guy, adjusting his glasses. "We went through Carl Tracey's statements and cross-checked with those of others, including Pauline Vachon and Homer Godin."

"And made a list of what it might mean if he was telling the truth," said Isabelle.

Gamache nodded. Listening. He had his own notes beside him on the sofa.

"He said she was alive when he left her," said Jean-Guy. "If that's true, then someone else murdered her. If that's the case, my money's on Pauline Vachon. With or without Tracey's knowledge."

"But probably with," said Isabelle.

By habit, they glanced at Gamache to gauge his reaction, but the Chief was noncommittal. Simply listening. Though it seemed to Jean-Guy that Gamache was struggling to remain focused.

"Is something wrong?"

*"Non, non,* go on. Pauline Vachon. I'm following."

Jean-Guy glanced quickly at Isabelle, who'd also noticed the uncharacteristic distraction.

"I'll get to that later," said Jean-Guy, "but for now let's go back to what Carl Tracey told you when you first visited his home. Before Vivienne was found. He said they'd both been drinking. That was later confirmed by the autopsy report on Vivienne's blood-alcohol level."

*"Oui,"* said Isabelle. "So that much was true. He said she was drunk. That was an exaggeration. They had an argument. She told him the baby wasn't his."

"This's directly contradicted by Monsieur Godin," Jean-Guy pointed out. "In his statement, he said Vivienne wanted to sneak away. That she was afraid of her husband. She'd never have provoked him like that."

"So does that mean Homer was lying?" asked Isabelle.

"It could mean that Vivienne meant to sneak away," said Jean-Guy, "as she told her father, but then had a drink. Maybe for courage. But it backfired. She had too many, and things got out of control."

"So let's say Vivienne had just enough alcohol to lower her defenses," said Lacoste. "She said things she hadn't planned to. What does Tracey do? He hits her. Then he said he left her, alive, and went into his studio to start a new piece but passed out instead. When he woke up, Vivienne was gone."

It was the picture of a catastrophically unhappy home. Of a sick relationship. That could not possibly continue. And into which a baby was going to be born.

Unless something changed.

"Can that be true?" asked Jean-Guy. "Are we supposed to believe that Tracey left her alive?"

"For now," said Gamache. "For argument's sake. Yes."

They sat quietly, trying to argue.

"So," Jean-Guy finally said. "Who killed her if not Tracey?"

They looked at Gamache.

He had no definite answers, though he had spent the better part of the night looking into the dark corners of the case. Beyond the malice, to where some fact, some feral truth, might be waiting to be found.

"Pauline Vachon," said Isabelle. "She had motive. She wants desperately to get out, to have a better life. And she's brighter than Tracey."

"That's not saying much. Henri here is brighter than Tracey," said Jean-Guy.

The shepherd raised his head and swiveled his mighty ears toward Jean-Guy. He was not, they all knew, a dog of great intellect. The main purpose of his head seemed to be to support his formidable ears, which were tuned to key words. Treat, dinner, walk, Henri.

Henri kept all he needed to know, all that really mattered, safe in his heart. Where there was not need of words. Except, maybe, good boy.

Armand lowered his hand and stroked Henri until the shepherd dropped his head to his paws.

"Pauline Vachon could plan it and pull it off," Isabelle was saying. "Shoving a woman who'd had a few drinks, who wasn't expecting to be attacked, from a bridge wouldn't take much. Those bruises could've been made by anyone."

"And the boot prints," said Jean-Guy. "She could've been wearing Tracey's. Trying to implicate him."

"But how did she arrange to meet Vivienne on the bridge?" asked Isabelle. "There were no calls into the house that day and only those two numbers dialed out."

"Tracey told Vivienne to go to the bridge," said Jean-Guy.

Isabelle stared at him in disbelief. "Now, that's really stretching it. You actually believe she'd go? To meet her husband's lover? All Vivienne wanted was to get as far away, as fast as possible. There's no way she'd agree to meet Pauline Vachon on a lonely bridge at night. Why would she?"

"To confront Pauline," said Jean-Guy. "To give her hell. Suppose Tracey tells Vivienne he's meeting his lover on the bridge, knowing she'll go there."

"Come on. Maybe on paper that works, but in reality?" said Isabelle. "Everyone who talks about Vivienne describes a woman frightened out of her wits."

She looked over at Gamache, who was considering it.

The scenario Jean-Guy described was possible. Just. In normal circumstances a wife might go to confront her husband's lover. Except these were not normal circumstances.

"Why the bridge?" he asked. "If they wanted her dead, there're easier ways. Why go through all that rigmarole?"

"Rigmarole?" asked Jean-Guy, always amused when Gamache used odd Anglo words.

"Yes," said Gamache. "It means either taking or luring a young woman to a bridge and throwing her off."

"Really?" asked Jean-Guy.

"*Non.* But it does mean making something complicated that could be simple. There's something else that argues against Vachon," said Gamache.

"What?" asked Jean-Guy, not liking the sound of that.

Gamache picked up the notes at his side and, putting on his reading glasses again, scanned them until he found what he was looking for.

"*Stuff's in the bag*," he read. "*Everything's ready. Will be done tonight. I promise.*" Gamache looked up at them. "The messages between Carl Tracey and Pauline Vachon on the day of the murder. And her reply: *Finally. Good luck. Don't mess it up.*"

"Pretty damning," said Isabelle.

"But the person it damns isn't Pauline Vachon," said Gamache, removing his glasses. "It shows that while Pauline Vachon knew about the murder plans, she wasn't actually there. So suppose there's another interpretation?"

"What?" asked Jean-Guy, not liking the sound of that either.

"Suppose Carl Tracey and Pauline Vachon were telling the truth."

"Oh, come on," said Jean-Guy. "You're kidding."

"You think I'm joking?" Gamache stared hard at Jean-Guy. "Just suppose that this exchange"—Gamache held up the page and shook it—"is about Tracey's pottery. He was out of clay and went to the art-supply store. The Instagram post originated from there. We know that. And we found a new bag of clay, unopened, in his studio. *Stuff's in the bag. Everything's ready. Will be done tonight.* He might've been referring to new works."

They stared at him in disbelief. Did Gamache really think that was possible?

"So you're saying Tracey didn't pack Vivienne's bag?" asked Jean-Guy. "That Vivienne did, and she tossed in those abortion pills even though she was well along in her pregnancy? The clothes she packed were for summer, even though it was minus five degrees that night. Why'd she do that?"

Gamache turned to Isabelle. "You answered that yesterday."

"I did?"

"*Oui.* And so did Madame Fleury, when we talked with her about the shelters."

Gamache looked at Jean-Guy, though try as he might, Jean-Guy couldn't come up with anything.

But Isabelle did. "You mean my overnight bag. I keep it in the car, in case."

"*Exactement*," said Gamache. "In case. Simone Fleury said many abused women pack a bag and keep it hidden. Sometimes for months—years, even. Ready to grab when the moment is right."

A knot was forming between Jean-Guy's brows.

Was it possible?

And suddenly Vivienne came into stark relief. A shattered, frightened young woman. Her bag packed. Waiting for her chance. Waiting. Enduring the loneliness, the humiliations. The beatings.

And when she was pregnant, deciding she really did need to leave. For her baby.

This one she'd save. This one she'd protect from Carl Tracey.

It would explain the timing. And it would explain the clothing.

"She packed in the summer," he said. "And the bag sat in her car since then."

"Until Saturday," said Isabelle.

"I think so, but there's a problem with that, too," said Gamache. "How did it get into the river? Would Carl Tracey or whoever killed her know it was in her car? Presumably he didn't realize before, so why would he look for a bag after he killed her?"

"She must've taken it out of the car with her," said Isabelle.

"But why?" asked Jean-Guy, imagining that cold night. On the bridge.

"Maybe she was getting into another car," said Isabelle. "Her lover's?"

"But wasn't she going to drive to her father?" asked Jean-Guy.

"She might've changed her mind," said Isabelle. "Tracey also said she told him she was going to 'the' father, not 'her' father."

"But how would the lover know she'd be there?" asked Jean-Guy. "Vivienne only called those two numbers. And one of them was a wrong number."

"It might've been prearranged," said Isabelle. "Every Saturday night. Tracey would either be in the local bar or passed out drunk at home. They'd meet on the bridge. Maybe that's why she told her father not to meet her. Her plan was to talk to her lover, tell him about the baby, and with luck he'd take her away. She'd call her father later and change the plans."

"So she goes there," said Jean-Guy, "meets her lover at their normal place, takes the bag from her car to put in his, and he kills her. Why?"

"The baby," said Isabelle. "Vivienne might've really believed it was his.

366

He didn't want the complication in his life, the burden. He might've pushed her away, too hard, and she fell through the railing."

It fit. Some loose ends still. Like Fred. But the rest fit.

"Shouldn't Cloutier and Cameron be here by now?" asked Beauvoir, looking at the clock. "You called them more than an hour ago. Cameron for sure should've arrived."

"I didn't call them," said Gamache.

"Why not?"

Gamache paused to corral his thoughts. This was delicate but needed to be said.

"We talked about jealousy. Agent Cloutier said it turned Vivienne's mother against her own daughter. That bond between Homer and Vivienne was so strong, no one else could get in. The only way to break it was to get rid of Vivienne."

"But Mom's dead," said Jean-Guy. "She didn't kill her daughter out of jealousy."

"*Non*, I don't mean her. I mean someone else who wanted a relationship with Homer. But who might've also run up against that unbreakable bond. Someone who might also need to get rid of Vivienne."

"Lysette Cloutier?" asked Isabelle. "You think she killed Vivienne?"

Clearly, Isabelle did not.

"I don't know," said Gamache. "I doubt it, but since we're looking at other possibilities, that one comes to mind. How many murders have we investigated where a relationship was at the center? Where jealousy had turned to hatred. To murder."

"We need to speak with her," said Jean-Guy.

"Let me do it," said Isabelle.

"There's something else." Gamache handed Jean-Guy his notebook.

As Jean-Guy read, his eyes opened and his brows shot up. Then he handed it over to Isabelle, who looked at it, then over to Gamache.

They knew then why Chief Inspector Gamache had seemed distracted. And why he'd been so insistent they consider other options.

"I think we should call them now," said Jean-Guy. "Don't you?"

# CHAPTER THIRTY-SEVEN

⌒

While they waited for the two Sûreté agents to arrive, Lacoste went back over the forensic evidence. Beauvoir read the reports on Vivienne's finances.

And Gamache went for a walk. To think.

He strolled once around the village green. His hands clasped behind his back, he watched Henri and Gracie playing in the mud.

Reine-Marie might not thank him for this, he thought.

"Come along," he called to them, and together they walked up the road out of town. Stopping on the crest of the hill, he turned to admire the view, which stretched past Québec and well into the Green Mountains of Vermont.

The snow was heading off somewhere else but had left a centimeter behind. It was, he knew, almost certainly the last snowfall. The end of a season. And the beginning of another.

He brushed off the bench that he and Reine-Marie had placed there for all to rest on.

As he did, familiar words were uncovered, etched deep into the wood.

*Surprised by Joy*

And below that:

*A Brave Man in a Brave Country*

Marilynne Robinson's words always made him think of his father and mother.

*"I'll pray that you grow up a brave man in a brave country,"* he whispered. *"I will pray you find a way to be useful."*

Would their prayers for him have been answered?

But mostly he thought of his grandchildren. Florence, Zora, Honoré. And soon, a new granddaughter.

He closed his eyes. Briefly. And tried not to think that the country they'll grow up in won't be his own.

Then, opening his eyes, he looked at the white world and thought of the white whale. That devoured reason.

*All that most maddens and torments; all that stirs up the lees of things; all truth with malice in it.*

That was where the quote ended, for him. He didn't know the rest. But in the small hours, in front of the fireplace, while Reine-Marie and Homer slept, while Henri snored at his feet and Gracie ran free in her dreams, he'd looked up that quote and read the rest.

*All that cracks the sinews and cakes the brain; all the subtle demonisms of life and thought; all evil . . .*

It was difficult, in this peaceful place, looking out over the quiet little village just waking up, to imagine the torment that cracks the sinews and cakes the brain.

But it existed. He met it every day. The subtle demons of life and thought.

That turned something horrific into something acceptable. That turned a crime into a punishment. That somehow made it okay to push a young, pregnant woman off a bridge to her death.

That twisted reality, until malice and truth were intertwined and indistinguishable.

Had the demons caught up with Lysette Cloutier, in love with Homer? Had they caught up with Cameron? With Pauline Vachon? Carl Tracey?

He was honest enough to recognize that it wasn't just murderers who harbored those demons. Cops did, too. He did, too.

His prejudices. And preconceptions. His blinders. And blunders. And outright mistakes.

He heard a car approach. Then slow down. And stop. He heard Henri's and Gracie's collars clink as they raised their heads and looked.

The car idled by the side of the road.

Then silence.

Gamache did not look behind him but continued to stare off into the distance, into the wilderness.

He felt the presence first, then saw it out of the corner of his eye.

"*Clare, Clare, do not despair.*" Gamache spoke the words slowly, deliberately, sending them out over the peaceful village below. "*Between the bridge and the water, I was there.*"

Then he turned and faced the person standing beside the bench.

"And so were you."


Clara stared at the closed door to her studio. Then went in.

Turning on the lights, she stood directly in front of her easel. Arms at her sides. Shoulders back. Almost at attention. A coward caught. Called out. And facing what was coming.

She lifted her chin in defiance and stared at her works. Daring them to do their worst.

And they did.

As she watched with growing dismay, the tiny paintings shifted before her eyes and went from something brilliant to something less than brilliant. And another shift.

*My God,* Clara thought. *They were right.*

The critics.

The gallery owners.

Dominica Oddly.

The assholes on social media. So filled with bile they were easily dismissed. One described her as a painter whose art began with an *f.* That juvenile comment got hundreds of retweets. Someone else said she was an artist who painted only in brown.

And she saw now that it was true.

The miniatures were shit.

It wasn't that she'd tried to be bold and failed, it was that she hadn't tried. Exactly as Oddly had said. She'd whipped them off without thought. Without feeling. Without caring. Fooling herself into believing that because it was a new medium, new territory for her, it was a brave experiment.

It was not.

She had betrayed the gift. Cheapened it.

Sitting down on the stool, she felt the lump forming in her throat.

When she was able to move, she took the miniatures off the easel, got out a hammer. And went to work.

Then she placed a clean canvas in front of her. And stared at it. White. White. It grew larger and larger. Huge. It was taunting her, daring her to approach.

"You'd better sit down," said Gamache.

And Bob Cameron did.

He felt the holster on his belt push into him. As though reminding him it was there.

There'd been something in Chief Inspector Beauvoir's tone when he'd called and invited him to the Gamache home. Not the incident room, as he'd expected. And it was put in the form of an invitation. As though he weren't an agent to be ordered but a civilian to be invited.

He'd suspected then, but now, looking at Chief Inspector Gamache, Cameron knew. That they knew.

"Does your wife know?" Gamache asked.

"*Non*. How did you . . . ?"

"The phone number. Your personal cell phone. Not your home number, not your work number. But you have another cell phone. When I looked up your file this morning, to call you, there it was. It's a single number off the one Vivienne was calling over and over on the day she died. She was calling you. You must've known we'd find out."

"Why would you? You were so focused on Carl Tracey, I thought you wouldn't get there."

What Cameron said was true. With, Gamache recognized, a touch of malice.

"Yes," said Gamache. "That was a mistake. Being corrected now." He put out his hand. "Your weapon, please."

"You know I didn't kill Vivienne, don't you?"

"I know you lied. I know you were her lover. I know you were on that bridge."

"But not that night."

372

Still, Gamache's gloved hand was held out. Steady. It would not move until Cameron's weapon was placed in it.

"Are you afraid I'll use it, *patron*?" asked Cameron.

"Give it to me," said Gamache.

"I didn't kill her."

"Give it to me."

And finally Cameron reached behind him and brought out the gun. And placed it in the Chief Inspector's hand.

"*Merci.*" Gamache put it in his coat pocket. "Before we get to how it ended, tell me how it began."

Superintendent Lacoste pointed to a chair at the kitchen table.

They'd moved from the living room into the kitchen, where Homer, still in his bedroom, couldn't hear what they were saying.

"Sit down, please."

Agent Cloutier raised her brows but did as she was told.

Her mentor stared at her for what seemed an eternity. Chief Inspector Beauvoir was also there. Looking at her. His face stern. His eyes watchful.

She knew that look.

It was the one he gave suspects. She didn't have to wait long to have it confirmed.

"As you know, Agent Cloutier, when we investigate a murder, we look for motive. You have a motive."

"*Pardon?*"

"Homer Godin."

"I don't understand."

"Of course you do. You understand too well. I can see it in your eyes."

Agent Cloutier was silent.

"Tell me about your relationship with Homer Godin," said Lacoste.

"There is no—"

"Enough. It's time for the truth. You clearly care for him. His wife's been gone for five years now. He's free. You're free. Have you told him how you feel? Or is something, or someone, stopping you?"

But still Cloutier remained mute. Partly out of fear of saying too much. But also, now, she found herself incapable of describing feelings that had run so deep, for so long. That had been the undercurrent of her life, for so long. And with each passing day, week, year, getting stronger.

She could feel herself growing fonder and fonder of her best friend's husband. Even while Kathy was alive. And yes, part of it was the tenderness Homer showed his infant daughter. His patience. His gentleness with her, so in contrast to Kathy's abruptness. Her efficient care. Her rules and rigid structure for the day.

Kathy couldn't help it. It was who she was. And Homer was who he was. And Lysette was who she was.

She never acted on her feelings, but she did visit when she could. To see Kathy. To see her goddaughter. To see him.

And then, after Kathy died, that heady mixture of guilt and excitement. Of hope and longing.

Allowing herself to imagine what life might be like. If—

And then, that first time she'd caught him looking at her with tenderness. That first small smile.

"What happened, Lysette?" Lacoste asked.

Even though she knew it was a trap, Lysette was too tired to avoid it. And she realized she wanted to talk. About Homer. About Vivienne. About what happened.


"You know how it started," said Cameron.

"And you know you need to tell me yourself," said Gamache.

Cameron, more used to action than talk, put up his hands in an instinctive defensive maneuver, then lowered them. He searched his vocabulary for unaccustomed words. Some way to describe feelings. Overwhelming. Unexpected. Unwanted.

From the moment she'd opened the door and he'd looked into Vivienne's eyes, he'd been branded. The emotions painful and permanent.

Gamache looked into that broken face and felt his pain. It was, Gamache knew, a hurt that went far back. Deep into Bob Cameron's earliest memories.

Here was a man born into chaos. Into abuse. Forged by it. Molded and shaped, literally, by it.

Some with similar upbringings grew up to be abusive themselves.

But some found the space between the bridge and the water.

Gamache had seen this man play football. Had seen his almost maniacal need to protect his quarterback. Even taking penalty after penalty to hold off those who'd hurt his teammate.

It had cost him his job.

But Bob Cameron couldn't help it, Gamache suspected. It was ingrained, as surely as those scars and smashed bones.

The need to protect. First his mother and siblings. Then his teammates.

And now he was a Sûreté officer. Protecting the population.

And Vivienne Godin?

"How did it start?" Gamache asked again.

"The moment she opened the door that first time," said Cameron. "She was polite. Dignified, even. She thanked me for coming but asked me not to arrest her husband. That it would only make things worse."

He paused, to remember. It seemed so long ago. And he was getting confused now, with images of his sister's face. His mother's. His own, in the mirror. Damage that could never, ever be repaired.

Gamache waited, giving the man the space he needed.

"She smiled then. And her lip split open, where he'd hit her." Cameron raised his finger to his own lip and touched it. "It bled. It caused her pain, but she still smiled. At me. I knew then."

"What did you know?"

"That I loved her."

"But you didn't know her."

"I knew enough."

Gamache paused. And believed him. "What did you do?"

"Nothing, not then. I gave her my card and asked her to call."

"Did she?"

"Not me. But she did call 911 again. I went out, and again she refused to let me into the house. I could see him. I could smell the booze. But there was nothing I could do. I asked her to meet me that night, after he went to bed. At the bridge."

"You knew it?"

"From hunting. Yes. It was close to her home and private."

Gamache said nothing. They were almost there. Almost.

"It was summer. Dark. Hot. She was there when I arrived."

"You had sex?"

"We made love."

But that wasn't the end. Not yet. Not even close.

"You confronted Tracey outside the bar in town," said Gamache. "More than once."

"Yes." Cameron was defiant, still far from willing to admit it was wrong.

"You told him to stop hurting his wife."

"Yes."

"It didn't work, of course. As she predicted, it only made it worse," said Gamache.

"Yes."

"When did your affair start?"

"Last July."

"How often did you meet?"

"Every Saturday night. At midnight. By then Tracey was drunk and passed out."

"And your wife? Didn't she suspect?"

"I always took the Saturday-night shift at work. No one else wanted it. It was quiet, so I could get away."

"Last Saturday night?"

"No, no, you don't understand. I broke it off. In the fall."

"Why?"

"I didn't want to lose my family. My job." He paused. "Have I lost them?"

"Why didn't you tell us this?"

"I knew you suspected—"

"You knew because I came right out and asked, and you denied it."

"Because I knew how it would look. And I knew I hadn't killed her. Vivienne was gone. Carl Tracey killed her. Admitting the affair would just muddy things. Hurt the investigation."

"You mean hurt you."

"No."

"She was calling you." Gamache pushed. "You'd given her your private cell-phone number. You told her only to call in an emergency. And she hadn't called. Hadn't needed to, until that night. She told her husband she was going to meet her lover—"

"Not me."

"The father of her child—"

"Not me."

Hearing the anger in Cameron's voice, Henri got to his feet and turned to face him. A low, low growl in his chest. Little Gracie stood beside him, all eyes. Barely larger than Cameron's boot, she tried to stare down the man who loomed over them.

"Stop lying." Gamache dropped his hand to Henri's head. To reassure him. "It was your number she was trying to call. The affair wasn't over, was it?"

"It was."

"She wanted to meet you earlier. That's why she called." Something about that statement gave Gamache a moment's pause. But he had to press on. "She didn't get through to you, because she'd written your number down wrong. One digit was off. So she showed up at the prearranged time. Midnight. And there you were. For the regular assignation."

"No."

"Expecting sex. Instead she told you she was pregnant and the child was yours. She might even have believed it. She told you she was leaving her husband, for you. She had her duffel bag over her shoulder. All packed. Had been for months, waiting for the right time. And this was it."

"No." Cameron shot to his feet.

Gamache could see the veins throbbing on Cameron's forehead as the big man tried to control his anger.

"It was over. I wasn't there."

Gamache also got up. And got right into Cameron's space. Into his face. "What did she do? Threaten to go to your wife? Your work? And when she refused to just go away, you pushed her."

"No."

"You pushed a pregnant woman to her death."

"No, never!"

Cameron heaved off and gave Gamache a mighty shove. Propelling him backward.

Henri barked and crouched, prepared to lunge.

"Henri, stay!" Gamache commanded as he regained his balance.

And Henri did. As did Gracie. Just. It clearly went against their every instinct.

Because he was prepared for it, had intentionally provoked it, Gamache had staggered but managed to keep to his feet, despite the force of the blow.

Which was far more than a young woman taken by surprise could possibly have done.


"Vivienne happened," said Lysette Cloutier.

Lacoste recognized the look in Cloutier's eyes. It was the expression of someone who'd made up her mind to walk off a cliff. And was just about to do it.

Still, Isabelle coaxed her forward. "Go on."

"Homer and I hadn't been intimate yet, but it was close. We finally admitted our feelings. I wonder if you know what that's like? To be in love with someone for years, maybe decades, and then, in your forties, to have those feelings returned. It felt like a miracle. It was a miracle. But Homer said he owed it to Vivienne to tell her, before we took it further."

Lysette lowered her head and narrowed her eyes. Then she raised her head. High. And looked directly at Superintendent Lacoste.

"I didn't kill her."

"What happened?" Lacoste asked.

She noticed that Beauvoir had turned back to his laptop and was reading something. A message. But she kept her focus on the middle-aged accountant–cum–homicide agent. Cum suspect. In front of her.

"Vivienne told him to break it off."

And there it was.

"Why?"

"Why did she do anything?" Long trapped deep inside, Cloutier's demons finally split the sinews and came tumbling out. "Because she was weak and afraid and needy and manipulative."

"What was she afraid of?"

"Of not being the center of Homer's life. She'd managed to come between Homer and Kathy, and now she came between us. I should've seen it coming, but I thought it was specific to her mother. A teenage thing. She was all grown up now. Married. It never occurred to me she'd tell him it was her or me."

"Is that what she said?"

"Yes."

"And what did Homer do?"

"You know what he did. He broke it off."

"He chose his grown married daughter over a woman he loved?"

"Yes."

"Why?"

"Obviously he didn't love me enough. Didn't love me as much."

"As much as Vivienne?"

"As much as I loved him."

"What did he do?"

"Nothing. He just said we couldn't see each other anymore."

"And you accepted that?"

"What could I do?"

Lacoste looked at her. They both knew what she could've done. Might've done.

"How long ago was that?"

"Almost a year ago. We haven't seen each other since then. Until he emailed and told me Vivienne was missing."

"Where were you on Saturday?"

"It was my day off. I was at home doing laundry. Chores."

"Alone?"

Lysette nodded. Always alone.

"Did you go down to see Vivienne? To confront her?"

"Of course not. It was over and done with almost a year ago. Why would I do it now? What're you saying?"

"I'm saying things grow. Fester. Time doesn't always heal. Sometimes it makes things worse. Is that what happened to you, Lysette?"

"Of course not."

"Did you think about it, about him, every day?"

"No."

"Did you think about what might've been, if Vivienne hadn't done that? How your life would be so different?"

"No."

"Did you arrange to meet her? Offer her something she wanted?"

"No."

"Money, maybe?"

"No."

"Did she suggest the bridge?"

"No."

"Did you push her off?"

"No!"

"Did you want her dead?"

Pause.

"Yes."

# CHAPTER THIRTY-EIGHT

⌒

As soon as Reine-Marie walked into the kitchen, she could see she was interrupting.

"I'm sorry," she said, stopping at the door. "Is something wrong?"

"*Non*," said Isabelle. "We were just chatting."

Though that was clearly not true.

"I was going to make breakfast," said Reine-Marie, going to the fridge. "Why don't you continue your chat in the study?"

Isabelle Lacoste smiled and nodded. "*Merci*. I think we will."

"Where's Armand?"

"Out for a walk. He took the dogs. Is Monsieur Godin still asleep?"

"Yes," said Reine-Marie. "I looked in but didn't want to disturb him. Is Jean-Guy with Armand?"

"*Non*," came the familiar voice.

Jean-Guy had gone to the study to print something and now returned to the kitchen holding the papers. "But I do need to find him. Be back soon. Don't let Isabelle eat everything. You know what she's like."

Reine-Marie smiled and watched him go.

The home settled. The bacon sizzled and popped. The coffee perked. The fire in the woodstove roiled as the women went into the study to continue whatever they were talking about, and Jean-Guy left to find Armand.

⌒

A mist was rising from the thinning layer of snow. The air warmer now than the ground. Giving the pretty village an otherworldly feel. Except for the mud.

Beauvoir's boots made a thucking sound as he walked quickly toward the bridge and the sandbags still in place against a threat no longer there.

The three huge pines, around which all life in the village revolved, stood in front of him now. Partly obscured by the mist. As though they existed in both this world and the other.

Whenever he and Annie visited with Honoré, Jean-Guy would bring him to the green to play. Sometimes, as he sat on the bench and watched his son, Jean-Guy had the oddest feeling that the little boy was playing not among the trees but with them.

He was almost at the bridge on his way to the incident room, where he expected Gamache had gone, when he noticed movement up on the ridge of the hill out of town.

Gamache and Cameron were standing, facing each other. It looked natural enough. But it was the posture of the dogs that alerted Beauvoir that this was not a pleasant discussion. For any of them.

And he knew what they must be talking about.

Picking up his pace, *thuck, thuck, thuck*, he headed up there. As he approached, he heard Cameron shout, "No. Never."

He saw Gamache get right up into Cameron's face.

While he couldn't hear what the Chief Inspector said, he could hear Cameron's reply. Another "No" blasted.

Cameron raised his hands.

Henri crouched.

Gracie barked.

And Armand braced.

When the blow landed, he staggered back.

Beauvoir shouted.

But neither heard.

They continued to stare. Cameron at the man accusing him of murder. Gamache at a man who could so easily be provoked into an act which, under different circumstances, would prove fatal.

"Are you going to lay charges?" Beauvoir asked as he and Gamache walked a dozen paces away from Agent Cameron.

Gamache looked behind him.

Cameron wasn't watching them. Instead, he gazed, dazed, out over the village.

Gamache wondered what he saw. The forests and mountains, the shifting reds and purples of the sunrise, with the mist rising pink-tinged below?

Did he see Vivienne? As she hung between the bridge and the water.

Cameron's huge hands were grasping the back of the bench. So that the words etched there now read "surprised by—"

The joy had disappeared.

"For assault? *Non*," said Gamache. "We're after bigger fish."

"A whale, even?" asked Beauvoir. "Look at this."

Gamache took the paper, then reached into the breast pocket of his coat and brought out his reading glasses. But they were broken.

Wordlessly, he replaced them and squinted to read the printout.

He made a guttural noise that sounded like "Huh." Then his eyes focused on the man in front of him. "What do you think it means?"

"I have an idea, but I think we need to ask him."


Homer Godin looked down at the printout.

He'd stared at it for a while, clearly trying to focus his mind.

They'd left Cloutier and Cameron in the kitchen while the senior officers met with Homer in Gamache's study.

"Viv's bank statements," he finally said, raising his eyes to Lacoste, then over to Beauvoir.

"Yes. They show that every month since last July you transferred two thousand dollars into her account."

"True."

"Why?"

"She asked for it. Said they needed it to pay their mortgage. I didn't want her to be homeless."

"And yet, it just sat there, accumulating," said Beauvoir. "There's eighteen thousand dollars in that account."

Homer shook his head. "Maybe she didn't need it after all."

"Then why did she keep taking it?" asked Beauvoir. When Homer didn't answer, Jean-Guy went on. "I think she was saving up. To leave Tracey. I think that was her plan for a long time."

"Could be," said Homer.

"I think with a baby on the way, she decided now was the time to get out and start a new life, with the money you'd given her."

"I hope so." Homer seemed confused now. As though what Beauvoir described were still possible.

Beauvoir looked over at Gamache, then to Lacoste, all thinking the same thing.

Homer Godin was not a rich man. He'd labored all his life. Had a modest home he'd paid off. Lived a modest life in a small Québec town.

These sorts of sums would almost certainly clean him out. And then some.

He seemed to follow their thoughts. "She said she'd pay me back. She'd get a job when she could. What would you do?"

And there was that question again. Variations on the theme that had haunted them since this case had begun. How would they feel, if . . . ?

What would they do, if . . . ?

If Honoré came to his parents, in distress, and needed more money than they had?

If Annie went to her parents . . . ?

If money would solve the problem?

They'd pay it. And more. To save their child? They'd give all they had. And more.

As Homer had.

"She called you on Saturday morning, telling you she was finally going to leave Tracey, is that right?" said Lacoste.

"Yes."

"Think carefully, Monsieur Godin," said Lacoste. "Did she say she was coming to you or going to someone else?"

"Me. Who else was there?"

"Tell us about your relationship with Lysette Cloutier," said Lacoste.

Homer was shaking his head. "Vivienne wouldn't go to Lysette. They barely knew each other."

"No, I don't mean that," said Lacoste. "Your relationship with her."

"How'd you know about that?"

"She told us."

"She shouldn't have. It was private."

"She didn't want to," said Gamache. "She had to be pushed, hard. But she finally told us."

"What did she say?"

"I think you need to tell us what happened," said Beauvoir.

Homer raised his head and looked stubborn. Then relented. "Doesn't much matter. We tried, and it didn't work."

"Why didn't it work?" asked Gamache.

"It just didn't. I thought of her as a friend. She wanted more, but I didn't. Couldn't."

"Did you talk to Vivienne about it?" asked Lacoste.

Homer looked surprised. "About Lysette? No, why would I? There was nothing to talk about."

Beauvoir looked at Gamache, then to Lacoste.

"So who's telling the truth?" asked Lacoste. "Lysette or Homer?"

The senior officers had walked to the incident room, where they could talk without fear of being overheard.

"Maybe Homer gave Lysette the impression that Vivienne wouldn't approve," said Beauvoir. "Without actually saying it."

"You mean he blamed his daughter?" asked Lacoste. "Is he that much of a coward?"

Beauvoir remained silent, not bothering to tell her how often he'd made up all sorts of far-fetched stories to get out of relationships. Granted, that was when he was younger.

"Could happen" was all he said.

"Or maybe Homer didn't outright blame his daughter," said Gamache, "but Cloutier did. Maybe it was easier on her feelings to think Vivienne forced it, rather than that the man she loved rejected her."

"Easier to blame someone she already didn't like," said Lacoste. "And she might've even believed it."

"If she really got it into her head that Vivienne stood between her and Homer," said Beauvoir, "that sort of thing can eat away at a person. You said it yourself, *patron*. It's a simple, clean motive. Most are."

It was true. When the mist and smoke and fireworks dissipated, what was left in a murder investigation could be rendered down to a few words. Greed. Hate. Jealousy.

But really, it was even simpler than that. Even those words had a common parent.

Fear.

Cameron was afraid of losing his family.

Cloutier was afraid of losing Homer.

Pauline Vachon was afraid of losing her ticket out.

Carl Tracey was afraid of losing his home, his studio, his pottery.

If Vivienne lived.

"But how would they set up the meeting?" said Beauvoir. "There's no record of a call between Cloutier and Vivienne."

"True," said Lacoste.

They'd checked all the calls into and out of the farmhouse, going back months. It was not as arduous as it sounded. There were hardly any, and those there were, were easily traced.

"One of the things I don't understand," said Gamache, "is why Vivienne didn't leave earlier."

"She had to get up courage," said Lacoste, a little surprised by the question. "We've talked about this. Lots of abused women never leave—" Her phone buzzed. "Sorry. *Allô?*"

"A message just came in," said Agent Cloutier. "I'd asked the forensic accountants to look into the bank accounts of all the people involved."

"Yes? And?" asked Lacoste.

"I've forwarded it to you."

Lacoste went to her emails. "Got it." She clicked on it. "What'm I looking at?"

She waved the others over to her laptop.

Gamache and Beauvoir bent and stared at the screen while Lacoste put Cloutier on speaker.

"Scroll down," said Cloutier. "To the bottom link."

Lacoste did, and clicked. "But this's Monsieur Godin's bank account."

"I didn't ask for it to be part of the search," explained Cloutier. "But his name must've been on the list of people involved in the case. So the forensic accountant included him, I guess."

They looked at the numbers. Twenty thousand dollars had been transferred into Homer Godin's bank account on Friday. And taken out in cash that afternoon.

"It's a mortgage loan," said Cloutier. "You can tell by the code attached to the transfer. He must've taken it out against his house."

"Why?" asked Beauvoir.

"I don't know," said Cloutier. "But I thought you should see it."

"Anything in the other accounts?" asked Lacoste.

"Tracey's massively overdrawn, and Pauline's credit cards are maxed out."

"And Vivienne was sitting with eighteen thousand dollars in her account," said Beauvoir.

"And twenty thousand in cash with Homer," said Lacoste. *"Merci."*

Lacoste hung up, and Beauvoir looked at Gamache, who'd cocked his head to one side. Considering.

"Must've been for Vivienne," said Lacoste. "Don't you think? She knew she was leaving Carl and asked her father for more money."

"When? And wasn't the eighteen thousand enough?" asked Beauvoir. "This would give her almost forty thousand. Why would she need that much? And in cash? And why didn't he tell us about it?"

"He had other things on his mind," said Lacoste.

"And he just forgot about the twenty thousand?"

"Maybe he did tell us," said Gamache. "Well, not us exactly, but Lysette Cloutier. She says they hadn't kept in touch since he broke it off, but that might not be true. Homer didn't say they'd lost touch. Maybe he asked her advice on how to raise the money."

"Yes, she's a trained accountant, after all," said Lacoste. "So he asked her, and she told him about the home loan. Maybe that was the final straw for Cloutier."

Beauvoir was nodding now. Following the logic. "She could see that Vivienne wasn't just ruining their lives but now was bleeding her dad dry. So she arranges to meet her."

"To kill her?" asked Lacoste.

"No, probably not. But to have it out with her, finally."

"Why would Vivienne agree to that?"

"Maybe Cloutier told her she had the money," suggested Beauvoir. "Vivienne chose a spot close by, where she'd had private meetings before."

"The bridge," said Lacoste.

"The bridge," he said.

Despite her affection for the woman, Lacoste could see it now. Could see how an uncomfortable confrontation could spiral out of control.

"Only Cloutier was lying," said Beauvoir. "She didn't really have the cash, of course. When Vivienne realized that, she'd be furious. Might've even attacked Cloutier, who pushed her away."

And through the railing.

"But if it was all triggered by that twenty thousand, why would she tell us about it now?" asked Lacoste.

"She'd have no choice," said Gamache. "The information was in the email about all the finances. She'd know we'd work it out. What I'm still wondering is why Homer didn't say anything about that loan."

"He might've worried that it made Vivienne look bad," said Beauvoir. "And it does. Taking so much money from her father, then running away with a married lover."

"No. It makes her look like a woman who's been beaten for years and was now desperate to save herself and her unborn child," snapped Lacoste. "Was it a series of decisions a healthy person would make? Probably not. But who can say what any of us would do to survive? You want to know what I think actually happened?"

She looked at her two colleagues.

"Please," said Gamache.

"I think we were right all along, and this's just complicating things.

I think Carl Tracey killed his wife. Maybe he knew about that secret account, maybe he didn't. Either way, he wanted to get rid of her. With Pauline Vachon's help, they came up with the plan to throw her into the river. And you know what?"

"What?" said Beauvoir.

"He might be a moron, but it looks like it worked. We can't get him. He's going to walk free."

"Oh, shit," said Jean-Guy, hanging his head.

Isabelle was right.

"I think we need to speak to Homer," said Gamache. "Find out about the money. At least this's new, and admissible."

"Yeah," said Beauvoir, getting up. "Untainted by that goddamned poisonous tree. But before we do, I want to go back over the evidence one more time."

"Again?" asked Lacoste. "I have it memorized."

"Again," said Beauvoir. "I'm not giving up on Tracey yet. There's something in there we've missed."

They spent the next hour sifting through evidence. Testimony. Events. They knew it by heart. They knew it was futile. That the search would prove fruitless.

And it did.

Finally Beauvoir stood up and yanked his coat from the back of his chair.

"Nothing. Let's go speak to Homer about this money. Maybe something will come up."

They had nowhere else to turn. Just this one slender thread to follow.

Reine-Marie greeted them at the door, and when Armand asked about Homer, she pointed upstairs.

"He went to his room right after you left."

Jean-Guy climbed the stairs, and from the living room they heard him knock. Then knock again.

"Monsieur Godin, it's Jean-Guy Beauvoir. I'm afraid we have some more questions."

There was silence.

Armand and Isabelle looked at each other, then started up the stairs. But only got halfway before Jean-Guy appeared on the landing.

"It's empty. He's not there."

"Bathroom?" asked Gamache, taking the stairs two at a time.

They searched the upstairs, but there was no Homer.

"When was the last time you saw him?" Armand asked Reine-Marie.

"Right after you left. He went straight to his room."

Gamache looked at his watch. "Over an hour ago."

"Cloutier! Cameron!" Beauvoir shouted as he walked quickly toward the kitchen. The two agents came out. "Where's Monsieur Godin?"

"In his bedroom," said Cloutier.

"He's not."

"Could he have slipped out?" said Gamache. "Taken Fred for a walk? There's a heavy fog, so we might not have seen him."

But on hearing his name, the dog appeared at the kitchen door. His tail slowly swishing back and forth.

"I'm sorry," said Reine-Marie. "I thought he was in his bedroom."

"It's not your fault at all," said Armand. "Your—"

Anticipating the question, she put her hand in the pocket of her cardigan and brought out her car keys. "I made sure I had them on me."

"Well done," he said with a smile. "That's a relief. That means he's on foot."

Beauvoir was in the study, using the landline to warn the agents guarding Carl Tracey's home.

"How long will it take him to get there?" asked Cloutier.

"At least half an hour, walking along the road, in good conditions," said Gamache, going to the kitchen as he spoke.

The others followed him.

"He's not there, *patron*," said Cameron.

But Gamache didn't answer him, choosing to answer Cloutier instead.

"He probably took the woods at first, so we wouldn't see him, then cut back onto the road. Once he sees the Sûreté car at Tracey's place, he'll head into the forest, to avoid being seen."

As he spoke, he opened and closed drawers.

"I've been through those woods—it's not easy going. I'd think it'll take him a good hour or more." Once again he looked at his watch.

Homer would be arriving right about now.

"Damn." Armand turned to Reine-Marie. "The carving knife's gone."

She paled, visualizing the large, sharp knife.

"I just called Tracey's home," Lacoste reported. "No answer."

"We've gotta go," said Beauvoir.

# CHAPTER THIRTY-NINE

A nything?" asked Beauvoir.
He'd slammed the car door, not trying to be discreet. Just the opposite. He wanted to make noise. Let Homer know they were there.

"Nothing," said one of the agents.

"Did you speak to Tracey?" asked Beauvoir. "Warn him?"

"We knocked on the door, but there was no answer," said the other agent. "Without a warrant, we didn't think we should break in. But we've been watching closely, and no one's approached the house."

He looked at his colleague, who nodded agreement.

"You did the right thing," said Beauvoir.

Homer had been gone for just under an hour and a half. He should be there soon. If he wasn't already.

Beauvoir looked around and considered the options.

They could go into the woods and hope to find Homer.

They could go into the house and take Tracey into protective custody.

They could leave him there as bait, stake out the house, and arrest Homer when he appeared.

Or they could do nothing. And let Homer do what he came to do.

Jean-Guy Beauvoir knew he'd never do that. But still . . .

"I'm going to get Tracey," he said. "Bring him into protective custody. We'll knock down the door if we have to."

"I'll come with you," said Lacoste. "You two come with us." She indicated the agents who'd been on duty. "You two"—she pointed to Cloutier and Cameron—"stay here and watch the road."

While clearly not happy about being left behind, they had no choice.

Beauvoir looked at Gamache, who was scanning the tree line. "*Patron?*"

"I'll stay out here."

His eyes returned to Beauvoir, briefly, before coming to rest on the two officers. Cloutier and Cameron.

Beauvoir couldn't make out what Gamache was thinking.

"Monsieur Godin isn't armed, is he?" asked one of the agents.

"He has a kitchen knife," said Gamache.

She gave a snort. An old man with a kitchen knife.

"Not much good against . . ." The agent placed her hand on her gun.

"You're not to use that," said Beauvoir. "Unless there's absolutely no other option. Understand?"

"*Oui, patron,*" she said, immediately dropping her hand to her side.

"And don't be fooled by his weapon," said Gamache.

The agent looked unconvinced. But she was young and didn't understand that Homer Godin wasn't an old man with a kitchen knife. He was a father with nothing to lose.

Isabelle Lacoste studied Gamache as he scanned the terrain, his eyes narrow as he tried to penetrate the mist rising from the snow in the fields.

She'd asked him a few weeks back, over drinks at the bistro one Saturday when she and her husband and children were visiting Three Pines, why he wanted to return to the Sûreté.

He was still on suspension at the time. He could easily just quit and get on with his life.

The Chief had smiled broadly. "I could ask you the same thing. You have even more reason to leave the Sûreté."

He'd glanced over her shoulder, to the door between Myrna's bookstore and the bistro. And saw, yet again, Isabelle Lacoste crumple to the floor. Shot. Her last act had saved all their lives. She'd done it knowing full well it would cost her her own.

Fortunately, she didn't remember it, so great was the trauma.

And Gamache could never forget, so great was the trauma.

But she'd recovered. Fought her way back, one excruciating step at a time.

*Things are strongest where they're broken.* If ever there was a person who proved that, it was Isabelle Lacoste.

"Honestly?" Isabelle said. "I didn't think I would, but then I realized I missed it. So?" she'd pressed. "Why do you want to go back? We both know you could name your job outside the Sûreté. You could run for Premier and probably win."

"Now there's a terrifying thought," he'd said. But she'd earned the right to a truthful answer. And so, after a pause, he gave it to her.

"It's where I belong. We're all handed a cup. This's mine."

Lacoste stared at him. Seeing the ghosts in his eyes.

The horrific decisions, the terrible orders conceived and carried out. The consequences of leadership.

As long as Armand Gamache carried the burden, no one else had to. He was already shattered. The damage done. The cup to his lips.

On seeing the sadness in her face, he smiled. "Not to worry, Isabelle. Maybe I'm being selfish." He leaned toward her and lowered his voice. "After all, it's how the light gets in."

That conversation flashed through her mind, more as a feeling than actually verbatim, as they stood on the side of the road, the icy mist seeping into their bones.

Beauvoir started down the drive.

Lacoste turned to Gamache. "You sure?"

"I'm sure," he said. "Be careful. Tracey has knives, too."

As Beauvoir and the others approached the house, Gamache signaled to Cameron to walk to the far side of the field and hold the position.

"And me?" asked Cloutier.

"You stay here, by the car. We'll need you when we find Homer."

"He won't listen to me."

"I think you'd be surprised."

Gamache walked along the slushy road, in the opposite direction to Cameron, who was now barely visible through the mist.

Gamache heard Beauvoir on the other side of the house, knocking on the door.

"Tracey, it's the Sûreté. Chief Inspector Beauvoir."

Gamache took a few steps off the road, onto the soft grass, soaked by melting snow.

There was a door back there. Closed. It led, he knew, into Tracey's studio.

As he got closer, he saw the boot prints.

He stopped. And stood absolutely still.

He heard pounding now. Beauvoir. At the door. Trying to get a response.

But there was no one there to respond, Gamache knew. At least no one alive.

He turned and shouted to Cloutier. "Homer's already been here and gone. Beauvoir needs to get inside and find Tracey."

"Yessir."

She ran down the drive, sliding slightly in the mud but keeping her footing.

"He's here," she shouted. "Homer's here."

At the door, everyone turned.

"How'd you know?" demanded Beauvoir.

"Chief Inspector Gamache told me. Said to tell you to go inside. Tracey might be—"

"*Merde,*" said Beauvoir, and reached for the door handle as the two agents reached for their guns.

"Holster them," said Lacoste.

The door was locked, and solid. They threw themselves against it, just as Cameron arrived. The human battering ram.

Putting his shoulder to it, the door burst open.

As he rushed in, Beauvoir wondered, very briefly, where Gamache was.

# CHAPTER FORTY

⌒

"Tell him I'm following Homer," Gamache shouted after Cloutier, as she ran to warn Beauvoir.

Then he turned back to the prints.

One set arriving.

One set returning.

Gamache followed the boot prints into the forest.

After a few steps, he paused and looked around. He knew then where Homer was heading.

No longer needing to follow the prints, Gamache moved through the woods as fast as he could, weaving between trees. Brittle branches scraped his coat, his hands, his face.

Once he had to stop as the mist grew thick and he lost his bearings. But he reoriented himself and pressed on.

It took ten minutes of slipping and slogging through mud and ankle-deep slush before he broke through to what was little more than an overgrown path.

He could hear labored breathing ahead of him, but it wasn't until he turned the corner that he saw.

Homer. On the bridge. The mist rising from the Bella Bella almost enveloping him.

But he wasn't alone.

Carl Tracey's body was slung over his shoulder.

"Homer!"

Godin turned.

"Here," shouted Cameron from the back of the house. "In the studio."

Beauvoir hurried back there, expecting to find Tracey, either cowering behind his pots or dead. Instead he found Cameron standing by the back door.

"Godin must've gotten in this way," said Cameron.

"No sign of Tracey?" said Beauvoir, pushing past Cameron. "Jesus, there're footprints coming and going."

"There's blood on the floor," said Lacoste, pointing to the stains. "Not a lot. Someone's hurt, but doesn't look like a fatal stabbing. There'd be lots more blood."

"And a body," said Beauvoir.

He stepped outside and saw what Gamache had seen. Not just two sets of prints, but one was deeper than the other.

"Homer must've taken Tracey with him."

"And the Chief's following them," said Lacoste, pointing to another set of prints.

"Oh, God," said Cloutier, and when they turned to her, she said, "He shouted something I didn't hear. I should've stopped and asked, but I just kept running."

Lacoste turned to Beauvoir. "He thinks we're right behind him. He thinks he'll get backup."

Cameron started past Beauvoir to follow the prints, and the man, into the forest, but Beauvoir stopped him.

"Wait."

Every fiber in his body wanted to run into the woods. He could feel the others straining to do the same thing.

But he remembered the Chief's advice.

Think. Take a breath. Take a moment. Just a moment. To think.

So now, almost vibrating with the need to act, Jean-Guy Beauvoir thought.

"Godin's taking Tracey to the bridge." Turning to Lacoste, he said, "Take the car. You two go with her." He pointed to Cameron and Cloutier.

"You?" she asked.

But Jean-Guy Beauvoir was already doing exactly what he always did. He was following Armand Gamache.

By the time Lacoste reached the car, Jean-Guy Beauvoir and the other two agents were well into the forest. Racing through the mist and trees.

"Drop him, Homer."

Godin, twenty paces ahead, was heaving for breath.

"Put him down." As he spoke, Gamache approached, reaching into his pocket as he walked toward the bridge. Not for the gun still resting there but for his phone. As Homer watched, Gamache stopped, pressed a button, and placed the phone on the ground, propped against a rock.

There was no reception there, he knew. It couldn't send, but it could record.

Homer, with Tracey unconscious and slung over his shoulder like a sack of potatoes, said nothing. Did nothing. Except stare at Gamache and gasp for breath.

Gamache approached, slowly. His hands out in front of him. He couldn't see the knife. It was possible Homer had already used it. And dropped it.

Was Carl Tracey dead?

But Gamache, who'd seen many, many bodies, didn't think so. There was still a pink hue to Tracey's hands as they hung limp. And there was no trail of blood, no sopping stain on Homer's coat, as there would be if he'd stabbed Tracey to death.

Homer backed up a step. Two. Toward the gap in the railing, mended only with yellow police tape.

And Armand knew what he planned to do. What he'd planned all along.

He would follow his daughter into the water. And take Tracey with him. Only parting ways in the afterlife. As Tracey went to hell, and Homer went . . . ?

"Fred," said Armand.

For a moment Homer looked confused. Then spoke. "Keep him. He's yours."

"No, I mean, why didn't Vivienne take Fred with her when she left?"

He glanced behind him. Nothing.

He'd expected Beauvoir and Lacoste to be there by now.

He was running out of time, and Homer was running out of bridge. Gamache's only hope was to distract him long enough.

"It doesn't make sense," said Gamache as he stepped onto the bridge. "She wouldn't leave without her dog. I don't understand. Do you?"

Tracey made a sound, and Homer tightened his grip on him.

If Gamache had hoped to engage Homer, break his focus, he'd failed.

Homer looked blank. But not confused. He was certain about the only thing that mattered now.

Gamache tried again. Anything to stop Homer's slow progress toward the edge.

"There's something else bothering me," he said. "Tracey was at the art-supply shop Saturday morning. Why didn't Vivienne go to you then? Why didn't she leave earlier?"

Again, nothing. Just the vacant stare.

Tracey moved now, groggy, and again Homer tightened his grip on him.

*Stay still*, Gamache begged the rousing man. *Don't move.*

"You took twenty thousand dollars out of the bank. To give to Vivienne?"

"Yes."

Simple question. Simple answer. But at least an answer. It gave Gamache information, but, equally important, it created a tiny crack in Homer's focus. And, maybe, time for Jean-Guy and Isabelle and the others to arrive. If he could just engage Homer.

Though Armand was far from sure that it would matter.

Homer took another step backward.

"She asked for the money?" he said.

"Yes."

"To raise it, you had to take a mortgage out against your home."

Homer gave one curt nod.

Gamache took another step. Farther onto the bridge.

"Did you ask Lysette Cloutier about that? About how to do it? Did she know about the money?"

"I don't know, I might have. It doesn't matter."

Homer still looked dazed, but now something else had crept into his eyes. It wasn't quite fear, but he was wary.

*Now, what,* thought Gamache, *could a man willing to kill himself be wary of?* Something to do with Cloutier?

"What is it, Homer? What do you want to tell me? What do you need to tell me?"

"I loved Vivienne."

"I know you did."

"I have to do this. It's my fault. I have to make it right."

"It's not your fault, and this won't make anything right, Homer. You must know that. Following one terrible act with another doesn't balance the books."

"All those years of hurt. All the pain." Homer was pleading with him now, trying to get Armand to see. To understand. "All the times I should've stopped it but didn't. Kathy begged me, but—"

"There was nothing you could do. You sent Vivienne money, you mortgaged your home. You tried to see her, to help—"

Annie's father stared at Vivienne's father. His mind racing. Trying to get a hold of something, anything, that would penetrate Homer's resolve.

But everything he said seemed to be making it worse, if that was possible.

Homer hefted Tracey further onto his shoulder. Tightening his grip.

"You're wrong," said Homer. "About everything. This isn't a terrible act. It's the one decent thing I can do for Vivienne. To make up for all the damage. All the pain I caused her. I owe her this. You're right. This might not . . . what did you call it? Balance the books? Not even close. But it's all I have left."

Armand heard a car door slam and saw Homer's eyes flicker over his shoulder.

"*Patron?*"


The sight that met Isabelle Lacoste was chilling. But not surprising.

Vivienne's father was about to make good on his promise. He was about to throw Vivienne's killer off the bridge. The only question was whether he'd go over with him.

But that really wasn't in doubt, she knew, as she looked at his face.

Beauvoir could see light through the trees. The opening. The road.

They were almost there.

He couldn't hear anything from up ahead, for all his crashing through the branches and undergrowth.

But as soon as he broke through, he saw the Sûreté vehicles and, racing around the corner, saw immediately what was happening. He skidded to a stop.

Armand felt the heft of Cameron's gun in his pocket and considered drawing it out. Considered using it, to wound the man. Bring him down.

But decided against it.

Homer was too close to the edge. In every way. It would propel him over.

And the threat of being shot wouldn't make him drop Tracey. It was no threat at all to a man about to do something far worse. It might even be a kindness.

A coup de grâce. A battlefield execution. To end his agony.

Beauvoir had moved to one side of the road while Lacoste took the far side. They inched along the soft shoulder, where the forest met the road. Once or twice, Homer's eyes flicked in his direction. The man clearly saw what Beauvoir was doing. And didn't care.

Beauvoir's breathing settled, but he remained taut, prepared to move fast. Though, like Lacoste and Gamache, he suspected it would not be nearly fast enough.

Gamache had an idea.

Wild. Desperate. And maybe the only thing that would stop Homer Godin from throwing Carl Tracey off the bridge.

"He didn't kill your daughter."

"What?"

"Tracey. He didn't kill Vivienne."

The words, like a soft bullet, entered Vivienne's father. And he stopped.

Beauvoir and Lacoste glanced at each other. They were on either side of the narrow road, with Gamache between them, up ahead. On the bridge.

They knew what he was doing. And it seemed to be working.

Homer Godin was a decent man. Driven mad by grief and despair. But he had no desire to kill anyone, except the person who'd murdered his daughter.

If Gamache could convince him that Carl Tracey was innocent, at least of the murder . . .

"Who?" was all Homer could say. All he needed to say.

His eyes wide, fixed on Gamache.

Armand had no idea what to say. Though he knew it didn't matter.

He just had to come up with a name. Someone. Anyone. Would do.

Anything to get Homer to drop Tracey and step away from the edge.

He was just about to say the name of the one suspect not actually on the bridge, Pauline Vachon, when from behind him, came a voice.

"I did."

Homer shifted his gaze. And while Gamache was tempted to look behind him, he didn't.

Didn't have to. He knew who'd spoken.

"I'm sorry, Homer."

Lysette Cloutier had walked to just a few paces behind Gamache. And now she stepped forward, until she was beside him.

Beauvoir moved swiftly forward until he had one foot on the bridge. His hand on the rickety railing. He was just a few paces from Homer, could almost, almost reach out and touch him.

Homer was staring so intently at Cloutier, standing in the middle of the road, that he didn't notice Beauvoir off to the side.

Now Beauvoir stopped. Not wanting to spook the man.

"Lysette?" whispered Homer.

"I'm sorry," she repeated, her words coming out on a sigh. "It was an accident. I didn't mean to. It just happened."

"Why're you saying this?" he asked.

"Because it's the truth. I was her godmother. I'd promised to look after her. You'd told me about Carl, about the abuse. She needed support. Needed money. To get away. I felt awful that I hadn't done more, done anything, to protect her. I'd promised Kathy . . . promised you . . ."

"Stay back," Gamache whispered as Lysette took a step toward Homer.

"I'd saved up some money. I called her a week ago. Told her I'd like to give it to her. She said she needed time to get things in order but that she'd meet me here, on Saturday night. She'd sneak away after her husband was drunk and passed out."

Homer was staring at her. He looked confused, and Gamache wondered how much he was taking in. Out of the corner of his eye, he saw Beauvoir almost within reach of Homer.

The mist rising from the Bella Bella was burning off in the early-morning sun.

They could see clearly now. Finally.

"I got here first. Those boot prints were mine. When she arrived, she got out of her car. She had her duffel bag over her shoulder. I was about to give her the money when she said she was pregnant. A girl. A daughter."

Lysette looked down.

No one moved. No one breathed.

They were there now. At the end.

Lysette mumbled something, and Homer shouted, "What's that? I can't hear. What're you saying?"

"She was so happy to tell me that. About the baby. I don't know what came over me, Homer." Lysette's eyes and voice both rose. "I said something I shouldn't have. I told her I hoped her daughter was kinder to her than she'd been to her mother."

There was silence then, except for the Bella Bella rushing beneath them.

"She was standing about where you are," said Lysette. "She got upset. Started yelling at me that I didn't know. It just . . ." she searched for words. "It just all came out, of both of us. She started screaming that it was all her mother's fault and how dare I . . ." She heaved and caught her breath. "And I shouted back. Defending Kathy, even though I knew, I knew Viv was right. Oh, God."

They were frozen in place. A tableau. Waiting for the rest.

"She came at me, and I pushed her away. And . . ."

And.

Homer, perhaps in shock, maybe intentionally, loosened his grip on Carl Tracey.

And Tracey, coming to, flailed as he fell to the ground.

Kicking. Twisting.

Hitting Homer in the chest and sending him backward.

405

Gamache jumped forward, but Beauvoir got there first.

Homer's arms pinwheeled as he stumbled. He reached behind him. Desperate for something to grab, to stop his fall.

But there was nothing there. Just air.

His eyes wide with terror, Homer Godin began to go over the edge. Beauvoir got a handful of Homer's coat and for a moment the momentum stopped. But Homer was too far gone.

Beauvoir, still clinging to his coat, felt an almighty yank as Homer disappeared.

Dragging Jean-Guy with him.


Time seemed to stand still.

Jean-Guy felt, for a moment, as though he were hanging in midair. Neither flying nor falling.

He'd let go of Homer. The man was gone. Vivienne's father was gone, into the river. And Jean-Guy was turned to the bridge. Reaching for it. But it was just beyond his grasp.

He was falling.

Annie. Annie. Honoré.


And then he fell.


It all happened so fast it seemed in slow motion.

Gamache leaped off after him. Following Beauvoir over the edge.

With one hand, he grasped the post. With the other, he reached out.

Reaching, reaching.

Jean-Guy's hand was stretching out toward him. Jean-Guy's eyes, pleading.

Then their hands touched, and gripped.

There was a yank, as Jean-Guy's fall was stopped. But not for long,

Gamache knew. His arm and shoulder had been wrenched. Slivers from the rotten wood were pushing into his palm. Making it slippery with blood. He was losing his grip, on the post. On Jean-Guy.

Jean-Guy was staring up at him. Eyes wide with terror.

Neither spoke. Neither could.

In a moment they'd both be in the river. The freezing water closing over them. Not able to breathe for the shock, the cold, the turbulence. The roiling. Turning them over and over. Their bodies hitting rocks and tree trunks.

Until all struggle left them. All breath left them. And finally all life left them, as their bodies bobbed and thumped down the Bella Bella. Past St. Thomas's Chapel. Past Miss Jane Neal's home. Past Clara's. Past the old railway station.

Under the stone bridge they'd go. And come to rest at the bend in the river.

He held Jean-Guy's frantic eyes and saw his lips move. Annie.

And Armand could see what Jean-Guy was about to do.

"Don't," he rasped. "You. Dare."

But Jean-Guy did.

Knowing Armand could not hold him and keep a grip on the bridge, Jean-Guy opened his grip. Released his hand.

Jean-Guy Beauvoir let go.

But Armand did not. He closed his hand even tighter, even as he felt Jean-Guy's fingers squeezing through his own.

All this took just moments but felt like an eternity.

Just as his hold slipped completely, Armand twisted and heaved. Throwing Jean-Guy as far as he could. Toward the shore.

The effort pulled his hand from the bridge and turned his body onto its back, so that for a moment Armand was looking up. At the sky. Into the April sunshine.

Reine-Marie. Reine-Marie.

He heard a splash as Jean-Guy hit the water.

Then his back arched and arms spread out, and he saw the river roiling below.

～

Armand had managed to throw Jean-Guy clear of the worst of the torrent, but still he'd splashed down in deep water. Arms flailing, trying to get his head above the bone-chilling water, he felt the current grab him, sweeping him out into the river.

Just as he was about to go under, hands gripped him. Water washing over him, retching and coughing, he felt himself pulled to shore.

He looked up, through the brilliant sunshine and cascading water, to where he'd come from.

Afraid to see a void where Armand had been.

Eyes screwed shut, Armand prepared to hit the water, then fight for his life.

But instead he was jerked to a stop.

The blood rushed to his head, mixing with the rush of the river below, until the sounds were indistinguishable. Water into blood. Blood into water.

Then he looked up, into the smashed face of Bob Cameron. The tackle. Penalized for holding, too often and too tight.

Holding on, tight.

As Armand hung there, suspended. Between the bridge and the water.

# CHAPTER FORTY-ONE

～

Reine-Marie hugged him.

And he held her.

Finally letting go, Armand asked, "Is he all right?"

She nodded. "Hot bath, warm clothing. He's in the kitchen by the fire. Annie's on her way down. Homer?"

Armand shook his head.

Reine-Marie sighed. "God." Then she turned and embraced Isabelle.

When they entered the kitchen, Jean-Guy got to his feet. He was clutching a blue blanket around his shoulders and looked a little, though Armand would never ever say it to his face, like Ruth. From Clara's portrait.

Jean-Guy would not appreciate being told he looked like the old poet. Never mind the Virgin Mary.

When he'd gotten to the rocky shore, gagging and heaving, Jean-Guy had first made sure Armand was safe. Only then did he focus on the person bending over him.

Wiping the Bella Bella from his eyes, Jean-Guy looked at Isabelle Lacoste.

Through chattering teeth he managed, "Thank you. Thank you."

"Don't thank me," she said, putting her warm coat over Jean-Guy's shoulders. "I just arrived. He got to you first."

She pointed to the person collapsed next to him.

Soaking and shivering, there was Carl Tracey. He'd seen Beauvoir fall and had slithered quickly down the embankment to the river.

"You?" said Beauvoir.

"Yeah, well," mumbled Tracey through blue lips, "sometimes ya gotta do something stupid."

Hands trembling, Jean-Guy took off the warm coat and gave it to Carl Tracey.


Safe now, warm and dry in the familiar kitchen, Jean-Guy walked over to Armand and, without a word, embraced him, then took the bandaged hand.

"*Merci.*"

They'd said the word together.

"Homer?" Jean-Guy asked as they subsided with groans into comfortable chairs by the woodstove.

"Found at the bend in the river," said Isabelle.

Where the Bella Bella left Three Pines.

"Where Vivienne was found?"

Armand nodded.

He'd stood on the banks of the river and waited for the divers to bring Homer ashore.

The coroner, Dr. Harris, also waiting, noticed Armand's hand wrapped in a scarf. She'd taken the splinters out and put on disinfectant and a bandage.

Lysette Cloutier had asked if she could be there when Homer's body was brought in. They'd agreed, and while Lacoste directed the recovery efforts, Lysette had stood next to Gamache, squinting into water that now gleamed and danced with reflected sunlight.

Finally, when Homer was back, Gamache turned to her and asked, "Why did you do it?"


"Is she arrested?" Reine-Marie asked.

"Not yet," said Isabelle. "She's outside with Cameron, waiting for the coroner's car to take the body away. I wanted to speak with you." She turned to Jean-Guy. "I think you should be the one to lay the charges and take her in, if you're up to it. Your last arrest. It was manslaughter, of course."

"No it wasn't," said Armand. "She was lying."

"It was premeditated?" asked Jean-Guy. "She planned it?"

"We'll let her explain," said Armand. "She wants to talk. I've asked Cameron to bring her here, once she's seen Homer off."

They'd get the truth this time, with or without malice. But first, Armand wanted to tell them what Homer had said to him on the bridge.


After the coroner's car drove away, Lysette Cloutier and Bob Cameron joined them around the woodstove.

Reine-Marie, having heard what happened, gave Bob Cameron a bear hug. As he accepted the embrace, he breathed in the subtle scent of rose. And below that, barely there, a hint of sandalwood.

"*Merci*," she'd whispered into his ear. "*Merci*."

Lysette was trembling so badly with cold and shock that Armand did up a hot-water bottle while Reine-Marie wrapped her in a heavy Hudson's Bay blanket.

"Better?" she asked, and got a small nod. Warmer, if not better.

When they'd settled in again, hands around mugs of hot sweet tea, all eyes turned to Lysette Cloutier, who sat staring into the fire.

"I have a few questions, Agent Cloutier," Beauvoir said, pulling the blanket tighter as another wave of shivers passed through him. "To get things straight."

She nodded. No more fight left. Nothing to fight for anymore.

"If you killed Vivienne, why did you get us involved? Why tell us she was missing in the first place?"

"I had to. How could I explain to Homer if I didn't? Besides, this way I could see what was happening."

"Not just see but influence?"

"If necessary, *oui*."

"That Saturday night she was killed, you said you met Vivienne on the bridge. How did you arrange that?"

"Like I said, I called and we set it up."

"But there're no records of your calling their home in the days before her death."

"I called from another line."

"*Non*. Every number is accounted for. Every call. There weren't many, so it didn't take long. There were no calls from an unidentified number." Beauvoir put his tea down and leaned toward her, lowering his voice. "So how did you do it?"

"I called," she repeated.

"Why're you lying?" asked Beauvoir. "You know you didn't do it."

"What?" said Cameron, looking from Beauvoir to Cloutier. Then back to Beauvoir. "Didn't do what?"

"Agent Cloutier didn't kill Vivienne," said Chief Inspector Beauvoir.

"So it was Tracey," said Cameron. "We were right all along." He turned to Gamache. "You told Homer that Tracey didn't do it, but that was a lie. You just wanted him to drop Tracey."

"*Non*," said Gamache, holding the gaze of the man who'd saved his life. "I wasn't lying. We were wrong all along. I was wrong. I'd warned you not to assume Tracey was guilty, and then I fell into the same trap. The evidence against Tracey was strong but circumstantial. He was vile, but he was also telling the truth. Those posts between himself and Pauline Vachon were about the clay. That night, after their fight, he left Vivienne bruised but alive. Carl Tracey did not murder his wife. She'd arranged to meet someone else on that bridge."

His gaze was so prolonged, so considered, that Cameron shifted in his seat. His large body tensing. His damaged face alert. It felt like that moment just before the quarterback called out the last number. That moment, suspended in time, just before they passed the point of no return.

Gamache turned back to the others.

"Before you arrived, I tossed things out to Homer, trying to break his concentration. Anything that came into my head. And what did were the two nagging questions. Why didn't Vivienne take Fred with her when she left home?"

Once again, on hearing his name, Fred raised his head. Not looking at the one who'd spoken. He was looking for someone who still hadn't returned.

"The other was, why didn't she leave earlier that day?" said Gamache. "When Tracey was at the art shop."

"There's only one answer," said Beauvoir. "She didn't leave in the morning and she didn't take Fred with her to the bridge that night because she didn't intend to go. Not yet, anyway. Her plan was always to leave with her lover."

He stared at Cameron, who sat up straighter. The scars on his face turning white against his flushed face.

"But the call to her father," Cameron said, his voice raised. "She told him she was leaving that night. Coming to him. Not to me. Him."

"No," said Beauvoir. "Vivienne never planned to go to her father."

"She lied to him?" asked Cameron.

"No," said Beauvoir.

"So what does that mean?" said Cameron. Then his face cleared. His eyes opened wider.

"Her father lied?" He looked from one to the other of the senior officers. "I don't understand. Why would he lie?"

"Did you know?" Isabelle Lacoste asked Cloutier.

Lysette Cloutier was very still for what felt like a long time. Balancing on the knife edge.

"I suspected. Not right away, but there were things I knew."

"Like what?"

"On her deathbed Kathy didn't just ask, she begged me to protect Vivienne. Not guide her, not watch over her, but to protect her. This was before Vivienne had even met Carl Tracey. So who was I supposed to protect her from? It didn't occur to me at the time to wonder. I was so upset I didn't think more about it, about the wording. But later—"

"Last summer. When Homer said Vivienne told him to break it off with you," said Gamache.

"I began to wonder."

"What?" asked Cameron, trying to catch up.

"Why she'd do that. Again, at the time I was so hurt I just accepted it. Accepted that Vivienne was jealous and controlling and demanding of all her father's attention. But then I got to wondering if it was more than that."

"What?" demanded Cameron. "I don't get it."

"Don't you?" asked Gamache. "The money from Homer to his daughter. His decision to break off a relationship not with just anyone, but Vivienne's godmother. Who is also a Sûreté officer."

"The payments into Vivienne's account started last July," said Lysette. "Exactly when he ended the relationship. When I saw that, I wanted to believe it was a coincidence. But things started adding up."

"What was the money?" asked Cameron. "What're you saying?"

"Why did Vivienne marry Carl Tracey?" Beauvoir asked. "Several people asked that question. We asked it. Why would a supposedly smart young woman marry a man so clearly violent, abusive? Madame Fleury gave us the answer."

"The devil she knew," said Gamache. "The damage done. Homer talked about that on the bridge. I didn't understand at the time, I was so focused on just trying to stop him. But when we were waiting on the shores of the Bella Bella for his body to be brought in, I went back over what he'd said. And then I realized something. He actually confessed."

"Oh, my God," said Cameron. "He beat her, too? When she was growing up?"

"I think you saw it, without realizing," said Gamache. "When she opened the door the first time. Last summer. You saw the look in her eyes. You recognized in them what you see in the mirror. It was, I think, one of the things that drew you to her. A mutual hurt that went back to the earliest memories. Of course she'd marry an abusive man. It was all she knew, all she thought she deserved."

Gamache looked at Cloutier. "When did you begin to suspect?"

"I didn't, not really. Not until I saw those payments."

"What were they?" asked Cameron. "Blackmail?"

"Restitution," said Lacoste. "Vivienne was already planning her escape last summer. About the time she miscarried. She probably suspected that Tracey had something to do with it. She knew she needed to get out, but she also needed money. So she contacted her father and demanded payment, for all the pain."

"And if he didn't pay," said Beauvoir, "she'd tell her godmother all about it. I doubt Vivienne even knew that you and her father had grown close."

"So Homer broke it off with you and paid," said Gamache. "Over and over again on the bridge, he told us about the pain he'd caused Vivienne. The hurt. He even said that his wife had begged him to stop it. I thought he meant stop Tracey abusing their daughter. But standing by the river, quietly, going back over it, I remembered that Kathy had never met Tracey. She couldn't have meant him. So who did she mean? There was only one answer."

"She was begging me to protect Vivienne from her father," said Cloutier. "From Homer. And I didn't. Worse, I'd fallen in love with him. I didn't see it. Didn't want to see it."

"None of us did," said Gamache.

"But you couldn't have saved Vivienne if you had." Cloutier's voice rose. "I could've. You didn't promise to protect her. I did. But instead I actually blamed Vivienne for being cruel to her father. For cutting him out of her life."

"So that's why Tracey killed Vivienne," said Cameron. "He knew about that money."

"But how would he?" asked Beauvoir. "Would she really have told him? I think if she was going to confide in anyone about the money, it would be someone she trusted. A lover, for example. Don't you?"

His voice had grown quiet. Almost a whisper. As he locked eyes with Cameron across the fire.

Cameron flushed red, almost purple. And closed his hands into fists.

"There was something else Homer said on the bridge," said Gamache. "Before you all arrived. Or, actually, something he didn't say."

He looked at the circle of faces, all of them focused on him. Even Cameron broke contact with Beauvoir and shifted his gaze.

"When he was preparing to take Tracey with him, he said it was punishment for all the years Tracey had hurt Vivienne."

"Yes," said Cameron. "Exactly."

"You're not listening," said Beauvoir.

"Wait," said Lysette Cloutier, who understood what Gamache was saying. "Wait. That can't be true."

"Yes it is," said Lacoste.

"What?" said Cameron, looking from one to the other.

"Homer Godin was punishing Tracey for abusing his daughter," Beauvoir explained. "But not for killing her."

He let that sink in.

"He never once said that, not on the bridge anyway," said Gamache. "Before, yes. I think he'd convinced himself Vivienne's death was Tracey's fault. If Tracey hadn't been abusing her, she'd never have needed to get away. Never have needed to demand the money. Never have needed to meet her father on the bridge."

"And Homer would not have killed her," said Beauvoir.

The words sat there. No one protesting. No one denying them.

It was, finally, the truth.

Lysette Cloutier hung her head, dropping it toward her heart. While Bob Cameron, wide-eyed, absorbed what had been said.

"I should've seen it sooner," said Beauvoir quietly. "Only two numbers were called from the house that day. One a wrong number. The other was to her father. Vivienne was on that bridge to meet someone, and it could only be the one person she'd spoken to that day. Her father."

Finally it was that simple. That obvious.

"But what about Fred?" asked Reine-Marie. And once again the dog raised his head. Then lowered it to his paws. "Why did she leave him behind?"

"Her plan was never to go away that night," said Armand. "She wanted to get the money from her father, then return home and talk to you." He turned to Cameron. "That's why she didn't leave when Tracey was at the art store, and that's why she didn't take Fred to the bridge. You didn't break off the affair last fall, did you?"

"No. I broke it off just after Christmas. I couldn't do that to my family."

Gamache nodded. "I think she genuinely believed the child was yours."

"She wanted to tell you," said Beauvoir, "and see if maybe—"

"I'd go with her," he said.

He didn't tell them what his answer would have been, nor did they ask.

"She called over and over, trying to get through to you," said

Beauvoir. "She finally gave up and went to the bridge to meet her father."

"But if she'd refused to see him since she left home, why agree to meet him that night?" asked Cameron.

"Yes," said Cloutier. "The money could've been wired into her account, like all the rest. No need to see him at all."

"The baby," said Beauvoir. "That changed everything. The idea of being a parent changes you."

Cameron nodded. Remembering his own mounting terror as his first child grew in his wife's womb. That maybe he'd be his father. Maybe he'd be impatient. Cruel. Violent.

Maybe he'd lash out. With fists. With a belt. With a baseball bat.

"She needed to face her abuser," said Cameron. "Look him in the eye. Confront him."

As he'd confronted his own father. Before his son was born.

Only then did he know, in his heart, that he would love his children, protect his children. He would never hit them. And he had not.

"Yes," said Beauvoir. "Vivienne met her father on the bridge for one reason. To look him in the eye and tell him what he'd done to her. She had to do it for her own sake, but also for her daughter's."

"It wasn't about the money," said Lacoste. "That was the excuse to get him there."

There was silence as some looked down at the floor, some stared into the fire, and others looked out the window, at the bright, cheerful day. At the three huge trees, swaying, playing in the breeze.

"Do you think her plan was to kill him?" asked Cameron.

"No," said Gamache. "If it was, she'd have taken Tracey's rifle. She had no weapon. I think it was as Chief Inspector Beauvoir says. She wanted her freedom. Not another burden. Killing her father would've bound him to her for the rest of her life."

But oh, thought Armand, the courage it must have taken to face him. And in doing that, turn her back on all the justified rage. All that had maddened and tormented her her entire life.

To rid herself of all the subtle demonisms of life and thought, Vivienne had to stand on that bridge and face them. Face him.

Her courage was almost unimaginable.

And once free . . .

"Something went wrong," Beauvoir said quietly. "Maybe she tripped. Maybe he pushed her away. If he did, I don't think he meant to kill her."

But maybe that was wishful thinking.

"I realize now that he almost told me what happened," said Armand. "That afternoon, when the case was thrown out. We stood out there"—he nodded toward the path along the Bella Bella—"and I told him how sorry I was. He talked about forgiveness and asked if some things were too horrible to forgive. I thought he was talking about Tracey's acquittal. He asked if a sincere apology really helped." Armand looked into the fire, remembering Homer's worn face. The exhaustion in those eyes. "I think he told her, on the bridge that night, how sorry he was. And asked forgiveness."

"Do you think he meant it?" Reine-Marie asked.

"I want to believe he did. Yes."

Mostly, though, Armand hoped and prayed that the last thing Vivienne Godin saw wasn't the monster, coming at her out of the dark again. But her father, reaching out. Trying to save her.

They'd never know the full truth. But they could hope.

# CHAPTER FORTY-TWO

⌒

S o I'm confused," said Gabri.

"We know you are," said Ruth, patting his hand. "And so's Olivier. Gays and confused."

"Homer killed his own daughter?" said Gabri, ignoring her.

"It looks like it," said Olivier.

They were sitting in the bistro over after-dinner drinks.

Gabri was shaking his head. "It's all so sad."

"And confusing?" asked Ruth.

"Yes. Why would he do it?"

"Those cops explained it all," said Ruth. "Weren't you listening?"

"By 'those cops,' you mean Armand, Jean-Guy, and Isabelle?" asked Olivier.

"Whoever. But yes, that's what they said. Homer did it."

They, of course, had said slightly more than that.

The villagers had seen Armand and Jean-Guy, Isabelle and the other officers return to Three Pines that morning.

Jean-Guy, wet, cold, bruised, had gone straight to the Gamache home.

While Armand, disheveled, slightly wild-eyed, hand wrapped in a scarf, had walked with Isabelle and the others to the path through the woods. That took them to the bend in the river, where the Bella Bella left Three Pines.

A few minutes later, an ambulance, Sûreté cars, the coroner returned.

Homer was discovered exactly where Vivienne had been found. Knocking gently up against a huge tree trunk.

Only then did Armand and Isabelle return home, watched by Clara, Gabri, Olivier. By Billy Williams and Myrna. By Ruth, with Rosa, who was silent for once. Though she did watch Armand with sad eyes. But then, ducks were often sad.

By that afternoon the sun was out in full force. Snowdrops and fragrant, delicate lily of the valley were beginning to appear. Crocuses broke through the grass of the village green.

Life had not just been restored, it had burst forth, as Isabelle and Jean-Guy, Armand and Reine-Marie walked into the bistro.

They joined Clara and Ruth and Rosa by the fieldstone fireplace. Billy Williams sat at a distance from Myrna but stole glances at her. Catching her eyes once, he smiled. And when Myrna smiled back, he blushed and looked away.

Olivier brought them cafés au lait and warm almond croissants, then perched on the arm of the large chair, next to Gabri.

The fire crackled in the background as they heard what had happened.

Ruth looked down at her thin, veined hand, holding Gabri's pink, pudgy one.

*You would have a different body by then,*
*An old murky one, a stranger's body you could*
*Not even imagine, and you would be lost and alone.*

But not lost, she thought.
And not alone.

That evening, Clara was in her studio. Ruth's final comment as she left to head home, ringing in her ears.

"Maybe there's a reason they call it a stool," she'd said, nodding to where Clara sat in front of the easel. "Something to think about."

Fuck, fuck, fuck. But this time it didn't come from the duck.

Once she stopped muttering, Clara turned to Myrna, who was sitting on the sofa, her bottom resting on the concrete floor. Her knees up around her ears.

"Homer kept saying he was going to kill Tracey," said Clara. "He even tried. Why would he do that if he knew Tracey hadn't killed his daughter? Was it an act?"

"I don't think so," said Myrna.

"You think Armand and the others might be wrong, and Tracey really did kill Vivienne?"

"No. I think Homer was mad with grief, with guilt. I think he couldn't bear to accept what he'd done. All those years of abuse and then being responsible for Vivienne's death."

"And his granddaughter's."

"Yes. I think his own self-loathing and his anger at Tracey for his abuse of Vivienne got all mixed up. He saw himself in Tracey and decided both must die. It's pretty obvious by what Armand said that Homer meant to take his own life, along with Tracey's. Both must go into the river."

"To be cleansed?" asked Clara.

"To be punished."

"You think his grief was real? It sure seemed real. Fooled everyone, including Armand."

"I don't think anyone was fooled. I think Vivienne's death destroyed Homer. I doubt it was on purpose. I want to believe he went to the bridge to try to make amends."

"I don't understand," said Clara. "He beat her. His own daughter. A child. God knows what else he did to her. And now what? You're saying he really did love her?"

"I'm saying people change." She held up her hands to ward off Clara's protests. "I know, it's easy to say. And it doesn't undo the damage. But we've seen changes of heart. Changes of perception. It happens. Racists, homophobes, misogynists, they can change. And some do."

"Truth and reconciliation," said Clara.

"Yes. The truth must come first. And then, maybe, reconciliation. Maybe."

"You think Vivienne and her father might've reconciled?"

"Maybe. I think getting the courage to confront him was the first step. If not to forgiveness, at least to healing. And I think Homer's willingness to meet her, and to take the money, shows that maybe he wanted that, too. Maybe."

"He killed her," Clara reminded Myrna. "Then he was willing to see Carl Tracey tried and convicted for something he himself did. Hardly the acts of a contrite man."

"True." Myrna pushed herself out of the sofa. "I guess I just want to believe."

Just as she'd wanted to believe, desperately, that Clara's miniatures were brilliant.

But that had proved a delusion. Dominica Oddly had made that clear. And had, with a few well-turned phrases on her site, destroyed Clara's credibility as an artist.

Her gallery had dropped her. Collectors were returning paintings. Social media was on a feeding frenzy.

Myrna looked at the tiny paintings, nailed to the wall where Clara had put them. Where she could always see them. A reminder. A warning.

Oddly had been right about them. But she'd also been wrong. She might have a duty to tell the truth, but there was no need to be so cruel.

"Are you going to do a portrait of her?" asked Myrna.

"Her who? Vivienne? I never met her."

"No, you know who I mean."

Myrna waited for the answer. That would reveal so much about her friend's state of mind.

But Clara didn't answer. Or maybe she did, thought Myrna, as she watched her friend stare into the vast, white, empty expanse of canvas in front of her. And put down her brush.


Jean-Guy Beauvoir pulled the car in to the now-familiar yard, and he and Armand got out.

The donkeys noticed first. Coming over to the fence to greet them.

"What do you want?" demanded Carl Tracey, once again standing at the barn door with a pitchfork. "Come to arrest me? I keep telling you, I didn't kill Vivienne."

Jean-Guy looked at the man and felt a wave of revulsion. He might not have killed his wife, but he beat her. Isolated her. Tormented her.

But Carl Tracey had also done something else.

"*Non*," said Beauvoir. "I've come to thank you. For saving my life."

He didn't offer his hand. Couldn't take it that far. But he did look Carl Tracey, his unexpected savior, in the eyes. And saw there surprise. And even, maybe, a softening? A hint of what this man could have been, might still become. Might actually be, deep inside.

Carl Tracey's actions on the bridge had been instinctive. Maybe, below all the rot, there existed some timid decency.

"Yeah, well, a blow to the head'll do that."

Was there, as he said it, the smallest possible smile?

"And I came to apologize," said Gamache. "For having you arrested, charged. I was wrong, and I'm sorry."

"You're kidding," said Tracey, scanning the woods, the road, behind the Sûreté officers. "This's a trap, right?"

Did Carl Tracey go through life looking for, seeing, manufacturing traps set by others, for him? How, Gamache wondered, must that affect how he sees the world?

It didn't forgive the abuse, the violence. It wasn't Gamache's to forgive. But it might help explain it.

"No, no trap. An apology."

While Jean-Guy backed the car up, Armand watched through the windshield as Tracey fed the donkeys carrots and scratched their long noses.

Superintendent Lacoste crossed her legs and smoothed her slacks. And looked across the coffee table at Chief Superintendent Toussaint.

It had been a week since the events in Three Pines, and her leave was coming to an end.

She was meeting with Toussaint to tell the head of the Sûreté which job she'd accept.

"I saw your tweets, Isabelle," said Madeleine Toussaint as they settled into the comfortable armchairs in the sitting area of the office. "Defending Chief Inspector Gamache. You didn't hide your identity."

"Why should I?"

"Because you used your rank. You were posting not as a private citizen but as a senior officer in the Sûreté. Making it look like the official Sûreté position."

"As it should have been. I waited, you know, for someone more senior to defend him." She glared at Toussaint. "And when that didn't happen . . ."

"There're issues you're not aware of."

"What issues exactly make it okay to attack our own?"

"I didn't attack him."

"Oh, no? You think I don't know where that video came from?" Lacoste demanded.

"What video?"

But Lacoste had seen the surprise in Toussaint's eyes. The tensing of her body. A spasm of alarm. Of fear even.

"When the shit was flying, he made sure it didn't stick to you," said Lacoste, leaning forward. "You do know that Monsieur Gamache was the one who recommended you for this job."

"He's not the only reason I got it."

"True. You got it because the Premier asked you not to defend Monsieur Gamache in the hearings and you agreed."

"That's a lie."

"It's the truth."

Toussaint's jaw clamped shut, and her eyes hardened. The problem with going up against Isabelle Lacoste was that she was a hero. Unassailable.

And a die-hard defender of Gamache.

"Be careful, Isabelle. It's never a good idea to catch a falling knife."

Toussaint knew that while Superintendent Lacoste might be beyond reach, Gamache was not.

When the smoke had cleared on that final, fateful raid and Isabelle Lacoste lay in her own blood, Chief Superintendent Gamache had to answer for his decisions.

Madeleine Toussaint had known, even as she stood in those woods surveying the wreckage, that he could never really explain his actions to anyone who wasn't there. Even as they made sweeping arrests, in the most successful raid in decades, the vultures were circling.

Politicians desperate to rid themselves of this inconvenient person. A vicious and ravenous social media, desperate for fodder.

On his last day in command, before being suspended, he'd recommended Toussaint for his job. A black woman, a Haitian. They'd stood in this office. He shook her hand and told her she'd be great. But he had one request.

"Don't defend me, Madeleine. You won't win, and they'll come after you."

"But—"

"Promise me."

When the board of review took their shot, no one in power had stepped in front of Armand Gamache to stop it.

Chief Superintendent Gamache had gone down.

And Superintendent Toussaint had risen up.

But what no one expected, was that Gamache would actually return. Would accept such a demotion.

With the departure that evening of Jean-Guy Beauvoir to Paris, Gamache once again took over the homicide department. Respected by colleagues and subordinates, he was viewed with suspicion and worse by those who feared the power he wielded. No matter his official rank.

And Madeleine Toussaint had grown used to her own power. Used to the office. The deferential looks. The salutes. The respect of her community.

She wasn't about to give it up. But to hold on to it, she had to diminish Gamache. And that meant one thing. A purge of his most powerful supporters.

"I've been looking at your health records, Isabelle." She nodded at the dossier on the table between them. "The Sûreté demands a certain level of fitness, especially in its leaders. We have to act as role models."

"Yes," said Lacoste. "I know. I also know there are different sorts of fitness."

The words hit home, but Toussaint tried not to show it. "I'm sorry to say we'll have to pension you off. While you'll keep most of your salary and your benefits, I'll have to ask for your ID and your weapon back. Your security code will no longer be valid."

If she'd expected an argument, Toussaint was disappointed. Isabelle Lacoste just nodded and put her hand in her pocket to bring out her Sûreté ID.

But instead what she brought out was her cell phone. Propping it against some books on the table, she hit play.

Chief Superintendent Toussaint watched with thin lips and narrow eyes.

She watched Jean-Guy Beauvoir dive across the screen. Reaching for the falling man.

She watched as he grabbed a handful of the man's coat and hung on, even as he himself was dragged over the edge.

Her eyes widened as she watched Gamache leap forward. No time to think. He reacted instinctively.

She no longer saw him. He'd disappeared over the edge of the bridge. But she did see his hand. White-knuckled. Gripped onto the foot of the post.

As she watched, the hand began to slip.

Her mouth opened a little as the finger slid off. Isabelle Lacoste leaped forward to grab the hand. But someone was there before her. The former tackle, Cameron, was on his belly, reaching over the side.

There were shouts for help. Cries for help. A splash.

All this the Chief Superintendent knew. She'd read the report. But knowing and seeing were two different things.

Lacoste picked up her phone and turned it off.

Then she took an envelope out of her pocket and, placing it on the table, slid it toward the Chief Superintendent.

Isabelle Lacoste knew that the doctored video purporting to show Gamache killing unarmed kids had come from Toussaint.

It was done to discredit her predecessor, not expecting the real video to be found and released by some crazy old woman in a village that didn't even, officially, exist.

And now it was gaining ground. Overtaking the fake.

Gamache's own reputation was not only being restored, it was growing.

And this video, if released, would put the final lie to Toussaint's doctored effort to show Gamache as a psychotic coward.

"What do you want?" Toussaint asked.

"That"—Lacoste gestured toward the envelope—"is the job I want. The job I will have."

Toussaint nodded. Knowing, of course, what it said.

While Gamache could not be made Chief Superintendent, Isabelle Lacoste could.

Toussaint picked up the envelope, tore it open, and read. Then she looked across the table at Isabelle Lacoste. Perplexed at first, then realization growing.

"You must be kidding."

# CHAPTER FORTY-THREE

—

W e need to go," said Annie. "They've almost finished boarding."
Armand's Sûreté credentials had gotten him and Reine-Marie past security. They stood with Annie and Jean-Guy by the gate at Trudeau International Airport.

Honoré was in Reine-Marie's arms while Armand and Jean-Guy struggled with the travel stroller.

"Here," said Reine-Marie. She handed the child to Annie, walked over to them, pressed a button, lifted some nylon, and up it folded.

The two men nodded to each other, Laurel and Hardy style.

*Hm, hm, hm.*

"Can I leave him here and bring you to Paris, Maman?"

"Oh, don't ask me twice," said Reine-Marie, taking Honoré back.

Dropping her face to his hair, she took a deep breath, then handed him to his grandfather.

The Air Canada representative approached. "I'm sorry, but we're closing the gate."

"*Merci,*" said Annie, and looked at her father.

"See you soon, buddy," Armand whispered to the tired child, almost asleep in his arms. "You'll love Paris. What an adventure you'll have. And you'll see your cousins Florence and Zora."

He held Honoré in the pocket of his shoulder, resting his cheek on the little head, for a moment. Then he kissed his forehead and whispered, "I love you."

The boy put his small hand on his grandfather's large one. Holding it there.

"Dad?" said Annie, putting out her arms.

Armand handed Honoré back to his mother.

"Before I go, I want to give you this," said Jean-Guy, holding out an envelope.

"Money?" asked Armand, as he took it.

Jean-Guy laughed. "*Non*. A name. The person I'm recommending as your second-in-command."

"Hope they're better than your last one," said Armand.

"Hard to be worse," agreed Jean-Guy. "It is, of course, your decision."

"Does this person know?"

"They applied. And yes, they do know about the recommendation." He nodded to the envelope. "I used one of the things you taught me, when making my decision about your second-in-command."

"You mean the four statements that lead to wisdom?" asked Armand.

Jean-Guy shook his head.

"The three questions to ask yourself before speaking?"

Again, Jean-Guy shook his head.

"Then what?"

"Sometimes you just have to do something stupid."

Armand raised his brows, and Annie turned to her mother.

"Oh, dear God, don't tell me that's the lesson he's taken from Dad?"

"I thought your dad got it from him."

Armand put the envelope in his pocket. He knew the name it contained. Bob Cameron. A lowly agent. Not even an inspector.

Gamache hadn't considered him. Cameron had potential, but still, giving him such a promotion would be a hard sell to his superiors, and the rest of the unit. But if someone can drop far, maybe he can also rise fast.

Armand put out his hand to Jean-Guy, who took it and held it. And looked into those familiar eyes. And saw that, after all these years, after all that had happened, after all the pain and hurt, one thing had not changed.

In those eyes he still saw kindness.

And Armand, looking deep into Jean-Guy's, saw below all the pain, all the hurt, all the ghosts, a gleam. A beam. Of kindness.

"I'll find a way to be useful," Jean-Guy whispered. *"Patron."*

"And so will I. *Patron.*"

Then he embraced Annie. "I love you. Take care of yourself. If you need anything, anything at all . . ."

"I know, Dad. I love you, too."

The young family disappeared through the door, Honoré holding up his hand to wave goodbye.

It was the secret wave he and his grandfather had worked out after Great-aunt Ruth had shown the boy the one-finger wave. Papa had explained that really, three fingers were even better. For the three pines.

Armand raised his hand and waved back.

Then they were gone.

To start their new life in the City of Light.


Once home, Reine-Marie poured them each a scotch while Armand walked Henri and Gracie. And Fred. Slowly around the village green.

He looked up as a plane moved overhead. Among the stars.


The next morning the villagers gathered to dismantle the wall of sandbags. All danger was past.

Then, led by Myrna, they walked down the path beside the Bella Bella, past young fiddleheads and lily of the valley and crocuses in the woods, to the bend in the river.

Lighting candles and a stick of dried sage, they smudged the area, blessed the area, said a prayer for the dead and the living. Then all walked back to the bistro for breakfast.

But Armand and Reine-Marie stopped at the bench on the village green. A peaceful place in the bright sunshine. They watched robins hop on the grass. They smelled woodsmoke and mud. And sweet pine.

Armand put his hand into his coat pocket and felt the envelope there. He'd forgotten it but now brought it out.

"What's that?" Reine-Marie asked.

"From Jean-Guy. His suggestion for my second-in-command."

After he'd opened it, he smiled and put it back in his pocket. Beside him, Reine-Marie closed her eyes and tilted her face up.

Then they walked back to the bistro to join the others.

Unheard by anyone else, Armand bent down and whispered to Ruth. "I forgive you, but don't ever do it again."

"Do what?"

"You know." While he couldn't bring himself to say the words, especially to the elderly woman, even this elderly woman, he brought out his phone and showed her. The Twitter handle @dumbass. And the link to the real Sûreté video of the raid on the factory. There were other posts by @dumbass, defending Gamache. But when the video went up, they'd stopped.

There was no longer any need to defend him once that vile video went viral.

"How did you find it?" he asked.

"I didn't. You think I'd defend you?"

"I do."

"I would," the old poet admitted. "I did. But that's not me."

Armand stepped back and stared at Ruth. He knew her to be many things, but never a liar.

So if she wasn't @dumbass, who was?


Madeleine Toussaint sat at her desk and opened her computer.

Putting in her Sûreté code, she went back over her posts, aimed at Gamache, and deleted them all. Pausing just a moment at the final one.

Then Chief Superintendent Toussaint hit delete. And @dumbass disappeared. Never, she prayed, to be found. Because if anyone knew . . . If the Premier found out she'd defied him, and defended Gamache by posting the real video . . .

It was an act of contrition. An amend. And now they were even, and she owed her former mentor nothing.

Looking across the room, her eyes fell on the last remnant of the last occupant. Something she kept meaning to take down. But had kept up. The framed poster, nailed to the wall by the door. The first, and last, thing seen each day.

*Noli timere.*


Armand sat on the sofa beside Reine-Marie and reached for the café au lait Olivier had brought them.

He seemed distracted, but now he reached into his pocket and handed Reine-Marie the envelope. "You might want to read this."

"Jean-Guy's recommendation?" She put on her reading glasses. "Will you take it?"

"I think so."

Armand watched her face as Reine-Marie read. He saw the smile. And relief. As she stared at Jean-Guy's familiar hand and the name he'd so carefully written.

Armand's new second-in-command.

Isabelle Lacoste.

Reine-Marie lowered the paper to her lap and looked into the fireplace. Everything might be all right, after all, she thought.

# ACKNOWLEDGMENTS

This book was initially going to be dedicated to my wonderful agent of fifteen years, Teresa Chris, in thanks for her own dedication to the books. She was the first publishing professional to believe in Gamache and Three Pines.

But, having said that, I decided to dedicate *A Better Man* not to my agent, but to a dog. (Sorry, Teresa . . . )

Bishop, the golden retriever who shared Michael's and my life for many years, died while I was writing this book. In fact, I almost changed the name of the dog in the book from Fred to Bishop, but for some reason, "Fred" just worked better. Besides, that was the name of my assistant Lise's dog, who also died while I was writing *A Better Man*. He deserved to be remembered, too.

Bishop is the last in a long line of golden retrievers who have shared, and improved, our lives. Who taught us how to be more generous, more kind, way more forgiving. More patient. More human.

Our first golden was Bonnie.

I'd wanted a dog for a long time. Michael did not. Just before we got married I somehow convinced him that a puppy would be the perfect wedding gift to each other. It was, for Michael, the same as giving each other razor-sharp teeth, pee, poop, and tumbleweeds of hair.

He was not enthusiastic.

After our honeymoon we picked up Bonnie, all eight weeks of her, and brought her home.

She immediately peed. Then cried all night.

In the morning I came down to find Michael cradling her, and Bonnie curled, asleep, in his arms.

She was forever his. And he was hers.

Each successive dog, over twenty years, tolerated me and bonded to Michael. Which, I must say, was fine with me. I loved seeing the joy in both their eyes when they spotted each other.

Not long after Michael was diagnosed with dementia, our last golden, Trudy, passed away. Michael came with me to the vet, and watched, befuddled by what was happening. Upset that I was upset, but not quite grasping why.

For weeks, Michael looked for Trudy. And asked where she was. It broke my already fragile heart.

A month or so later, knowing our distress, Kirk came by and said he'd heard about an old dog, a golden, whose family could no longer care for him. Would we like to meet him?

Michael was doing his ever-present jigsaw puzzle when Bishop arrived, just for a visit. Bishop took one look at Michael, walked over, placed his teddy chew toy on Michael's lap, sat down, and barely left Michael's side, until the day Michael died.

Bishop was our miracle dog. Our gift from a loving Higher Power.

He was dedicated to Michael. And so, after Bishop's passing this spring, at the grand age of fourteen, it seemed only right to return the favor, and dedicate *A Better Man* to a wonderful dog.

Indeed, to all our dogs.

To all the cats, horses, birds, gerbils, fish, and animals who make our lives so much better. Who give up their freedom, for us.

I now live apparently alone, but in reality I live with Bonnie, Maggie, Seamus, Trudy, Bishop. And Michael. Ever-present and immortal.

There are also some humans I want to acknowledge.

Of course, Teresa Chris, my patient (dear God, let that be true) literary agent.

My wonderful editors, Kelley Ragland, Hope Dellon, Ed Wood. My publishers, especially Andy Martin with Minotaur/St. Martin's Press in the U.S., and Louise Loiselle with Flammarion Québec. Thank you to Paul Hochman and Sarah Melnyk.

To Jamie Broadhurst and everyone at Raincoast Books.

Two people in particular, both lawyers, helped with ideas for *A Better Man*. Thank you to Laura Marr and Mike Conway.

Thank you to my family, Rob and Audi, Doug and Mary, to the nieces and nephews, for all your support and patience. For being happy for (though no doubt kinda surprised by) my success. For cheering me on, especially when things got tough. All this would be hollow, meaningless, without you to share it with.

To Kirk Lawrence and Walter Marinelli, Rocky and Steve Gottlieb. To Jon and Cotton and Betsy and Tom and Oscar and Brendan. To Hillary and Bill and Chelsea and Marc. To Danny and Lucy. Normand and Peter. Robert Bathurst, Ann Cleeves, Rhys Bowen. To Rosemary and Will and David. Kim and Deanna and Sylvie and Nathalie and Erin, Guy, and Jackie, and my neighbors in Knowlton, and, and . . .

Special thanks to Linda "In Scotland" Lyall, who manages the website and now answers, with Lise's help, most of the mail, though I read it all and do answer some. I met Linda face to face for the first time in fifteen years this summer. She's as beautiful as she is kind.

And finally, to my assistant, and great friend, Lise. Without her, there would be no books. Lise does so much for me it's impossible to list it all. But mostly, she's my friend. My confidante.

These books are about community. About love and belonging. About the great gift of friendship.

How lucky I am to live in Three Pines. In every way. With you.

We are never alone.


Louise Penny